RESTORATION

♦ ♦ ♦

A novel

J.G. Follansbee

For my future grandchildren

CHAPTER 1

♦ ♦ ♦

PEOPLE WORK IN THIS UPSIDE-DOWN PIE TIN?

Junie Wye rolled her eyes. She prepped herself for an about
face and a run back to the public car that had dropped her off at the
entrance to the derelict, saucer-shaped visitors center. She wanted
nothing to do with the place, but the soles of her shoes, despite her
raging desire to mount an escape back to San Francisco before it
was too late, stuck to the stained sidewalk.

She couldn't disappoint her father. Turning up her classic
Greek nose at the brutalist architecture, Junie imagined him
directing workers to pry out the letters that once hung on the wall
by the glass doors. Reversed shadows of unbleached concrete
made the old name easy to read: "Arroyo Grande Reclamation
Project." Removing the name was part of taking down the bone-
white decommissioned dam looming behind the center. "It's one
step toward fixing the planet," her dad said.

*Why does Dad need me here? It's hot enough to bake
something in the pie tin. I'll end up a cinder.*

She knew why. Support. A shoulder to cry on, though he'd
never put it that way. Control over a teenager. That was more like
it. "Face-time matters," he said. She growled. *Bullshit.*

After two and a half days in the car, Junie was crabby from a
rough night's sleep as the car's AI drove the 1,380 kilometers
northeast to Utility. She would've arrived sooner, but she had to
stop a couple of times to avoid feeling imprisoned in the two-
seater. The countryside east of the Cascade Mountains was nothing

but a sea of dust and sagebrush. A few orchards of apple and pear trees were an improbable green in this wasteland. She missed the home smell of ocean and cypress.

She'd rather be a million other places, but her father was right about one thing: The cinnamon-red basalt columns that rose in cliffs either side of the arroyo, like old-style bar codes, were breathtaking.

Sweating in the 43-degree heat, she cussed at forgetting her sun hat, and she fought an urge to retrieve it from the car, because she might climb back in and tell the AI to screw this place and take her back to her friends. She and Ed fought about it for days, but she promised him she'd come to Utility. *Dammit.* She had to, because she was 17 and still his responsibility, and he couldn't raise a child from 1,380 kilometers away. *Child? Who made up these stupid rules?* The day she turned 18, she swore to him, she'd steal money from her college fund, buy a plane ticket, and be back in time to entangle herself with Alex and watch the sunset from Golden Gate Park. She secretly hoped Ed would fail again, so she could go home sooner.

Fuck it if I don't love my dad and want him to be happy. And so I'm here.

Her surprise arrival was sweet revenge. Ed budgeted four days for the car and three days in hotels. He assumed Junie preferred to sleep in a bed rather than a public car's uncomfortable cot. Junie was outdoorsy in only a fair-weather way, despite a half-dozen summers at a Girl Scout camp in the Sierra Nevada. Rock climbing, hiking, gossiping, enough to last the rest of the year. *Maybe not gossiping.* It was true she preferred a mattress and sheets to a sleeping bag, but roughing it in the car was worth the chance to get to Utility a day early and see Ed go ape shit.

Pausing on the sidewalk, she shaded her eyes to study dark streaks on the looming dam's—*What's it called? Spillway. Where's the water?* A car with flashing yellow roof lights accelerated out of the nearby "authorized only" parking lot, teasing her curiosity. She watched the car for a few seconds as it raced toward the concrete monster like a police car chasing a robber. After half a kilometer or so, it halted among other vehicles with strobing lights.

Junie stepped through the glass doors into an arena-like open space under the pie tin's roof. The space was empty and deconstructed, as if a parasite had eaten out the interior, leaving a scattering of lonesome cubicles. The contrast between the desert air and the A/C in the building raised goose pimples on her butterscotch skin. She stepped up to a decrepit security bot.

"Excuse me, I'm here to see the project superintendent."

"Junie-girl!" Edward Malcolm Wye's baritone echoed in the cavern of the repurposed building. It seemed to add 10 centimeters to his 188, as well as his open-mouthed smile. Junie's heart melted and she rushed to her father, her tenny-runners silent on the bare concrete floor. Father and daughter hugged, and she took in the smell of his broadcloth shirt tinged with coffee and maple from his breakfast cereal. For a moment, she forgot her resentment of his demand that she move to Utility. For the moment, she let herself be his favorite only child.

She stood on tip-toe to kiss his cheek. "Surprise!"

"You're supposed to be here tomorrow." Ed wasn't angry, just a little nonplussed. "I've been in meetings all day, and I didn't think to check your progress."

"I didn't see any reason to wait, Dad."

"We're in an emerging situation, and I can't break away right now."

Junie had no idea what "emerging" meant, but she took satisfaction from flustering her father. The triumphant feeling faded quickly. He was working, and by the look of the people around him, doing something important. "Sorry, Dad."

"No, I'm glad you're here." He returned the kiss.

Ed made quick introductions for Junie: A well-dressed, if

dowdy woman who was mayor of Utility, and a craggy-faced, calloused man who had to be at least 80 years old. *Culchies all.* After a minute of negotiation, the group allowed Junie to come along on a site tour.

God, it's like I'm on a boring field trip. Junie donned a safety vest and a hard-hat labeled "Visitor." Led by the mayor, the group made its way outside to an observation area on the southwest lip of the canyon spanned by the dam. The wooden platform was temporary, unlike the old public platform at the visitors center. Below was the answer to Junie's water question. *There's a brown shitload of it.*

It had been raining like crazy in Canada, the mayor said, and all that water was backed up on the cougher—*What?*—more than was planned for. Junie accessed Wikipedia via her minds-eye to look up the technical terms. The data appeared in her field of vision, though it was an illusion programmed into the implants behind her ear, which fed impulses directly to the occipital lobe of her brain.

Coffer: A watertight enclosure pumped dry to permit construction work below the waterline, as when building bridges or repairing a ship.

The mayor kept going, saying the sheet piling was at its limit and the diversion channel was maxed out. *Speak English, woman.*

Sheet piling: A form of driven piling using thin interlocking sheets of steel to obtain a continuous barrier in the ground.

Junie guessed that "diversion channel" meant the man-made cut in the rock that let off the pressure behind the coffer. Russet water from the upstream flood event surged at the temporary dam, reluctant to bend toward the diversion channel. The only thing between the pilings and the bone-dry, 200-year-old concrete of the Arroyo Grande Dam was the yawning space of the construction pit. The vehicles with the yellow flashing lights raced across the

6

top of the dam.

Junie watched her father talk with the VIPs. He and the mayor were friends from when he grew up in Utility. She was the head of the committee looking at hiring Ed for the job. The old man was on the committee too. Her father was the only finalist who hadn't withdrawn, and he worried that he might not get another job offer for a long time. So much had gone wrong with his work since her mother died, even before. It was part of the reason she came to Utility. Ed needed her near, to know she was safe. *And a shoulder to cry on.*

A vibration shook the ground under Junie's feet. It felt strange, not like earthquakes in California. More like someone dropping a heavy piece of furniture. She texted Ed via her minds-eye: What's going on, Dad?

We're perfectly safe. He didn't attach an emotional signature to the text, but Junie sensed his apprehension.

A notification appeared in Junie's minds-eye. The local network was sending her a video, emblazoned with the tulip logo of the Bureau of Environmental Security. Part of the tour presentation, the moving image was a drone's-eye view of the dam.

No one has built a dam of this size in North America for a century. Most of the economically viable dam sites were used up by the 1960s, and their reservoirs are the source of 20 percent, maybe more, of man-made atmospheric methane. It's 84 times more potent than CO2 as a greenhouse gas.

The information was straight out of Junie's environmental history book.

If you take into account the ecosystem destruction, not to mention the extinct Columbia River salmon runs, and the main justifications for dams—hydropower, irrigation, and flood control—fall apart. The average atmospheric temp is up three degrees since the 20th century. The planet can't handle dams any longer. Arroyo Grande has to come down.

The old man growled and said something about "bessie propaganda."

Another notification interrupted the video. It ordered everyone away from the observation point, but no one in Junie's group moved when they saw the trouble below them. A section of the coffer bowed out like an infected pimple. The welds on the sheet piles had split. Geysers of water under pressure streamed through the broken seams.

Junie gripped the wooden rail as she saw workers on the pit floor tens of meters below scrambling to the single construction elevator. Water from the artificial lake held back by the coffer streamed into the pit. "Dad, those people will drown if they can't get out."

"There's enough time if they hurry." Her father's face was creased with worry.

Human-sized robots jumped off the coffer and scrambled to the dam's face, climbing U-shaped pieces of rebar pounded into the concrete. Junie thought they were good handholds, and some of the workers had the same idea, because they started up the dam face hand-over-hand. They tired quickly, stopping to rest as the bots passed them with little effort. A robot lost its grip and fell at least 50 meters, barely missing a man before it splashed into shallow water at the bottom of the pit. Pumps lifted the seepage water 50 meters, the coffer's height, and dumped the water back into the reservoir, but they were failing one-by-one. About halfway up the dam face, one of those platforms that window washers use on high rises rested against the concrete. Safety lines dangled from the top of the dam to the platform and below it. Workers at the top threw more lines down. Soon the lines draped like spaghetti and Junie worried they'd tangle.

"Dad, some of those lines aren't anchored properly." The climbing instructors at summer camp had drilled her in setting lines and triple-checking knot strength and quality. A poor knot was a prelude to a fall. Her father didn't respond to her observation. Junie was ready to jump down from the platform and fix the problems, but the near panic was like a barricade across a road. *I feel like I should do something.*

Several lines rubbed against the concrete as they swayed under the weight of the terrified workers. Junie watched with horror as one of the lines showed signs of parting. She turned to get her father's attention, but Ed and the others were distracted by something Junie couldn't see.

`Dad, these ropes aren't going to hold all those people.`

The silence in reply to her warnings was maddening, as if she didn't exist. Seeing a coming disaster compounded by idiocy, Junie waved at the worker below her, pointing out the fraying lines. They ignored her as well, or they were too far away to hear. She was about to run over to her father to yank on his shirt like a toddler, but he and the others had disappeared, forgetting Junie on the platform. The scene below was chaos, as seams in the coffer opened up and let water gush into the pit. A chain link fence was the only barrier between the platform and the flat top of the dam, and the fabric was rusted and frayed.

To get to the workers on the dam top, she'd have to break the rules, trespassing in an area marked "Danger" and "No admittance" in signage and blinking warnings in her minds-eye. The unfamiliar working landscape was frightening in itself. She'd never visited a construction site before beyond the temporary office at previous projects where her dad worked. But nobody noticed, except her, the concrete cutting through the ropes like a dull saw.

What do I do? I have to help, but no one will listen. She'd seen a climbing accident once. One of the girls at camp didn't belay a line properly and it slipped. The climber fell only two meters, but her left leg shattered into a compound fracture. Junie imagined a worker falling twenty or thirty meters, and she closed her eyes to blot out the imagined carnage.

Junie had to go down there and tell somebody what she saw, or one of those workers climbing the dam face was going to die. She climbed over the platform's makeshift railing and ruined her tenny-runners as she scrambled over the rock. Dust enveloped her as she stopped to push through an opening in the fence. Focused on the rescues, no one on the construction crew stopped her or called to her. She glanced around for robots patrolling the fence, but saw none. She hid the blaring warning in her minds-eye.

On the top of the dam, surrounded by heavy equipment and escaping robots folding themselves into storage, she waved her arms and yelled, again trying to get the attention of a man in a yellow, stained shirt. Junie grabbed his arm. He glanced first at his arm, then her. She didn't belong there, and he didn't expect her. He mouthed *What in h—*.

"Mister, there's a rope over there about to part." Junie pointed at the line that worried her. Robots and autonomous vehicles swerved around the pair. They argued for a minute, but Junie persuaded him to take a closer look. The fibers on the rope's outside layer had already worn to fuzz. The worker cussed and they peered over the edge. They saw a rowboat with a half-dozen people bobbing in the rising water. A few others clung to floating objects, like shipwrecked sailors. The worker shouted, and together, he and Junie pulled the line up.

Junie retied it properly around the base of an old lamp post. She asked for a knife, thinking to cut away the damaged portions of the line. The worker apologized as he handed her a pocket knife. She didn't have time to splice the line, and she wasn't sure how, in any case. She sat crossed-leg and thought back to the advanced climbing demos. She had the videos stored in her minds-eye account, but she didn't want to waste time searching. She gathered up the rope at the frayed point and tied an alpine butterfly, shortening the line, but taking the load off the weakened point. The worker watched in front of her on his haunches, while a drone floated overhead. They tested the knot, let the line back down, and someone grabbed it. The knot held perfectly.

`Junie, what the hell are you doing?` It was her father.

`Putting that rock climbing experience to use. These guys have no idea what they're doing.`

`Get out of there before you hurt yourself.`

`You ought to be more worried about this project.`

"Don't argue with me." Ed appeared out of nowhere, mad as a cornered cat. "Here hardly ten minutes and you're already making trouble. You!" He pointed at the worker. "Take her to the visitor center."

The worker was about to say something in defense of Junie, but her father stormed away. Meanwhile, the sound of metal scraping and tearing signaled the failure of the coffer, but as Junie watched the water pour through the breach, the last of the construction crew made it to safety, either at the top of the dam or above the water level. Men and women lay on the concrete sweating under a jury-rigged tarp. A few had passed out from the heat. Ambulances and fire trucks with rescue equipment arrived, lights and sirens blaring, but Junie didn't see anyone seriously hurt. Her escort was pulled aside by another supervisor and Junie reached out to a trundling robot carrying water bottles. She opened one and gulped it. She started handing them out to the exhausted.

The pandemonium eased as ambulances carried away the injured. She was exhausted herself and angry at her father and the other adults. At least the hapless worker mouthed an embarrassed "Thanks" as he lifted one end of a stretcher. She made her way to the visitors center parking lot and climbed into the public car, now surrounded by police cars and emergency vehicles, though no humans were in sight. Wiping the sweat and dust off her face and arms with a wet cloth, she darkened the windows of the car and changed into fresh clothes.

I don't want to be here.

She toyed with the idea of telling the car to take her home, back to the Bay Area and her boyfriend and her friends and real family. *If the kids my age are anything like the rubes here, I'll go completely crazy.* Her dad had yelled at her for trying to help after he ignored her warnings. That hurt. She thought her dad needed her, but now she wondered if she was just in the way. *If I hadn't been there, someone might have died, but no one cares.* When she was really pissed off at her father, she thought about her mother, wondering what she might say or do. It was easy to imagine soothing words from her or a sympathetic touch. *You had to die on El Capitan, didn't you? Why couldn't you die of old age, like everyone else?*

Junie told the car to reconfigure the seats to a cot, and she lay down with her arm over her eyes, hoping to keep the tears hidden, even from herself. After dozing a few minutes, she sighed, put the car seat back into normal travel mode, and ordered the windows back to transparency. She punched in a destination to the car's AI, and left the ridiculous pie-tin building behind.

CHAPTER 2

ED WYE OPENED THE DOOR to the old visitors center onto an argument between a 30ish man in a loose tie and an older man in a hardhat and safety vest that bulged over his paunch. Holo-displays flickered. A robot trolley bumped against a wall. Mountains of papers on hand-me-down desks threatened to fall and crush an unlucky bystander.

The chaos that engulfed the project superintendent's office upset Ed as much as the collapse of the coffer and Junie's out-of-bounds behavior. He was happy to see her, but she got into trouble, and when he scolded her, she disappeared. He cussed himself under his breath. *That girl causes me no end of grief.* He was used to her quirks, however, and as he stood in the midst of the cubicles, he sensed Junie was the least of his problems.

I must've been mad to say Yes to Grace's job offer.

Next to him stood Connie Gasca, the project's operations supervisor, introduced to him hastily by Mayor Grace Cromer as reporters descended on the elected official. Dressed in a zipped-up safety vest and hard hat, Connie gave him a thirty-second summary with enough detail to impress him on her competence. Ed set his hands on his hips, and got his bearings. "Is this a project office or a middle school classroom?" Ed said, using what Junie called his "daddy voice," a baritone growl.

"Who the hell are you?" The question came from a ruddy-faced man.

"Your new boss."

"That's what you think."

The man glanced at Connie, whose eyes flicked to the private offices. Ed perceived a private understanding that unnerved him. With Connie leading, they passed a door to a compact office with the name "Gasca" taped to it. In contrast, Ed's office door had nothing but a small rectangle of adhesive left from the tape that held up the name of the previous occupant. *At least it's what I'm used to, a corner office.* He laughed under his breath.

Ed opened the door to find a tall man with his back to him. Ed swallowed. The man of 60 or so wore the forest-green uniform of the Bureau of Environmental Security. The uniform fit on his athletic frame like a second skin. Turning from the window as if he had occupied the office for years, the officer's flinty gray eyes met Ed's, and he lifted a corner of his thin mouth. "Ah, Mr Wye. I apologize for the surprise. I wanted to see you as soon as I could." The pips on the man's tunic collar next to the golden tulip marked him as high-ranking.

"Not at all, um..."

"Gerard Rossmann." He extended his hand. "Deputy Inspector General for the Pacific West bioregion."

Rossmann's grip was as firm as wound cords. He gave the clasp a tiny flick, like punctuation on a sentence, adding emphasis to his unspoken claim of rank over Ed. The Bureau of Environmental Security made a show of bringing in locals to advise it on major decisions, such as hiring superintendents on major projects. It gave the appearance of local control, or at least input, on big decisions that affected ordinary lives. Though Mayor Cromer made the formal job offer to Ed, the deconstruction was a BES project. Rossmann was Ed's boss.

Connie shuffled out of Ed's office and closed the door, leaving the two men alone. The office was bare and the desk empty, save for the holo-emitter. Ed noticed a separate door that led directly outside, like an emergency exit, or a bolt hole. "General, it's a pleasure to finally meet you." *Best for me to be diplomatic.*

14

Because of his position in the BES, Rossmann was the most powerful man within a couple of thousand kilometers.

"I'd offer my congratulations on your appointment, Mr Wye, but I'm afraid it might come across as sarcasm, given what's happened today."

"I'm appreciative nonetheless, General." Ed cleared his throat. Rossmann had a whiff of Ed's father. "How can I help you?"

"I know you are very busy, so I will come to the point, away from prying eyes." Rossmann glanced through an interior office window looking into the chaos. Connie and the other workers tried to appear uninterested. Rossmann gestured to the exterior door.

Once outside, a uniformed young woman drew up, along with a security robot. It resembled a dark-green ostrich without a neck and head, and it walked on its two legs as if stalking the trio of humans, rather than watching for danger. News chan drones buzzed overhead, lured by the newly flooded construction pit. Rossmann and Ed ducked into a large equipment shed. The human guard stood at ease, while the bot watched the equipment yard. *I don't qualify for bodyguards.*

"Today's incident was not an accident, Mr Wye," Rossmann said.

The statement took a moment to sink in. Once it did, Ed struggled to hide his anxiety from the general, knowing that the sensors in the bot's egg-shaped body recorded his breathing, pulse, and muscle tension, as well as sniffing the air for pheromones indicating his state of mind. "You mean the coffer failure was deliberate?"

"I suppose doubts are natural. It'd be foolish to brief you before you accepted this job." Rossmann held out his hand to his aide, who handed the general a tab. The woman's tunic bulged at her waist, suggesting a standard automatic pistol, rather than the bulkier staser, though Ed was no expert on weapons. Rossmann glanced at the tab before giving it to Ed. "Ordinarily, I'd share a document over the com network, but this is too sensitive."

Ed skimmed the email, more from an inability to concentrate due to Rossmann's stiff presence than impatience at his obtuseness. Phrases jumped out at Ed: "Illegal deconstruction," "bessie lies," "any means necessary." Ed rubbed the back of his neck. He'd seen this kind of rhetoric before. The BES was the most unpopular agency in the government. The arguments in the text were disjointed, but the meaning was clear enough. "You're taking this threat seriously?"

Rossmann regarded Ed with disbelief, then relaxed. "It fits a pattern. I hesitate to use the word 'terrorists'—the word is thrown about too much—but these threats are growing in scope and vehemence. Not only the actions, but the timing is no coincidence, Mr. Wye."

His meaning struck Ed like a bullet. "You're saying the sabotage—if it was sabotage—was timed to coincide with my arrival?"

His own shadow of doubt crossed Rossmann's face. "I can't prove that, but I don't believe in coincidences." He pursed his lips. "There is a substantial faction, perhaps a majority of people in this part of the bioregion, concentrated in Utility, that hate this deconstruction. They will do anything to stop it. Today's incident was a delaying tactic." Rossmann halted and faced Ed. "I, on the other hand, will do anything to see it completed in an orderly manner."

"Why don't you arrest these people?" Ed held out the tablet, as if the question was written on it.

The general failed to hide his embarrassment. "We don't know who they are."

"You mean with all the security assets you have, you can't find them?"

"The cell is using quite sophisticated methods."

"What about this signature?" The words were in a script Ed

16

didn't recognize.

"The language is a dialect of Pashto. It translates roughly as 'Our Land, Our People.'"

"Why would someone from Utility sign this in Pashto?"

Rossmann grew impatient. "It's a joke of some kind. Malcontents like to do that sort of thing." He waved at the tab. "It's not relevant, anyway. The dam must come down. Safely, of course, with no muss or fuss."

"You have a job to do, General. So do I." Confidence was the best response, though Ed imagined his knees wobbling.

"I will be watching you carefully, Mr Wye." Rossmann's face was stony as the basalt on the cliffs above the dam. For a moment, however, he regretted his hard edge. He touched the back of Ed's arm with an open hand and smiled with aristocratic restraint.

Ed fought the urge to recoil. "I know what's at stake, General."

"Just so we're absolutely clear, Mr Wye, let me explain those stakes. The BES and the Interior Ministry are behind the controlled deconstruction of the Arroyo Grande Dam. It's the last piece of a decades-long project to return the Columbia River to its natural state. The people placed everything run by the old American land and resource management bureaucracies into our hands with one goal in mind. Our mission is protection of Mother Earth, and her restoration, if possible." Rossmann straightened his back, as if preparing to recite an oath. "We will accomplish this restoration, Mr Wye."

Did we do the right thing after the Year of Storms? Was the danger from the changing climate so terrible we had to give up so much to these people? It was an endless debate on the news chans, the chat chans, and the c-tribes on the com net. Ed did not participate in these debates. To him, the decision was made a long time ago, and he had to make his way in this new world.

"Nothing will stop our plan," Rossmann said, "including threats against you."

Ed was taken aback. "I don't read that in the email."

"You didn't read far enough."

Ed scrolled further into the diatribe. *"No one at the site is safe,"* the text read, *"from the night custodian to the project superintendent."* The impassive security bot and the armed woman loomed larger in Ed's consciousness.

"You're a man who does his due diligence, Mr Wye, so I'm sure you know that the first superintendent resigned after a year, and the second superintendent resigned after three weeks."

"That was in the local media reports."

"Those reports were incomplete. Both received death threats, though neither suffered an actual attack. At least they didn't report one. The first superintendent was an independent unmarried woman, an admirably tough woman, if I may say so. The second super was a man with a wife and two young children. Understandably, he could not take any chances."

Ed imagined the frightened family packing belongings in a public van and running for safety. *Is Junie in danger?*

"Rest assured, Mr Wye, you and your daughter's safety are a top priority for us, and not just because we are committed to this project. You needn't worry."

Easy for him to say.

"You can also rest assured that once the project is complete, you will receive all the support the Bureau can offer. We take care of our own."

He knows everything about me. All the accusations against me. All never proven.

"Your reputation will be greatly enhanced, perhaps even restored, Mr. Wye, once you successfully bring down the Arroyo Grande Dam. I will personally do everything in my power to assist you in any effort, private or public, that you may pursue."

The content of Rossmann's offer encouraged Ed, but it masked the real message. He sighed. The day was full of threats. First, the coffer dam's collapse threatened to set the project back by weeks, if not months. If Rossmann was correct, the saboteurs had succeeded, temporarily. Second, the threat against Ed's life by the deconstruction opponents elicited a sense of bodily dread he hadn't felt since he first heard the manner of his wife's death ten years previous. He shuddered at the memory of her recovered body.

However, it was Rossmann's threat, oblique but pointed, that made Ed's mouth go dry, once he grasped its meaning. He had taken this job in large part to rehabilitate himself in the eyes of his peers. After so many years of failure, he wondered if his colleagues back in San Francisco and Silicon Valley's rarefied investment world would ever greet him again as an equal. A high-profile success could reestablish him as a man to be reckoned with. Rossmann, in his own way, agreed, while implying that if Ed failed to take down the Arroyo Grande Dam, his career, possibly his life, would be over. He would never escape his past, never shrug off the label of "fraudster." The BES took care of its own, but it never forgot, either.

What about Junie? Should I send her home? No, she's my daughter. I'd worry myself insane if she were far away.

"General, I appreciate your support. I feel safe here. I grew up in this area. I know these people. I'm going to see this project through."

♦ ♦ ♦

Ed lifted the plastic louvers over his office's exterior window, which looked out over a patch of anemic sagebrush. His last office was on the 39th floor of a new office tower in downtown San Francisco, and he could not recall a time in his old digs watching a security bot stow itself in a BES vehicle before driving off.

His office door opened after a light knock. Connie poked her head in and Ed gestured for the ops supervisor to sit. She had a hint of epicanthic folds over her dark eyes. "I heard you were assessing the damage from the flood."

"That's what I came in to talk with you about." Connie studied her tablet, glancing up at him as if confirming a piece of unexpected information. "It's pretty bad."

"Let's have it."

"Ten major pieces of earth-moving equipment at the bottom of the pit, dozens of smaller pieces, tools, and so on. There's the coffer itself, and the derrick barge is partly sunk."

"What about the pumps?"

"They couldn't keep up with the inflow, so I had the operators shut them down for now. No point in burning them out."

"Good." Ed was only a few hours on the job, but he already felt he could depend on Connie. *Can I depend on anyone else here?* "Let's get the department heads in the conference room right away."

"Yes, sir."

"By the way, what's your title?"

"Assistant project superintendent, operations."

Ed assessed Connie as friendly and business-like, if standoffish. She had seen two supers come and go, one after he had no time to learn the job. She wouldn't take any emotional risks on him for now. She had the institutional memory he needed, and she knew almost as much about the real story behind the project's workings as the receptionist and the bookkeeper. "The title's new? I saw the paper sign on your door."

"I was the first hire, after the first super, that is. I haven't got around to getting a nameplate."

Connie knew her priorities. *She probably deserves more money than she's making.*

A thought about Junie flashed in his mind. *Does she deserve more than I can give?* He hadn't heard from her since her car departed, but she'd been out of touch for days in the past, so he

20

wasn't concerned. *She's never been here before. Maybe I should worry.* He waited for a snarky text from her announcing she was 100 kilometers away and accelerating. If she did something like that, would he send the override command to the public car's AI and force her to come to Utility?

Asking her to leave her friends behind in San Francisco and come here was like asking her to remove her own teeth with pliers. If he let her stay, she argued, she promised to talk with him every day, even twice a day. Ed could not accept the deal. He had friends who tried to parent long-distance, but the results were sub-optimal, from his perspective. He was a man for whom in-person conversations with his daughter were as important as eating and sleeping. Even after a century of network technology that made distance as meaningless as national borders, nothing substituted for a hug after a long workday or a coffee shared on a lazy Saturday morning. Not yet, at least. *Have I asked her to sacrifice too much?*

In the conference, Ed greeted the engineers and foremen and women. Ten minutes after the meeting started, the office staff and the line staff were at each others' throats, each blaming the other for the coffer failure. After a half-dozen "Excuse me" and "I'd like a moment, please," delivered in his best non-shouting, authoritative voice, a few in the room turned his way, and the others followed their leads. After high school, he moved away to Seattle and then San Francisco. Coming back, he thought he knew how to talk to local people, but the skepticism in the stony faces argued otherwise. *I'm a stranger here, in more ways than one.* Ed noted who listened, who had ideas, and who nodded in agreement. Connie scribbled on her tablet. By the end of the discussion, most of the group knew what to do next. Ed also knew which people he would fire.

None of them mentioned the threats.

He returned to his desk and rested his eyes, imagining a list of names, collaborating with Connie and the HR AI, and drawing a line through the ones he would let go. He'd done it before, right before giving speeches exhorting everyone to carry on. For a time, he wasn't an executive, but an executioner, albeit without the mask to hide his identity. The thought turned his stomach. That day would be terrible for everyone.

The 30ish man whose avatar labeled him Chandra stood at the door. "I'm sorry to interrupt, Mr Wye, but something urgent has come up."

"Come in, Ramesh."

"Well, sir..." Ramesh tapped his tablet and the holo-emitter radiated a simplified image of the Arroyo Grande Dam over Ed's desk. "The flooding caused a problem." The display zoomed to a section of the dam below the crest of the spillway. The image showed a series of red dots in an irregular line. "We've embedded several hundred sensors in the concrete to monitor vibrations throughout the structure."

"Why, Ramesh?"

"Millions of tons of water have pushed against the dam for nearly 200 years, and we wanted to know what the release of pressure might do."

"Makes sense."

"Everything was nominal until the water came back." Ramesh touched the screen. A more or less vertical, irregular red line appeared from the spillway to the foundation. "A crack, probably caused by the inflow and reapplication of the water pressure."

"Christ, if the water got to its max level, we'd be talking as high as 7000 kilopascals in the grout holes at the base."

"The pressure's not that high, because the water is lower," Ramesh said, "but it's enough to scare the shit out of us."

"I'm with you there. How far does the crack extend horizontally?"

"We don't know, sir, but there's no seepage visible on the downriver side of the dam. It could be just a surface crack."

If a saboteur attacked that crack with explosives, the whole thing might come down, and take Utility with it.

"Connie, what's the status of the pumps?" Ed said.

"Operational. We just have to restart them."

"We need to get the water out of the pit as soon as possible."

"But the coffer isn't repaired. That'll take at least a week."

"Let's get as much water out of the pit as possible to relieve pressure on the dam face. What about the dive team?"

"I've ordered the submersible from the marine construction and salvage people."

"Have them send a couple of divers as backup." Ed said. "We can't take any chances of a breakdown slowing repairs. Ramesh, we need to step up monitoring of the crack. I'd like a daily report." Ramesh and Connie turned to leave. "Send the safety team in here. I want to know the notification protocols to the authorities if we think something nasty is about to happen. When was the last time we had a drill?"

Ramesh and Connie looked at each other.

"That'll be on the agenda, too."

"Knock, knock." Grace Cromer appeared at the door, beleaguered.

"Are the reporters fed?"

"Fed, but not full. I have a lot to answer for, apparently, that's not my fault."

"Hazards of the job." *How much does Grace know?* Rossmann warned Ed against discussing his suspicions about the coffer collapse, though the threatening email was sent to dozens of people. The BES knew more than Rossmann was telling, no surprise, and he would tell Ed more when the time came. In the meantime, Ed should avoid fueling speculation in his office and in the media.

A half-dozen old-fashioned framed photos on the office wall distracted him. Ed liked history, but as a former tech entrepreneur, he found history was a shackle as much as anything else. The black and white images were labeled with hand-lettered notes, such as "First Concrete Pour, December 6, 1935," and "West Powerhouse, January 1940." The photos were familiar; copies lined the walls of every public building and school in Utility, including the ones he attended as a kid. One photo was unlabeled, but it showed people dipping nets into a roaring falls and pulling out large fish. The salmon had since gone extinct.

"That dam built this town," Grace said, noticing Ed's interest. "It's a shame it has to come down."

"If you don't mind my saying, Madame Mayor," Connie said. "many people are happy to see it come down."

Ed turned on the air conditioner, which shuddered like an old cat. Who would threaten, or kill, to keep the dam whole, or maybe take it down early to forestall...? His mind spun like a turbine. He remembered a story from World War II, of missions flown by bombers against European dams with specially designed bombs. The plan worked. *A specially built drone—*

"Have you heard from Junie?" Grace said.

Grace's question brought Ed back to the moment. "Radio silence."

"I wanted to tell you. She's on the news."

"No." *God, Junie could become a target.*

"I'll send a link to your minds-eye."

It was a news chan vid of Junie watched by a worker as she made some sort of a repair to a line. The image was fleeting, but Junie's face was clear. She was in control, and his instinctive concern gave way to guilt when he happened across her warning texts. She'd taken the initiative, something he'd taught her since the day she was born. His final emotion was amazement.

"Damn," Ed said.

Grace chuckled. "That's either fatherly pride or a subtle freak-out."

"Not sure which myself."

"It ought to be the former. Junie's quite a young lady."

Ed was used to praise for Junie, though it never got old. In some parallel universe, Grace might've been Junie's mother, instead of Marcy. Ed and Grace dated in high school, and they both went to Stanford, but their personal lives had diverged. Professionally, though, Grace had stuck with him through the best and worst of times. She recruited him for the deconstruction job— no doubt with Rossmann's blessing—making the stakes for his success even higher. She threw him a lifeline when no one else would. Ed tested the chair behind his desk. It squeaked. She could just as easily cut the lifeline.

"What have I gotten myself into, Grace?" He recalled the furtive looks of the staff as he met with Rossmann. "I feel as if people are measuring me for a coffin."

"It's not personal, though I did hear something that... Well, maybe I shouldn't say."

"What?"

"There's already an office pool."

Connie blushed.

Ramesh fidgeted.

Ed was puzzled.

"On how long you'll last."

That was the nut of it. Everyone expected him to fail, and someone, or some few, would do everything they could to make him fail. Catastrophically, if necessary. In an instant, his view of Utility changed. Who had the motivation or the means to stop him from doing his job, to do him in? From now on, he would have to be on his guard.

"I'll have to throw in a few euros. Are you in?"

Grace laughed. "I'm too much of a politician to give you a straight answer to that question, Ed. Good luck. I'll show myself out."

Ed tried to read her face, to read her mind, to suss out the unspoken, the secret. She was one of the recipients in the threatening email. It's easy, though, to send an email to yourself from a masked account.

He blinked, deliberately. *Now I'm getting paranoid.*

"Wait." Ed needed to shake his anxiety with a gesture. He got up from his chair, closed the office door, and lowered the blinds over the window that looked out on the open office. Gossip was one of the most important currencies of a small town, and he wasn't about to enrich anyone. He thought he could count on Connie and Ramesh's discretion, though he barely knew them. "I know I'm repeating myself, but thank you again, Grace. I needed this break."

She grinned and kissed him on the cheek, lingering for a half-second. Her scent didn't match the one he remembered from high school.

CHAPTER 3

♦ ♦ ♦

"FUCK IT." Junie reached for the AI interface on the car's dashboard. "Fuck it if I'm going to abandon all my friends in the Bay Area for a MON swarming with rednecks and culchies." She reprogrammed the car to take her back to San Francisco. The car had settled onto the westbound lanes of the interstate after she ordered simply "West, by fastest route," in the parking lot of the pie-tin building. Her fingers hurt as she punched the buttons with the new commands, as if her animus would make the AI pay closer attention.

The "Save" button was a blue oval on the holo-display, and it reminded her of her father's blue broadcloth shirts, the ones every businessman had worn for a hundred years, and the feel of it on her cheek when she had hugged him in the visitors center. He was happy to see her, and she him, and only Alex made her close to as happy. He'd asked her to come to Utility and help him with his new life. *When do I get what I want?* She pondered a decision. *Should I stay or should I go?*

That's the trouble with Dad. He trusts me. He trusted her with everything after her mother died. She practically raised herself as he pursued one enterprise after another, though her mother's social circle was wide and loving. Junie was never without a place to hang for a day or two while her dad flew around the planet pitching his latest new thing. Years ago, an old guy on a news chan called him a "serial entrepreneur." A month or so ago, a tongue wagger compared him to a serial murderer, because he managed to kill everything he started.

Junie would've punched the wagger in the neck, if she could.

Cooling down, she texted: Dad, I'm taking a look around. Not exactly a lie, but not exactly the truth. He could call up a map and see where she was and her direction of travel, but she liked to go off on her own. She sent the text so he wouldn't come unglued.

Thanks for letting me know. Her dad's text came back within a few seconds.

Junie had seen things go up and down with her dad her whole life. He said it was part of the world of getting pigs to fly, that is to say, starting up businesses with small chances but big potential profits, not that she understood or cared about business. Things went haywire in the spring of her junior year at Sierra Vista High School. Some of the California tech money in that school went back to the 20th century, and the kids let you know it. Junie knew Ed had a bit of that from her dead grandfather, but one day the bottom fell out of his world, and hers. The worst sign was her com allowance. Without asking, Ed cut her com services to text and voice and unsubscribed her from the emo-sig augmentations. She had a shit-fit. *How the hell was I supposed to know what my friends were feeling? Their avatars were fucking blank. It's like shaking someone's hand and having your sense of touch turned off.* Her father realized his mistake and added the emo-sigs back to her com account, but he complained about the cost.

Things got really bad at the start of the summer. Ed spent every day and night at home. It annoyed Junie, because she liked her independence, though they talked and texted every day when he was on one of his trips. She asked what was wrong, but money talk bored her, and she tuned out his explanations. She felt guilty, but there it was. *At least he didn't chew himself into a blank-eyed stupor with prescription mist.* Some of her friends' parents took that route and never returned.

Dad, are you going to make me go to
school tomorrow?

Yes.

Figures. I wonder how far behind the rubes are.

Junie's circle included the math geeks, science nerds, and
spectrum dwellers, though she counted herself in the subgroup of
members with decent social skills and fashion sense. She'd catch
the math errors of the AI cashiers at the mall. She once proved a
rounding error in a physics class, which pissed off the teacher so
much that he called Ed. *Dad laughed and bought me sushi when he
got off the com with the jerk. I wish he were that cool all the time.*

When he gave her the news that he was taking a job 1,380
klicks away, and that she had to come with him, she lost it. Her
yelling, door slamming, hairbrush throwing, and similar acting out
went on for days. *He ripped my life in half.*

Her social life cratered before she said tearful goodbyes to her
closest friends. A lot of the so-called friends stopped pinging or
texting weeks before her departure. One of them let slip that Junie
no longer mattered, now that she was moving to the Middle of
Nowhere. One posted in a com-tribe: "We feel sorry for you. It's
like you have terminal cancer." The pity was humiliating. Her com
net social tribes dwindled to two or three with a few kids each. As
she cruised in the public car, grateful that there was still such a
thing as friendship, Junie closed her eyes to commune with her
remaining chums in the virtual hideout from parents, teachers, and
cops. Images, voices, text, and emotions floated in her
consciousness, shared on the com net via the implants behind her
right ear, freshly tuned as a gift from Ed for agreeing to come to
Utility with no more fuss.

"Hey."

The single syllable in Alex's voice blew away Junie's c-tribe
trance. Coming out of it was a little like waking up from a nap.
"Hey, there."

"I just got off work."

29

"Cool." Junie wished she hadn't run out of over-the-counter mist. "Everything okay?"

"Sure. Well, maybe not. I mean, I left work, and I started walking to your place to surprise you, and then I remembered you weren't there anymore."

The pain of saying goodbye to Alex flooded Junie again. On their last night together, for hours, she nuzzled him in that space where his athletic neck muscles curved into his broad shoulders. "Sorry I wasn't there." In the public car's uncomfortable seat, Junie wrapped her arms around herself. "You probably still smell like garlic anyway."

"Canned tomatoes, cilantro, mozzarella, all the pizza ingredients."

Junie giggled. Alex did that to her. "I miss you, baby."

"Me, too." Alex cleared his throat. "Are you alone?"

"If you don't count the people in the other cars, yes." Privacy in public cars was an aspiration at best, but the risk of discovery was small. "What are you thinking?" *I know exactly what Alex is thinking. I want it too.*

"Do you want to sig-up?"

Without answering, Junie opened a private chan, started the app, and found her boyfriend on the net. The connection was strong and the feelings flowed as if their spirits merged in a higher reality. Every tendon and fiber relaxed, and Junie's virtual body blended with Alex's, as if they flew as one. She loved the sig matrix that simulated the space between the stars and planets. It was her favorite set of sensory images. It made her feel as if she and Alex commanded the universe beside the other gods and goddesses of the past ten thousand years. The climactic moment was as intense as a supernova.

Junie gasped for breath and the world around her returned. "Alex?"

"Yeah."

"That was amazing."

"Yeah, but..."

"But what?"

"I still miss you next to me."

Her chest tightened, and she swallowed, as if the act could push her emotion far enough away as to make it invisible. Junie hated tears, thinking them maudlin and manipulative. Again, she thought of punching instructions telling the car to head back to the Bay Area, but she didn't.

"I miss you too." Junie cleared her throat. "You're still coming to Utility in a couple of weeks, right?"

The pause lasted longer than Junie expected. "Sure. Everything's set."

"You'd better not change your mind." Junie was playful. "I have plans for you, and they include spending most of the time in my room."

"What about your dad?"

"He'll be at work. He won't care."

"Sounds great." The emo-sig over Alex's avatar showed delight and lasciviousness.

"That's what I like to see." Junie sigged satisfaction. "See you in two weeks?"

"Um-hmm."

"Love you, baby."

"See you."

Alex closed the private chan. *That was sudden. He didn't say "I love you" back. What's he thinking?* Junie could not rebuff unease about her boyfriend, but she always felt that way when they said goodbye, virtually or in person. Another wave of anxiety pushed out worries about Alex. When her father saw the monthly com bill, he was bound to ask her about the sig-up. Strictly speaking, she was underage. She thought up an answer: *Don't worry, Dad, I'm monogamous, and I'll pay for the sig-up when I have the money.*

♦ ♦ ♦

The car signaled her travel time and distance: 90 minutes and 100 kilometers, and her misery increased with every klick. The joy of the sig-up with Alex had faded into a memory that felt 100 years old. In her imagination, Ed scolded her for ignoring the crystalline, parallel lines of the basalt bluffs above the road, or the deep, hurtful blue of the August sky. *I don't want to be here.* Like a whining puppy, the car's AI picked at her mood, notifying her of a tourist snare with an intriguing name: "Grandfather Cuts Loose the Ponies." It was an excuse to delay the inevitable. She instructed the car to find the nearest parking and stepped out into the heat. With her straw hat as shade, her minds-eye linked to the local network node.

The virtual guide invited Junie to walk a short gravel trail to the steel sculptures for a close look. The site had nothing more than the parking lot, a recycling can, a garbage can, a food waste can, a portable composting toilet, and a stained canopy tent protecting a few boxes of fruit from the sun. Next to the canopy was a car with faded paint and a patched body. Hunger wormed its way into Junie's mind and she approached the fruit: apples, apricots, and peaches, labeled with a hand-painted sign as "local." She picked up one of the peaches, the color of 14-carat gold. She returned it to the box. A grizzled woman left the car.

Another movement, animal-like, but cautious, caught Junie's eye. She ignored it.

"That's the best local fruit, lady." The woman gestured towards a sign that warned against overnight camping. "Rast Orchards, right next to the lake."

Rast? Like the old man in the site tour?

"Would you like a taste?" The woman removed a covered

plate from behind one of the boxes and offered it to Junie. "The peaches couldn't be better."

The juices on the slices of golden fruit glistened like dew. Junie took a slice and tasted it. *Wow.* "How much?" The woman wasn't using the net to advertise prices.

"Five euros for the peach, three-fifty for three apricots, two for the apples."

Junie had no idea whether the prices were fair or not, but she hadn't tasted anything like the peach in the Bay Area, not even at the farmers markets. "I'll have two of the peaches, please."

The woman flicked open a paper bag. Junie picked out a pair and the woman laid them in the bag as if the fruit was a family heirloom. Junie waved her com ring over the beat-up receiver on the table and got the debit notification in her minds-eye. The woman dropped a paper napkin in the bag. "Enjoy the heat."

Junie acknowledged the woman and again, the shadow caught her attention. The angle of the sun distorted the height and weight of its owner. She looked about, more from curiosity than fear, and saw nothing.

The guide directed Junie's eye to a ridge 300 meters away, where 15 wild horses galloped in a rough line, heading south. Junie lifted one of the peaches to her mouth and bit in. Sticky juices ran down her chin. She slurped and blessed the woman at the table for throwing in the napkin. The trail climbed toward the ridge, ageless in the desert. When the life-size, two-dimensional sculptures were built in the 20th century, the sculpture avatar label said, wild horses had disappeared from the area. A patina of rust covered the objects, but the sense of wind in the manes of the horses was as fresh as the breeze from the river valley below that rustled Junie's dark hair. *The mustangs are back from extinction, and it's the sculptures that are trapped now, like me.*

Junie finished the peach, a meal in itself, and she dropped the pit into the paper bag. The elevation at the sculptures gave her a birds-eye view of the parking lot. No one had come to look at the iron ponies besides her. The grizzled woman was in the car, reading or sleeping. Junie made her way back to her car, and a second before she waved her com ring over the car's door latch to unlock it, she saw the creature, as insubstantial as the shadow it cast. That's how she was trained to think of it. It was a disidentified. Male, he was not a vagrant, or homeless, or derelict, though he appeared as much to Junie. He was a man socially executed for unspeakable crimes, a human with no identity, no records, no birth certificate, no death certificate, not in any database, and therefore, by some legal definitions, not alive. He lived an unexistence.

On his forehead was a raised welt in the shape of a tulip. All dissed were welted, and this one was an environmental criminal.

The creature was ragged, filthy and starving. He trembled in the heat. He pawed through the food compost can, his back to Junie. *Another centimeter and it might fall in.* He fell onto his haunches, and he sobbed. If Junie were home in the Bay Area, she would have driven off without even seeing the dissed man. In the bald landscape of the desert, he stood out, like a full moon on a clear night. He noticed Junie, and he turned to crawl away.

With one arm. Junie's jaw fell when she realized that the man pulled himself on the dust with one hand, his left. The other was missing, along with his arm up to his elbow, and Junie remembered a story put out by the Bureau of Environmental Security in her c-tribe and thousands of others six months previous.

The story went like this: An illegal forge was discovered in some remote place; Junie couldn't recall the name. The blacksmith fabricated ironwork for wealthy people, using techniques from the 19th and 20th centuries. He made the mistake of using coal as a fuel source, despite warnings from the BES inspectors. An electric furnace powered by a bank of solar cells wasn't traditional enough for his work. He fought them in court, arguing that he qualified for an exemption under a "traditional arts" provision of the anti-carbon laws. When he lost, he bought smuggled coal on the black market. A few of his customers didn't care; they had the money to pay the premium for gray-market goods. The blacksmith was afraid, however, and he armed himself. One day, a force of BES militia and security bots showed up at his forge. They surrounded it as if it were the hideout of a criminal. A security bot fired its staser, and the smith was severely injured. He survived, but he was dissed.

He lost most of his right arm.

Junie had no way to know whether the dissed man below the sculpture of horses reveling in their freedom was the blacksmith, but seeing him filled her with sorrow. Since childhood, teachers and other adults trained Junie to avoid contact with the people whom the government said did not exist, who had been sentenced to a social death. They warned her of fines and imprisonment if she spoke to him, but here he was, or someone like him. *How do the bones of the invisible break and their cuts bleed?* When he saw Junie's paper bag, he licked his cracked lips and made tiny motions with his mouth, as if imaging himself eating the peach.

Junie realized the dissed man had seen her purchase. Dissed were tolerated around non-dissed. Bold ones could take food from stores without consequences, because they were officially invisible, though most avoided crowds. The wretchedness of the man—calling him "it" was forgotten by Junie for the moment—made her ill. Not physically sick, not nauseated, but her heart hurt, and she didn't understand why. *He's not a thing that has social substance. He's less than a feral dog or cat. At least animals exist in public records.* This creature did not, but Junie could not escape the fact that she shared a heritage with him in a primal way. His DNA still functioned, despite the law. His cells made the proteins that sent chemical signals to neurons experienced as starvation.

Junie removed the peach from the paper bag. It was as round and fuzzy yellow as the sun that beat down from the cerulean sky.

She bent to the asphalt. The dissed man flinched and tensed, preparing to run, but he watched the peach as if it were the last one in existence. Junie set the fruit on the asphalt next to the painted white line of the parking space. A moment later, she was in her car, the AI taking her back to the freeway. In her rear view mirror, she saw the dissed man holding the peach in his hand, uncertain of its reality.

♦ ♦ ♦

The car signaled the final kilometers to Utility and Junie took the measure of her new town. She'd made her decision. She couldn't abandon her father. Maybe it was the wretchedness of the dissed man that put perspective on her predicament. Compared to its problems, hers were nothing. That said, Utility disappointed her with its old buildings, men wearing shit-kickers and ball caps, women wearing shit-kickers and cowboy hats, an excess of pickups, and not a single *izakaya* in sight. *Where the hell am I going to get decent* edamame? The downtown morphed into a residential neighborhood. The car pulled into a parking lot behind a group of modular apartments.

I'm here.

A smiling Ed came out into the waning light, lanky but well-muscled in jeans and a plain green t-shirt. The car's gull-wing door opened and Junie embraced her father in the breezeway's shade. It was a more relaxed reunion than at the visitors center. Her simmering resentment gave way to the feeling she had when he returned from a business trip. Reunion is a sweet emotion founded on the threat of parting once again. This time was different; she was coming to him, rather than him coming home.

"Welcome to Utility," her father said. "Again."

"Hi, Dad." Junie sent commands via her minds-eye to the car's AI, which opened the cargo bay. She lifted a shoulder bag and ordered the suitcase out. It followed her and her father down the breezeway.

"How was your trip?" He sounded awkward, as if still trying to regain his balance from her earlier surprise.

The disaster at the dam might have something to do with it. "Good. Dull."

"All your stuff arrived a couple of days ago." Ed said. "It's in your room."

"You haven't unpacked it?"

"Hell, no. You'd shoot me if I did. It's still in boxes."

Ed climbed a flight of stairs to the second floor of the building. Junie followed, with the suitcase close behind. Her father touched the biometric pad on the door labeled "4."

"God, this place is small."

"The rent's cheap." Her father stood in the hall and pointed out the apartment's features. "Quick tour: Living room, kitchen, my bedroom, bathroom, your bedroom, bot closet."

Junie and her father lived in a succession of places, starting with a thousand-square-meter house in the hills above Palo Alto. A year later, while she was in middle school, after her mother died, they moved to a smaller house, then to the townhouse where she lived now, or rather until she and her father moved out. "Are we really that poor, Dad?"

"It's a fringe benefit, Junie-girl. We're lucky." Ed opened the blinds on the window, which looked onto dun hills dotted with artichoke-colored bushes. "My job pays pretty well, so we'll be able to trade up someday."

"If I live long enough," Junie said.

"Look over there." Her father pointed out the triple-paned window of Junie's room. His finger tapped the glass. "See that patch of green? That's the high school."

Junie glanced out the window, but she didn't want to think about school at the moment, Instead, she knelt in front of the moving boxes, her back to her father. The inventory displayed in her minds-eye: favorite dolls, books, tablets, art projects, wall posters, holo-pics, gifts, memories that belonged to her and her alone. Secret things from Alex. All the objects she cared about were here.

"Aren't you interested in your school?"

Junie wheeled around, her tension and resentment released, like he'd pulled a trigger. "What the hell? You ripped me away from my school in my senior year, for fuck's sake. All of my friends are there. I've known them since pre-school. We all got coms together. They were my first c-tribes. When I got my license, I drove them around until they got theirs. I'd probably go into the Army with a few of them."

"I know this is hard..." Ed's eyes widened.

"Instead, you take a shit job in a dried-out husk of a town and you expect me to be interested in my new school?" *I have no friends here, and now I have no friends back home.*

"Junie, I'll help..."

"I don't want your fucking help. I'm your prisoner." She rapped her forehead. "Here, diss me. I have no life, anyway. *You're going to pay a price for this.* You're a selfish jerk. When I turn 18, I'm out of here." That hurt him, and Junie regretted it, but she kept quiet. It was the same old arguments, even the words were the same every time.

Her father wrung his hands, as if he wanted to reach out, but didn't, because she was 17 and too old for a comfort hug from daddy. *Alex will hold me soon.*

"I'm sorry, honey." Ed's apology was for the pain, not the move. "I didn't have any choice. If I could've afforded an apartment for you back home or even a room in a friend's house, I would've got one." He slipped down to the carpet and sat cross-legged, his back against the wall. He focused on a corner where the wall met the ceiling. The register hissed with cool air. "To be honest, I think I would've missed you too much. Maybe I brought you here because I'm selfish."

I would've missed you too, though why is beyond me. "Okay, Dad."

The doorbell rang.

"I'll get it," Ed said.

Junie felt filthy. "I'm going to take a shower."

As he trod down the hall, Junie logged in to the house network and accessed the front door security camera. Ed opened the door and accepted a package from a delivery bot. After bathing, Junie met her father at the kitchen table. "What is it?"

Ed opened the seal and removed an electronic document. He swiped through the first few pages. He set it down on the table and crossed his legs on the sofa in the living room. He was soon lost in thought.

"What are you thinking about, Dad?"

He stuck his chin on his palm. "Casinos, if you can believe it."

"You mean Las Vegas?"

"No, more like how people take risks. Big gambles, in particular. You commit or back away. People in business like to think it's rational, but it isn't. They call them 'choices,' but it's the same thing as throwing dice. Sometimes it isn't much different than Vegas. My choices haven't worked out lately, and they've hurt people."

Junie picked up the document, but all she understood was "United States Bankruptcy Court" and her father's name. The words "Summary Judgment" terrified her. "What is it?"

"The end of a long story."

"What story?" Her father could be cryptic.

"A dream. My dream. The last in a long line of dreams." He stared at the powered-down black screen of the television, which reflected a tired face. "The liquidation is complete. My business is gone, dismembered, like when they used to slaughter cattle."

Dismembered. Slaughter. Fear stabbed Junie's gut. "So we really are poor?"

Ed reached out with both hands. "Junie, come here, please."

Junie let her father guide her to the sturdy coffee table in front of the sofa. She sat on the edge.

"Juniper, I know my work doesn't interest you, but you should understand that I had many debts. I owed banks and suppliers a lot of money, millions of euros, and I couldn't find a way to pay them. It's so damned unfair. You plan everything down to the last detail, and things still go bad." His voice broke, and he coughed. "It's happened too many times in the last few years, especially since your mother died, and I couldn't find any investors willing to take more chances on my ideas."

"You couldn't make pigs fly."

Ed grinned. "True. But listen, sweetheart." He patted Junie's knee. "I've got a job, a good job, and we're not going to starve, or live on the street. I'm going to finish taking down the dam. If things go well, and everything works out, there's a good chance we'll go home when I'm done." *He thinks of the Bay Area as home, like me.* He considered his next words. "I know you miss Alex and your other friends. I grew up in Utility, and I wanted the hell out as soon as I could. But right now, I need to be successful here, and I need your help. Will you help me, please?"

Junie sniffed as gravity proved stronger than her ability to hold back her tears.

"I'm so happy you're here. Nothing is more important to me than you."

In a stupid, crazy way, Junie was happy, too.

CHAPTER 4

COVINGTON RAST INSTRUCTED HIS PICKUP'S AI to head home. Planting the new section of drought-resistant saplings on his Frenchman's Road property was done, and the field bots were secure in the truck bed. The road dipped into a shallow side canyon, and he caught a glimpse of the partially drained Arroyo Grande impoundment, like a half-empty glass of water. He felt half-empty himself, played out by the battle to keep his dam, his water, and his way of life. *I'll never give up. I'll do whatever it takes.*

He lifted the lid of a cooler, removed and opened a bottle of convenience-store beer, and sipped it. Cov was tempted to hand another bottle to his grandson, but he was eighteen, too young in Cov's book for alcohol.

"Don, I want to finish up the northeast section on the homestead by Friday night. Clear?"

"Yes, sir."

"Mmm." He saw the young man every day from sunrise to sunset, except when he was at school, and every day he looked more and more like his father. Dark curls, broad shoulders, regular features, a generous personality, unlike his grandfather. *More like his father.* The thought hurt Cov and made him proud as a strutting rooster. A physical piece of Marshal lived on in Don, and a spiritual piece, too, though Cov was not one to credit the latter to the supernatural. The world was more random than people wanted to admit. *No god worth a damn would've let a son like mine die too soon.*

Or kill Cov's wife with stomach cancer.

Or let a good-for-nothing like Marshal's wife take a breath. *How could the mother of my grandchild abandon him?*

"Have you contacted those colleges, Don? You're going to be 19 soon. What did they tell you?"

The young man tapped on his tablet. "They won't even look at me until the disidentification is overwith."

Damned bessies. "You ought to be ready to click submit one minute after your sentence is done."

"Yes, Grandpa." Don rolled his eyes. "You know I want to get into college as much as you want me to. You don't have to remind me every day."

Don was right to be impatient with his cranky grandfather. Cov was an old man, and though he felt fine, death was not far away. Don had to learn how to run this business and take over soon, or Cov couldn't be certain that some lawyer or BES fuck-up would decide that fruit growing was not going to work after the dam came down. *If I can't stop it.* Time was running out, and he depended on Don. He patted his grandson on his knee and grinned. It was as close to a physical expression of love and appreciation as he could manage. Don looked up and let his eyes go soft in response.

I'm fighting for him.

The beer encouraged a mild stupor in Cov, and he let his mind drift. The four-lane highway opened up to the double cable-stayed bridge named for the last governor of Washington State before the country was reorganized by the bug huggers. The new political boundaries were based on biomes and eco-regions. *How the huggers got the Canadians to agree to the same thing still mystifies me.* The powers-that-be left the smaller jurisdictions alone— counties, cities, school districts—but old timers such as Cov had trouble thinking in terms of "Pacific West," "Salish Sea," and so on. California managed to keep its name, if not the old state boundaries. The Warming had changed everything. Young people like Don had never experienced winters with snow that stuck or summers without warnings to stay indoors or risk baking to death in the heat.

People were displaced, but Cov and most of Utility blamed the government, not the Warming. One of them was Rodrigo Slane, a balding, tobacco-stained, blob of a man. He'd lost his business running barges up and down the river.

"You can thank the bessies for that," Slane said over a whiskey. "My pop gave me the business after I left the Navy." The conversation took place after one of the sham BES "public input" sessions about the Arroyo Grande deconstruction plans. "I wanted to stay with my boat, but they made me scrap it." Slane winced. "I hurt my back a few years ago, and I had no place to live. A cousin here in Utility put me up."

Cov regarded Slane in the darkness of the tavern. "Why don't you do something about it?" He'd known Slane and his father, seeing him at meetings of various ag and commercial associations with interests on the river.

"What can I do?" Slane's eyes had lost all hope.

"Listen to me. The BES may have the bots and the guns, but we know the land and the people. They're intruders. We can fight this. People up and down the river have had enough of them. A few people, determined people, can change the world."

Rast thought he saw a spark in Slane's eyes

They kept in touch.

They made plans. Cov's money and connections, and Slane's practical know-how in artificial intelligence—he'd managed a small fleet of automated tugs and towboats in the Navy and on the river—made a good combination.

Edward Wye was on his hit list.

"Don, you know about the new water allocation schedule the

bessies put out?" Cov had more mundane things to worry about at the moment.

"I'm looking at the tables now, Grandpa." He rubbed the fuzz on his chin. "I've been running simulations on our allocations and I can't make them work for us."

Condensation from the beer bottle dripped onto Cov's denim bib overalls. "I've tried some myself. The way it looks, we'll have to take another thousand hectares out of production to keep the operation going."

"Not a lot of options, except..."

Cov guessed what Don had in mind. "What the Halstons did? Sell out?"

"They're retired now and living on the coast."

"I'm not ready to retire," Cov said. "I'm not giving in to the bessies. They're bound and determined to restore this area to like it was when the Indians ran around here. Nothing but sage and greasewood." The beer loosened him. He straightened in his seat and pointed in a generally eastern direction, toward the capital. "Taking the dam down will drive everyone out of the county faster than buying them out. Damn it if I'll leave to please them. They'll have to carry me out of here feet first."

"There might be another way, Grandpa." Don folded his arms and stretched his feet out. The dust was thick on his boots. "The Fredericksons traded land for water."

"Is that a fact?"

"So I've heard."

"Old man Frederickson's been quiet about it. On the other hand, it's not something you tell your neighbors." Cov sipped from his bottle as he considered the idea. "You know, there's that section on the ridge that's never amounted to anything. It's been fallow for years. Do you think the bessies might take that for some extra water?"

"I wouldn't mind gettin' rid of it," Don said. "Working that section is a pain in the ass."

"Let me think about it. Wouldn't hurt to try, as much as I hate the bessies."

Everything would be fine for us if the dam stayed put. The new deconstruction superintendent, Wye, was Cov's newest problem. Much as the BES wouldn't give up on taking down the dam, Cov would not give up on delaying the project or somehow killing it. Don, his oldest friends, even his own inner voice, told him it was a lost cause, but it was a personal matter, as much as a business matter. The dam was part of him, the same as the basalt and the dust. *We need to get rid of Wye.* He'd seen the video of Wye's daughter, and he had to admit to himself a certain admiration for the child's pluck. She'd earned his respect. He'd take no pleasure in taking down Wye, if only for her sake.

I want to know about Wye, more than what's on his resume. The background check showed that the new superintendent had failed at practically everything he'd done since graduating Stanford's business school. Failure was a red flag for Rast, but the check turned up nothing illegal. The old man was certain the investigators had missed something. *I want to know his ruinous secrets.*

That was Slane's job, among others.

The truck climbed a long switchback up the bluffs on the other side of the river. The glare off the water was cut into sections by a thin black line, the coffer dam, broken near its midpoint. Cov didn't know how long Wye would take to fix the coffer, but fix it he would, Cov was certain. Wye had everything to gain by a success, mostly his reputation. A man's reputation was worth more than gold, in Cov's eyes, or water, for that matter.

The pickup pulled into the long driveway to the collection of buildings that formed the headquarters of the Rast operation. Cov and Don exited into a blast of heat, but Cov didn't mind. The heat was like the light that struck the leaves of his apple and pear trees and forced the chlorophyll in the leaves to make the sugars that the trees stored in their fruit, which he turned to money burning a hole in his pocket. It was a glorious cycle. Of the two other main ingredients in this recipe, there was one in abundance, carbon dioxide. A dangerous over-abundance, the scientists said, and it was true, but Cov minded it less than the city people and bug huggers.

"The water monitors in the northeast section say the flow's down by half, Grandpa," Don said. "What's that about?"

Water was the final ingredient in Cov's recipe for making money, and the thought of it disappearing made his heart ache. "Let's go take a look."

Cov walked his orchards whenever he could, letting an all-terrain cart trail him like an old horse. He glanced with envy at Don, whose gridiron-trained legs were powerful enough to get him from one end of a hectare to another, while Cov's creaky bones would demand help before Don noticed the distance. Eighty-three years of measuring progress one step at a time took something out of a man. Here was a smart young fellow willing to learn the family business, though Cov questioned Don's judgment sometimes. Choices of friends, crazy-ass ideas, youthful indiscretions. He felt the need to knock some sense into him on occasion.

"Do you think we should change out these driplines for conventional watering?" Cov knew the answer to the question, but he wanted to know the boy's mind.

"Grandpa, you know the Bureau agents get upset when growers use those old-style watering systems." In the way of all young people, Don admonished Cov as if the elder had gone senile, though Cov was a sharp as the day *he* turned eighteen. "You've already been cited for using non-standard line diameters," the boy added.

God damn those bessies. Cov was middle-aged when a series

of hurricanes unlike any seen in history swept up the east coast of the US and Canada. A third of Florida was submerged. New Orleans was evacuated and never rebuilt. New York's financial hub decamped 100 kilometers west. The bug huggers got scared and convinced the president and the Canadian prime minister to create the Bureau of Environmental Security to force change. North America was trailing the Europeans, China, India, even Africa. The scientists said it was too little too late; climate change was hitting its stride. No one ever listened to climate scientists, and BES got more powerful every year. *Next thing you know, they'll tell me when and where and how much I can piss.* "You're right, son. I forgot."

Grandfather and grandson walked between a section of six-year-old apple trees and a section planted a few weeks ago. Along a row of new planting, a robot crawler laid down 1.5 centimeter hose with sensors that better regulated the water flow. A second robot worked in compost made from the old trees pulled last year. The system cost Cov a fortune, but the fines for water overuse rose every year even as the BES planned to take away the biggest source of water for 100 kilometers in all directions.

Cov's knees hurt, and he put his hand on his grandson's shoulder. He was damned if he was going to call on that cart to get him to the monitor locker. Don was a good 15 centimeters taller than Cov, and the old man took comfort in the strength of Don's trapezius and deltoid muscles. Full-contact football might be dead as a spectator sport in the big cities, but out here in the country, it was a fine way to toughen up a young man who'd have to deal with bug huggers and bessies. Cov had played right tackle himself at Electric City High School. "What's the telemetry saying now, Don?"

Cov could've checked the readings himself via his minds-eye and the farm's com network, but the human voice was a beautiful thing. He drove everyone crazy with his vintage Johnny Cash and

Porter Wagoner recordings.

"Same readings as before, Grandpa. Damnedest thing."

Cov saw the monitor locker near the fence line, but the view was blocked by a newly planted pear tree. He came around it and saw the red tag. "Oh, fuck. Not again."

Don knelt on the dirt and let his tablet pick up the ID signal from the tag. "Overuse again, Grandpa. The citation says we're 10 percent over the allocation."

"How is that possible?" Cov threw up his hands. "We've changed out the entire drip system to the new standards."

Don studied the tablet. "Here's the email with the notification of overuse. Something about the updated water allocation schedule for all agricultural operations in Douglas County."

Cov snarled.

"They don't tag you if you respond within 10 days, Grandpa."

"I know that, for God's sake."

"Then why didn't you..."

"Because I can't stand dealing with those people. They can come on your land whenever they please and look for any tiny thing that's wrong. I'm so sick of them. They're not interested in 'saving the planet.' They're trying to get rid of good farmers because we don't fit their way of thinking."

"It might help if you read your email once in a while."

Cov's blood rose. "Don't talk like that to me, boy." *God damn if he isn't right, though.*

Unperturbed, Don examined the tablet. "We could pay the fine right now if you give me your access code. Either that, or you can appeal the fine, but the water allocation will still be 50 percent of the contracted amount while you appeal."

"You're talking like a lawyer."

"It's right here on the citation."

"Pay the damned fine." Cov queried his bank account's access code for the day and texted it to Don with double-encryption.

"Euros, renminbi, or dollars?"

"Dollars, son. Always dollars."

The account was debited.

"Water's flowing again." Don smiled in relief.

Cov felt a bolt of pleasure as well. He and Don worked on the problem like partners, instead of grandfather and grandson, despite Cov's admonition demanding respect. Don was a young man who deserved a chance. *I just might give the operation to him before I'm gone.*

"The water's flowing, Don, but it's not enough, not if we have a hope in hell of making a profit this year. The fruit'll be smaller, and those people in Seattle want fruit that fits in your hand like it was grown for it." Cov held out his mitt and made a fist.

"We'll figure something out, right Grandpa?"

"Yes, son." *Son. When did I start calling him that?* Cov stole a glance at Don's scalp, but the juvenile disidentification dissing brand was hidden under hair matted by a mesh ball cap. He thanked the fates that Don broke the species protection laws before he was 21. The judge placed him in Cov's care. Otherwise, Don might've been lost to him.

The hair on the whore's little boy is the same. Cov didn't need his minds-eye to remember the child's face, bright as an angel's. It saddened Cov that the little boy would never know his father, Marshal, and that he would never know his half-brother, Don, if Cov had anything to say about it. But Cov could not abide Syren Ioannu, no matter if she was the mother of his grandchild. She was nothing but a high-class prostitute, and what's worse, leader of River Defenders, the local bug huggers. *And Rossmann's bitch, I'm sure of it.*

Grandfather and grandson turned toward some idle machinery. *I should put more money aside for his college.*

"What are they teaching you in school these days, Don?"

"Same old shit."

"Any interesting shit?"

Don shrugged. Cov learned to read his grandson's shrugs, and this one meant, *Maybe*.

"What about that history class?" Cov hated history when he was in school. The older Cov got, though, the more he liked history. Learning about history these days was an exercise in understanding the arc of his own life. "What time period are you studying?"

Don lifted his eyes, which were hidden behind sunglasses. "American history. First half of the 20th century."

"World War II? A relative of yours won a Medal of Honor at Saipan." *He's never heard of Saipan.*

Don kicked at a stone, as if reluctant to discuss the subject. "Before that."

"World War I? The Great Depression?"

"Yeah, the Depression."

"Good. That was an important time for your family."

Don took longer strides, putting distance between himself and Cov. It surprised the old man. "What's your hurry?" Cov caught up, and huffed. "What's the matter?"

"Grandpa, I know you're mad about the dam."

Cov stopped, and after a few steps, Don stopped as well. "I don't understand, son. What's that got to do with your history class?"

"It's just that, the book we have to use..."

"Yes." The word came out as a growl. Textbooks were a constant headache in the Banks Lake School District. They told local history in a way that irritated all the old families, but the district bureaucrats said their hands were tied by the capital. "What is it this time?"

Don lifted the ball cap from his head and ran his hand through his sweat-soaked hair. The dissing brand was pronounced. "The dam was a mistake. That's what the book says. President Roosevelt was wrong. The people were wrong. It was wrong to destroy an ecosystem so that farmers could grow crops in a desert. It says..."

Cov leaped toward his grandson and struck him in the face with his fist. The old man surprised himself with the burst of angry energy. Pain shot through Cov's hand into his arm, reminding him of the time he sent the wrong command to a seeder and the AI crushed his leg against a wall.

Don tumbled backward, ass in the dirt, sunglasses flying off. He scrambled to his feet and crouched, nearly in a three-point stance, as if ready to rush his grandfather. "What the hell? What was that for?"

"They're jackasses! Every one of them!" Cov shook his bleeding fist at the boy. "Your great-great grandfather Rast was hungry. Starving. The dam project came and he could work again. Feel like a man again."

"Yes, but—"

"But nothing." The voice of Cov's mother telling him the family story was as clear in his memory as the day she passed. "He saved his money, bought some land, the land you're on right now." *Unlike his feckless brother Julian, who abandoned the family. That's what Mother said.*

Cov grabbed a handful of Don's shirt. "Get up." Cov sent a command via minds-eye com to the cart's AI and it sped toward the pair, stopping a meter away. "Get in." Don complied, answering a fear borne of years living with a unpredictable man. Cov took the command seat, and the AI rolled fast over the dust and crumbly clods of dry soil past the boundary into government property. *Drones will be staring down at me in a New York West minute.* The cart halted twenty meters from a jumble of basalt stones. Cov eased out of the cart. "Come on, you pup."

Cov's anger eased, but not his passion. Next to him, Don rubbed his swollen lip, and they stood at the edge of a bluff. A stab of guilt penetrated Cov. "I'm sorry, son. My temper... It gets the better of me."

Cowed, but attentive, Don nodded in acknowledgment, if not forgiveness.

Thermals from the floor fifty meters below lifted the old man's white hair. Above them, a turkey vulture kept an eye out for an opportunity. The glare off the water below them was harsh in the waning afternoon. "Don Rast, let me tell you what's important. Look at that and you tell me what you see."

A shrug. "It's the reservoir."

"No, son. It's what's in you. That is what gave you life. If it weren't for that water, you wouldn't be here. I wouldn't be here. Nothing about you would exist." Cov raised his hand, his index finger under his grandson's nose, like a staser's emitter. "You listen to me. Don't you let anyone ever tell you that reservoir, that dam, was a mistake. It's a gift from your great-great-grandparents to you and to me."

"The book said the dams made the salmon disappear, and birds, and plants."

"That water belongs to human beings as well as fish and birds. God gave us this place, and we made something of it with that portion that belongs to us." Cov noticed the water stains on the far wall of the canyon, exposed when the engineers drew down the reservoir to prep for the dam's removal. "There was nothing here, and we made it alive. It's people like Cromer and Wye that want to take it away. I won't let it happen. To me. Or to you. Is that clear?"

CHAPTER 5

JUNIE OPENED HER EYES in a mild panic as the wake-up call rang in her minds-eye. She was due at school in a half-hour, and the wake-up message told her that breakfast was in the fridge. She jumped in and out of the shower in record time. Her father wanted to accompany her to the school office on her first day, but she preferred to play out the ritual on her own. They compromised on her clothing. She had something flashy in mind, but she agreed to dress in her most conservative clothes, at least on the first day. A touch of lip gloss and mascara was all she had time for.

The brisk two-block walk to school distracted her from her first-day anxiety, and she arrived as a bell rang, an obsolete sound she heard in old movies, but nowhere else. *Why a bell?* Her minds-eye listed a bunch of school networks that would notify students on class changes. *Maybe it's an old tradition.* Small towns held on to traditions with a death grip, her father said. Back home, traditions were disrupted, not followed.

Kids raced up to the school's doors, some glancing, staring, or gawking at Junie. The strange looks embarrassed her, but they deserved a similar attitude, because their clothes were five years behind the current fashion. *No, that girl's got some fashion sense, and maybe her in the viridian.* Tucking her discomfort into an emotional corner, Junie walked in the main entrance, and opened the glass door labeled "Office."

The office bot was designed to look matronly. "May I help you?" The voice was feminine and mature.

"My name is Juniper Ellen Wye. I'm a new student."

"A new student?"

A minds-eye notification confirmed that the bot recognized Junie's digital ID. "My dad sent in the papers. I have a copy if you need it."

"Wait please while I confirm your registration."

Junie tapped her foot and glanced around the office. No humans were in sight.

"Botswanan vegan dishes will be hard to get in our cafeteria."

That's because you people live on fucking Mars. "I can be flexible."

The school's colors were blue and white, judging by the pompoms over the trophy case.

"I've sent your network credentials to your com account, Miss Wye. You're on the seniors net and in the school's c-tribe. Be sure to check-in frequently for announcements." A hall pass appeared in Junie's minds-eye. "You're late for your calculus class with Mr Henderson, but I'll excuse you, seeing that it's your first day."

"Thank you." Junie turned to leave. *Silicon sow.*

"Miss Wye?"

"Yes?"

"I've been authorized to give you a warning." The bot's affect was flat, though stern. "We recognize you're new here, and that you're transferring from an urban district, but..."

Who's "we"? "Is something wrong?"

"We have a dress code, and your outfit is not appropriate."

Oh, shit. Junie flushed, understanding the stares on the school's doorstep. *Even the AI thinks I'm half-naked.* The windows of the school office reflected Junie's image, but she could not understand the problem. She felt perfectly comfortable, even drab.

"Your clothing is fine for today, Miss Wye." The bot's reassurance was hollow. "We'd recommend a visit to Coulee Plaza for a more conservative outfit. You'll find several national stores there. I've put a mall directory in your student folder, as well as a copy of our dress code to help you pick something out."

"I see. Thank you, I guess." *The local mall knows how to promote its tenants. I'll bet the school gets a cut, the misers.*

After logging in with her new credentials, she opened the dress code, and compared it with her outfit. Junie debated whether to be horrified and embarrassed, and race to the mall now, or to be cool and confident, certain that her clothing, hair, and makeup were perfectly acceptable back home, and that if Julius Rast High School didn't like it, then its dress code was stupid, and fuck it. *Easy decision.* She followed the waypoints in her minds-eye, knocked on Mr Henderson's door, and walked in.

Junie halted as the door clicked behind her. Two dozen students sat at desks. On the wall opposite was a poster on orbital mechanics, which piqued Junie's interest. She had a thing for astrophysics and planetary astronomy. A middle-aged, indifferent man with a paunch stood in front of the class. *Mr Henderson.* Her guess was confirmed by his avatar on the school's network. Glancing about, Junie enjoyed the dropping jaws of the girls and the wide-eyed stares of the boys. Another piece of her wanted to hide. She pulled her shoulder bag in front of her, protectively. It was a birthday gift from an Italian friend in one of her c-tribes.

Henderson caught Junie's entrance. "Yes? Ah, I see." A notification in Junie's minds-eye told her he had accessed her identification folder. "Class, this is a new student, Juniper Wye. Please make her feel welcome."

No one spoke. No greeting pings or un-ID'd texts popped up in Junie's minds-eye. She forced a tiny smile. *First impressions, girl.*

"You can take any seat, Juniper."

"Junie, if that's alright, sir." She edged toward an open seat.

"Junie, then."

A boy coughed behind Junie. *Did that fuck say "whore?"*

Junie coughed herself and made a quarter-turn, saw the culprit, lifted her hand, and flipped him off.

The entire row stifled giggles.

Henderson didn't notice. "We're starting a new unit today on Navier–Stokes equations, which are all about the motions of fluids. The engineering specialists in the room are already familiar with these, but we're going to do fun things with some of the derivatives." The teacher made a circling motion with his hand, and the holo-emitter rotated a 3-D graphic. "Junie, I bet your father knows these equations backwards and forwards. He's the new project superintendent at the dam, correct?"

All eyes were on Junie again. *Why do teachers always single kids out?* "Yes, sir."

"Good. Now, I want everyone to get into your teams and decide on an approach to solving this problem."

A set of parameters appeared in Junie's minds-eye. *Hmm. These guys might not be so far behind as I thought.* Squeaking and dragging sounds sliced the AC'd atmosphere as students re-positioned their desks. Junie found herself with two other girls.

Junie waved her hand. "Hi."

The room buzzed as students talked.

"I'm Tiffany." A blond girl with pink lip gloss held out her hand. Junie shook it. The grip was firm, though her hands were thin. *Queen bee.*

"My name's Trudy." *Overweight, but pretty.*

"Let's get down to business." Tiffany swiped her tablet. Junie glanced and saw the parameters proposed by Henderson. A bot drone the size of a hummingbird hovered over the group for a second or two. It moved on to another team. The pink-lipped girl tapped and the solutions appeared on Junie's answer sheets.

"Showoff," Trudy huffed.

"Now," Tiffany said, "on to more important things. Tell us all about yourself, Junie."

Junie glanced at Henderson, who was bent over a student,

pointing at his tab.

"Don't worry about him." Tiffany waved. "He knows I'm a star mathematician, so he never comes over. I want to know more about you."

Junie had not yet made up her mind about Tiffany, but talking let her relax. "Well, I'm 17. I'm a vegan. I listen to Hindi Mistress. I..."

"That's not what I mean, June. I've already read your student bio."

A nosy bee too. The school must have imported the Sierra Vista profile. "Not June. June-ee. What else do you want to know?"

"Where did you get that... look?" Tiffany's eyes scanned Junie's outfit as if they were a pair of dressmaker's lasers.

Junie grew suspicious. *Is she going to cite chapter and verse of the dress code?* Tiffany's clothes matched the code to the letter, though they were elegant and well-made. "I don't know what you mean."

Tiffany leaned in. "I can tell by your outfit that you are a risk-taker. Your ensemble says you don't care what other people think. You're a woman who owns herself."

You ought to see my party clothes. "Thanks, I think." She appreciated the compliment.

Trudy nodded. "Tiffany is in the marketing and finance track. Does it show?"

"The problem is, June..."

"Junie."

"...that no one here will take you seriously, even if you were a straight-A student at your old school."

Junie remembered the office bot. "The artificial intransigence in the office said I should get something more conservative."

"The gadget has an IQ south of zero, but it's right on that point. What are you doing after school?"

Junie shrugged. "Going to the mall?"

"You have passed your first test, young one."

◆ ◆ ◆

Junie and Tiffany rendezvoused at the transit stop in front of the school's main entrance. Tiffany called for the bus via her minds-eye. Trudy showed up and Tiffany agreed to let her join the outing. The quieter girl was a rocky planet to Tiffany's main-sequence star. Junie wasn't sure what her own role in this solar system might be at this point.

Riding the bus with new acquaintances, even likeable ones, was more awkward than sitting next to a stranger. You can safely ignore strangers, but not people who have taken an interest in you. Tiffany broke the tension. "So, June, er, Junie, what was the dating scene like at your old high school?"

Junie was glad for the safe subject. "I don't know. Same as other schools, I guess." Gossip was not her forte, and she wasn't ready to open up quite yet.

"Oh, please. You're more sophisticated than that. On a scale of one to ten, with one being chaste as a convent and 10 being group orgies every weekend, where was your school?"

Trudy giggled.

Junie considered the question, recalling the extra hours of homework, advanced placement classes, and the six weeks of required overseas travel for juniors and seniors. Her junior trip was to Florence, Italy. "I don't think anyone had time for orgies. I'd say something around a four."

"Interesting." Tiffany's made-up eyes narrowed, analyzing the data. "I'd put Rast High at about the same."

"Utility is different than San Francisco, Tif," Trudy said. "Junie's 'four' might be a 'six' here."

Tiffany touched up her lip gloss. "How do you compare the boys here with Sierra Vista?"

Junie was on firmer ground with this question. "I've had one insult me already."

"There's a few good men," Tiffany said, "but the positions they occupy on the curve is about this big." She held her thumb and forefinger a centimeter apart.

"Don't look now, but here comes someone at the avoid-at-all-costs end." Trudy glanced at the bus door. It admitted a boy—Junie would call him a young man—in jeans and a t-shirt. *The national dress of Utility.* His knapsack appeared empty. He had broad, strong shoulders and graceful hands, dark, unkempt hair under a ball cap, and a mild, confident manner. He sat near the front of the bus, away from the trio of girls.

"Nice," Junie said.

Tiffany shook her head as if Junie was about to jump off a cliff. "No, no, and no."

Trudy's woven brow showed agreement.

"What's wrong with him?" Junie said.

"Damaged. Seriously damaged." Tiffany pointed to her head, just above the hairline.

"Oh." Junie understood. "He's been dissed?" The last word in her question was half-whispered.

"The details are murky, but it happened a couple of years ago."

Juvenile disidentification was less serious than the adult punishment. The brand was put under the hairline to hide it, and it gradually faded until it was gone, unlike the permanent brands on people like the man at the fruit stand. The prohibitions against contact were less stringent, but most people avoided juves out of habit. Junie glanced at the boy again and again, avoiding his return gaze. "He seems like an alright guy."

"You're not supposed to talk to him or associate with him or anything until he turns 21," Trudy said, "unless you're related, or you're a teacher, or something."

"You don't know him, do you?" Tiffany's tone was scolding.

"Of course not," Junie said.

"Better keep it that way."

His open, friendly face was like a magnet to Junie. She fantasized about touching his hair and scalp, feeling for the brand. "What's his name?"

"Don Rast."

"Rast? Like the school?"

"Some ancestor or something, a million years ago."

Tiffany noticed Junie's stubborn interest. "That ring on your finger tells me you have a boyfriend."

The thin gold band broadcast her and Alex's commitment on the public net. "Yeah, so? What business is it of yours?"

"What would he think about your wandering eye?"

Junie's face reddened. "It's like admiring a painting. Look, but don't touch."

"Good girl. Keep it that way."

The bus stopped at the main entrance to the Coulee Plaza. Junie made a face. She'd shopped at malls in Redwood City that made Coulee Plaza look like a shoebox. The collection of stores hadn't stocked anything worth wearing for half a decade, in Junie's judgment. Ordering online might be a better idea; the major retailers had her measurements and preferences in their databases. Junie decided the social value of the trip was more important.

The girls got off the bus by the back door, away from Don Rast, but after two steps, Tiffany halted abruptly. "Shit."

"What is it now?"

"Social leper alert." Trudy echoed Tiffany's attitude.

Another bus had come up behind Junie's and dropped off a tall woman with a child, perhaps four or five years old. *Mother and son, but she's different.* Like Don Rast, the woman sparked Junie's curiosity. She was refined, even in the simple clothes of a mother accustomed to cleaning off baby urps. Tiffany and Trudy curved away from the family, dragging Junie along. "Is she another dissed? If so, you have a lot of them living here."

"Don't be dumb. The town hates her."

"What the hell for?" Junie glanced over her shoulder at the woman, who picked up her fussy son and walked toward the department store. "She looks harmless. What's her name?" Her avatar on the com net had a privacy icon on it. Same with the boy.

"Syren something or other. It doesn't matter. She's that River Defenders woman. They want to take down the dam."

"It's coming down anyway, so what's the problem?"

"We hate her. That's all you need to know."

"She's pretty in a mature sort of way. I wonder if she was a model before she got married."

Trudy laughed. "You ought to hear the rumors. Nympho. Men at her door at all hours, who knows what for. I could go on."

"Please don't." Something didn't add up for Junie. *The woman reeks suburbia, but she holds her head up.*

Tiffany cocked her head. "Don't you care about reputation at all?"

"Not if I've never seen her before."

"Junie, my new friend," Tiffany said patiently, "don't think your San Francisco ways cut it here in down home Utility. You have a lot to learn."

Junie needed time to discuss Tiffany's prejudice against a woman who appeared as normal as any mom, but she was distracted by the foray into the fresh mall, even if it didn't meet Junie's standards. To Tiffany's credit, she used the anchor stores as convenient paths to the specialty retailers inside the mall. The thin, but well-proportioned girl hiked as if she had a homing instinct. Junie picked up her pace to keep up. Trudy trailed, huffing and puffing. The shoppers turned a corner and halted at a store Junie never expected to find in a MON.

"MON?" Trudy said.

"M-O-N. It means, 'middle-of-nowhere.'"

"That's not a nice thing to say about a place."

"Get over it, Gert." Tiffany dived into a closeout rack at the entrance.

"I prefer 'Trudy.'"

The girls swept through the tiny retailer, and Junie didn't have the heart to tell Tiffany and Trudy that the racks were full of last year's styles. Tiffany and Trudy picked out three tops and two pairs of casual slacks for Junie that she considered acceptable, if restrictive. The store network accepted Junie's credit request. *Thanks, Dad.* The girls headed for the transit stop.

Tiffany's arm leaped out like a barrier. "Crap."

"What the hell is wrong now?" Junie stumbled, then saw the problem. Don Rast waited under the sign.

"I'll cancel the bus call," Trudy said.

Junie thought her two new friends were off their rockers. "He's just a guy. We don't have to talk to him, or even stand next to him." She remembered her encounter at the horse sculptures on her way into town.

Tiffany and Trudy pressed Junie to go back into the mall, but Junie had had enough. "It's been fun guy, but I'm tired. I'm going home."

"How?" Tiffany said. "You don't know your way around."

Junie waved her off. "I've gotten myself around the Bay Area since I was ten. I think I can find my way in culchie-town."

Her two new friends gave her a dirty look, and Junie felt a twinge of guilt at her insult. They'd been nice to her, the new girl. Her feeling was replaced by an inexplicable sadness when Don came back into view, because he was untouchable. *He's dissed, and I love Alex.* When a memory of Alex's failure to say "I love you, too" during their sig-up returned, Junie felt overwhelmed, and she shook her head like a puppy shaking off a hoard of buzzing flies.

♦ ♦ ♦

Powerhouse Boulevard split Utility in two, its four traffic lanes and center turning lane carrying AI-driven public cars, private cars, buses, and convoys of freight-carrying trucks north to British Columbia, and south to California. Winding her way on foot toward home as evening approached, Junie hurried across the always-busy state highway, taking the nearest of a half-dozen pedestrian bridges. She was halfway across when she saw the child.

The toddler sat in the wrong place, a deadly place, a low asphalt rise with ancient splotches of yellow paint. Vehicles passing under Junie's bridge like a raging two-way river drowned out the toddler's cries. She couldn't make out the baby's gender, but its face was streaked with tears. It was so out-of-place, like laughter at a burial, that Junie skipped a breath. How could it have wandered into the middle of the road without instantly dying?

A second cry, this one audible, pulled her attention to the road's verge. A woman dressed in faded, patched, but neat clothes, screamed at the child, her words masked by the *thrum* and *pop* of tires on pavement.

Junie yelped in sympathy, looking up and down the bridge for help. It was empty except for lengthening autumn shadows. The girl joined in chorus with the woman—Junie guessed she was the baby's mother—but neither heard the other over the traffic. The frightening scene struck another odd chord. The centralized traffic control network recognized when a pedestrian needed to cross a road, and it sent signals to the vehicles to stop and let the pedestrian cross. The system was not foolproof, but none of the vehicles recognized the mother's need to reach her baby. It was as if she didn't exist.

The woman was a disidentified, Junie realized. *So many*

around here.

The mother had no way to reach her child. The vehicles sped by at 120 kilometers per hour. Even if the scattered headlights of cars and trucks illuminated her and the drivers manually slowed, they would never see her in time to stop. Because the AI-managed controllers ignored the woman, and because the child might panic and walk into certain death, Junie ran. It was that or see a baby squashed like a bug. The image caught in her throat. She ran to the platform at the end of the bridge, squeezed between a fence post and a concrete wall, and slid down a narrow trail to the roadbed. *I have a habit of jumping fences in this town.* Along the way, she passed a tattered bag with a random collection of foraged cans of food and found objects.

She met the woman on the gravel border. A half-second of recognition passed: the dissed woman of the ordinary citizen, Junie of the tulip-shaped welt on the mother's forehead. Junie thought of the dissed man at the horses sculpture. The barrier between mother and stranger vanished when both heard the child's wail. The women were now allies to save an innocent.

Cars and trucks roared by, the passengers little more than smears of flesh in the windows. Junie yelled into the woman's ear. "How did she get over there?"

"I don't know!" The mother's eyes were raw with fright. "I got the com implants installed when she started walking, but they haven't worked right, and then I got this..." She pointed at her welt. "...and no one will help me fix them."

Junie laid a hand on the woman's arm in reassurance. Ed Wye's daughter had already committed a felony just by talking to her, and touching her compounded the crime. She didn't care.

"Have you called 9-1-1?"

"No! Please don't call them. If the police see this, they'll take my baby away from me."

A fleeting thought of sympathy for the cops' viewpoint crossed

Junie's mind, but the danger was not the child's fault. *I'll try to help first and call the cops if I can't.* She had one chance, and it was a leap of faith.

A ghost of white paint covered a part of the pavement at Junie's feet. The residential street behind her once met here as an intersection before the road was reconfigured. Normally, Junie could walk to an intersection and cross without breaking her stride. The traffic AI knew she was crossing and stopped vehicles before she arrived at the curb. Junie stood at the rushing highway's curb, but nothing happened. Vehicles sped by as if she were a shrub or fence post. Or a disidentified. *Why aren't they stopping? Bad signal?* For an instant, she felt the mother's terror.

The signal appeared strong, but the AIs weren't as reliable as people imagined. Ten meters distant, visible, then blocked, then visible like a rotoscope image, the child watched Junie while the baby's mother held her hands palms up and out, begging the child to stay put. Junie called up a little-used app in her minds-eye and sent her xGPS location and a command. She closed her eyes and imagined what she wanted. As if she were a biblical saint favored by the Christian god, the traffic in both directions slowed to a stop.

The silence broke Junie's concentration, and she ran across the road to the hump of asphalt. The child lifted its arms and Junie picked up the girl, who held the young woman tight as a constrictor.

The traffic controller didn't wait for her. Junie stepped off the island, then jumped back to safety. She heard the characteristic squeak and whoosh of air brakes' release, and a train of three trucks rolled in front of her, blocking her way. If she didn't move, she'd be trapped with the child. Beyond the trucks, cars rolled forward, told by the traffic control AI they could continue on their way. Junie didn't wait to see if the AI would obey her command a second time. She pushed out in the traffic, dodging the accelerating truck and cars. It was only ten meters. *Keep alert!* She caught a glimpse of gape-mouthed passengers.

Junie handed the child to its mother, who sobbed in relief.
"You need to leave," Junie told the woman. "The people in the cars
probably called the police. They'll be here soon."

The mother understood. She mouthed a thank-you, daring not
to hug Junie or touch her, for Junie's sake and her child's. The
mother whispered into the child's ear. The toddler lifted her face
from her mother's shoulder, and waved goodbye. Junie watched her
go, the baby's dirty hair framing a gap-toothed grin. Her rescuer
laughed and waved back. *Where will you go now, little one?*

Giving the woman and her child a moment to find their way
up the path, Junie followed the trail to a bench on the bridge
platform. The pair were already out of sight. Junie sat on the
bench, feeling heavy as lead, and she shook with adrenalin and the
comprehension of what she had risked. Unbidden sobs of relief and
fear came in gasping breaths and she wished for her father to carry
her home as the dissed mother had carried her toddler, enfolded in
perfect safety.

She could've died. I could've died.

After a moment, her sobs subsided, and she pulled a scrunched
handkerchief from her pocket to wipe the tears from her eyes and
the sweat from her neck. The memory of the child's face stayed
with her, and Junie wondered about its present and future. She
wanted to know the girl's name, but doubted she would ever learn
it.

CHAPTER 6

THE TOP-FLOOR HEARING ROOM—once the drunk tank of the county jail, according to a tourist brochure—was standing-room only. Knots of people chatted and sipped civil service coffee. Ed glad-handed local officials and business people in his best confident CEO role-play. *They want to see if I can take punches.* In Ed's minds-eye, the chairs in the front row and the head table showed floating avatars with his name and Connie's. Ed spotted Ramesh standing against the back wall, although his presence wasn't required. Media drones hovered in their designated corner.

The second door to the hearing room opened and a man in a forest green uniform with four pips on his collar entered. Gerard Rossmann's stern eyes scanned the room and the occupants, noting the names and status of everyone in his presence. His gaze fell on Ed, and the superintendent felt as if a large truck had passed the building, setting off vibrations in his body.

Privately, before the hearing, Rossmann told him the BES had to put on a show of investigating the coffer collapse. "Under no circumstances," he said, "are you to detail suspicions about a cell of saboteurs, unless I tell you to." Despite the emailed warnings, no one had claimed responsibility for what the general still believed was an act of sabotage. He had shared with Ed the handful of messages and c-tribe postings, which were sparse but precise and consistent enough to be credible.

"They may try to intimidate you," Rossmann said, "to scare you off. It happened to your predecessors."

The hairs on the back of Ed's neck stood up. He was sure the saboteurs were in the room watching him.

Rossmann sat down at the center of the head table. On the left edge of his name plate was the flag of the United States of America. On the right was the flag of the BES, its golden tulip mirrored by the tulip on Rossmann's collar and on his network avatar.

Rossmann tapped the gavel and stepped through the preliminary rituals and introductions, and Ed accessed the courthouse's camera network. The first view showed a BES security bot outside the second door to the hearing room. Ed switched to a bird's eye view from over Rossmann's shoulder. Besides himself and Connie, Ed recognized a calm Grace Cromer, a deceptively frail Covington Rast, and a mesmerizing Syren Ioannu.

She had come to his office the day after the collapse. She preferred the shorthand "Sy." Tall and dressed in a way that showed her figure while muting the sexual overtones, her jet hair framed an oval face with cheekbones a rock climber could rappel. "Mr Wye, I know I'm disturbing you at a difficult time, but..."

Her handshake was firm and friendly. Ed had no trouble applying the adjective "beautiful" to Syren Ioannu, though her manner suggested she was of two minds regarding her physical attractiveness. Her intelligence was manifest in her intense eyes, but her full breasts and hips sent his amygdala into overdrive.

"Mr Wye—"

"Ed."

Her slight grin was a thank-you. "Ed, I wanted you to know that we'll offer you all the moral support we can."

"We?"

"I'm sorry. I should've said that I'm representing the local chapter of River Defenders.
Are you familiar with us?"

It's the most powerful private environmental organization west of the Continental Divide. "I've heard of it."

"We worked very hard with the Bureau of Environmental Security to heal this human-inflicted wound on the Columbia River. It's the biggest wound remaining. We want a positive future for the river on behalf of our children. I have a four-year-old son. Do you have any children?"

"A daughter." *Who might be in danger from extremists on either side.*

"The project has been... troubled."

"The last superintendent barely had time to collect his first paycheck," Ed said.

"He was unable to stand up to people whom I can only think of as reactionary."

Does she know I've been threatened? "I know the dam removal is controversial, but I take it that the decision is final, or I wouldn't have been hired."

"To these people, a decision they oppose is never final."

Ioannu's remark brought Covington Rast to mind. He called her an "unlicensed whore" during a discussion about River Defenders. Ed wasn't sure what the old man meant by "unlicensed," or even "whore," a word as forbidden in polite society as racial, gender, and identity epithets. Maybe he meant it as a slur against an "easy" woman, but Ioannu didn't strike him as the type. Her face was determined, but it had a poise that underlined her confidence. He perceived an emotional parapet few men or women scaled.

Ed flashed on an article on one of the news chans. River Defenders was once called River Revolution, and it had a militant arm that committed acts of sabotage against energy companies, timber companies, and any other organization it thought was hurting the planet. That was decades ago, before the Year of Storms changed everything and ecological values once thought

69

radical went mainstream.

Ed liked Sy. She reminded him of the powerful women he knew in Silicon Valley, with whom he felt comfortable. Unlike Rast, who relied on intimidation, Ioannu relied on charm. Ed respected that. *I wonder if Junie would like her.* "I'm genuinely thankful for your support, Sy. I'm going to need it. The project's back to square one, almost." Ed took a leap of faith. "I hope I can call on you if I need any assistance with the authorities?" He was thinking of Rossmann, but his libido kept begging for attention, like an enthusiastic sixth-grader.

In the hearing room, Ed lingered on the security camera's view of Sy's face. As he beheld her, she turned to the lens, as if she knew who was staring. It wasn't possible, because the public network stats showed a dozen anonymous avatars accessing the view, but he couldn't shake the feeling. *Are they all looking at her?*

Rossmann interlaced his fingers on the table. "This is an administrative proceeding, not a criminal proceeding. We are not here to assign blame, though we will find a cause for this event." Rossmann's reputation mirrored the Bureau's relentlessness. Rossmann had rolled up oil smuggling rings, exposed reforestration fraud, and stomped out a water war—a shooting war—in the old Four Corners region. Ed was sure he wasn't the only one in the room intimidated by the officer.

A young man in a BES uniform with one pip on his collar sat at Rossmann's left and handed the general a paper.

Rossmann swiped through the first few pages. "We'll begin with statements from the principles. Mr Wye?"

Ed recounted the events of the disaster, summarizing the documentation submitted to the BES investigative office in Eugene.

"WE NEED THAT DAM."

The male shout came from the audience, but Ed didn't recognize the voice. Everyone's head swiveled to find it. Most nodded in agreement.

"STOP TAKING IT DOWN. WE NEED THE DAM."

The second voice was female, but it was unclear who spoke up. The net traffic on the room monitoring cameras spiked, but the identification software was too slow to pinpoint the speaker.

Rossmann's tapped the handle of the gavel on the table, his insistence turning everyone's heads back to him. "This is an official proceeding. Everyone will observe silence while the witness speaks."

"BRING THE RIVER BACK."

"RESTORE THE RIVER."

The third and fourth voices were also unfamiliar. Sy looked about as if surprised. Muffled "shooshes" filled the atmosphere. *Maybe I should've expected a demonstration. The removal issue is still hot.* This time, Ed resisted the temptation to turn around, but Connie glanced back. Barely a week into his tenure, Ed already thought of Connie as a friend, as well as a colleague. Her subordinate status was irrelevant. She'd spent the better part of the last 48 hours going over the details of his report to the BES, prepping the holo-presentation, and correcting his grammar.

`I don't see who's speaking, sir.`

"Silence, or I will clear the room of spectators." Rossmann's voice was firm, but restrained. "We are not here to reopen debate on the dam's removal. That decision by the Interior Minister is final. The Columbia River will run free, whatever it costs."

"YOU MEAN WHATEVER IT COSTS THIS TOWN."

Blood rose in Rossmann's face. The young, uniformed man whispered in his ear. The general frowned, displeased but placated. "However, in the spirit of transparency and respect for people's views, we will take public testimony after the witnesses make their presentations."

Connie's graphics and photos shone on the screen behind Rossmann, but a haze of distrust and hostility from the audience rattled Ed. After he finished, the inspector general took his time with one of the documents. Ed called up the hearing's public chat feed and found the usual vitriol directed at the BES. Ed didn't understand people's anger at the Bureau. After a hundred years of weak environmental agencies and political compromises with polluting industries, the BES had pushed them aside and managed to get something done on climate change and all the deadlocked environmental issues. The agency was respected, if not popular, in the urban areas. *If it weren't so heavy-handed, it might have support out here in the boonies.* No more outbursts erupted from the audience.

"Mr Wye, I want to go over a couple of points. You say that welds meant to strengthen the joints between the coffer sheets were inadequate."

"Yes, sir. We examined the placement of the welds and bracing and they were spaced too far apart. Not by much, but enough to weaken the entire assembly. They weren't to spec."

"How do you mean?"

I thought he didn't want to talk about sabotage. "They didn't follow the approved design."

"Go on."

"Under the extreme pressure of the water from the flooding, the coffer sheets were pushed apart and the welds broke."

"And this is contrary to the records?"

Ed cleared his throat. "Yes, there are discrepancies between what the records say and the actual distances."

"What about the independent inspections? You do have independent inspections done of this work as it's completed, don't you?"

"Of course, sir." Ed wanted to roll his eyes, but he kept his face impassive. "Their records match the project records. That's obviously a problem, but we haven't been able to track down the discrepancies."

Rossmann made a note with a stylus. "Mr Wye, do you have any explanation for these discrepancies? Even preliminary? Speculative?"

A bead of sweat dripped down his chest under Ed's shirt. Had the A/C failed? "We're still looking into what happened, General Rossmann." He didn't want to commit to a hypothesis yet.

"Do you think it could've been deliberate?"

Ed glanced at Connie, who bit her lip. Despite Rossmann's insistence on secrecy, Ed needed to confide to someone, and Connie got the story. Ed said, "We can't rule out that possibility."

"WHAT DOES HE KNOW? HE CAN'T DRAW A STRAIGHT LINE ON GRAPH PAPER."

A few in the audience tittered.

Rossmann's face flushed as he tapped the gavel, harder this time. "This is the last time I will warn the spectators. Another outburst and I will tell security to escort everyone out."

The room fell quiet. Ed felt the artificial breeze of the HVAC on his neck. It didn't soothe the sting of the anonymous insult, which was closer to the truth than the speaker imagined.

Grace texted him: You're doing fine, Eddie. Let me know when you've looked at those docs from San Francisco.

The text snapped Ed back into the hearing. The night before, Natalie Wong, an old friend in Silicon Valley circles, had sent him a proposal, cc'ing Grace. He was up half the night reading it and running the numbers.

Rossmann continued. "Local opposition to the deconstruction is no secret. We've investigated a number of threats to the project, but so far, they've been unsubstantiated rumors. Mr Wye, I suggest you include sabotage as one of your hypotheses."

"WHAT THE HELL DO YOU TAKE US FOR?" The voice— the same as the one who spoke the first time—was followed by hushes from the back rows.

He's throwing chum to attract the sharks.

Rossmann's ruddy faced burned. "Very well. Securi..."

The young officer whispered in Rossmann's ear again, and the elder calmed down.

A saboteur inside the project? The idea shocked Ed. He could not imagine any of his immediate staff involved in monkey-wrenching. They were professionals, many with their whole careers ahead of them. Connie was a local, but Ramesh, the lead engineer, was new to the area. He'd brought his extended family with him. No one in his office had a stake in saving the dam, as far as Ed could tell. *It's only been a week, though. Do I know any of these people?* He knew less about the deconstruction crew. He guessed the majority grew up in Utility or nearby, but he had no clear idea. *I haven't fired anyone yet, so who's mad at me?*

Rossmann laid his tablet on the table. "What is the status of the coffer at the moment?"

Ed relaxed. He could talk about progress, rather than problems dropped in his lap. "We've repaired the breach, added more bracing, and we've begun pumping out the water from the pit." Then Ramesh's most recent report came back to him, and his self-possession vanished. *What do I say?* "However, we've discovered further problems."

"Yes?"

Ed realized he should've informed Rossmann before the hearing. Powerful people hate surprises. "We've found a network of cracks in the dam. It's more than what we'd expect from normal age and settling."

Behind Ed, feet shuffled on the carpeted floor.

"Is there any danger to the public?"

Ramesh responded to Ed's similar question with a shrug, explaining that he didn't have enough information. "We don't think there's immediate danger of a breach, General, but we're working with local emergency managers on notification procedures."

"Indeed. It would seem that demolition should proceed as quickly as possible."

Half the audience shifted and grumbled. Above and behind Rossmann was the Grant County seal. In its center was the watery spillway of a dam flanked by a man holding lightning bolts and a woman with a horn of plenty full of fruits and sheaves of wheat. It advertised the town's dependence on the dam.

"Do you have an estimate of when you can begin actual demolition?" Rossmann said.

"Two weeks, maybe three. We have extra pumps online to keep water pressure against the dam as low as possible."

Rossmann appeared ready to close the proceeding when the younger officer stayed his hand. "Oh, yes. I nearly forgot." The elder officer laid down the gavel and pointed at a lectern. "I'll now take 20 minutes of public testimony. If you have something to say..." Rossmann addressed the audience. "...come up here and say it. Keep it to two minutes and keep it on point. If you start wandering around, I'll cut you off." The younger officer handed Rossmann another paper. "The first name on the sign-up sheet is 'Rast.'"

Covington Rast lifted himself off his chair in the second row. As he edged past protruding knees in the tightly packed chairs, a balding florid-faced man in a t-shirt caught Ed's gaze. The hostility in his eye was palpable, and Ed remembered his name: Rodrigo Slane, an ex tugboat captain. Ed had shaken his hand at some open house or other. His unkempt hair and paunch contrasted with Rast's hobbled dignity. Slane was one of those men who are invisible, until provoked. *I've provoked half the town, merely by breathing.* At the moment, all eyes were on Rast as he approached the lectern.

Rast flinched. A high-speed object crashed through the window, its rotors blowing the cloud of safety glass into a swarm of bee-like shards. Rast ducked, and the drone flew straight at Ed. He cried out as a rotor sliced into his raised forearm, tearing away shirt fabric and skin. The flesh's resistance confused the drone's AI and it flew off to regain control.

"Everyone down!" Rossmann barked. Most of the crowd disobeyed, rushing for the door, including Ramesh.

As if afraid of the general's order, the drone sprang straight for the drop ceiling, smashing tiles to dust. Ed's throat closed. The top button on his shirt was choking him.

"C'mon, son!" Rast had grabbed his shirt collar. The octogenarian dragged Ed toward the wall away from the drone and its whirring blades. Before Ed had a chance to speak to the orchardist, a glint of enamel caught his eye. The security bot stood at the open second door. Just as it deployed its staser, the drone recovered its bearings and bore down on Ed. He raised his sliced arm and the bot fired its staser once. The noise level fell as the flying object crashed to the floor.

"Be still!" Rossmann's voice was muffled, but strong. "The security bot will kill you if you move." An instant later, the bot stowed its staser, and posed at-rest. "The sec-bot's on stand-by. Is anyone hurt?"

Ed heard sirens and footsteps in the hall. Rast had gone. A light fixture on the floor trembled. Someone was underneath it. Shaking from adrenalin, Ed crawled toward the victim on hands and knees, thinking it might be the elder. Broken glass cut Ed's hands. He lifted a wrecked fixture and found Sy. "Are you hurt?"

She shook her head No, but Ed didn't believe her. Dust covered her face and hair. Her network avatar displayed a medical emergency icon, but at Level 1, indicating superficial injuries. He wanted to get her to help as soon as he could.

First responders called out, searching for victims, their boots crunching debris. Ed got to his feet and motioned them over. Two knelt over Sy. He backed away a step, but stayed with her.

At that point, Ed noticed the series of parallel lacerations on his arm, like claw marks. The pain went from fuzzy to biting. He dropped to a chair, and a responder wrapped a dressing around the dripping wounds.

Connie examined the destroyed drone. Rossmann stood over her. "What the hell happened?"

The inert drone had the logo of one of the construction subcontractors on its side. Connie glanced at Ed. She was mystified. "The sec-bot turned its brain to mush, I know that much."

A new set of sirens wailed, their screaming magnified by the mangled window. Hot air from the outside drifted in, and when Ed heard the doppler effect drop the whine to a bass note, signaling they had passed the building to another emergency. The dressing's pain killers and emergency nano-bots were already taking charge of the wound. Ed tapped into the security camera network with his minds-eye, selecting exterior views. He zoomed in on a vehicle. "Oh, Christ."

It was a bulldozer, running over cars parked in the street and taking out storefronts. The subcontractor's logo was on its empty cab.

"Connie! I need you."

Ed stumbled out of the hearing room, a mix of terror and a sense of responsibility driving him. He jumped down two flights of stairs. He pushed on a door's panic bar and winced at the returning pain. Sunlight blinded him for a second, and Connie nearly collided with him in the alley. A police car flew past, sirens and lights wailing. Down the gap between the courthouse and another building, the bulldozer took out a corner of the courthouse before caroming back into the street.

"Connie, I don't see the dozer on any network."

"I don't see it either. It's not listening or sending."

"Fuck." Without a wireless signal, no one could access the on-board computer and the AI. "Why didn't the kill switch work?"

"I don't know."

All AI-enabled devices, from medical nano-bots to passenger aircraft, had a built-in kill switch if wireless systems failed. *Someone must have disabled the kill switch. Not an easy thing.* "Connie, I'm going to climb on and see if I can force it into safe mode."

Ed ran after the dozer, which poked along at a slow walking pace. Memories surfaced of driving dozers as a nineteen-year-old in his father's construction company. The blades of the crawler track clanked and tore the concrete pavement. Ed found handholds and footholds, and he pulled himself up to a narrow walkway along the side of the giant machine. The dozer plodded for another storefront and plowed into its plate glass. Ed raised his hands to protect himself from falling debris.

The dozer made a slow turn back into the street and lurched over a parked car. Ed reached for the dozer's door handle and pulled. It didn't budge. A long scratch and crease in the metal showed where the door had bent and jammed. Ed pulled hard and steady and the metal door moved enough allowing him to slip inside. The control panel was dark as coal. He punched buttons and pushed handles, but nothing happened. The dozer continued like a boulder down a hill, unstoppable.

Ed texted Connie: `The controls have been disabled or disconnected from the driver box. Do you know where it is on this model?` He waited for her response. Her silence worried him. `Connie?`

`The online manual says the driver box is under the seat.`

Ed squeezed into a corner of the cab and removed the seat as the dozer headed toward a parked truck. The driver box, a shielded compartment containing the on-board computer and other electronics, was labeled with the manufacturer's logo and maintenance login instructions. Without wireless, the instructions were useless. He didn't have a cable for the backup access.

The dozer plowed into the parked truck and peeled away the composite skin as if it were an orange. The machine turned again, but not as much as before. It headed straight down the street, as if taking a break from its mission of ruin. A black shape, the size and shape of an ostrich but with no neck or head, appeared in front of the dozer. *Shit! It's fucking trying to kill me.* Ed laid as flat as he could on the cab's floor and the dozer shook as the security bot's staser hit the dozer blade at full power. Ed glanced through the windshield and saw Connie pleading with Rossmann. The bot fired again with no effect on the dozer. It trotted away. Ed expected it to find a more vulnerable spot on the dozer and fire again. *I'm in the most vulnerable spot.*

The dozer ignored the bot, but it reconsidered its path and changed course for a six-story building. Ed was horrified when he saw the name on the storefront. The dozer was about to demolish a hospice. Workers in white uniforms carried patients out the doors in their arms or on rolling stretchers, but Ed couldn't believe they would get everyone out in time. Ed stared at the driver box. He sent a text to Connie.

It felt like hours passed before she appeared at the cab's broken door and handed Ed a tool. "Get away, Connie!" In the cab's confined space, he swung the six-and-a-half kilo sledgehammer on the box as hard as he could. Blood oozed from underneath his sliced skin, dripping onto the sledge's grip, making it slippery. *Fuck, it hurts.*

Sparks flew as the steel hammerhead smashed on the box. The box was designed to withstand electronic brute force, not mechanical brute force, but Ed had so little room to work, he couldn't bring all the hammer's kinetic energy to bear. Sweat dripped from his chin as the dozer crept toward the hospice. "Get away! Get away!" He screamed at the scurrying figures. At the fifth hit with the sledge, the casing broke, exposing the plastic inner housing of the computer.

Ed felt the crawler track lift the dozer over the curb. The masonry of the hospice was centimeters away. Two hits with the sledge shattered the inner housing, and Ed swung the hexagonal head a last time on the exposed circuits. The bio-logics splattered as if he'd smashed a tomato. Bits of achromatic pulp slapped his face. The dozer's blade crunched into the masonry and the circuits arced. Ed smelled burning meat. The dozer halted with a shudder of death.

Ed released a held breath. His hands shook with adrenalin. *If someone's trying to scare me, he's doing a pretty good job.*

CHAPTER 7

♦ ♦ ♦

THE REPORTERS AND NEWS CHAN TRUCKS outnumbered the victims of the deranged drone and berserk bulldozer who waited in the Grant County Community Hospital's emergency room. Ed's hands were wrapped in a temporary dressing, along with his arm. Doctors, nurses, and med-bots cared for the half-dozen injured, including himself. It was random and pointless, like the terrorist attacks of the early 21st century.

"Dad, how long do you think it'll be?" Junie raced from school when he texted her with the news. A new friend, Tiffany, gave her a ride to the hospital.

"Could be a while. Other people are hurt worse than me." One of the injured was in serious danger; an old woman's cloned heart had failed as she was pulled out of the way of the dozer. "You don't have to stay."

"I want to stay." Junie swiped through a public tablet. As Ed read over her shoulder, her attention was elsewhere. He saw her eyes flick back and forth between an article on the Pluto landing and a young man at the elbow of Cov Rast. The elder's head was wrapped in layers of bandages. They exchanged a glance. Ed offered a silent thank-you for pulling him away from the drone. The elder met Ed's eye, but did not acknowledge his adversary.

Ed noticed Junie linger on the youth. "Do you know him?"

"How could I possibly know him? I've only been here a few days."

"No need to be snippy. I was just asking."

Junie shrugged. "I've seen him at school and around town."

"Do you know who he is?"

"Don Rast."

Ed wanted to ask more questions, but Junie turned her body away from him. The conversation was over, which left Ed speculating on the young man, Rast, and Junie's interest. His daughter sighed and slumped. "What's wrong?"

"Alex."

"Umm." Ed braced himself for bad news.

"He's not coming. He just texted me."

"I'm sorry." Junie mentioned the visit two or three times to Ed since the moment she arrived. Her disappointment was obvious. "Did he say why?"

"A practice entrance exam."

"Sounds like a good reason."

"His parents spy on him all the time. If he isn't studying for MIT or Harvard or Hyderabad Polytechnic, he's a fuck-up." Ed knew that voice. She was making excuses for her boyfriend. Ed met him twice, once at a school function, and the second time when he picked her up for a party at a girlfriend's house. He was smart and appropriately deferential. Ed liked him.

"Ask him to re-schedule. Maybe the next week?"

"He already did. In two weeks."

"Well, then. Don't be so disappointed. Scheduling stuff is hard, particularly if traveling is involved." Ed reflected on how desire for an absent beloved slows time to a crawl.

"He knew about the exam a month ago. So why didn't he tell me and pick a different day to visit?"

Ed had no answer. Even in a time of virtual companionship, when you could feel every emotion of a partner, assuming you had the right com plug-ins, nothing substituted for a lover's physical presence. "Long-distance relationships are frustrating."

A notification appeared in Ed's minds-eye calling him to the reception desk. A nurse bid him to an examination room. Junie followed.

The exam room had two beds. The nurse directed Ed to the empty bed and promised to come back. Sy Ioannu was in the other bed. She lay back, a light sheet over her up to her waist. A robot dressed her bare arm. Her rolled up sleeve revealed a few centimeters of an elaborate tattoo, but Ed couldn't see enough to make out its meaning. Sy's eyes were closed. *Is she sedated?* She opened her eyes and adjusted the position of her head. Ed's blood pressure spiked, betrayed by the insistent beeping of the monitor. He wanted to hide. *Do all men react to her in this way?* Ed swallowed. "Hi."

"Hello." Sy brushed tendrils of dark, wavy hair from her face.

"Are you badly hurt?"

Sy glanced at the robot working on her arm. "Cuts and bruises." She blinked. "You can hardly see them now." Even prone and in pain, the woman was graceful.

Ed noted the reversed location of the proverbial shoe. This time, it was Junie's eyes that flicked back and forth between Ed and Sy as she silently speculated. His daughter was partly curious, partly protective of her father's emotional life. He was equally protective of her heart, but he raised her to live and think independently, up to a point, and he hated lecturing her. Nonetheless, he observed her blind spots. Her relationship to Alex was fraying, and he would know soon enough if its end was on the horizon.

"Thank you, by the way," Sy said.

"For what?"

"You were one of my rescuers."

Ed remembered pushing debris off Sy's body. "I did nothing. The firefighters were the rescuers."

"I feel I owe you something." She smiled in a way that was appreciative without conveying expectation.

Dad, watch yourself. You're drooling. Junie appended a rolling-eyes emoji to her text.

What is it about Sy Ioannu that makes me feel 14 years old?

The encounter was interrupted by General Rossmann, who entered the room as if he owned the hospital and the town. He had no visible injuries, though his uniform was peppered with dust and dirt. "Mr Wye, I'd like to speak to you."

A pang of anxiety focused Ed's attention. "How can I help you, General?"

Rossmann's gaze fell on Sy.

"General Rossmann, this is Sy Ioannu. She's part of a group supporting the removal..."

"We've met." Rossmann's remark was familiar with a touch of indifference.

Who's the Nazi? Junie texted to her father on their private channel.

The nurse returned with a tray and pushed past Rossmann. She either did not know or did not care that his word was law when it came to environment of the Pacific West bioregion. The nurse unwrapped the bandages on Ed's hands and sprayed them with an anesthetic.

Junie looked away. Sy closed her eyes.

Rossmann watched the nurse remove bits of glass with tweezers. "You're hands are badly cut, Mr Wye."

"I'll be back at work tomorrow." Ed winced, more at the size of the shards of glass than any discomfort.

Rossmann peered over the nurse's shoulder. "I'm bringing in my own investigative team. I expect your cooperation."

"Of course, General." Snooping bessies made a complicated situation even more convoluted. It was a relief for Ed, though. They would do a better job of finding saboteurs, assuming they existed. Ed could get back to taking down the dam, if he survived long enough. "I'd appreciate it, General, that next time you turn your bots loose, you keep me out of the line of fire."

An unhappy blaze rose in Rossmann's eyes. "Stasers operated by security bots are very precise. It did not miss."

"I'm glad to hear it."

Rossmann relaxed. "You'll also be glad to hear that we've recovered much of the DNA information storage strands from the biologics you, er, bludgeoned. The repair and programming enzymes as well."

"That should provide you several leads."

"Under other circumstances, maybe. Trouble is..." Rossmann paused to study the nurse, who exercised the discretion of all medical professionals, that is, ignoring anything that didn't concern her. "The trouble is that virtually all the maintenance enzymes were disabled."

"Which means?"

"The DNA instructions—the biologics programming, if you will—decayed into gibberish within minutes of your assault."

"I didn't do anything wrong, did I?"

"Not technically, but you made my investigation that much harder."

"My apologies." *I doubt he appreciates sarcasm.*

"Don't get me wrong, Mr Wye. You saved much of downtown Utility, and we did learn one thing."

"Yes?"

"Whoever is sabotaging this project has deep resources. DNA reprogramming is difficult and expensive."

Rossmann reached for the handle of the exam room door. "There is a conspiracy in this community to stop the deconstruction that is as monstrous as I've ever seen, Mr Wye. And more dangerous." He turned to Sy, as if she were an afterthought. "Ms Ioannu, I hope you are back on your feet soon."

"I expect so."

Rossmann grunted. He opened the door. "Oh, and Miss Wye, a

word."

Ed's heart jumped. *What does he want with Junie?*

"The Nazi Party was a gang of thugs and mass murderers of the mid-20th century, as I'm sure you'll remember from school. I hope you're not comparing me or the Bureau of Environmental Security with them?"

Junie went white. "No, sir."

Rossmann smirked and departed.

Junie lowered her head and muttered, "He's still a Nazi."

The nurse grinned.

Ed nudged his daughter. "Be careful, Junie-girl. The bessies aren't evil, but they have a reputation for ruthlessness. That's what makes them scary."

"And effective," Sy said, as her med robot stowed itself in its bay. "Gerard Rossmann is actually a sweet man, in his own way."

"Really?" Ed said. "How do you know him?"

"It's a long story." Sy's eyes lifted. "If you'll let me make you dinner, I'll tell it to you. Tonight?"

Ed couldn't say no to Sy's invitation, in part due to her role as a leader of the minority of Utility residents who supported the dam removal, and in part due to the sheer magnetism of the woman. He could not help himself.

♦ ♦ ♦

Ed endured Junie's mocking with stoic good humor as she picked an outfit for him at once casual and stylish. "She has a reputation as a 'loose woman,' Dad." In front of his bedroom mirror, Junie held up one tie, next to her father's collar, then discarded the idea of a tie altogether.

"How do you know so much about her?"

Junie related the sighting at the mall and Tiffany's assessment.

"Utility is one of the most gossipy places on the planet," Ed said. "It's one reason I left for the Bay Area. It's stifling."

"She's beautiful. She's got a confidence anyone would admire."

"Agreed." Ed thought Sy was one of the most beautiful women he'd ever met.

"I don't think she cares that much about what people think about her or her son."

"You're sure about that, after a ten-second encounter without speaking to her?"

"She reminds me of me," Junie said.

They laughed together. Ed hadn't dated any woman for more than a few months after Junie's mother died, because he didn't want the complications of a relationship as he pursued his ventures. His travels offered plenty of opportunities for friendships and physical intimacy, mostly with women who shared his interests and focus on business and technology. *Natalie Wong, for one.* It was too soon to tell if Sy fell into that category. For one thing, he had to keep his distance because of her political status. Furthermore, she flustered him, and he didn't like it. Ed had trouble figuring who she was. *I can't shake the feeling that she's after something.*

The gate to Sy Ioannu's front yard opened to a garden of native plants and shrubs, arranged in a bed of alabaster gravel raked like a Zen garden. The flowering season was months in the past, but Sy had found a way to introduce a splash of yellow. He knocked on the door and sent a polite greeting via the net account for house guests.

I'm in the kitchen. Let yourself in.

Ed opened the door to a solarium. The glass was at an angle to catch the morning sun in winter, and despite the heat outside, the room was cool in the shade as the late summer sun set behind the hills to the west above the house.

Sy's melodic voice came from somewhere inside the house. "I'm running late and the kitchen's a mess. Can I bring you a glass of wine?"

"Sure." Ed's voice caught, and he cleared his throat. "I was worried I'd be late. Are you sure you're not tired from all the excitement this morning?"

"I'm fine. I'm glad you came. It's better to talk about scary events, don't you think? Better than letting them get to you."

An outdoor set of table and chairs was decorated with flowers and settings for two, minus plates. Ed took a seat on a wicker sofa that made the characteristic creaky, rubbing sound when he put his weight on it. Painted and glazed terra cotta sculptures of similar style were set everywhere in the solarium, like an outdoor art gallery in a fertile desert.

"Here you go." Sy handed him a glass of red wine. "I hope you like it. It's local." She looked fresh, but not girlish.

"I'm sure it's fine." He swirled the wine and tasted. "Very good! I have to ask, are the sculptures yours?"

"Something I work on whenever I can."

Ed nodded, unsure what to say next.

"Excuse me, I have to tend to the meal." Sy wore a full-body apron that had been washed a hundred times. "Do you like Greek food?"

"Love it." *Not too much enthusiasm, buddy.*

"I'm so glad." Sy returned to the kitchen.

Ed sipped the wine, which was as good or better as any he had tasted in California. The thought led his mind to Grace Cromer, and her insistence that he look at the attachments from Natalie Wong in San Francisco. Grace's enthusiasm for the project was on target, as usual, but why she wanted him to comment and offer suggestions puzzled him. Grace was an angel investor in the last two of his business ventures. She believed in his ideas, but they had failed. *All of my ideas have failed, except the first.* However, Grace had hired him to take down the Arroyo Grande Dam, and that job would take two years. *Is she trying to get rid of me already?*

Sy returned with plates of food and set them on the table. A small bowl sat on the large plate next to the entree. She was still wearing the apron. For an instant, Ed caught a look that measured him.

"I'm sorry to be so rushed. I'm a terrible hostess."

"It's alright. I'm enjoying the wine."

"I can hear my mother scolding me. I'll do better." Sy gestured at the food. "The dish is a vegetarian moussaka my grandmother made. The soup is a traditional bean soup."

Ed's mouth watered, even though he was not fond of bean dishes. "It looks delicious."

"One more thing." Sy departed again. Ed left the sofa and took a seat at the table. Sy returned within seconds, and he was halfway out of his chair when she returned. "Don't get up." Sy set down a wicker basket and a small plate. "Bread and olive oil. Staples of Greece."

Sy had removed her apron. She wore a blouse and pants that were sexy without immodesty. Her arms were covered from shoulder to wrist, perhaps to hide the artificial skin covering her injury, but she wasn't flushed or sweaty. *Poised and polished.* Sy refilled the wine glasses. "Don't wait for me, Ed."

"My friends call me 'Eddie.'"

"I'm honored you consider me a friend."

Ed tasted eggplant, fresh tomatoes, lentils, oregano, and black pepper. The feta cheese melted in his mouth. "Wow. I don't think I've ever had this before. What did you call it?"

"Moussaka. It was usually made with meat until the anti-methane regulations. Beef is too expensive for most people now."

"It's delicious."

"My grandmother said vegetarian moussaka was better anyway."

"I thought lamb was a meat of choice in Greek food."

Sy gave Ed a dirty look, then grinned. "Not in this house. And not in many other houses that call themselves humane after the Warming."

Ed finished the moussaka and ate a polite amount of soup. He sipped the last of his wine. "That was amazing. You should open a restaurant, Sy."

"I would much rather entertain a single guest than a bunch of strangers night after night."

"Are you working? I mean, do you have a job?"

She glanced away, with a hint of coy. "Yes, of a kind."

"What kind of work do you do?"

"Entertainment consulting."

Ed sensed that Sy was reluctant to go into detail about her work. Everyone deserved privacy, an increasingly difficult-to-find commodity in a networked society. Ed was tempted to do a quick net search on Sy as he ate, but he resisted. He had his own secrets, and he respected Sy's right to keep hers. "Consulting. I see. Is that how you came to know General Rossmann?"

"In a manner of speaking, yes." Sy looked thoughtful. "He was an up-and-coming officer in a new agency. I was rising in my chosen work. We helped each other. It was a long time ago."

"Did you love him?" Ed gasped for air. "Oh god, I'm sorry. That's none of my business. I've had too much wine." *That stuff is pretty powerful. I've only had two glasses.*

Sy laughed, a sound Ed liked. "That's a perfectly good question. The answer is no. We were close friends and I respect him a great deal, but we weren't in love. We keep in touch."

Ed made a connection. Sy was a newcomer to town, Junie said, and the woman across from him described an old friendship, perhaps more than a friendship, with Rossmann. Here they were, in the same town at the same moment during a crisis. Coincidence? Did Rossmann have an arrangement with Sy, or did she have a hold over him? What did she want?

"Ed, may I ask you a professional question?"

"Sure."

"Is the dam safe?"

"Perfectly." Ed hoped she wouldn't challenge him for specifics. The dam wasn't about to fail, despite the cracks, but it wasn't the safest place in the world these days. Much of Utility was on a plain below the dam, above the old floodplain to be sure, but no one could guess what might happen with a sudden collapse, not without years of engineering studies. Rossmann's conspiracy was the true threat. Ed wanted to share his fears with Sy, but he pledged confidentiality to the general on the emails and other communications. *Perfectly safe? I must be drunk.* Ed put his hand over his glass when Sy offered to pour again. She didn't push it.

"That's a relief. Now, I have... Oh, I'm terrible about prying."

"Go ahead. I really don't mind."

"A few minutes ago, just before we began eating, you looked troubled. Was something on your mind? I'm sorry if it's none of my business."

Am I that transparent? "Well, I received some news, but..." Ed decided to stop talking.

"I'm sorry. Mother always said I should listen more and talk less. 'Two ears to listen, one mouth to speak.'" Sy touched a linen napkin to her full mouth. "I've made baklava. Would you like some?"

Ed wanted to lay out his thoughts to Sy as if they had known each other since childhood. The warmth of the solarium and the deliciousness of the food, and his desire for this woman made him want to open his heart. His imagination flashed on Junie's teasing, which doused the fire. *I can't become besotted with Sy now.* He remembered Junie's disappointment with Alex, and her interest in Don Rast. *There's trouble coming for her, and for me.* "The baklava sounds excellent."

Sy returned from the kitchen with a small plate of four finger-length slices of the layered golden pastry.

"You're an accomplished baker, too."

"You're so generous."

Sy set her chin on her palm, a gesture that signaled to Ed an openness he had never seen before in anyone, not even his long-dead wife. "It's not an offer of another job, Sy, but it's almost the same thing. An old friend sent me a business plan and some technical specs for a new energy venture. They're in the process of putting together an executive team, and the hint is pretty clear that I'm a good fit for CEO."

"Sounds really exciting."

"It does to me, too." Sy leaned inward, waiting for Ed to say more. "But I've just moved here. I've taken a new job for an important project. More importantly, my daughter just moved here, and she wasn't happy about it."

"Kids can adapt to anything."

"That doesn't apply to 17-year-old girls."

Sy laughed again, and it sent a thrill up Ed's spine. "You're right. I remember being 17, and worried about everything that a woman in her forties ought to consider trivial."

"Junie is the most important thing in my life. I won't screw that up." *Unlike I've screwed up so much else.*

"You're a good father, and a good man."

The statement warmed Ed, but it wasn't the content, so much as the undercurrent, a feeling of support and understanding. Sy was not only a peerless hostess, brilliant chef, and a perfect conversationalist, she had a unique power to create a sense of well-being almost spiritual in its depth. As he looked upon her face, it transfigured into the most beautiful object he had ever seen, orders of magnitude more beautiful than a sunset or the Milky Way on a moonless desert night.

The cry broke the spell. Sy looked over to the door leading to the kitchen, and a boy child stood at it, tears streaming from its face. "Mommy, I'm scared." *Her son, just as Junie described.*

The child's mother stretched our her arms, and a stab of jealousy pierced Ed's heart as Sy gathered the boy in her embrace. The feeling embarrassed Ed.

"What happened, darling?" Sy said.

"I'm sorry, Madame." The nanny robot rolled into the solarium. It was the latest Japanese model, built for child care and elder care. Only the wealthiest families could afford them. "The child had a nightmare. The EEG monitor failed to pick it up before he awoke. I apologize."

Sy ignored the robot, instead kissing the tow-headed boy and letting him rest her head on her breast. "I'm so very sorry, Eddie. This is Mason. Robots are only so useful when it comes to sensitive little boys."

"He reminds me of Juniper at that age."

"Can you wait a while until I put him back to bed?"

Ed wanted to stay. Being with Sy was like going home after a long trip. "It's late, and I have to be at work tomorrow. And Mason needs you." The goodbyes were slow and polite. Ed was not angry at the child for interrupting the moment. He sympathized with Sy, who had to cope with the skinned knee or unexpected illness. *More than I did when Junie was small.* Ed reflected on the vision of Sy's face, and a feeling gnawed at him, that it wasn't all it seemed. *The wine, probably.* He set his doubts aside. As he closed the garden gate behind him, he noted an emptiness in his heart that he vowed to fill again with Sy Ioannu.

CHAPTER 8

◆ ◆ ◆

THE HOUR BEFORE MIDNIGHT bestowed on Cov Rast a rare
phenomenon coveted by him and his generation: quiet. Not a true,
dead silence, but the out-competing of human-made sounds by
natural sounds. A stuttering breeze rustled the fallen leaves of the
mature maples, leftovers from a time when parks departments
watered their parcels. A pair of tired crickets rasped in the dry air.
The few man-made sounds at this hour—the crunch of the tires
from the occasional car, the *whirr* of the blades from a passing
police surveillance drone—were muted.

The park was a quiet place from which to watch Syren
Ioannu's house.

The front door opened and Ed Wye emerged, saying his
goodbyes. The elder couldn't hear their conversation, but he knew
the movements. Cov half-expected them to kiss, then corrected
himself. *Whores don't kiss their johns.* Cov intended to speak with
Sy earlier in the evening, but he held back when he saw Wye
approach her door. Cov had ensconced himself on the bench, his
arthritic knees making it hard to move, and waiting for Wye to
leave was better than trying again the next night. *I need to see the
young one.*

Sy stood at her door as Wye climbed into a public car at the
curb. The auto pulled away, and Cov wrenched himself to his feet.
The crickets' chirps marked the slow beat of his footsteps. He
thought of his time in the Army, doing house checks in Kyrgyzstan,
hyper-alert for an ambush. He wished he held his old rifle for

comfort's sake, not for violence. He hated guns after seeing what they did to the bodies of men, women, and children. These days, Sy Ioannu and River Defenders was his enemy, less lethal, but just as stubborn and relentless. She wanted to destroy his way of life, the same as the terrorists in the 'stans.

And here he was, hat in hand, ready to ask for something only she could give: access to the boy.

He announced himself the old-fashioned way: a knock on Sy's door. The door opened.

"Did you forget something, Eddie? Oh, it's you."

The cyprian's head and body were in silhouette, backlit by the house's interior lights. Cov's hearing was good, but his eyes weren't the same, despite enough corrective surgeries to replace both. Cov grinned. "Eddie, is it? Best friends already?"

"I make friends easily, Cov."

"I'm sure you do. May I come in? It's getting chilly out here."

"It's late."

"Only take a minute."

Sy stood aside. The air in her solarium was as dry as outside. Cov failed to understand her fascination with cacti and succulents. The abstract forms and unyielding spines made him think of the drying of his world, the slow receding of the water that shaped his identity as an orchardist.

"Something to drink, Cov?"

He scanned the room for a seat and chose the wicker sofa. He grunted as he lowered himself. "It's getting so I can't walk across the street without being winded." Two wine glasses were on the table, the red dregs collected at the top of their stems. "Ice water, if it's not too much trouble."

After fussing in the kitchen, Sy set a glass in front of Cov. She waited opposite him on the edge of her chair, as if ready to open the door at a second's notice. Her message was clear: *I tolerate you in my home because I have to.* Cov sipped the water. "I know you don't like me, Sy..."

"That's not true."

Lying whore. That's what Cov's mother would have said, if she were alive. *Street-walking trash.* The image was old and inaccurate, but it was the sentiment that counted. Cov's mother, who rarely cussed or raised her voice, might have spat on Sy's floor, the worst insult imaginable. Times had changed, though. It was an enlightened age. *Unlike me?* He let out an involuntary "Pfft."

"What's so funny?"

"I was thinking about my mother. And yours."

"My mother?" Sy was taken aback, her eyes widening.

"I believe in due diligence. About everything."

"What's that have to do with my mother?"

"When Marshal told me about you, I had to check you out. Your mother and grandmother were quite the movers and shakers, reformers in the best sense of the word." Cov's comment was not meant as a compliment. "I'm sure you disappointed them."

Cov enjoyed watching Sy wrestle with her rage. *She can't do a damn thing about it.*

"If you were not Mason's grandfather, I'd throw you out."

"Did your mother disown you when she discovered what you'd done? Where was your father, by the way? Fucking some other whore?" Cov laughed with the cynicism of too much knowledge. "No, that's not fair. He was probably loyal to the core, for business reasons, I imagine."

Sy fell into a familiar defensive mode. They'd discussed her professional history before. "Cov, I know you don't believe it, but my mother and grandmother and the other sex workers—"

Cov laughed again, but not so loud as to disturb the boy, whom he guessed was sleeping.

"—who changed everything are heroes to many, many people."

"Not in my world."

"You'd be surprised."

"All your ma and grandma and the others did was get the government off their backs. Hmm. That makes me wonder. Did they ask while they were *on* their backs?"

Sy went white. Cov was ready for her to slap him, but she held her temper. *C'mon baby. If you can dish it out, I can take it.* Cov sighed. "I apologize, Syren. It's late and I'm tired." He threw his head back in a silent cry. "There's too much change in the world! Why can't things settle down? Give us a chance to get used to things. To catch up. My grandmother complained about Martin Luther King, a half century after he changed everything. My mother complained about Harvey Milk and gay rights, a generation after that was settled. It just never stops. Now I have to put up with unions of whores that get preferential treatment from dumb-ass politicians, in exchange for what?"

"Safety, justice, health care, a living wage, a recognition of reality that we're here, we've always been here, and we're not going away." Sy put her hands together, as if praying that Cov would understand. "Would you rather we go back to being victims?"

"I wish the world would go back to some kind of sanity!" Cov's throat nearly closed from his anger, which had less to do with Sy's chosen profession, then the slipping away of his world in the waning days of his life. "You're threatening everything my family has worked for. My grandmother and mother were heroes too. Two hundred years we've worked this land, but you've been here fewer years than the five fingers of my hand." He held up his calloused fingers. "Why should you rise while we fall?"

"It's not a zero-sum game, Cov." Her voice was gentle, seductive. "We can both win as the world changes."

Cov sneered. "You should talk. You didn't abide by the rules." *She's not only a harlot, she's a cheat.* Unlike his mother, were she alive, Cov didn't care about Sy's trade of sex for money. It was the cheating that angered him. It was the dishonesty. Sy's dishonesty. *Marshal's dishonesty.* "I'm curious. What exactly did you do to yourself? I've always wanted to know."

Sy folded her arms, protecting herself against another of Cov's assaults. "You tell me. You seem to know already."

Cov shrugged. "I only know what the Cyprian Association knows, or at least what the Bay Area media found out after you disappeared. 'Daughter of Cyprian Rights Leader Loses CA License Over DNA Mods,' or something. It was never clear exactly what kind of modifications."

Sy leaned back on the couch. For the first time, she looked ashamed.

"Oh come off it, Sy. Everyone from pro athletes to fashion models do it. Bending the rules to gain an advantage. I'm in business, too, remember? It's a competitive world. A base pair here, a subtracted sequence there. What's an extra chromosome between friends?"

Sy's eyes were fixed on a cactus.

"Trouble is, only the fools get caught. What's it feel like to cheat on your law-abiding brothers and sisters in the union?"

"All right, Cov, I'll tell you." She pinched her skin, lifting a sample to show Cov, or punishing herself. "Chameleon and cuttlefish genes."

Cov's jaw dropped. "Jesus God, I wouldn't have believed it, if you hadn't said it yourself. You're a shapeshifter."

"You make it sound like I can turn into a lizard or a cephalopod."

"No, but you can make a man completely insane with lust. They see their wildest fantasies when you want them to."

Sy relaxed, and inched toward Cov. He swallowed when her affect changed from fury to lasciviousness. She opened her full mouth slightly, and Cov swore her appearance softened. Her tongue moved inside her mouth. His groin stirred, and he was afraid he might reach out to touch her. "It only works if you have working balls." She glanced down as his crotch. "Yours don't."

Bitch. The insult cut to Cov's core, but he was wise enough to recognize a provocation, and old enough that his blood couldn't rise as fast as it did when he was a young man. That distance and experience allowed a rumor to surface. A contact at the dam told him the BES snoops had linked the DNA programming in the out-of-control dozer to the project's local network AI. Investigators were interviewing everybody, even the carpenter's apprentice.

A thought brought Cov up short. Sy had modified her DNA to gain a business advantage. Could she be connected to the sabotage? Cov dismissed the idea—he knew little about the technology, and Sy wanted the dam down—but doubts lingered. *Does she know who's involved?*

Cov's mind turned to his other nemesis. "I'm sure you've been honest with Ed Wye about your intentions."

The cyprian returned to her seat, in repose. "And by that you mean..."

"Does he know about you?"

"Does it matter?"

"Of course it matters, but that's what I can't figure." Cov cocked his head, as if looking at Sy from a different angle. Her spell—if that's what it was—wore off in a blink. "What do you gain by seducing Ed Wye, beyond offering a nice welcome gift from a fellow bug hugger."

"I have at least as much to gain by helping Eddie... Ed succeed as you do by manipulating him into failure, the same way you discredited and ran out his predecessors."

Cov grunted. "Touché." He interlaced his fingers. "Apparently, your attentions didn't help the previous supers."

"You're mistaken—"

Cov tuned out Sy's attempts to defend herself. Instead, his mind cast back to the lonely months after his wife died, the loss of connection and physical intimacy as painful as a surgery without anesthetic. Visiting a licensed cyprian occurred to Cov, but the echoes of his mother's voice kept him away, and he suppressed a modicum of admiration for Sy. Cyprians were closer to the ancient idea of courtesans than the prostitutes that just did an act for cash. Cyprians were courtesans for the masses. That's how they won over the public.

Cov observed the trade regulations work wherever they were adopted, and Utility was a good quarter-century behind the trend, but he would never support them publicly. If adopting the sex regs ever came up again before the council, he'd lobby against them. He had a reputation to maintain. Nonetheless, Utility would adopt the regs eventually, Cov foresaw, just as it had buckled under the pressure of urbanites combating climate change as the average temps rose and kids could no longer go out in July or August even to swim in the reservoir for fear of heatstroke.

He drew the line at the dam.

"Are you ashamed of me and Mason?" Sy said.

Cov startled out of his reverie. "What?"

"Are you ashamed of us?"

The question got to the heart of the matter. The first part was easy to answer; Cov was not ashamed of Sy. *I can't be ashamed of a stranger, though I've known her for five years now.* Cov's check-ins were more about the boy than the mother. "Mason is my own blood. Shame is irrelevant."

"You wouldn't say that about Marshal. You never talk about him, ask about us, anything." Sy shifted in her seat. "I don't hate you, but you hate him."

The whore has a point. Am I ashamed of my own son? "My feelings about my son are none of your business."

"I think they are, Cov. I have a stake in this. Marshal was the father of Mason, your grandson."

"Marshal took up with a... cyprian after his divorce and got her pregnant. How did that happen, by the way? Aren't you people supposed to have the best contraception and end pregnancies early?"

"Do you wish that I'd had an abortion?"

"That's not what I meant."

"Mistakes happen. Marshal was just another client at first. But when the CA found out what I'd done to my genes, he kept coming to me, as a friend. Everyone abandoned me, except him. You should be proud of him."

"He was an idiot. You lied to everyone. You deserved to be thrown out on the street. Then you got pregnant..."

"And Marshal brought me here to your unending regret."

"You let yourself get pregnant because you knew Marshal was a decent man who wouldn't abandon his child and his mother. You *are* a whore." *I can't forgive him.*

"You're ashamed of Marshal. I know it because you've never told Don that he has a half-brother."

"How can you know what I tell Don and don't tell him?" *What she says is true.*

"Call it an instinct. I've seen Don around town. He's like his father, handsome, warm, and decent, despite his dissing. You're proud of him, aren't you?"

Cov was so proud of Don that he thought his heart would burst. Don was the best grandson a man could have, and Marshal was the best son a man could have. Father and son worked together in the orchards for most of Marshal's forty-eight years. He was steady as a rock to the point of stubbornness sometimes, but Cov admired that strength. Marshal knew who he was until April left him. Cov noticed something about Sy's face. It had the openness that got men talking. Marshal and April talked for hours about everything. *April's openness was real. Is Sy's just a substituted DNA gene sequence?* "I am proud of Don."

"Why don't you feel the same way about Mason?"

"Who says I don't?" The defensiveness in Cov's tone shocked him. Cov was a man sure of himself, certain that after 83 years he had figured life out. Few mysteries of day-to-day living remained. He knew what to do, except how to feel about Mason. Or about Marshal. *How many years does it take for a man to get over the suicide of his only son?*

"I think you may hate Marshal. You hate him for killing himself, and you're ashamed of him."

Cov's anger rose. "You are the one who deserves my hate. You drove Marshal insane with your freakish genes, let yourself get pregnant, then extorted money from him to keep you and your bastard son in a house you don't deserve. You all but pushed him off that bluff. When I had to scrape his brains off the basalt, I thought of you. And then you had the gall to lead a bunch of bug huggers that wants to get rid of the dam. You're trying to destroy me, first through Marshal and then the dam. If you want me to hate someone, you're the best candidate I can think of."

Sy blinked, but otherwise did nothing. "Why would I do anything like that to a man I loved and who loved me?"

"Whores can't love."

"Neither can old men."

"No, we're just pickier." Cov took a long draft of the water. The ice clinked in the glass. "I want to see him."

"Now?"

"Now."

"What if I said No?"

"I'll cut you off. No more bank transfers from the money that Marshal set aside for you. You'll lose everything."

"You promised to honor his wishes."

"Promises to the dead are nothing to the living."

"I'll take you to court."

Cov laughed. "Don't make threats you can't carry out. Exposure wouldn't do you or Mason any good."

"Your threats are as empty as mine. Besides, I have a job, a legitimate job. I can make my own way."

"Shilling for the bessies can't possibly pay enough to keep you in diapers and bots." Cov shifted. "I just want to look at him."

Cov observed the debate in her eyes. She believed her son deserved to know his family, but Cov knew the argument: He was a relic of the oppressive, ignorant past that could do more harm than good to the boy. *Maybe so, but Mason is my blood.* Sy sighed and rose from her seat. "Come then."

The cyprian led Cov out of the solarium down a hall to the darkened child's bedroom. 2-D pictures of puppies and construction equipment hung on the walls. The nanny bot was docked in the corner, its green ready light comforting and frightening. A toy car bot skittered out of Cov's way, and he feared Mason might wake. He didn't, sleeping deeply, covered by a blanket with shimmering holograms of cartoon characters. The child was small for his age, an infant in a three-year-old's body. *Just like Marshal at that age. His mother kept him at her breast much later than most babes.* Cov opened his mouth to share this memory with Sy, but changed his mind. She didn't deserve the gift.

Instead, Cov gripped the edge of a dresser and dropped to one knee to be nearer the child. He gritted his teeth to get through the pain, and it passed quickly. He was thankful when Sy moved a half-step back, giving Cov some room. Grandfather laid a papery hand on the grandson's sandy hair, murmuring a blessing.

CHAPTER 9

♦ ♦ ♦

JUNIE CHEERED as the "Electrons" of Julius Rast High School scored a touchdown against the Moses Lake High School "Chiefs." She jumped up and down as if the concrete bleachers were a trampoline, but her participation was spiritless. Alex had pinged her and sent this text: Something's come up. I can't come this weekend.

Why not? Junie added a bawling emoji. The feeling was half-joke, half-sincere.

School stuff. Mom says that comes first.

Tell your mom that your g-f needs her b-f.

I'm a senior. Mom says I have to ace everything. You're a distraction.

A whistle blew, signaling two minutes left in the game.

Ditched again. The problem was the two emotional signals attached to Alex's text: disappointment and relief. *He's forgotten that he set the emo-sigs to auto-generate.* The second emotion alarmed Junie. Attaching emo-sigs to one-to-one communications was common, but when people forgot about the automated features and how they often misread the sender's emotional state... *Divorces have been caused by less.*

Do you think I'm a distraction?

No.

Action on the football field brought Junie's mind back to the game. A ref-bot signaled a—what was it?—someone broke the rules. Mr Henderson, who directed the ref-bot squad, announced the punishment, or whatever it was called. *Penalty.*

Maybe I did something wrong, something that pissed off Alex. Is it me? Did I make you mad or your mom mad?

No.

Liar. *Why am I having trouble believing him?*

You didn't do anything. I'm sorry. OK? I see the pissed-off emo-sig. Fuck, it's just that... I'm still coming to visit. Okay? I just don't know when. Maybe around Solstice?

Bullshit. Alex always spent the solstice break with his father diving in Hawaii. The joy of the rescue at the highway dissipated. Anger and hurt simmered now in Junie. She'd seen this before with friends fighting with boys and in the rom-coms on the chans.

Action on the field banished Junie's melancholy temporarily. A Chiefs player flung the football in a perfect arc down the field. Junie marveled at the player's instinctive grasp of ballistics and timing combined with Einstein's vision of a warped reality as the ball followed a gravity-bent curve of spacetime. As the ball fell, a flash of powder blue leapt in front of the Chiefs' player. Number 86, Don Rast, his hands high in the air, snatched the ball from its trajectory and brought it to his breast. He cradled it like a baby as he tore down to the opposite end of the field and into the end zone.

The Electrons' touchdown hammered a final nail in the coffin of the adversary's hopes for victory. Despite Alex's upsetting cancellation, Junie screamed herself into hoarseness, a mass injury not usually noted by the anti-football moralizers. It afflicted every one of the thousand or so students, parents and hangers-on at Rast Field, apart from the unfortunates from Moses Lake.

The endorphin high didn't last. The memory of Alex's texting pushed back into Junie's consciousness. Alex, you're breaking up with me, aren't you?

What? Why would I do that? I love you. His emo-sig was sincerity.

That can be faked, even on the net. Despite her doubts, Alex's declaration soothed her. OK. Sorry. I just miss you, that's all.

Me too. I'll be in touch. OK?

Fine.

The doubts lingered. Alex's behavior fit a pattern. After the first football game she attended, Junie shared images with her San Francisco c-tribes to universal derision. The pics and videos confirmed that the culchies out in the sticks of Pacific West lived outside civilized norms. The only football worth playing was the "beautiful" version. Alex called Junie's peers in Utility "troglodytes." She didn't like it. *The people around here may be a little behind the times in some ways, but they aren't knuckle-dragging cavemen.* Junie chose not to share photos from her second game, and after more insults and questions about her sanity, she changed the minds-eye privacy settings to exclude her geolocation to everyone except Alex, her Utility friends, and her father. She was done explaining herself to the Bay Area people. *They don't respect me anymore. Do I still respect them?*

She fingered the thin gold band on her finger, given to her by Alex the day before she left for Utility. He was her best connection to her old life. They would go hiking in the Santa Cruz Mountains, or sailing out of Half Moon Bay, or clubbing in Haight-Ashbury. The music was loud, the mist barely legal, and he was the sexiest man alive. She closed her eyes, and she felt his hands, powerful from daily gymnastics practice, around her waist.

Tiffany texted Junie, because being heard over the screams of the Electrons' fans was impossible. What's up with you?

Junie gave her friend a sheepish look without answering.

Tiffany wasn't fooled. Boy trouble. I can smell it. She attached a concern emoji. Alex, right?

Junie stared ahead.

`Want to talk about it?`

`No.`

`Suit yourself.`

Junie wasn't ready to admit that Alex was probably pulling away. He was not the type of guy to just drop her, which made the situation harder. Junie almost wished he'd remove the "attached" icon from his avatar. A public statement like that, and she'd know where she stood. It would hurt, but it would be over sooner, like ripping off an adhesive bandage.

The game was over, but a local radio station was interviewing Rast High coaches and players on the field. Junie found the stream chan. The host interviewed all the scoring players, except one.

The oversight troubled Junie. The stands were emptying, leaving the field much quieter. Junie, Tiffany, and Trudy stood in a knot with other seniors. Junie tapped Tiffany's arm.

"What?"

"The radio people didn't interview Don. They were talking to everyone who scored, but not him."

Trudy sneered. "He's dissed, remember? *Persona non grata.* You can't interview a non-person."

Don sat on the team bench by himself.

"Don't talk to him." Tiffany gave Junie a stern look.

"Who says I'm going to?"

"I told you he's damaged goods."

"You're imagining things. He looks lonesome. It's not fair."

"Just sayin'." Tiffany wagged her finger at Junie. "Give yourself a chance to bounce before letting another man catch you on the rebound."

"I don't know what you mean." Junie joined the students and fans who poured onto the field in the victory celebration. She drifted toward the Electrons' Friday night hero. Tiffany shook her head No, but her warning carried no weight. Junie found Don unwinding athletic tape from his ankle. "That was the most beautiful thing I ever saw."

Don was wary. "What?"

"The catch. The, um, interception, and the run. It was as beautiful as anything at the San Francisco Ballet."

Don scanned the area around him. "Thanks, but you're not supposed to be talking to me in public." He removed his helmet, and the disidentification welt bulged where the helmet's lining pressed into his sweaty hair. "At least back out from my bubble."

Junie stepped back to the regulation three meters distance from a disidentified felon. It felt weird, even wrong, after ignoring the rule by giving a dissed man a peach and rescuing a child in danger of getting run over. *Why is it so easy for me to disobey the rules here?* "I'm sorry. I don't want to get you in trouble."

Other fans waived at Don, a concession to the cause for the victory celebration. Don met their eyes in silent gratitude. If he spoke to them, they would also be guilty of violating the punishment statutes. He played for the Electrons under a special permit from the juvenile justice authorities, and no one wanted to endanger his status. A potential league championship was at stake.

Junie wished she could add him to the c-tribe of her friends, or even set up a private channel, but that was a worse violation of his punishment than physical proximity or conversing. His relationship icon was "unattached." She had an idea. Making a half-turn to her left, she spoke as if on a voice call. No one stood next to her. If a policeman challenged her, she could claim to be speaking aloud on a priv chan. "It's so unfair. If this were a thousand years ago, you'd be carried on everyone's shoulders and given a laurel crown."

"It's alright, Junie."

If you were Alex, I would be smothering you with kisses, but he's fourteen-hundred kilometers away. There's no one to kiss you.

The crowd cleared off the field as the players disappeared into the locker room. Junie waited for Don to leave, but he stayed put.

"Aren't you going inside?" Junie said.

"I have to wait for the locker room and the showers to empty."
Junie imagined Don naked.

"You don't have to wait, Junie."

"I don't feel right leaving."

A police surveillance drone sped overhead, its blue and red light flashing, like a oversized bumble bee on a life-or-death mission.

"Please, Junie. I'm not alone. Grandpa is in the stands. He waits to take me home."

Junie scanned the scattering of fans still in the bleachers. She didn't see Cov Rast. The network reported his presence, though.

Don picked up his helmet. "The shower's clear. I have to go now."

The clack of Don's cleats echoed inside the locker room before the door closed behind him. Junie climbed a short flight of stairs to the parking lot. Most of the cars had driven away. Tiffany's car was gone; Junie would catch up to her later. Junie lingered near the bleachers, unable to decide whether to leave or wait for Don. Covington Rast shuffled near.

"You're the Wye girl." The old man, a fresh scar on his forehead, leaned on a cane. "I remember you from the dam, when the coffer burst. Quite a performance on your part." He scanned her up and down. The gesture did not bother her. "Have you seen Don?"

Junie suspected he knew exactly where his grandson was. "He went into the locker room a minute ago."

"So you know him, do you?"

"I've helped him with homework once or twice."

"At school, for academic purposes, so as not to violate his sentence."

Junie felt interrogated. "Of course, Mr Rast."

The old man grunted. A moment of awkward silence passed between Junie and Cov Rast. Junie heard the trudge of feet up concrete steps, and Don spotted Junie. By habit, he circled around her, maintaining the legal distance, a thoughtful gesture, signaling a desire not to endanger her. Their eyes met for a half-second, and he lifted a corner of his mouth. The Rast's car pulled up and grandfather and grandson drove away, leaving Junie alone in the lot. Night had fallen, though the field lights pushed back the darkness. Junie wished she had brought a sweater.

She walked the two blocks home. Alex's cancellation pressed on her. Hanging out with Tiffany and Trudy was less attractive than before. A text came through. It was from Covington Rast.

```
I'm sending this because Don is
prohibited from contacting you by his
sentence. He says he needs more help with
his calculus homework. He wants to know if
you will come over for a visit tomorrow.
```

◆ ◆ ◆

The public car ferried Junie beyond the town limits, across the river, and up into the hills. Her anxiety spiked. She was already jittery about the visit; her father's attitude didn't help. He had no problem with a friendship with Don, as long as she observed the regulations and kept the interaction to academic help. A citation for illegally associating with a dissed person might hurt her chances for acceptance at a good college. He was skeptical, however, of Cov Rast's motives for allowing her into his home. It seemed inconsistent, given his vehement opposition to the dam removal. Junie cared little for dam politics, but the tension in her father's voice put her on edge.

Tiffany was relentless in her warnings. `He's hot, but at least wait until the welt's gone.` Back in San Francisco, Junie knew of girls who dated dissed guys, and their reputations suffered. Junie was certain Don was different, though she couldn't put her finger on why. *It's only school work. Alex is my boyfriend.*

The car turned off the two-lane paved road onto a gravel road, kicking up dust as it passed hundreds of trees, all the same height and the same species. Concerned the car's AI was broken, she came within seconds of ordering it to turn back, but the xGPS showed the car was on target. The road opened out onto a manicured garden with real grass. *Grass in a desert?* Don came out of the front door and greeted her. She wore a simple short-sleeved shirt, jeans, flats, and no makeup. She flinched when he ignored the bubble.

"Sorry," he said. "I should've told you. The three-meter rule doesn't apply at home."

Junie nodded, happy as if she had heard a pleasant secret. She followed Don into the house, which smelled of organic fertilizer and old clothes.

An elderly voice boomed. "Who's that, Don?"

"Junie's here, Grandpa."

The old man appeared, his hand braced against a door. "Nice to see you again. Junie, is it?"

"Yes, Mr Rast."

"Your avatar says your name is 'Juniper.' Unusual for a girl."

"My mother was Scottish. Juniper is used in Gaelic saining ceremonies."

"Saining?" One his scraggly eyebrows arched.

"A blessing, for protection."

Cov Rast's skepticism was evident. "Well, I guess I would expect that from a city woman." He turned and disappeared. His voice resounded from another room. "Why can't people these days name their kids something normal?"

Junie whispered, "What was that about?"

Don rolled his eyes. "Don't worry about it. He gets cranky around strangers."

Don showed Junie into the dining room. The large ancient table was covered with a clean cloth and decorated with a vase and fresh flowers. *For my benefit?* The thought warmed her. Junie removed her tablets from her shoulder bag while Don fussed in the kitchen. She glanced around at the dust collectors and holo-pics. One showed a young Don with a middle-aged man with the same curly hair, though less of it. A slightly younger Cov Rast rounded out the trio. Don came back from the kitchen with fruit drinks.

"Who's the third man in the picture?"

A shadow crossed Don's face. "My father."

Junie glanced around, peering into the spacious dining room where she saw Cov's feet stretched out from an easy chair. "Is he here?"

"He died a few years ago."

"Oh. I'm sorry."

The feet in the dining room pulled up closer to the hidden body.

"It's alright." Don kept his eyes away from Junie. "It was an, um, accident."

Family secret. A bad one. Junie knew better than to pry, but an instinctive sympathy welled up in her chest. Don had told a lie, and he was ashamed of it. It was easy to forgive him. They barely knew each other. *I'm here to help him with his homework, not gather intelligence.*

Don and Junie worked for two hours. After a month or so in Utility, Junie learned that she was ahead of most other Rast High students in math skills, but not by much. Mr Henderson knew his business, but Don was not a natural math talent. He struggled, but Junie didn't mind. He listened to her and picked up some of her problem-solving techniques. She relaxed as they talked about the calculus problems, school, friends, and random things. *He is different.* Sitting next to Don, the air was crisper, her hearing sharper, her awareness of the world magnified by his presence, like those military network add-ons she had heard about. *I miss Alex.*

"I need a break." Don sipped the last of his drink. "Refill?"

"Thanks."

He brought back a fresh drink. "Let's go outside for a while."

Are you with him? The text came from Tiffany.

Go away.

That means Yes. Can you keep your hands off him?

Fuck off.

That means No, probably not. Don't say I didn't warn you.

Junie put a temporary block on all texts so she wouldn't be interrupted by stupid friends. Tutor and student took a break. Outside, under a mature fruit tree, where the shade cut the heat by 10 degrees, she glanced up at Don's face, and she saw the prominent Adam's apple and strong chin. He rested his right hand on his left shoulder, as if embracing himself, and he winced. "Is something wrong?"

"It's nothing. I'm always sore after a game. It's better after a day or two."

Junie wanted to massage out the pain, but before she could work up the courage, he started for the barn. He looked back. "Come on. I'd like to show you something."

Sunlight streamed through spaces between the old sheets of roofing metal, highlighting the buzzing flies like searchlight beams. The fragrance was strong, but not overwhelming. The concrete floor was dusty, but swept.

"Over here," Don said.

Two horses stood together in a large stall. Don patted one of them. "This is Delia. The other one is Frankie."

"Wow." Junie had never seen a horse up close before. "Are they yours?"

"Technically, they belong to the ranch, but Grandpa put me in charge. I've taken care of them since I was ten."

Delia pushed her nose at Junie, taking a sniff, and letting it out, mussing Junie's hair.

"They're amazing," Junie said. "Do you ride them?"

"Not if I want to avoid a fat fine from the bessies."

"I don't understand."

"Riding's illegal now. Something about damage to horse's spines or legs or something. City people made the government pass a law."

City people. That includes me. It seemed that adults' only role in life was to take things away young people might enjoy. "Hey, it's not my fault."

"Actually, I could ride Delia or Frank, but I'd have to get a special license. Hours of training and exams. It's a huge hassle. Only rich people can afford it."

"So why do you keep the horses?"

"Grandpa says it reminds him of the first Rast who farmed this property. He used draft horses for a few years before he could buy a tractor. And the guests like them, especially when we let the horses run loose in the pasture."

"Guests?"

"We've got a cottage, which we rent out to visitors. They come over from Seattle and the Bay Area. We rent out these, too." Don loosened a thin rope and pulled off a heavy tarp. He opened a small cabinet and removed a cloth and began wiping the robots down.

The bots gleamed in the filtered sunlight, and if not for their absolute stillness, as if made of ice, June would have mistaken them for real horses. One of the two bots was the color of liquid mercury. The other was the color of Black Hills gold. Junie touched their cold metal skins.

"This is what the visitors ride now, instead of flesh and blood animals," Don said.

"They're beautiful." Junie liked how her reaction pleased Don.

"Would you like to ride one?"

Junie nodded eagerly. "But, don't go to a lot of trouble on my account."

"No trouble. They're on a low-power standby. I have to do a weekly systems check anyway. They're pretty high-maintenance bots, but they earn a lot of money for us." Don removed a tablet from a shelf and swiped into an app. Junie swore she heard the bots take a breath.

"Which one would you like?" Don said.

Both were beautiful works of industrial art, but Junie was already in love with the golden horse. Don touched a button, and he guided Junie back a couple of paces. The bot woke up with a slight jerk, and stepped off its power pad. "Everything checks out. Batteries at 100 percent." He touched the tablet again, and the bot clip-clopped out into the yard. It lifted its head high and flicked its ears as if checking for danger. Opening a closet door, Don removed a saddle and a helmet.

Doubts welled up in Junie. "I've never ridden a bot before."

"This model is designed for all skill levels up to beginning dressage." Don placed a blanket over the bot's back. "I'll set the rider skill level to 1. The only setting lower is zero, for little kids. The horse doesn't even move at that level." He tightened the cinch on the saddle, and draped a bridle over the horse's head. The bot opened its "mouth" as if accepting the bridle. Junie almost believed the machine had a heartbeat and an animal's consciousness.

"Why isn't the horse the same color as Delia and Frankie?" Both were a dark brown with a white patch on their foreheads.

"The dealer told us riders prefer the unreal colors. The bot manufacturers have gotten so good with mimicking behavior that the true horse colors made the bots seem too real, and that scared off buyers." Don wiped down the bot's front legs. "Personally, I love these things."

115

His touch on the bots was careful, even loving, to Junie. "You remind me of the way people used to take care of the old carbon-fuel cars."

"Exactly," Don said. "Ok, she's ready."

"She?"

Don shrugged and grinned. "Why not?" He put out his hands and interlaced his fingers.

"Does she have a name?

"It should be over her avatar."

Junie had forgotten to check her minds-eye, and the horse had a bot avatar with a horse image icon and the name "Daisy."

"Weak name, but I won't argue with you."

Junie stepped on Don's open fingers; he was unconcerned about the dirt and dust on her shoes. She dropped on the saddle and the bot adjusted its stance. The leather of the saddle creaked. "What do I do now?"

"What do you want to do?"

"I don't know. Walk around?"

"Coming up." Don touched the tablet. "The kill switch is armed. If you get scared, just jump off and the horse will stop moving." The ground appeared miles away from Junie's perch in the saddle. *Great way to break an ankle.* The equine robot made a slight turn to the right, starting a slow circle around the yard. A few minutes later, it returned to its starting place.

Not so bad. "Will it follow my commands?" Junie said.

"Sure. Check the ranch software archive. There's a minds-eye app for issuing commands to the bot."

"I see it," Junie said. "Ok, it's installed."

"Set it to voice commands, and give it some simple instructions, like 'walk' or 'left.'"

Junie enjoyed a few minutes of directing the bot around the yard. It obeyed immediately, but smoothly, every movement graceful and gentle. "Don, this is incredible. Can we go for a

ride?"

Don shrugged. "Sure. It's better than going back for more calculus homework." Don saddled and mounted the second equine, named "Silver." He filled a large canteen with tap water and stowed it in a pouch on a saddle bag. He kept a watchful eye on Junie as she practiced giving commands to Daisy. He placed another large package in the other pouch. Junie wanted to ask about it, but kept silent.

"I'm going to set Daisy to follow Silver closely, as if it were following an alpha mare in a herd. You're not used to controlling Daisy, so this will be safer. Okay?"

Junie chafed at Don's protectiveness, but she accepted his rules.

Don nudged Silver, which accepted haptic input. They walked through an orchard, which Don said were pears, and they emerged onto a well-worn trail that wound up into the hills. The sun was an hour from touching the peaks of the hills on the western side of the river. A breeze kept the heat bearable.

The rhythm of the slow walk lulled Junie. "Don, what happened?"

"What do you mean?"

"The dissing. What did you do?"

He paused as if deciding how to answer the question. "A couple of years ago, I was out hunting jackrabbits."

Junie twisted her face in disgust. *Torturing small animals.* Because she was behind him, he didn't see her reaction.

"I fired a round, but I didn't watch where I was aiming. The bullet hit a wild horse."

How did you not see a horse in front of you?

"It was only a .22, but the horse was unlucky, and it bled to death. I called for animal rescue, but there was nothing they could do. It was a stallion in prime condition. The BES biologists were pretty upset."

117

"So you were punished."

"I was sixteen. I got the juvenile sentence. It'll be over by graduation, and the welt will go away by then. It's already starting to shrink."

Junie better understood Tiffany's reticence about Don. The previous spring, before moving to Utility, she took a course in environmental history, which was mostly about the Warming. The effects were worse than any scientist expected, and people demanded the government do something. Laws against environmental damage were expanded. Violations that police used to ignore now earned disidentification. Crimes against animals, especially protected species, were treated like many crimes against persons. Except for the most horrible crimes, almost no one went to prison. Erasing them from public memory was more humane. "You're lucky you didn't hit a human being with that bullet."

"Even if I had, it would've been an accident," Don said. "The lawyer Grandpa hired said it was like being charged with manslaughter."

"Were you sorry?"

"What kind of question is that? Of course I was sorry." Don nudged Silver, which pulled ahead a meter or so. Daisy picked up her pace, jolting Junie. *I deserved that. Don is nothing but kind to animals.*

They continued on the trail for a kilometer or so, and Junie drank in the stark undulations of the plain, dotted with sagebrush and cut by dry washes with stunted cottonwoods. The trail passed under a cliff made of basalt columns. They resembled the columns of a Roman temple, narrower than the carved marble columns, with no space between them. On the exposed flat planes of the hexagonal columns, someone had carved or scraped onto the rock. The lines of the images were gray, close to white, and they stood out against the red-brown patina of the ancient basalt. Junie identified birds, antelope, and human outlines with rays of light extending outward from their bodies. Some of the shapes were abstract, others random, but not natural. "Who made these?" Junie said.

"No one knows for sure. There were Indians here for thousands of years before white people came. There were Indian wars in the 1850s in the Spokane Valley and the Yakima Valley. All the Indians are on the reservation now."

The equines trudged into open country. "Don, are we going any place in particular?"

"I'd like to show you something else, if that's okay." Don turned around in his saddle. A thin trickle of sweat stained the back of his t-shirt. It highlighted his broad shoulders. "We can go back, if you like."

"No, I'm fine."

The young man nodded, and the horses took a branch of the trail, which was barely visible among the clumps of greasewood and exposed basalt blocks baked over 10,000 years to the color of dark bread. They came to a gully and Junie thought she heard voices, low, whispering. The sound sent chills up her spine. Though the sky was blue overhead, the gully was in shadow. Silver passed through a cut in an outcropping of basalt, like a gate. Don vanished for a half-second behind the branches of a tall shrub, its leaves the dirty green of late summer, and Junie's heart skipped. *If something happens, how will I find my way back?* Daisy picked up speed, trotting to return to her place behind Silver. Don rode as if nothing had happened. The ground became flat and sandy, and they passed through another set of shrubs.

"Here we are," Don said.

The settlement resembled a village from an underdeveloped country or one of the coastal areas plagued by Category Five hurricanes. A bearded man and a elderly woman came out smiling from a shack made of discarded planks and tin roofing. They stopped short when they saw Junie.

Junie inhaled when she saw the welts.

"Don't worry, Peter. She's okay." Don reached back to his saddle pack and removed the package that had piqued Junie's curiosity. "Here's the medicines and the other things you wanted."

Silver and Daisy stopped, and Peter accepted the package with a thank-you. On his forehead, and on the woman's, below the hairline of each, was a raised welt in the shape of a tulip. Junie was transported back to the parking lot below the sculptures of the running horses and the pitiable dissed man who might've been the blacksmith who might've lost his arm to the BES. Though Peter and his companion were whole, here was an entire community of the social dead, and Don was helping them.

Despite her sympathy for individual dissed, watching Don interact with a dozen at once frightened her. It violated everything she'd ever been taught. *They're criminals. They've hurt the earth. They are nothing.* She heard General Rossmann's voice warning her that she was watched. She imagined her father angry and her friends abandoning her.

When the little girl she rescued ran up to her, the joy of recognition plain as day, Junie ran again. This time, she was running away.

CHAPTER 10

COV RAST'S OLD EYES were no good in the dark. He was thankful for the security system, which tracked the young riders as twilight turned into night. After bedding down the equines, the Wye girl and Don shared a fruit cobbler in the kitchen. His grandson didn't touch her as Cov watched discreetly from the parlor, but Cov was a young man once, and he didn't need the silly emo-sig enhancements on his com to know every detail of what Don was feeling. *Awkwardness. Uncertainty. Longing.* They were the same feelings he had when he took Arlene out for the first time, when Cov was almost exactly Don's age. The woman who would become Cov's wife was different than Ed Wye's daughter. *Different, but not opposite. Arlene had spice too.*

After the girl drove away, Cov shuffled into the kitchen while Don cleaned up the dishes. "Pretty young lady."

"I thought you'd gone to bed." Don put on a mask of indifference.

"Pretty girl, I said."

Don pursed his lips.

Cov knew the sign. It kept a lid on emotions. "You're about fit to bust, that's what I say." The grandfather was not a man to burst out in laughter, but he was close, especially when his grandson's face turned the color of a Fuji cultivar. "Sit down, son. You and I need to talk."

"I'm tired. I want to sleep."

"This won't take long."

Cov poured himself a half-cup from the always-on pot. He drank it black, angling himself at the table and rested one arm on the bare top. Cov took a sip. "Good plain coffee." Don kept his eyes away from his grandfather, as if he had been caught stealing. "How much do you know about this Wye girl, son?"

"Her name's Junie."

"Junie, is it? Well..." Cov paused, taking in Don's quick defense of the Wye girl. "She's the daughter of Edward Wye, the project superintendent for the dam removal."

"I know. So what?"

"She's not from Utility or anywhere near here."

"And that matters?"

"No need to raise your voice to me. I think you ought to have some perspective on what you're doing. This Junie..." —Cov drew out the word like a mass of taffy—"...doesn't know us and doesn't understand our ways. Neither does her father."

"She understands more than you think."

Cov rubbed his hand under his chin, feeling the stubble.

"Junie's father practically saved the town," Don said. "Have you forgotten that?"

Cov touched the fresh scar on his forehead. The attempt by the opponents of the dam removal to scare the bessies and disrupt the project had nearly killed him. *How much does Slane know? He may have answers.* "Ed Wye is working for the Bureau of Environmental Security. He's going to destroy this community and your family."

"That's not Junie's fault." Don folded his arms.

"You're not taking her side, are you?"

"Her side?" Don's arms tightened. "She's just a friend." He shrugged. "She's different. Smart."

"A friend, you say. A bug hugger, most likely. Just like everyone on the coasts." Cov brushed a crumb off the table. "You took her to the camp, didn't you?"

"Yes," the young man whispered.

"Why?"

"It's important to me, to us. I thought she would understand." Don frowned.

"I take it she didn't understand."

Pain crossed Don's face. "It upset her. She was scared."

"Doesn't surprise me." Cov knocked on the table with his knuckle. He squinted with sarcasm. "Those people are environmental criminals. The worst of the worst. Shunned like lepers in the Bible." He grinned as if sharing a secret joke.

The old man switched to dead seriousness. "They're our people. A few of them are blood relations." He banged the table with his palm. "Punished by the bessies for trying to make a living on farms they're killing by taking away our water." Cov moved in his chair as if turning on an enemy. "Let me tell you what I did this week. Remember that lock the bessie water rats put on our water a couple of months back? They put it on again, even after I paid the fine."

"What?" The BES perplexed everyone, including Don.

"They said I didn't need that much water, that I was wasting it. But I could appeal their decision, they said. I went down there, went before a hearing officer downtown. I brought charts and graphs and showed how we'd spent hundreds of thousands of dollars on new equipment. We're the most efficient operation this side of the Canadian border, but we need just a few more cubic meters per day. Enough to count on both hands. And you know what he said?"

Don shook his head, fearful of what was coming.

"He said I was a dinosaur, and I should sell out to the government. 'We've grown beyond old ways like yours.' He said that, to me, Covington Rast. For five generations, my family has farmed this land, raised families, employed half of two counties. Well, fuck them if I'm a dinosaur. Fuck them!" Cov was half out of his chair, holding his finger in Don's face, like the barrel of a gun, as if his grandson was the cause of his troubles.

Don was unfazed. "I wish you'd told me, Grandpa. I'd have gone down there with you. Maybe I could've helped."

"I may be an old man, but I'm still in charge of this operation. Besides, I doubt you could've persuaded the bastard, him and his degree in environmental science from Harvard goddamn bug hugger University." The framed degree in Latin hung on the bureaucrat's wall.

Don reacted with distaste, and his grandfather assumed the young man felt the same distrust of outsiders as he. *Or maybe my breathe is stale.* Cov grinned to himself. Don was Cov's closest family, but they were sixty years apart. He was growing into his own man. Rast Orchards was always on the leading edge of the fruit business, though not the cutting edge. Don liked to learn about the newest gadgets and methods, taking chances untempered by painful experience. Cov, on the other hand, knew what success looked like, and in agriculture, you protect like a mother bear what little gains you might have.

Cov calmed himself. Age had slowed him, even his legendary temper. The two men sat in silence.

Don stirred. "She apologized, Grandpa."

"For what?"

"She was scared and tried to run with Daisy, but she didn't know the override commands and I caught up with her. She was mad as a wet hen, but I talked to her on the ride back. I explained what we're doing, giving our people a place to live until their sentences are up. We know it's illegal to help them, but I told her that we don't want our people wandering the streets like ghosts." Don rested his forearms on the wood. Each scratch and stain told a story of a meal or a family conversation. "She said she was sorry for being scared, for not trusting me."

"And you believe her?"

"Of course, I do."

"And you think she's suddenly got religion about the way we do things around here?"

Don let out a non-committal breath.

"Let me tell you something, son. Since the day she was born, she's been told by the city people and the bessies that anyone who violates the Carbon Acts and the other dumb-ass environmental laws are worse than murderers. What's killing a human being when people are killing the planet?" Cov laughed, as near to a guffaw as he could manage. "She and her father grasp our ways as well as anyone who lives in a manicured, germ-free, robot-run city can, which is this much." He formed a zero with his hand.

Don pitched his voice high, a sign of frustration. "What do you want me to do? I see her every day at school. She comes to my games. She helps me with my homework. Do you want me to ignore her?"

Cov was a hard man, but not a cruel man. *I've loved many times. And the first time is the hardest.* "I just want you to understand what you're doing." As the next thought formed in his mind, he glanced away from his grandson. "In fact, it would be good to stay friends with her."

"What do you mean?" Don puffed out his chest. *He is in deep.*

"Just be friends, like you said." Cov swallowed the last of his coffee. "She'll probably talk about her dad, maybe about his work. Tell me what she says. It might be useful."

"You want me to spy on her." His distaste had turned into derision.

"Watch yourself, Don. There's more to your girlfriend's father than you know, than maybe she knows."

"She's not my girlfriend."

"I'm going to tell you something I've learned after a bit of digging," Cov said. "Edward Wye was a wealthy man, rich enough 20 years ago to buy every farm within 10 kilometers of Utility.

Wind made him rich." Wind generators hummed night and day on thousands of square miles in the foothills of the Cascades. They had done so for more than a century. Next to farming, wind was the biggest industry in this part of Pacific West. "If things had gone his way, we'd look like paupers next to him. He's broke now, bankrupt. If he didn't have this job, he and his daughter would be on the dole."

Don listened closely. Cov was talking about a girl he was falling in love with.

"It seems that right after graduating from Stanford, Ed Wye filed a patent on a technology that reduced the amount of energy lost on transmission lines from the source down through the distribution network. The technology also doubled the efficiency of wind generators." Cov frowned in a kind of admiration he reserved for peers. "Something like that would be worth millions, maybe billions in license fees to all kinds of people."

Don scrunched his face, uncertain of his grandfather's meaning.

"That's how Wye got his money, back then, anyway," Cov relaxed into his chair. "The problem is, he stole it, the patent, the whole thing."

Don was nonplussed. "I don't believe that. Junie's father would not—"

Cov snorted, dismissing Don's skepticism. In return, Don mocked his grandfather's smugness. "How do you know this?"

"Public documents. News reports. It's all on the network, if you know where to look."

"When was this?"

Cov shifted, unwilling to give up the next fact, knowing it weakened his case. "Twenty years ago."

It was Don's turn to laugh. "I wasn't even alive 20 years ago. Why should I care about this?"

"The company had to change the designs of several projects to accommodate the inventor's patent requirements. Wye had to return most of the money he stole from the energy companies. He's never made that kind of money again. He's a fraud, Don, a fraud."

The young man shook his head.

Cov was gleeful. "Don't you see what this means, Don? We can get rid of another project superintendent, and maybe even that bitch Grace Cromer. They're friends from way back. I know it. She'd be tainted by all this."

Cov leaned into Don, who kept his eyes on the table. "You listen to me, son. You stay friends with the Wye girl. Take her out. Show her a good time. Buy her a case of mist. I'll pay for it."

Don face was fixated on the table. "She probably doesn't know anything about this lawsuit. It happened before she was born. Before I was born."

Cov ignored him. "If she says anything about her father or her father's work, I want to know about it."

Don's shoulders tensed, and the energy discharged like a spring when he slapped both hands on the table top, making a painful sound that resonated throughout the ranch house. He left the table, face beet red.

Cov blinked. *Some things are more important than a broken heart.*

The late season night insects buzzed outside the open kitchen window, and Cov regretted the coffee, if not the hurt he'd caused Don. The elder had trouble enough sleeping, and the caffeine wouldn't wear off for an hour. Instead, he enjoyed the steady *tick-tock* of the mantle clock, which his mother said was brought to the Rast homestead by a Model T truck. His reverie was interrupted by a notification in his minds-eye from the house network. He opened the front door to a short, balding man in a light jacket.

"Slane. It's about time."

"I know it's late."

Cov stood aside and directed the retired tug captain to the

kitchen. "Coffee?"

"I can't stay long." Slane took a chair, the same one Don sat in earlier in the evening. "How's your grandson?"

"Well enough." Cov poured the black liquid for Slane, though the guest didn't ask for it. Slane looked as if he'd thought long and hard about a problem, and he didn't like the solution.

"Did you look at those documents I sent, Cov?"

"Enlightening." Cov remained on his feet, but leaned on the counter. "What else have you found?"

Slane wrapped his hands around the half-full cup, as if trying to warm his hands, despite the pleasant temperatures. "I've stopped looking."

"I told you—"

"I've stayed off the net. It's not safe."

"Not safe for whom?"

"The bessies are thicker than flies on roadkill around here. I think it's better to keep a low profile."

"Why? All you're doing is research. I told you to learn everything you can about Wye. The patent stuff was good."

Slane pushed the coffee cup away from him. "Fine. I've got one more piece of information for you." He drummed his fingers on the table. "You've heard the rumors about Wye?"

"What's your version?"

"Some Bay Area investors are courting him with a new wind generation project."

"Doesn't surprise me. He's got lots of connections there. That's his background."

"Grace Cromer's involved."

"Indeed."

"It could be our chance."

"To do what?"

"Look, Cov. We both want to get rid of Wye. If we say he's thinking about quitting, it'll upset people, slow the project down, maybe enough to kill it. I know you're gathering information on Wye to discredit him—"

"What business is it of yours?"

Slane spoke with more confidence. "Don't get sanctimonious with me. You'll do whatever is necessary to save your business and your family's legacy." The towboat master's prominent gut brushed against the edge of the kitchen table. Slane lifted his hands and turned up the corners of his mouth. "No violence, but it won't hurt to put the fear of God into Wye."

"How so?"

"A word spoken or emailed here and there. There's his daughter—"

"You leave her alone." Don sprung to Cov mind. He did not want to rub salt into his grandson's wounds. Besides, Slane was too ridiculous a character to be a thug. "Thanks, but I prefer to handle things my own way."

"You haven't gotten very far on your own, Cov. Wye is working his butt off, and the dam is coming down by inches."

Cov let his eye settle on a corner of a chipped cabinet. Slane was right. Cov was losing ground, and he was ready to grasp at any straw.

"I want to say something more to you." Slane turned his head, afraid to meet Cov's eye. Slane let out a slow breath. "I came by to apologize."

"For what?"

Slane touched his hand to his forehead, in the same area where Cov had a pink scar. "I had a hand in what happened that day at the courthouse."

Cov almost laughed. He was amazed that Slane feared him enough to apologize for messing with the drone. Cov intimidated people, and it was a useful trick, sometimes, but he hadn't intentionally hurt anyone since a single fistfight in high school. *I've gotten more mileage out of that thirty seconds than anything else*

I've done in the seventy years since then. Cov was further
astonished that a man like Slane had the balls to pull off something
so brazen as attacking people in a hearing with a BES lackey who
reported directly to the Interior Minister.

"No one was supposed to be hurt, Cov." The man was shaking.
"I'm sorry."

Cov leaned over Slane, who shied. "You did the bulldozer too?
What the hell were you thinking?"

Slane lifted his face. His affect changed from intimidation to
fury. "I wanted to show the bessies that we mean business, that
we're tired of their picking on people, stomping on people to get
their way."

"And you were going to do that by wrecking half the town?"

"That wasn't what I wanted."

"And now Wye is a hero." Cov snorted. "Brilliant. Just
brilliant." Cov rubbed the back of his neck. "I suppose you had a
hand in the coffer collapse."

Slane's emotions shifted again. He was abject, supplicating, as
if confronted by a prosecutor. "No. I had nothing to do with that."

"The bessies think it was sabotage. It won't take long for them
to put two-and-two together. You're probably already in their
sights."

"I don't know anything about the coffer."

"Don't lie to me."

"I swear to God, Cov. Those systems are air-tight. Way
beyond what I know."

Cov believed the man. Children learned the technical
rudiments of artificial intelligence in preschool, and Slane's
experience with programming the AIs on his tugboats was nothing
complicated. The drone and the dozer were in the same league.
Cov doubted the man had the sophistication to break into a system
as secure, he supposed, as Arroyo Grande's, as well as tweak
welding bot instructions to simultaneously wreck the coffer while

hiding his subversion. "Do you know who did it?"

Slane closed down.

"If you know who fucked with that system—"

"I don't. I swear it, but..."

"But what?"

Slane ran a hand through his thinning black hair. "Something's going on, Cov. Something bigger than you asking me to find dirt on Wye. Bigger than my thing with the drone and dozer.."

"Spit it out."

"Sure, there's lots of people who agree with you and me, but you know it's mostly talk. I screwed up, yeah, but I'm seeing things on the com net, and chatter, and sideways talk. There's someone with serious chops attempting to hack into the local BES and the dam and the contractor's equipment. He or she or it may already be in there."

She? Sy Ioannu's face resolved in Cov's mind. *The whore knows a lot about DNA hacking or she knows someone who does, I'd bet.*

The captain's statements alarmed Cov. He'd not heard the man's story, and it was a rare thing that he was not aware of behind-the-scenes dealings in Douglas and Grant counties. He knew everybody and their dog. He knew whom they liked and hated. What's more, Slane's poking around on the net was bound to raise eyebrows, and Cov might be get caught up in some dragnet. Slane's usefulness to Cov was dwindling faster than a freshet after a downpour.

"Apology accepted, Rodrigo. I think you're wise to lay low."

Slane grinned. "Thanks, Cov."

"In fact, I think you ought to take a little trip. You look tired. Maybe to the ocean. I hear it's quite relaxing."

Slane grew suspicious. "You're trying to get rid of me."

"I'm concerned is all." Cov's eyes bored into Slane's. "For your health."

"Don't threaten me, Cov. We're friends, but I know a lot about you."

"Nothing the bessies don't already know. I keep my nose clean."

"Except for some friends you're hiding."

Slane meant the colony, but Cov wouldn't give the man the satisfaction of understanding the threat he posed. "I think you'd better leave Utility, Slane. I don't want to see your ugly face again. If I do, you'll never know what hit you."

Slane got the message. Cowed with a leavening of defiance, Slane adjusted his jacket, and a frightening fact dawned on Cov. Apart from the single notification when Slane appeared at his door, the expensive security system that covered every centimeter of his property didn't warn him he was coming. As the night insects escorted Slane's departure, Cov scrolled through the security cameras via his minds-eye. Slane was nowhere within five kilometers of his house and land, as if he were a ghost. He was already in a kind of hiding. Or someone was protecting him. *What if Slane is bait to get me?*

CHAPTER 11

◆ ◆ ◆

ED WYE LABORED to stay focused on the task at hand: triple-checking the firing sequences and geometry of the explosive charges with Connie Gasca and Ramesh Chandra. Screwing this up was unthinkable if he was going to bring down the dam with a minimum of fuss and earn a maximum amount of social capital in the eyes of his Silicon Valley friends, but two things distracted him. One was good news: the local cops had arrested Rodrigo Slane on a charge of hacking the drone and the bulldozer's security systems. Ed was relieved. He'd received another emailed threat the day before.

"We have warned you numerous times to quit the project or we will be forced to take stronger measures to persuade you. If something should happen to you or your daughter, it will be on your conscience, not ours."

Threats of bodily harm against him or Junie weren't in his job description, and he was by turns angry and frightened. He reported it to Rossmann, who repeated promises to protect him and his daughter with greater surveillance. Ed doubted Rossmann's omniscience, despite BES's legendary capabilities, but the project super had few options.

The next day, he congratulated Rossmann for the arrest. The general demurred, and he didn't take any public credit. That puzzled Ed, as if the general had nothing to do with the arrest or didn't care. After the news had a few hours to percolate in his subconscious, Ed reread the email. He had a hard time picturing a retired towboat captain composing such an articulate threat, though he barely knew the man. Doubts pricked at him.

The second thing that distracted Ed was the proposal from Natalie Wong. He bounced between regret and hope since reading the draft prospectus about the renewable energy venture. He obsessed over it, despite his best efforts to put it out of his mind, because it raised his hopes that he was not a wash-out after all. *Natalie wants me on this project.* Wong was one of the most powerful women in the San Francisco investment community, a long-time friend of Grace Cromer, and one of the first women he dated after his wife died. The relationship never flowered, but they remained friends, and they spent the occasional night at a VR movie or an art opening or in her bed. *She was a little too ruthless for me.*

The conflicting facets of his life pressed on him: Rossmann wanted him to finish the dam job; Natalie Wong was dangling a new future; Junie was settling in to Utility. At least the saboteur had been caught. Maybe.

All I want is to hold my head high among my friends. I am not a failure.

An image of Sy Ioannu resolved in his imagination. He couldn't help but linger on it. He reflected that while he was nominally in charge of many things—the dam work, Junie's upbringing, his career—women ran his life.

Ed rubbed his eyes, interlaced his fingers and rested the mesh of them on his light brown hair, like a soldier's helmet. "Run the simulations again, and I want you to add another random variable."

"Another one?" Connie's voice cracked from exhaustion.

Ramesh Chandra's shoulders slumped. "I can't think of anything more, Ed."

I'm not taking any unnecessary chances. "What about earthquakes? What's the average magnitude for the local geology in the past 100 years? Run the simulation with a 20 percent higher-than-average magnitude quake happening at the same moment as the trigger."

"Are you crazy?" Connie struggled against tears. "We're sitting on a cow pie of frozen black basalt 17 million years old. There's 200,000 square miles of it. What are the chances of a real earthquake actually happening anytime in the next 10,000 years?"

"Don't argue with me. Do it." *It's my neck on the block, not theirs.*

Ramesh put his hand over Connie's. They had all become friends as the project moved from utter chaos to a semblance of order. Ed depended on them in the same way he depended on air to breathe.

"Guys, I promise this is the last one. Let's take a look at the results, and then make the call."

Ed broke away, grabbed a stale cake donut from a plate in the break room, and stepped outside. He sat at a picnic table in the shadow of the work site office portables that gave a view of the whole project. The coffer seeped, but it was stronger than ever, and it would withstand another 1,000-year flood, assuming no sabotage. On the dam itself, robots and human supervisors set the final charges.

Ed let his mind wander, allowing himself a rare moment of respite from the strain. Sy Ioannu floated in his consciousness like a dancer. She had introduced him to the small, secretive community of activists who lobbied BES for the dam removal. He was circumspect with her, despite her friendliness and praise for his work. He could not take his eyes off her for more than a moment whenever she was in the room. She was different than other women in a way he could not pin down, and not just because she attracted him in an almost primal way. *It's like those urban legends of government spies tapping into your com and reading your thoughts.*

He brushed the donut crumbs off the table. His daughter

replaced Sy in his thoughts, like changing a com chan. She was adjusting to Utility much faster than he would have guessed two months ago. She'd changed her avatar to the blue lightning-strike of the Rast High School mascot. Her interest in Don Rast was problematic, and not just because the boy's grandfather was an adversary. She would mention a visit to the Rast ranch house for homework, and Ed would ask how it went, and she would not answer beyond generalities. *What do I do about Junie if the San Francisco thing is too good to turn down?*

A note in his minds-eye told him the updated simulation was ready. He gulped the last bite of donut and returned to the conference room. "What have we got?" A holo-emitter showed a 3-D image of the dam three meters wide by one meter high.

Connie stood to one side of the image. "Ramesh has programmed a magnitude 5.0 quake's P waves to arrive just as the first charge is set off, with the Raleigh waves arriving about five seconds later."

"Before the debris has settled," Ed said.

"Exactly."

"Good. Let's run it."

Ramesh touched a key and an arrow showed the first charge going off. "We've slowed down the action about 50 times." A moment later, the Raleigh waves hit. Back home in California, Ed felt the rolling motion several times during small quakes. As the last wave passed in the simulation, the entire debris field collapsed down the sides of the dam. Anything below the field would have been destroyed.

"Christ almighty," Ed said. He lowered himself into a creaky chair. "So what's the likelihood of such an earthquake hitting us?"

Ramesh swiped through a tablet. "I'd estimate the probability of it happening at just the right moment as, um, about as high as me suddenly turning into a white man."

Ed turned to his engineer and Connie giggled. Ed laughed

hard, grateful that Ramesh found a way to break the tension. *Make a decision.* "Oh, fuck, let's just blow it up."

"Really?" Connie's glee was catching.

"Nine a.m., tomorrow. Alert the media." Ed snorted and the emotional release was glorious.

The next day, after a fitful sleep, Ed arrived at the site and found Grace, reporters, and onlookers gathered at the viewpoint where he watched the coffer collapse on his first day on the job. Cov Rast was invited, but he did not appear. A white canopy protected a half-dozen people associated with the project from the autumn sun. Water bulbs chilled in a cooler. "I don't mean to make this a ceremony," Ed said to the gathering, "but I thought you'd like to see that we've reached an important milestone."

The crowd murmured approval.

"Stand by everyone." Ed texted Connie: `Thirty seconds.`

A siren sounded, rising and echoing like a flight of invisible birds between the basalt walls of the canyon.

A message appeared over the local networks, including the public network. `FIRE IN THE HOLE.`

The siren's whine faded to silence. "Keep your eyes on the dam, folks. Five, four..." Ed counted down and touched a tab button.

Nothing happened.

Ed texted: `What the hell?`

People in the crowd whispered in each other's ears. A few pointed fingers at Ed. He could imagine the jokes flying across the net.

`Come on, guys.`

Ramesh texted: `Software issue. We're looking into it.`

`ETA for a fix?`

`Found the bug already, but we have to`

reboot and go through the checklist. It'll
be an hour or so.

Ed turned to the crowd. "Sorry, folks. Software glitch. We're triple-checking everything. Please have some more refreshments. I'll keep you up-to-date."

The onlookers grinned. They hadn't lost confidence in Ed and the project. Just one of those things. Ed breathed a sigh of relief and chatted with the minor dignitaries.

Grace Cromer came over. "What happens next, assuming the software bug is fixed?"

"The excavators will move in and remove the debris. It'll take some time. It's almost like picking up broken glass. We don't want it to tumble down into the pit."

"Broken concrete is considered hazardous waste."

"We'll take it to a designated landfill. Once we've removed the old concrete, we'll set more charges and take the concrete down another five to ten meters, and so on, until we reach bottom."

"How long will it take?"

"A couple of years."

"That long?"

"It's delicate work. Remember that the structure's already cracked from the flood last summer." Monitoring showed the crack had stabilized. Connie and Ramesh had included the flaw in their simulations. "We want to do this right."

"The BES has more to investigate."

"Come again?"

"You haven't heard about the BES water enforcement officer?"

Ed shrugged. "I've been busy this morning."

"He was found bound, gagged, tarred, and feathered on the steps of the BES office downtown about an hour ago."

"Are you serious? It's like something out of the Old West."

An image arrived in Ed's public net account. A man was covered in a brown substance, probably not real tar, but sticky enough to hold onto hundreds of white down feathers, perhaps from a pillow. "That's terrible."

"Any thoughts on who might have done such a thing?"

"I wouldn't begin to guess, Grace. I'm not a policeman."

"The officer had issued a number of tickets to Rast Orchards. Covington Rast disputed the last one. This would be his style, his idea of intimidation masked as a joke. There's desperation in that kind of thing."

"Not even Rast is that crude."

"On the other hand, I can think of a dozen people besides Rast who'd like to send that kind of message. Some people around here live in the Stone Age."

The visceral suspicion of government, especially BES, was over the top, in Ed's opinion. *If our grandparents and great-grandparents had listened to the warnings before things went to hell, people wouldn't have handed environmental protection to a police force.* In public, he kept these thoughts to himself. He knew how to be politically acceptable, up to a point. He joined the Rotary Club and the Pioneers Club and dropped the occasional €10 coin into the fundraising jar for the food bank or the fight against the latest pandemic.

Years, maybe decades might pass, however, before he was accepted as a member of the community, despite the fact that he'd grown up in Utility. He was like the prodigal son, welcomed, if not warmly, and not yet forgiven. His father was a transplant from southern California, and around here, the sins of the father attached to the son when it came to origins. People from "elsewhere" were easily blamed for problems not of their creation.

Grace was successful as mayor because friends and relatives were aplenty, unlike Ed. People she went to grade school with still lived in Utility. With 20 years of experience in the high-pressure world of venture capital—her money came from her mother's savvy investments in land near coastlines flooded by rising sea levels—she straddled Ed's world and Utility's. Grace was one of

Ed's few adult friends; her early support of companies that profited from his patents made her wealthy independent of her mother's money.

Sy was another of Ed's friends, but he wasn't sure why. She was an outsider, too.

Connie sent a text: We've reset the countdown to thirty minutes from now. Ed watched the countdown restart via his minds-eye.

"Utility is changing, Eddie." Grace handed him a water bulb.

"I haven't been around here long enough to see it."

"People are taking an interest in the area. The dam removal is helping. People want to be near a flowing river. Some of the towns near the old dams are reviving after an initial out-migration. Land is cheap. Schools are adequate for people who can't afford teaching bots. Mother Nature is reasserting herself. I'm optimistic."

I'm not planning to stick around once my job is done. "I'm glad some people see what's happening as positive."

The guests and staff dispersed, leaving Grace and Ed alone under the canopy. Water in the diversion channel rushed below them. Grace swept her eyes across the canyon.

"Eddie, do you ever think about the age of this place?"

"Do you mean geological age?"

"Yes, but also in the spiritual sense. It's timeless. I know it's not static, but humans don't really grasp the true meaning of 'millions of years.' It's outside our comprehension."

"The universe is billions of years old."

"That's my point. It's permanent and ageless, for all intents and purposes."

"Maybe like long friendships." Ed patted Grace's arm. She glanced at his hand, and Ed saw a flash of anger. *I forgot these rural types aren't into tactile affection.* "Sorry, Grace."

Her round face softened. She patted his hand. "Nothing to be sorry about, Eddie. I was just thinking about Stanford, and how we crossed paths."

"It was better than the first time we were friends."

"We were both awkward 14-year-olds. You were geeky, but well-proportioned. I was smart, with enough hormones to choke a rhino."

"Funny. I don't remember that part. Just that you were nice to me and fun to hang out with."

"I held back. I was never an impulsive person." Grace laughed. "But I was in love with you, as much as a girl child can love."

"I thought about you after we lost touch," Ed said.

"I knew you went to Stanford. I wondered if we might run into each other after I transferred from U-Dub."

"We did."

"But it was different."

"Ten years passed. People cope with their hormones. Pain and pleasure season a person."

Grace turned to him. "Do you remember Roger?"

Professor Roger Saar. Ed forced his face to go blank, though he couldn't be certain Grace did not detect the ember that the name fanned. "Of course I remember Roger."

"I'm surprised. He's been dead for more than twenty years."

"He was one of my instructors. Classic prof, though more the tweedy stereotype than the engineering stereotype."

"A brilliant researcher. A dozen patents, and still in his thirties."

"I was sorry when he died." *I'm sorry I have to lie to you about my feelings about Roger.*

"Broke my heart." Grace was wistful.

"I didn't know you were close."

Grace moved in her garden chair, looking away from Ed. "We were acquaintances. I was thinking about how he died, taking his own life. Something broke his heart."

141

Ed was wary. "Why are you thinking about him now? It was 20 years ago."

"Middle-age, probably. Old friends. Missed opportunities. It's inevitable." Grace met Ed's eye. "You were part of that time of my life. I associate you with him. Hard not to."

An alarm went off in Ed's mind. "Do you have regrets? About investing in my patents and my research?"

Grace stared at him. "People who don't have regrets haven't lived a life. They haven't made mistakes. We all make mistakes."

Ed knew what she meant, and it bit him. The image of Roger Saar's name on the paper based on Ed's graduate research was burned in Ed's mind, followed by the patent application, and the excitement in the wind energy community. Utilities and manufacturers offered licensing contracts King Midas would envy. *All Roger had to do was share the profits with me, but he wouldn't.* Lawsuits, counter-lawsuits, and a judge's decision in Ed's favor. Roger was left with a token share, but he wouldn't let up. He forced a two-year investigation by the patent office, and the report found "insufficient evidence" for fraud on Ed's part.

But the doubts about Ed were chiseled in stone. The rumors were never ending, that he had stolen the ideas from Roger, not the other way around. For years, every news chan article about Ed had the phrase "once accused of patent theft" in them. It was as if he were Jean Valjean in *Les Misérables*, forced to carry a yellow passport of accusation forever.

Grace, however, had kept faith with him. He thought it was because of their long friendship. "Why did you stick with me, after everything?"

"Someone had to keep an eye on you." Grace winked, but it was the gesture of a cynic. It struck Ed that she had just lied, or told a half-truth, or meant something other than the face-value of the words. He dismissed the thought as a misfiring of his tendency to expect the words of business partners to have double or triple meanings, as if they were in constant negotiations for a better deal out of life.

Grace shifted in her chair. "Change of subject? Any more thoughts about the energy company proposal?"

"Grace, I can't tell if you want me to stick around to finish the removal job or to look seriously at ZephyrCom."

"I want you to use your talents in the most effective way possible."

"A politician's comeback."

Grace laughed. The crinkles around the edges of her eyes deepened. "I'll admit to a conflict of interest. I'm an investor in ZephyrCom, and I'm mayor of Utility." She shrugged. "Life is complicated."

"Thanks, but I'm a bad risk."

"You're making this project happen."

"So much could go wrong still," Ed said. "It's far from a done deal."

"Same with ZephyrCom. I think you ought to check out their facility and go see Natalie about it."

A day away from here might be a good thing, if only to see the country. "We'll see, Grace."

`Sixty seconds, boss.`

Ed got the crowd's attention, and counted down to zero. This time, when he touched the button on his tablet, puffs of dust raced across the top ten percent of the dam from one end of the coffer to the other. Powdery geysers followed the puffs as the initiating charges set off the main charges. An instant later, the top 10 meters of the dam lifted as if nudged by an off-balance child. The broken concrete settled back, and one or two tendrils of debris rolled down the visible face of the dam. In his minds-eye, Ed switched to a camera on the hidden side of the dam, and saw two or three similar tracks, but nothing unexpected. The airborne dust floated downstream in the light airs.

"There you have it, ladies and gentlemen. Deconstruction has begun."

Ed was exultant, as were the observers. Grace led a round of applause. For the first time since he'd arrived in Utility, Ed felt as if his life was moving forward. He had taken the first real step toward getting his reputation back. He returned to the project office and the staff had laid out a cake and snacks on the break room table. A little premature, Ed thought, but he didn't complain. A good day had had finally arrived.

After the party broke up, Ed returned to his desk, reviewed his email, and found a new message.

"You're killing us, Wye. We'll gut you like a fish."

CHAPTER 12

◆ ◆ ◆

THE NEW THREAT RATTLED ED, and he forwarded it to
Rossmann, just to feel like he was doing something. *At least it
didn't mention Junie.* Unlike the earlier threat, its crudeness might
have come from someone like Slane, but Ed wondered how the
man might've accessed the net through the jail's blocks on net
access. Maybe Slane's technical skills were better than first
thought. Maybe he had help.

A day off from the project, even if it was mostly business, was
more attractive than ever.

The rental public car was pricey, but Ed could expense it if he
signed on to ZephyrCom. Giving in to temptation, he decided to
visit Natalie Wong's research site. No one in the office gave his
announced absence a second look; everyone saw the pressure he
was under. In the car, he studied a new prospectus updated with
fresh and thorough financial projections. *Natalie's fingerprints as
always.* The kilometers passed quickly as the on-board AI guided
the car through the Cascade Mountain foothills toward the
Wanapum Indian Reservation.

How Ed managed to convince Junie to accompany him on his
day trip mystified him at first. He kept the details of the threats
against her vague for fear of alarming her and giving her an excuse
to run back to Sierra Vista. His invitation the night before was *pro
forma*, more a statement that he liked having his daughter along,
that maybe he should've invited her on these short trips more often
when she was younger. The trip to the research site would be a

long day, between the visit to the lab and the socially mandatory Winter Fair and Feed at the school later that evening.

He expected a No Thanks. Instead, she said Yes. Maybe it was a chance to get her own day off, or maybe she was bored. *Maybe she just wants to be with her dad?* He was happy Junie was with him.

His daughter dozed in the seat across from him. Her tablet was open to an article in a lefty news magazine with the headline, "Is the BES dissing too many people?" *Odd. She's never been interested in politics.* He dismissed the interest as youthful curiosity, reflecting on her more subtle reason for accepting his invitation. A few days earlier, on Winter Solstice Eve, things changed for her. She hadn't left for a party, as she announced at dinner. He found her in her room, crying.

"Junie-girl, you never cry." Ed stood at the door, uncertain whether to violate her space.

"Go away." She lay with her face in a pillow.

Ed bit his lip. He respected Junie's self-containment, perhaps too much. "Are you sick?"

"No. Go away!"

She's hurting, you idiot. There's a point in every father's relationship to his daughter when he teeters on the edge of ignoring everything she says and reaches out, and then stops himself for fear of crossing a boundary into a place from which he can't retreat without creating a scene.

Ed closed her door, and stood there, unsure what to do. Even as a baby, Junie was not a bawler. She'd whimper, mouse-like, which was more painful for him than the toddler meltdowns he'd witnessed. With her door closed, he heard nothing, and he imagined the whimper instead. He knocked lightly and turned the handle.

She didn't object when he opened it a crack. He feared a lashing out. She was curled up over a pillow, her eyes red and puffy. "Good lord, Juniper, what's wrong?"

She turned her head, but allowed him to come in. "This is what's wrong." A ping appeared in Ed's minds-eye, a shared image from one of Junie's Bay Area connections. The pic showed Alex embracing a girl Ed didn't recognize.

Boys were a verboten subject between Ed and his daughter. *The truth is, I don't want to know. I'm scared to ask.* Junie had told him about Alex, though not in detail. Ed assumed Junie was sexually active, not because he knew it for a fact, but because it was smarter than denying she might experiment with sex. *Thank God Marcy had the sense to be open with Junie about her body from the first day she asked about it.* He had the standard fears for her physical safety and her emotional well-being, but when his health insurance statement showed charges related to a doctor visit and a prescription for a common contraceptive, he was relieved. The law let her choose whether to keep the details of the visit and the medication to herself, but she didn't exercise her option. She trusted her father enough to let him know what was going on.

That's not to say Ed liked the situation. He had an instinctive suspicion of any male sniffing around his daughter. Junie was making her own choices, and like them or not, he had to live with them. Controlling his daughter was not possible. The sig-up fees that pointed to an encounter on her way to Utility were an expensive shock, though, and the discussion was long and tense.

"Read the comments," Junie ordered from her semi-fetal position.

The texts and emoji strings were cruel and painful.

"They're laughing at me. Alex is fucking around with some whore, and they're laughing at me."

"Does Alex know about this? Have you talked to him?"

"Of course he knows, Dad! The whole planet knows. BaseLuna knows. No, I haven't talked to him, and I won't talk to him."

"Why not?"

"He cancelled! Again!"

That was one thing that Junie did share about Alex, that he was coming to visit, first after Thanksgiving, then during the Solstice break. He'd bailed out on both.

"Junie, I know you were looking forward to seeing him, but I'm really not surprised."

"I don't want to hear about it."

"It's tough enough to have a relationship when people live ten minutes from each other. Long talks and sig-ups are no substitute."

"You're wrong. We love each other. It's different with us."

The furrow on Junie's brow meant Ed's appeal to reason hadn't completely failed. He patted his daughter's knee. "Talk to him. Maybe it's not what it seems. Maybe he's sorry." *It's a father's job to give his daughter hope, even false hope.* "Can I tell you a story?"

"No." The objection was weak.

"It's a short one. After your mother and I were together about six months or so—this is before you were born—she found me in a bar with another woman."

"That sucks. For Mom, I mean."

"She thought so. We had a huge fight about it. I tried to explain that the woman was an old girlfriend from high school. We were just visiting and catching up."

"I'm sure." Junie's cynicism swelled like a sprained ankle.

"The woman was Grace Cromer."

"Wait. I know that name."

"She's the mayor of Utility."

"You dated the mayor?"

"In high school. She later invested in companies that licensed my patents. You could say I made her rich." *That's pushing it, but let's keep things simple.*

"But you broke up with her."

"Grace? We broke up when I was 16, but we managed to stay friends. She helped me get this job." *Was she dating someone when I was working on the patents? I don't remember.*

"So you're saying that if Alex and I break up, he'll help me find a job when I'm old?"

"I'm saying that Alex may be innocent of what all those gossips are saying, and that you shouldn't feel threatened by a photo posted to a c-tribe."

"I don't think you get it, Dad. Look at his face. Look at the slut's face. It's more than a couple of friends hugging."

"Maybe." Ed remained neutral on the interpretation of a photo, but it was easy to see Junie's point. Alex's hands were on the small of the girl's back, where he could pull her close to the point of melding with her. His eyes were closed as he drank in the girl's scent. Looking at the photo roused an image of Sy in his consciousness, though they had done nothing more than shake hands. "All I'm saying, Junie, is to avoid jumping to conclusions or automatically agreeing with gossips who spread rumors." He wondered what the gossips might be saying about Junie and Don Rast, though he'd heard nothing.

As father and daughter made a wide turn in the rental car, its AI beeped a notification. Junie opened her eyes, and Ed saw a vulnerability exposed by the dying relationship with Alex. He could not fix it, even if he wanted to, and all Junie wanted for the moment was to shelter in his maturity and strength. *Such as it is.* Given what he sometimes thought was neglect of her when she was small, he didn't feel worthy of such trust. Here she was, however, proof enough that she thought he was worthy.

The research facility was in a remote valley of the reservation, which had made itself a haven for companies and government agencies interested in keeping prying eyes to a minimum. After the Indian gaming economy played itself out, the reservation's half-dozen tribes and bands fell into old habits of infighting, but the threat of poverty led them to cooperate on leasing land for research projects, as long as the land was restored to its original condition once the project was completed. The Indians proved to be discreet business partners, and Natalie Wong signed several contracts with them. After a gauntlet of security checks, the AI parked the car in front of a metal-sided building surrounded by 20-meter ponderosa pines.

A curly-haired young man in a lab coat stepped out of the building and waved at Ed in greeting. He introduced himself as Anders and an old-fashioned name tag labeled him "Dr. Folstad." He didn't look a day over 25. Junie studied him with more than casual interest.

"Ms Wong contacted me personally about your visit." Folstad's accent was minimal. He looked nervous. "We're so honored to have you here with your lovely daughter."

For an instant, Junie reverted to her four-year-old self and edged toward her father, as if needing protection from her own embarrassment.

"It was your work after Stanford that inspired our research, Mr Wye. I wouldn't be here if it weren't for you."

"Thank you, Anders. I'm having some trouble accessing your local network."

"No, Mr Wye, that's just our network security. We're very careful here. Let me send you credentials for a guest account." Anders was apologetic. "Unfortunately, I won't be able to provide one for your daughter."

"Not a problem, Anders," Ed said. "Lead on."

Junie nudged in protest.

The building turned out to be a modest, but well-equipped high-tech manufacturing facility with the latest 3-D printing technologies, growth media for bio-logic chips, and portable super-computers for DNA programming. The room was quiet as a church. "Are you the only researcher here, Anders?"

"Oh, no, Mr Wye. Everyone else is at a conference in Brussels."

"And you volunteered to stay behind?"

"I don't mind. I can get a lot of work done when it's quiet. I participate in the breakout sessions via minds-eye."

Folstad led them through the facility, his pride in the pioneering technology on full display. Junie listened politely, though Ed had trouble teasing out her interest in Anders Folstad as an intelligent, accomplished young man from an interest in the subject matter. The researcher brought them to a conference room set with a plate of goodies and showed a brief holo-presentation that Ed already reviewed as part of the ZephyrCom proposal. Ed waited politely until it finished. "Anders, have you been able to deploy any prototypes?"

"Yes!" Folstad's eagerness was child-like. "I wanted to show you what we've done." He stood up. "Will you follow me, please?"

The researcher and his guests retraced their steps through the lab, taking a turn to another exterior door, which opened to a grove of trees. The air was cool and birds flitted through the understory. "It's just 500 meters on this path. It's an easy stroll, Mr Wye. Or would you prefer a cart?"

"I'd prefer that." Junie pointed at an object plugged into a wall socket and covered with a fitted tarp.

"Junie, I don't think..."

"No, Mr Wye, it's all right."

Ed suspected his host of extra politeness. "Anders, we're not here to take advantage of your kindness. Junie hasn't ridden a horse for years." He turned to Junie. "You've never ridden an equine."

"I rode one at Don Rast's ranch. He'd showed me how. I've still got the controller app installed."

Junie hadn't mentioned the ride, which surprised Ed. He wondered if he should revise his strategy of watchful distance from her emotional life. A connection to the Rasts was not the same as having a boyfriend 1,320 kilometers away. *What else is she holding back about their relationship?* "But you're not on the net."

"I'll take of that, Mr Wye." A notification appeared in Ed's minds-eye. "I can give your daughter limited access, just to the equine. I'll keep on eye on things."

The app icon appeared in Ed's minds-eye next to Junie's avatar. "Anders, you're more than generous." *Is he falling over himself on my account or Junie's?*

"It's nothing, sir. I ride Peggy almost every day. It relaxes me." He removed the tarp, and the robot shivered, so much like a real animal that Ed forgot that its coppery skin was metal.

"Not too long, Junie." Ed felt the need to put a limit on things.

"Dad, I'm not five years old. Give me some credit."

As Anders cinched the saddle, behaving more like a stable hand than a scientist in his lab coat, Junie strapped on a helmet and lifted herself on the equine as if she'd ridden bots and real horses for years.

"Just point her down the trail." Anders gestured down the path. "Peggy knows the way."

"C'mon." Junie's under-her-breath command was confident, and the equine slow-walked into the forest and disappeared around a pair of pine trees.

Anders touched Ed's arm and he closed his mouth. "Shall we, sir?"

After months in a semi-arid desert, the grove was like an unkempt, but captivating garden. The trees were of similar age and size, suggesting the forest was logged decades in the past. Ancient stumps were covered with fungi and branches broken by wind and snowfall. The air was fresh and fragrant with pine sap and the decay of needles. Ed thought of the time he and Marcy visited the graves of his parents when Junie was five. His mother died three weeks before he started his freshman year at Stanford. His father died six months later. Both had chosen promession, and by the time they showed Junie the grave sites on the private forest land, the freeze-dried dust from both bodies had long decayed into the humus of the forest floor. The graves were marked only by GPS location, but Ed knew the spot from a lichen-encrusted boulder on the slope. The site had a timeless magic to Ed, changing with the seasons, but permanent, at least at a human scale. To Junie, Ed repeated the few family stories he kept, such as the time the family traveled to Cape Canaveral to watch the launch of the Mars astronauts. Marcy was the keeper of the histories for both families, as wives and mothers tend to be.

Junie was curious, but unmoved emotionally, as near as he could tell. At that age, dead grandparents were important to her because they were important to him. Marcy wasn't even sure her parents were alive.

Not a single day passed when Ed did not think of Marcy, but after eight years, the memories were more rational than emotional. They were recollections of facts and stories, rather than sharp pains. Scars hid his loss, but at times like now, when a walk through a forest elicited memories of holding his wife's strong climber's hands as their daughter ran ahead, a dull pain returned. He'd loved no woman since.

The path arced to the right and opened to a large, green, flowered meadow with three towers topped by wind generators. All were turning, but Ed's eyes locked on the horse cantering along the edge of the meadow, carrying a slim, but strong young woman whose dark hair bounced on her shoulders. Junie and Peggy came around toward him, and his daughter grinned wide. Ed's throat caught, because he saw Marcy in the set of Junie's mouth and himself in the Roman nose and a melding of father and mother in the skeptical, worldly glint of eyes which underlined the fact that she knew a lot more than anyone gave her credit for, particularly her father.

"I have some water, if you're thirsty, Mr Wye."

Ed swallowed. "What?" He looked at the proffered bottle. "Yes. Thanks."

"You might want to log into the monitoring site. I'll show you some of our latest advances."

Ed called up the local wind maps and weather forecasts. Windspeeds were zero to five kilometers per hour. The air was still at ground level, but the blades turned with the vigor of a gale. "Walk me through it, will you?"

"We've developed a new blade design, which was badly needed to catch up to the newer generator designs that don't depend on vanes. We've also developed industrial DNA and AI upgrades to get more of the kinetic energy of the moving air."

Junie spurred Peggy into short gallops, and Anders' animation jumped. "Here's the breakthrough, Mr Wye." Anders described an improved efficiency technology, some of which Ed didn't immediately grasp, though he was reluctant to show it. The researcher's enthusiasm was infectious, which was as important to the success of a new product or technology as the science and engineering. Anders made a perfect poster boy. "And it's all thanks to your patent work twenty years ago. We've built on it to create something that will reduce the costs of generation by 10 percent and the transmission and distribution losses to less than one-half percent over the longest transmission lines." Anders directed Ed to a set of graphs on the network that weren't part of the ZephyrCom docs he had. The efficiency curves were impressive.

"What about the costs of upgrades and deployment?"

"I'm not really familiar with that part of the business, Mr Wye, but we're trying to make retrofitting as easy as possible."

The ZephyrCom prospectus addressed this, noting that upgrades to older wind power generation facilities would be expensive. Some of the farm infrastructure dated to the late 20th century. The pitch was the quick amortization of the upgrade costs. Deployments of new systems would be substantially cheaper, but energy companies were notoriously conservative, and they would not tear down functioning, paid-for systems generating profits until the last possible minute. Anders' assurance that easy retrofits were a priority satisfied this problem.

From a power generation perspective, tearing down Arroyo Grande is non-sensical, but political priorities rarely match economic models.

Ed and Anders chatted for a few minutes on technical matters, and Junie brought Peggy to a halt. She was sweating, but the grin was as wide as ever. "I think I've had enough. Thank you so much, Mr Folstad. Peggy is amazing."

"Anders, please." The researcher blushed as he took the bridle and led the group back to the lab.

♦ ♦ ♦

Ed and Junie stopped at the apartment long enough to shower and change, and they were out the door again. The politics of small towns dictated that Ed appear at a minimum number of public events. The annual Winter Fair and Feed in the high school gymnasium qualified as one of the most important, according to Grace Cromer, who pushed Ed to attend. "The town resents the loss of the dam. Remember the dog-and-pony shows in front of New York West investors? Put on your happy face." For her part, Junie was upbeat, even energized by the day trip to the research lab. Perhaps better than Ed, she understood the social importance of the Feed.

Within three steps of entering the crowded, cavernous gym, Junie bolted for her new friends, Tiffany and Trudy, and left him to fend for himself. The "Fair" part of the event turned out to be a science fair showcasing the best science projects from the three elementary schools, one middle school, and the high school juniors. Ed forced himself to look into the maw of a baking soda volcano, answer a poll via his minds-eye on whether cinnamon, mint, or "plain" was the best flavor for gum, and attempt to navigate a 3-D randomized-path maze with a home-programmed AI bot.

The "Feed" half of the event was tolerable. The basic pasta and in-season marinara meal supplied by the PTSA was edible, though the cooks were wedded to the ancient institutional traditions of blandness demanded by public schools everywhere. The desserts, however, leaped from the other end of the culinary spectrum. The organizers made the dessert options a competition, complete with ribbons and prizes. The resulting pies, breads, custards, cobblers—most with local fruits—were enough to set diets back by ten years at one sitting. Ed's mother loved to make pies of all kinds, especially at holidays. He never got a birthday cake because his mother preferred piling candles on birthday pies. With the Feed's sugary bounty spread out before him, he piled samples on a plate.

A serve-bot rolled by and Ed lifted a coffee from the tray. The bot blew by so fast, he couldn't snag a sweetener pack and two-centiliter half-and-half. A four-piece jazz band struck up a tune at the other end of the gym. *Christ, the acoustics are as bad as a... high school gym.*

At the portable table, Junie dropped into the chair next to him. "Hi."

"Hi, Junie-girl. What's shakin'?"

Junie looked at him as if he had three heads. "Just checking in. Everything okay?"

"Almost. Could you do me a big favor and get me a sugar pack and creamer?" Ed pointed at his black coffee, already going cold.

"Can't you get it yourself?"

"Do something nice for your old man." He forced a grin.

"Fine." Junie departed in the direction of Tiffany and Trudy.

The image of her riding Peggy in the meadow was still fresh.

Connie, at the fair as an adviser to one of the high school teams, came up to the table with an elderly man in a partial exoskeleton. Supporting his legs and hips, the motors purred as they adjusted to his gait, but he struggled to sit without falling over. "Papa is still getting used to the upgrade, Ed. Do you mind if I leave him with you while I get some food?"

"Not at all." Ed extended his hand. "I'm Ed Wye."

"Robert Gasca." He lifted a corner of his wrinkled mouth. "Call me Bob." He twisted toward his daughter. "See if there's any fry bread, will you?"

"Sure, Papa."

"I like a good fry bread." Bob coughed as he winked. "I only met one white woman who could make decent fry bread. That was my wife. She's dead."

The elder spoke with the carelessness of the old, who speak the truth, knowing few people, least of all young people, will listen or care. Even with the exo, Bob shrank as he bent over the table, as if his back muscles switched off. His eyes were bright and penetrating. "You're the guy who saved the town from that loco bulldozer. I saw it on the news chan."

Ed grinned, unsure how to respond.

"You should've let it wreck the place. We'd be better off without it."

What should I say? "A lot of people could've been hurt."

Bob grunted skeptically.

Ed was in that classic moment with a stranger you dare not abandon, for fear of what other people might think. Ed did not want Connie to judge him insensitive or ill-mannered, but the tension was uncomfortable. *Where's Junie with the sugar and creamer?* For his part, Bob closed his eyes. Ed cleared his throat. "So, did you grow up around here, Mr Gasca?"

Bob blinked at Ed as if he didn't recognize him. "What? Oh,

157

sure. On the rez." Bob emphasized the final word as if he weren't sure if it was a good thing or bad. "Wanapum. Up north."

"Really?"

"Got out of there as quick as I could." Bob removed a handkerchief from a pocket and wiped his nose. "Hellish place."

"Where did you go?"

"MIT." Bob coughed into the handkerchief. "They took pity on a little Indian boy and bribed me to go to Boston."

Ed thought the old man was putting himself down to be polite. "What did you study?"

"Civil engineering. I suppose they thought I'd go back to the rez and dig sewers or something."

"You did something else then."

"No, I dug sewers on the rez. Lots of reservations. An MIT grad in Indian country, that's a big deal. Most of those people were dumb-asses, but I kept busy."

"And so you retired back here." Ed thought he was on firmer ground.

"Hell, no. The dam people hired me." Bob laughed. "Those dam people. Funny, huh?" His face was as plastic as an actor's. The laugh exposed full dentures. The smile took off ten years. "I upgraded all the powerhouses."

"That was good work back when we needed hydropower."

"It sucked." Bob blew out his disgust. "I hated every minute." He pointed a knobby finger at Ed. "When I heard they hired you, that was a good day. The other guys they hired were shit. They needed to be sent on down the road." He wafted his hand, dismissing the thought of Ed's predecessors. "I knew you'd get 'er done."

"What made you think that?"

"Just a feeling. 'He'll take the fucker down.' That's what I thought."

"I don't understand."

"That dam is a killer. It murders people. It murdered whole nations. It stomped on weak people like a kid stomping ants. That's what it did, back in the 1930s. We've never forgotten." He pointed at his head. "Not even a stroke could make me forget."

Connie returned with a plate of chili and a large piece of fry bread.

"You're a sweetheart, Concepción." Bob held his daughter's hand. "Thank you."

"I have to speak to a parent," Connie said. "I'll be back in a few minutes."

Bob scooped a mouthful of chili. It made Ed hungry. "I do like chili," Bob said, "but it gives me the farts." He relished the dish as if it were his last helping.

Junie dropped into the chair next to Ed. "Hi again."

"Hi!" Ed liked Junie's relaxed manner. It meant she was happy.

"Here's your order." She laid two sugars and two creamers on the table.

"Thanks, Junie-girl."

"Hello." Junie greeted Bob, who lifted his hand in salute while he chewed.

A steady stream of visitors came over to Ed's table, asking him to review one exhibit or another, but he didn't want to leave Bob alone. He liked the old man. Pretentiousness was as alien to the elder as oil is to water. He wondered if Bob could offer advice on some of the engineering problems he was facing.

Out of the corner of his eye, Ed saw Sy Ioannu. Mason was with her. He was just tall enough to peer over the edge of the table at the projects. Ed watched the woman for longer than he should. As leader of the River Defenders chapter, she needed to show the flag as well. Ed noted the quasi-warm formality of her conversations, especially with other women. There was an awkwardness, though. The talk was missing the instant

159

camaraderie most mothers with small children feel for each other. *Marcy and her friends were like that when Junie was a baby.* His daughter nudged him and he returned to his half-eaten plate of desserts.

"Nice to see you again, Ed." Sy materialized next to him, like a ghost. Mason clung to her leg, a stuffed animal under his arm. "Those desserts look heavenly."

"Would you like me to get you some?" Ed swore he heard Junie snigger, but she had the stuffed animal in her hand, animating it like a puppet. Mason was enthralled.

"Nothing for me, thanks." Sy watched Junie and Mason. "He likes you, Miss..."

"I'm Junie."

"Ed's daughter. Nice to meet you."

Mason nudged closer to Junie.

"You have a way with children."

"I was a sitter back home, I mean, in San Francisco."

"Mason is shy, and sitters don't always work out with him. My nanny bot can only do so much. Are you available to watch Mason for a few hours a week while I run errands and such?" Sy quoted a impressive rate.

Junie shrugged. "Sure, why not?"

"I'm so glad. I've got your contact info from your public profile. I'll be in touch." Sy picked up Mason and rested him on her hip. "I have to mingle. See you soon Ed, Junie, Mr Gasca."

Sy walked two steps and Mason squealed. Sy let him down and he ran back to Junie, who was holding his stuffed animal. She handed him the creature, and he thanked her with a hug in the guileless way of small children. He ran back to his mother, jumping with unfeigned happiness.

"Nice work, Junie-girl." Ed surmised that Sy's offer of work to Junie was as much about impressing her father than getting away from a demanding toddler for a couple of hours.

"You'll probably tell me to save half my earnings for college."

"Yep."

"I'm leaving you." With no further word, she departed.

Bob watched her go. "She's yours, eh?"

"Yes, sir."

The elder winked. "A beaut."

Ed hunted for Sy in the crowd. She was a like a magnet; it was impossible for him to take his eyes off her. Bob hacked, which broke the spell.

"Pretty gal," Bob said.

"I'm sorry?"

"Don't be stupid, Ed. You can do better."

"Come again? She's just an acquaintance."

"I'd want to fuck her, too, if my dick worked." Bob took another mouthful of chili.

Ed revised his opinion of Bob. He was more of a dirty old man than he first imagined. "I don't think your opinion is quite appropriate, Mr Gasca."

"Now you're defending her." He shook his head, as if disappointed by a promising student. "I like you, Ed, and I'd tell you to not be a dumb-ass, if I thought it would make a difference. It's too fucking late. You're screwed." Bob shook his head again, and bit off a hunk of fry bread.

Ed stared into his cold coffee, wondering if Bob had a point. Thinking of Sy reminded Ed that he was alone in Utility, with no close friends. He remembered their easy conversation at her house over wine and Greek food.

"Connie is a beaut, too." Ed remembered that Bob was her father. "I mean, she's..."

"I know what you mean, Ed. She's clever and works her ass off. She's got twice the smarts I have. I take up all her time when she's not working. Kinda kills the romance thing. The boys around here are all stupid anyway."

Ed had nothing to add.

"Sounds like you're making a nuisance of yourself again, Papa." Connie rubbed his back with affection.

"Old people are like that." The actuators in his exo whirred. "How else can you tell that we're still breathing?"

Ed hoped Bob Gasca would breath for many more years.

CHAPTER 13

♦ ♦ ♦

JOIN ME FOR BRUNCH?

The text from Natalie was the first to appear in Ed's minds-eye once the bio-logics underneath the skin behind his left ear sensed that he was awake enough to process network input with a semblance of rationality. The characters rolled into his visual field as he finished running an electric razor over his stubble, which showed more and more flecks of gray with every passing month. A cup of coffee from the serv-bot helped his synapses snap back.

I'd love to. Lots to report.

Natalie texted: I'll send a car in ten minutes.

Waiting by the hotel entrance, he collected his mental notes. The day before, she'd sent one of her Lexus-Mercedes to pick him up at SFO. Within an hour of landing, he was prowling the AfterCarbon Expo floor. The hotel and the premium ticket were part thank-you gift and part payment for a scouting mission, though Ed knew Natalie really wanted to talk about ZephyrCom.

The two-seater arrived on time and after it confirmed Ed's identity, he slipped inside. The other seat was empty; he'd be meeting Natalie alone. The hint of ocean in the air diffused the sunlight, which forced its way between the high-rises of downtown San Francisco. "Sunroof open, please?" The AI opened a panel and Ed reveled in the moist atmosphere, a contrast to the harsh dryness of desert surrounding Utility. The nearby ocean's pleasant mix of decay and fecundity countered his new jitters. *Good to be home.*

The car dipped into the underground garage of the newest

residential tower. He stepped out of the car, and a middle-aged, well-built man approached him. "Mr Wye? My name is Merson. Ms Wong asked me to accompany you to her apartment. I hope you don't mind."

"No, of course not." *A human valet. Incredible.*

The men boarded an elevator with only three buttons—43, 44, and 45—and the valet selected 45. After a buttery smooth rise, the door opened to a modest foyer with a wooden double-door opposite the elevator. Carved Chinese dragons writhed on each door.

Merson invited Ed to step through. "If you'll wait here just a moment, I'll tell Madame that you've arrived."

The valet departed, leaving Ed in an open living area with a ceiling five meters above him. The room was dominated by a large, gossamer sculpture that floated in mid-air, lifted by thousands of tiny lifting rotors. The artist managed to elicit a sense of wonder without overwhelming the viewer. The kinetic sculpture delighted Ed, much like the warm greetings from the c-suite executives that he encountered at AfterCarbon. A year ago, the encounter might result in a polite smile and wave, but little more, a clear sign of his status in the community. The new warmth puzzled him, until the CTO of a wave energy company revealed the secret.

"Natalie Wong thinks you're the cat's meow," the portly, red-faced executive said, imitating a cat's meow as he delivered the message. "Every time she shows up at an event or a conference, it's 'Where's Eddie Wye?' or 'Does anyone know what Eddie Wye thinks?' not that I ever get invited to those things. But that's the buzz around town."

Natalie's talking me up and parading me like a prized bull. Why?

In Natalie's suite, curving floor-to-ceiling windows covered the northwest quadrant, framing the Golden Gate Bridge on the left, Point Bonita in the center, and the Pacific Ocean on the right.

A three-masted windship sped into the strait, bound for the cargo terminals at Alameda.

"Impressed?"

Ed turned as Natalie strolled into the room. "Your place is breathtaking."

"I'm glad you think so, Eddie. It had better impress you, or I've wasted a lot of money." Natalie reached out to Ed with both her hands, and they embraced. "I've missed you. Honestly, I have."

Ed drank in the image of the most powerful woman financier and investor in California, some said North America. She wore her Chinese ancestry with pride, but six generations had passed since her ancestors came from the Pearl River Delta to sell groceries to immigrants working in California's gold fields and railroads. Over the succeeding generations, intermarriage with the other immigrants who dreamed of a new life in California had muffled her Asian features, leaving her skin a cream color and her eyes a deep blue under the hint of an epicanthic fold. Jet black hair framed a square face. The crinkles in the corners of her eyes belied her age, a year less than Ed's, and her body advertised the vanity of sculpting and genetic re-engineering. Ed was taller than Natalie by ten centimeters, but he couldn't help feel smaller in a grand space with a grande dame who made the future.

"I've missed you too, Natalie." Ed was happy to see his old friend, though he understood that he was closer to Merson in status than an equal to Natalie.

"Let's eat." Natalie led Ed through the formal dining area to a smaller room with a cloth-covered table set for two. A presentation of sliced apples, pears, and whole plums was partnered with steamed *har gow* and *shaomai*. "The apples and pears are from Wenatchee. Second rate, I know, compared to Utility's fruit, but Merson had trouble finding any from there. A rare failure for him." Natalie indicated a plate of *har gow*. "This one's shrimp. The other is pork. That was the one you like. Did I remember correctly?"

Ed nodded. "It looks delicious."

Merson walked in with a platter of teas. "Oolong, green, or chrysanthemum tea, Mr Wye?"

"Oolong, please."

The old friends sat facing the west and the Pacific Ocean. Ed cast his eye around the room. Chinese and modern paintings decorated the walls. Two holo-pics of a man and a woman floated over a table containing a bowl of fruit and a tea setting. "Your ancestors?"

"Yes, the ones who came to California. I owe everything to them."

"Everything."

"My ancestor started a grocery in 1856. His wife operated a brothel."

"That must be a little embarrassing."

"It was a traditional business. Very profitable and grandmother took care of her girls. They had to close it eventually. The wives of the upper-class white politicians would have none of it. The irony is that the first Cyprian Association brothel opened at the same location 250 years later." The address was in Pacific Heights.

"Amazing."

Natalie rested her hand on Ed's. "How is Junie?"

"Doing well. Adjusting to Utility faster than I imagined."

"And school?"

"She's always been an indifferent student. She's never found a teacher that really inspired her, but her grades are decent."

"Where is she going to college?"

"She hasn't decided yet."

"She must decide quickly, Eddie. She has a doctorate in her, I know it."

"I'm not so sure."

"Nonsense. I'll speak to her."

For a fleeting moment, Ed imagined Natalie as Junie's

166

stepmother, and saw them at each others' throats. Natalie was far too demanding and controlling for an independent soul such as Junie. Ed often wondered, however, if any kind of mother would have been better for Junie than none after Marcy died. Even Natalie could teach things to his daughter Ed never could, such as how to succeed in a world where testosterone still drove relations in business.

"Natalie, I appreciate your..."

Natalie chewed a bit of melon, and sighed. "I'm sorry, Eddie. It's just that I'm so glad you're back, and I like Junie, even if she's skeptical of me."

"She skeptical of everyone."

"A mind that asks questions is a mind that finds answers. She's a smart young woman, even if she doesn't know it yet."

Ed sipped his his tea. It was perfectly brewed. "What about you?"

"Same old same old." The hostess sliced off a hunk of steamed bun with shrimp. "Don't get me wrong. I love my work, but it's not as much fun when you don't have someone to share it with."

Ed worried that she might be hinting at rekindling their relationship. "I live far away now."

"Which pains me every day." She grinned. "I have fun, though. Merson keeps me on my toes, don't you?"

The valet had stepped back from the table. "Madame."

"He's my cook, bartender, valet, personal trainer, masseuse, and occasional therapist. He's better than a husband, because I can kick him out if he's too tough on me without paying lawyers through the nose."

A cruel woman. That's why I'm a little afraid of her. "Well, Merson, I'll say that this is one of the best brunches I've ever had."

Merson lowered his eyes in acknowledgment.

Natalie touched her fingers on a napkin. "Now, Eddie, what did you learn at the expo?"

In bullet point fashion, Ed laid out his view of the renewable and sustainable energy winners and losers among the companies on a list Natalie gave him, as well as a few he thought warranted a look. On one side of the philosophical spectrum were the geo-engineers, who insisted a planetary atmospheric makeover was the one and only way to bring the earth back into ecological balance. Ed regarded the strategy as irresponsible, dangerous, and unnecessary. On the other end was a small, but well-financed company that refined crude oil into the traditional fuel products, despite the functional global ban on fossil fuels. When Ed asked the sales person about the pricing model, he doubted even Natalie could afford a single liter, much less buy a license to burn it.

Natalie laughed. "I can afford a few liters." She queried Ed on all his points. "This is what I really want to know. Did you see anything that could challenge ZephyrCom's potential position?"

Ed knew this was coming. "That's hard to judge. Speaking to people at an expo gives you a skewed view of the competitive environment."

"I've been investigating half of the companies you mentioned for months."

"And I haven't really had time to analyze ZephyrCom's technological advances, despite their roots in my patents."

"That makes sense, but I'm not looking for your rational analysis. Your instincts are good. That's what I'm interested in." Natalie pointed to his belly. "What does your gut say?"

Time to fish or cut bait. Ed worried that he might be holding the knife at his own throat. "All other things the same, ZephyrCom has a lot to offer the market. It could work. It could be very profitable if the big utilities and generators adopt it."

"Let's say you're right. What would you do next?"

"Apart from making sure the technology works..." Again, Ed was prepared for the question. He loved the strategic planning and tactical analysis of bringing a product to market, particularly one that could change the face of a whole class of technologies, what insiders used to call "disruptive." He spelled out his approach.

Natalie listened, and when Ed finished, she asked to be excused. Her abrupt departure alarmed Ed, but he kept quiet, preferring to wait for the ax to be raised before ducking. *Natalie is the most ruthless businesswoman within 500 kilometers.* He remembered Natalie's text upon his landing: `Welcome back to the slaughterhouse`. Ed had been slaughtered himself in the technology abattoir by investors fattening up his or a partners' business before dismembering it for the profit. Sooner or later, everyone in the Valley was shot with a bolt gun, trussed up, and bled out. Did she think ZephyrCom was another sacrificial animal?

Ed glanced at Merson, who was as impassive as an executioner.

"Eddie, would you come in here with me?" Natalie stood in a door previously hidden in the wall.

Ed dropped his linen napkin on the table and entered a typical conference room, except for the antique mahogany table and the west-facing window. Two men in business suits sat next to one another. Ed didn't recognize them.

"Sit here, next to me," Natalie instructed her friend as she pulled out a high-backed chair at the end of the oval table. The diffuse exterior light illuminated her face. She introduced the two men as Mr Köhler and Mr Dharma.

Merson entered the conference room. "Your final guest has arrived, Madame."

"Grace!" Ed called out her name in spite of himself. *She's been in on this since the beginning.*

"So good to see you, Ed." They touched cheeks. The gesture was all-business, rather than warm, leaving Ed wary. He did not expect to see Grace at the meeting, despite her connections to the ZephyrCom project.

"Sorry to be late, Natalie,"Grace said. "The tube from Seattle was delayed."

"Why don't you ever fly, Grace?" Natalie kissed her on the cheek, also business-like.

"And hurl through the air at a thousand kilometers per hour when you can do the same thing on the ground?"

Ed said, "Why do I have the feeling that I'm the victim of a conspiracy?"

"I'll admit that Natalie and I colluded to get you here," Grace said. "But she brought me the idea and I encouraged it."

"Let's get right to the point, Eddie." Natalie poured herself a chai tea. "How do you like your job?"

Ed glanced at Grace "That's a hard question to answer, with the person who hired me in the room."

Grace listened without showing emotion. "Don't worry, Ed. I'm wearing my investor hat today. Utility might as well be on another planet."

"Well, the truth is, that I took the job because I didn't have many other options. I have Junie and I needed work. The doors were closed here."

"That's true," Natalie said. "Your last venture was a disaster, wouldn't you agree?"

Ed blushed. Though failure was a daily occurrence in the business world, he had lost virtually all his investors' money, as well as his own stake, without even a prototype to show for it.

"You've got a reputation as a failure magnet, Ed, at least in the Valley," Grace said.

"And I've never believed that, Eddie." Natalie said. "I've told everyone I know that you're a smart guy and a brilliant manager."

Just like the red-faced guy at the expo said.

"I've seen that it's true," Grace said. "The dam removal project was going nowhere, and you've put it on track. That's not a small thing."

"The fact of the matter," Ed said, "is that I've gotten the

project into a groove. I'm even enjoying it a little bit."

Natalie interrupted. "Let's be honest. Removing dams is a waste of your talent, Eddie. ZephyrCom needs a CEO that knows the business backwards and forwards, and even though you've stumbled lately, your brand still has pull in Brussels, Johannesburg, Delhi, a hundred places."

"I'm not so sure." *A risk-reward analysis of my recent record would be a joke.*

"Trust me," Natalie said. "Tell Mr Köhler and Mr Dharma about your strategic ideas, the ones you explained at brunch."

Ed had nothing to lose. He assumed they signed non-disclosure agreements. He laid out the basics for them. He found himself not only laying out a case, but arguing for it, as if he were its champion. He worried his tone might come across as desperation, rather than passion, but that was how he felt, frantic in his desire to convince the strangers that he was not in exile, not a failure, not a fraud, that he knew his business, despite setbacks, that he deserved to be where they were, instead of a backwater like Utility.

The two foreigners glanced at each other. *Exchanging texts.* Dharma reached for his tab and touched keys rapidly. Köhler addressed Natalie in German, his voice resonant and calm. Natalie answered at length in German, her accent indistinguishable from Köhler's. Ed suspected the thickset man spoke perfect English, and didn't require on-the-fly translation from his minds-eye. Ed had left his translator off. "I'm sorry?"

"Mr Köhler likes to play games," Natalie said with a sharp glance at the German. "He asked about the status of your original patents, and I explained that it shouldn't be a problem in the markets we want to exploit, particularly in Africa."

"There has never been a problem with my patents." Ed felt the need to defend himself in front of the strangers. "Just because that troll Roger Saar convinced an ignorant judge I stole something I owned doesn't make it true. I was exonerated."

Grace winced.

I shouldn't have said his name, but why would it hurt her?

The mayor touched Ed's arm. "You're among friends, Eddie. It's just due diligence. Gerhardt likes you."

"How can you tell?"

Dharma smirked, as if Ed shared his opinion of Köhler.

"Eddie, Mr Köhler represents nine percent of the capitalization in the European renewable energy market. Mr Dharma represents a similar amount in South Asia. I've committed 20 percent of the second-round financing, which gives me control of ZephyrCom's shares."

"What about Grace?" Ed said.

"I'm acting as a consultant to the project."

Ed's eyes narrowed. "Your job is to bring me aboard."

"It's true, Eddie," Natalie said. "I want you to lead the next phase of the project. I want you to bring this technology to market. You understand it. You know what it means, not only to us as investors, but to the planet's adaptation strategy. It's a second chance for you to make a difference."

And get back in the game. "It's tempting, very tempting."

"It's a big decision, Eddie. You should take your time, talk to Junie about it."

"She's already figured out what's going on."

"I told you she was smart," Natalie said. "You should listen to the women in your life."

Natalie ended the meeting by standing and offering her hand to Ed. It was an awkward move, but Ed recognized it as a sign to the foreigners, not to him. Ed felt the need to apologize to the German. "No need, Herr Wye," Köhler said. Dharma smiled broadly, showing perfect white teeth.

◆ ◆ ◆

After Natalie's car dropped him off at the hotel, Ed walked the half block to Market Street and took the cable car to The Embarcadero. Though he knew San Francisco like a native, he felt the need to do something mindless to let the information buffer in his brain empty. He mixed with the tourists at the maritime history park and he contemplated the big antique windship with the unlikely name of *Balclutha*. It was a great-grandfather to the modern windships that replaced the oil-fired monstrosities that crisscrossed the planet's oceans in the 20th and 21st centuries. He read pirate stories as a kid, and though he never saw himself as a windship sailor, a part of him wanted to stow away on one of the vessels ducking under the Golden Gate Bridge on its way to Singapore or Shanghai. *I said I would do my best to finish the dam removal, but Natalie's offer puts me back where I want to be.*

If he took the job, he wouldn't have to worry anymore about the threat against himself and Junie. *Is it smart, or am I a coward?*

Natalie texted: `Are you free for dinner? I promise no shop talk.`

Ed waited a moment before responding. `That's impossible for you, but I'll come anyway.`

`Six o'clock. Just come on up when you get here.`

Ed put on his new tie, reflecting Junie's tastes as much as his own, securing it in place with a diamond tie tack Natalie had given him as a wedding present when he married Marcy. Natalie surprised him by picking him up at the hotel herself. She wore a navy silk gown inspired by the traditional *ao dai* of Vietnam. Ed felt under-dressed. "I decided we should go out for dinner," she said as he buckled himself in. "South Asian okay?"

The pair sped toward Chinatown, taking the network of toll streets. The most famous of San Francisco's neighborhoods was a mix of immigrants, many third and fourth generation from

Afghanistan, Pakistan, and Kashmir, who took the place of the declining population of ethnic Chinese. The restaurant featured a human maitre d' and waiter, a pretty, if dour woman. Ed took the menu from her. "Human staff. Paper menus. You were always a woman with expensive tastes, Natalie. How is it that you hang out with a middle-class dullard like me?"

"I don't have to perform around you, Eddie. There's no pretense with you. You just...are. Don't take that the wrong way. I don't waste time with dunces, and smart people who have their egos under control are rare these days."

Mostly out of habit, Ed studied the network version of the menu, which included a detailed list of ingredients and available cooking styles. The waiter took their order and opened a bottle of wine. "Napa Valley?" Ed said. "I thought those vineyards disappeared a decade ago."

"There's a few micro-climates left that work for grapes and wine-making. It's a niche market now, and pricey, even for me."

They chatted over various subjects, and Ed appreciated that she didn't bring up ZephyrCom or the dam removal. Natalie was charming and beautiful. Men could never keep up with her, including Ed, which is why their relationship never flowered beyond common interests and the occasional night out. He hadn't seen her in five years or so, and she struck him as lonelier than ever.

"You're different from other men I've known. You rarely ask me for anything. I always come to you."

It's true. She sent me the proposal; I didn't ask her for it. "I feel lucky to be your friend, even though I might end up working for you."

"Hah! You're the one who brought up shop talk."

They laughed together.

"Seriously, Natalie, it's always been the work that interested me the most. Of course, that's easy to say when you don't worry where your next meal is coming from, or your child's. I came within a hair's breadth of that before Grace got me the dam removal job. It's actually been good for me. I thought I was a complete failure, that I'd gone from the heights of success to utter defeat. I've put the project on track, and it feels great. I want to see it through." *Do I really want to go to the heights where Natalie reigns?*

"That's why I talked this morning about making a difference, Eddie, because I know that's what you really care about. You'll make a difference in Utility, for sure, but ZephyrCom could change nations, maybe a continent or two."

The waiter brought a plate of Indian *mithai* to satisfy the diners' request for sweets, and they departed the restaurant, walking toward Huntington Park on Nob Hill. The fountains were among the few in the city with water, paid for by a local taxing district. They sat on a stone bench, and Natalie rested her hand on Ed's. After a while, they strolled to a corner of the park where Natalie called for her car. "Night cap?"

Ed nodded, not without a twinge of guilt. Natalie and he had known each other since his days at Stanford, and Marcy understood how close they were as friends. Around Junie's eighth birthday, Ed's marriage hit a rough patch, and Natalie was one friend who listened. Ed believed he and Marcy might have divorced had she not been killed in Yosemite Valley. They had gone different high-risk directions; he into entrepreneurship—the same path as Natalie—and Marcy up cliffs as smooth as glass. She had not survived, he barely. Junie was the thing that kept him alive afterward. The thing was, Ed felt closer to Marcy *after* she died, as if he was in love with a memory of her before their marriage failed. *Eight years later, I haven't let her go.*

The sun dipped below the horizon, leaving it a deep navy and purple along the edge of the world. They watched the stars from Natalie's living room. It was as if they floated in one of the

Branson Hotel chain's orbiters, with only the diffuse glow of city lights below the level of the windows signaling they were on the ground in a major metropolis.

"I should be going. I have a long flight back to Spokane tomorrow." Ed stood up and gathered his suit coat. His hand slipped from Natalie's.

Merson was nowhere near.

Natalie followed Ed to the door, her feet bare. For the first time that evening, she brought her eyes to his and held them, as if it would be the last time she would ever see him. A piece of Ed wished it were so, that he could leave and never see her again. He knew what she was capable of, and it scared him, as if dark matter from the most remote regions of the universe lived behind those eyes.

One time, he was on a team negotiating rights to expand a wind farm onto land in India considered sacred by an obscure cult of Jains. After a year of frustrating talks, their main temple was leveled by an explosion, killing the cult's leadership. Hardly two bricks or two human cells were found together. The government blamed terrorists. More importantly for Natalie, the impediment to the deal suddenly vanished, and she upped her offer the next day. Ed was one of the negotiators who initialed the contract.

No terrorist group ever claimed responsibility, and no one was ever arrested.

Ed swallowed. "Natalie, what do you want from me, at bottom, I mean."

Natalie pulled away. She walked up to the window glass, her shape outlined in the darkness. "I want a partner, a real partner. Not financial, not mutual business interests, but a partner who cares about what's going on here." She held her hand to her breast. "I'd like to ask you something, Eddie."

"Ok."

"If I had asked you to marry me, back before you married

Marcy, would you have said Yes?"

"Natalie, you never hold back, do you?"

"I did then, much to my regret."

Ed stood next to her. "I don't know what I would've said. We were both a lot younger."

Natalie returned and lifted Ed's hand to her lips. "Are we smarter now?"

"I don't know. More cautious."

"I don't want to be cautious, not tonight. I'm so tired of calculating everything. Aren't you?"

Ed didn't need his minds-eye to read Natalie's message. "You might be my boss soon. It wouldn't do for me to sleep with the boss."

Natalie smiled. "I'm not your boss...yet." She parted her lips. "Until then, we can be equal partners, at least for one night."

Ed kissed Natalie. She smelled of jasmine, and he struggled to keep his desire under control. Twenty years had passed, though, and neither of them was the same person. He had more self-control, more perspective. Sleeping with Natalie only complicated matters. *Junie would never accept her, and Sy Ioannu...* He stopped short, surprised that Sy had popped into his mind. Ed slipped on his suit coat, and said goodnight.

How far will she go to get me by her side?

CHAPTER 14

♦ ♦ ♦

WE NEED TO TALK.

Junie clenched her fists as she stared at the text from Alex in her minds-eye. When she got the text, her first sensation was a sharp pain in her stomach, just beneath her sternum. Her first emotion, upon understanding the text, was the terror that comes with knowing an awful future. Her fingernails dug into her palms, but she was unaware of the pain, focused as she was on fighting back her tears, which blurred her vision in the same way that space and time for her was twisted and stretched, turning the hallway between the classrooms of Rast High into an endless tunnel and her journey from fifth to sixth period into a milk run across a galaxy. The experience added up to a truth: Her relationship with Alex was dying, if not dead.

Talk about what?

About things.

The automated emotional signature on Alex's text was sadness and dread, but Junie's empathy for him was as a pebble is to a mountain, insignificant compared to the laceration on her soul. Junie's throat closed as if some devil choked her.

What sort of things? Junie swallowed hard when she sent the response.

Junie, you're making this harder than it has to be.

Junie debated whom she should hate more: Her father, for bringing her Utility, tearing her away from Alex, weakening the

178

bonds that left her relationship vulnerable to a break; Alex, for starting this thread, not to mention showing no fidelity to her around the whores at Sierra Vista; or her so-called "friends" back home, who took perverse delight in sending her images of Alex enjoying the attentions of half the sluts in the South Bay. Her inability to resolve the triple dilemma magnified the numbness that made the hall walk an endless trudge. Her feet felt as if they were weighed a thousand pounds.

~~Are you breaking up with me?~~ Junie backspaced out of the text, regaining a measure of self-control as she took her usual seat in physics. Is something bothering you?

I don't want to hurt you.

She laughed a little. The line was such a cliché, only slightly better than "It's not you, it's me," or the god-awful, "Can we just be friends?" Her laugh broke Tiffany's concentration. She glanced at Junie as the latter girl bent over her tablet, sniffed, and hated her body for giving away her emotional state.

"Are you alright?" Tiffany said.

Junie pretended she was fine, but she was not convincing.

"You don't look that good. Are you sick?"

Junie pinged Mr Henderson and asked to be excused. She was finished with the required questions, and she had no stomach for the extra credit problems. Henderson let her go. With Tif's eyes following her, she went straight for the bathroom, found a stall, and closed the door.

I'm alone. Do you want to use voice?
Not really. Text and sigs are better.
Coward.

She thought-sent the single-word text impulsively, and regretted it, but felt satisfaction, even glee. Her emotions fired at random, like the particles from a decaying radioactive substance. *Love is radioactive. Love decays.*

You're the one who moved away.

    You promised to visit, but you always
cancel.
    I have to prep for college.
    Always the same excuse. You were never
interested in coming here.
    Yes, I was! It's not my fault you're on
the fucking moon.
    People go to the moon every week. What's
your problem?
    You don't have parents watching you day
and night.
    Ditch them.
    Why don't you come here?
    I can't. I might not leave.
    Weak. Weak. Weak.

And on and on and on for 20 minutes. Junie missed her last class as she and Alex fought a silent thought-war over the com net, a battle as loud in emotion as it was quiet in anything the ear could perceive, except for Junie's sobbing. She perceived one or two knocks on the stall door from Tiffany and Trudy and half-heard her own shouted "Go away!" and then quiet as the next class began. That's when she walked out and down the side hall to the exit, not caring about dumb-ass hall passes or monitor bots with artificial intransigence you could fool with one hand tied behind your back.

    This isn't working any more. The emo-sig on Alex's text was implacability. I don't think we should see each other any more. Then he closed the connection, like slamming the door.

    As the [END] icon displayed in her occipital awareness, Junie jolted open the school doors until they nearly flew off their hinges. She took off at a run, her laced-up shoes slapping the concrete, her pack flagellating her shoulder blades. It felt good to run; the discomfort in her feet and the rhythm of her pack broke the steady beat of misery in her heart. After a couple of blocks, she stopped under a shade tree, abruptly disbelieving what she had just seen in her minds-eye. She scrolled again and again through the texts and sigs and even an image of Alex with probably faked tears as if she wanted to relive a nightmare to make sure it didn't happen that way and that she had misinterpreted something or he had said something he didn't mean to say and that everything was alright and it was just a misunderstanding because of the stupid com net and I'm sorry I called you a coward and I'm sorry I'm sorry and I'm sorry and can we just talk on the voice channel?

He didn't respond to any of her entreaties. Her tears flowed freely down the spillway where her nose met her cheek. The snot from her nose flowed freely to the point where she couldn't keep up with the sniffling and wiping with the crushed tissue in her hand, the last one in the package she carried in her pack. She felt as grotesque as the yellow-shirted, balding, beer-gut construction supervisor back at the dam months ago. *Love is ugly.*

`Notification: Babysit Mason, 15:00 to 17:00, Ioannu house.`

The calendar note was as routine as her morning wake-up call, but she welcomed it like a life ring thrown at her in a storm. She was due at Sy Ioannu's house in a few minutes, and as it happened, she sat on a bench directly across the street from the woman's home. Like the notification, the normality of routine provided a measure of comfort, and the pain receded, but only into a corner, poised to return at a moment's notice. She collected herself and cleaned up as best she could using a makeup mirror, ignoring the AI's suggestions on blush and liner. She was not in the mood to paint herself.

Patched up. Ready for work.

Sy opened the door as the house net confirmed Junie's identity. Mason wrapped himself around Junie's leg. She'd only watched him a few times since Sy's invitation, but the child thought of her as a big sister. "So heavy!" she said, as she lifted him onto her hip, then kissed him on a downy cheek. He wiped his cheek, belying his delight. He stared at her for a moment before Junie let him down. His eyes were exactly the same violet blue as his mother's.

"Mason, you're getting too big for climbing on people," Sy scolded with little conviction. "You're going to hurt your friend."

"She's already hurting." Mason ran off, leaving his innocent comment hanging in the air. The nanny bot followed him.

Junie's eyes fell to her feet as she realized her failure at covering up her distress. *I hope she doesn't say anything.* Sy measured the younger woman with a glance, and she stepped aside to let her in.

"I've only got a couple of errands today. I won't be long."

"That's fine," Junie said. "I'm a little tired and wouldn't mind going home early."

Sy hesitated. "It's warmer than usual today. You look hot. I'm getting you some water."

"I'm fine, Sy."

"Only take a minute. Have a seat in the solarium."

Junie did as she was told. She liked Sy and didn't have the energy to object. The room was Junie's favorite. She took in the art pieces, noticing a new one, brightly painted. Despite the sunshine, the room was pleasantly cool.

Sy returned with a glass. "No one in my house is allowed to have heatstroke. Sip slowly. You know the protocol."

The cool water was soothing. The under-the-radar fragrances of the succulents and cacti calmed Junie as well. Sy sat waiting. For what, Junie wasn't sure. Again, time was distorted, slowing to a heartbeat. The brutal moments of her argument with Alex resurfaced, and Junie struggled like Sisyphus to push her emotions away. *I can't lose control in front of Sy. What if it scares her? Would she tell Dad?* "I'm feeling better." She handed the half-drunk glass to Sy.

Sy sat before Junie, hands folded on her knees, the look on her face open, questioning, accepting, a silent offering of a friendly ear.

The dam burst. A fresh wave of tears and cries from the deepest part of Junie broke through, shaking her shoulders and body like an earthquake. In an instant, Sy was at her side, arms enfolding Junie as if they had known each other for decades. Sy stroked Junie's face as the girl lay on the woman's breast feeling every wave of pain as if her skin were flayed. Each brush of Sy's soft hands and each back and forth movement soothed the teenager into an almost meditative state. In time, Junie's emotions were less like knives and more like a fog that would lift as soon as the sun had a chance to burn it off. Reluctant to leave Sy's embrace, Junie eventually accepted a fresh tissue from Sy and let herself slump back into the solarium's sofa.

Silence was Sy's art. Patience was her craft, and in the fullness of time, she asked Junie, "Do you want to talk about it?"

"I don't know."

Sy waited a moment, then said. "The people we care about most, hurt us the most."

"Is it that obvious?"

In a flash, Junie understood the power of Sy Ioannu, why she was at once alluring and intimidating. By simply waiting and focusing all her attention on you, she could tear down any barrier. Despite the difference in ages, Junie was fascinated by Sy Ioannu. Her poise and confidence, unsullied by arrogance, were strengths worth emulating. Junie fidgeted. "It's just that… Why can't things be the way we want them to be?"

A shadow crossed Sy's face. "We think we have control, but we don't. Other people's desires get in the way."

An image of Alex with one of Junie's competitors resolved in her imagination. *I've failed with Alex.* "My boyfriend broke up with me." Saying the words out loud proved less difficult than Junie expected.

"I see."

Seeing no reason to hold back, Junie told Sy the story of the argument.

"He sounds like basically a good person, but young men, some of them, have a hard time staying with one woman. Did you expect him to stay loyal to you, exclusively?"

"Yes."

"What happened is not your fault. You're far away from each other, physically. Could that be the problem?"

A fresh wave of pain. "That's the other part of it, Sy. I didn't want to come to Utility, but Dad made me. I didn't want to choose between staying with Dad and staying with Alex. I thought I could keep things going with Alex. But I'm here practically on Pluto surrounded by culchies and now I've lost the most important thing in my life." Junie was embarrassed by her disrespect for her new friends. *They're good people, but I don't want to be here!*

"It sounds like your father is more important to you."

Junie had to agree, but she could not say it out loud. "I don't belong here."

"Have you considered that maybe you do? Have you thought that maybe in time, you would fit in?"

"You've got to be kidding me."

Sy laughed, a breathy sound hinting at deep experience. "I don't blame you for discounting the possibility. I sometimes think I'll never belong here, that I'll always be a stranger. Maybe even an outcast."

Sy's admission piqued Junie's curiosity. "Because you're for the dam deconstruction?"

"That's some of it, but I was thinking more about my family. You see, when I was much younger, only a few years older than you, I made some… choices, that weren't so smart. I have to live with the consequences."

Junie wanted to ask for more details, but she was uncertain how much to probe. "What sort of consequences?"

"It's a complicated story—"

Junie sensed Sy was not ready to explain the details.

"—but they meant that my mother was so angry, we haven't spoken to each other in many years. I didn't find out my grandmother had died until days after she passed."

Junie saw tears forming in Sy's eyes. "Can you tell me... I mean... I guess it's none of my business."

"Junie, you've been trusting enough of me to open your heart. I'll try to do the same." Sy cleared her throat. "Do you know the story of my mother and grandmother?"

Junie confessed she didn't.

"You know about the Cyprian Association?"

Who didn't know? People avoided the words "whore" or "prostitute." The accepted words were "cyprian" or "sex worker," at least for the licensed trade managed by the CA. "A rep from the union ran the sex ed program in my middle school."

"My grandmother founded the CA before I was born. My mother helped her build it into an international movement."

Junie was impressed. She didn't know much about the CA's history, though she understood that sex work was still frowned on outside the big cities where the CA was visible. Yes, cyprians sold sex in all its ingenious forms. They also listened to lovers with broken hearts. "What happened? Did you have a disagreement with your mother? What about your father?"

"My father was my mother's business partner, though he preferred a low profile." Sy sighed. "It's hard to explain, but I'd say that my mother and grandmother felt betrayed by my choices, especially as it reflected on the union and them. The story got out, and I was ostracized."

Outcast. "And that's when you came to Utility?"

"Not quite. During the trouble, a man whom I had... worked with, became lovers."

Junie put two-and-two together. "Mason?"

185

"He was our child. The father felt responsible for Mason and I, and he brought us here."

Junie glanced about her. "Where is he, the father?"

"He died shortly after we came here."

"That must've been hard, after what happened back home." *Back home! We're both exiles.*

"Yes, but Marshal—that was his name—provided for Mason and I in his will. Not much, but it helped me get this house, and my work for River Defenders pays our expenses. Mason and I made a new start in Utility. It's not the perfect place to live, but the schools are decent, and I think the town has a good future, despite what the deconstruction opponents say."

The comment made Junie think of old man Rast. And Don. "I guess you can get used to anything."

Sy took Junie's hands in hers. "I'm telling you this because you're hurting right now. It feels like nothing else matters, and that no one understands. I'm not going to pretend that I understand what happened between you and Alex, but it's only temporary. You'll survive it, just like Mason and I survived our ordeal. You might even come out stronger. Do you think that's possible?"

Junie agreed.

"I know you love Alex, but remember that he's just a young man. Your life doesn't depend on him. Perhaps he wasn't meant to be your life companion, which is really what people want."

"You have to embrace the pain, but not the pleasure." Sy's wisdom and compassion gave Junie strength. "The more you grasp pleasure, the weaker each subsequent moment of joy. The more you reject pain, the more enduring the hurt. Let yourself feel what you feel, Juniper Wye. You'll heal faster."

Another thought of Don Rast intruded into Junie's thoughts. She pushed it away, though she wondered if she should bring him up with Sy. *Is he my life companion?* Junie blinked, appalled at her own duplicity viz a viz Alex. Sy, however, had become a friend, not quite a confidant, but more than a single mother who paid her for child care. Junie respected Sy.

Mason toddled into the solarium, carrying a toy car. He sat on a braided rug, and he pretended to drive around the braids as if they were a road. Junie had forgotten that she was at Sy's house to watch the child. "I don't want to keep you from your errands."

Sy gathered her bag and keys. "There's always another possibility, Junie. Couples fight and make up all the time. Life's narrator likes to toy with her characters. Maybe your relationship with Alex isn't really over."

The potential for getting back together with Alex gave Junie hope that all was not lost, but the thought left her further confused. *I won't leave Dad to be with Alex. What if it's better that I let him go?* "I'm not sure, but he'll have to make the first move."

CHAPTER 15

◆ ◆ ◆

ED ARRIVED AT SPOKANE'S AIRPORT wishing he hadn't turned
down Natalie's offer of a helicopter ride to Utility after he left her
apartment. He wanted to be home and in bed. He was tired, and not
only because he slept all of two hours at his hotel. Thoughts of
Natalie and her attempted seduction kept him awake. Layered on
top was the exhaustion of carrying a problem that didn't have a
good solution: what to do about Natalie's offer. He wanted to talk
to someone other than Natalie or even Grace. Neither had an
objective point of view when it came to ZephyrCom. Junie was too
young and inexperienced to help him weigh the options. He wished
his mother was alive; she was a good listener. His father would've
told him to "get on with it." Marcy would've rolled her eyes. The
chill of the Columbia Plateau winter didn't help, and at the taxi
stand, he shoved his hands into his pockets.

"Ed! Ed Wye!"

He turned to the voice before the auto-cabbies had a chance to
compete for his business.

"Sy?"

She trotted up to him in shoes meant for display, not comfort.

"Ed, thank goodness I didn't miss you."

He smiled in spite of his surprise. "You knew I was here?"

"Junie told me you were coming in."

"Junie?"

"Don't be mad at her. Your profile only said 'Away from my
desk.' I tried to call you at the office last week and they told me

you had taken a couple of days off. Junie told me you had flown to San Francisco and that you were coming back today. I checked the flights from SFO and put two-and-two together."

"You came all the way to Spokane to find me?"

"I had some business here, so it was convenient."

Ed wasn't sure whether to be thankful or suspicious.

"Oh, come on," Sy said. "I was hoping we could share a public car back to Utility."

Sy was right. Ed wouldn't mind saving a few euros by doubling up. "Good idea, Sy." The pair boarded a shuttle to the public car lot and ordered a two-seater. Public cars were a crap shoot. In this case, the legendary stink was absent, and the AI understood the instructions the first time. Sy had no luggage, but her shoulder bag contained packaged veggie snacks and water. Ed remembered Mason. Mothers of small children know to carry exactly what's needed. She offered Ed a baby carrot. As he munched, his hunger grew, and he accepted another.

"No breakfast today?" Sy said.

"I was in a hurry to get out of San Francisco."

Sy nodded. "It's easy to forget eating when you have a lot on your mind."

Her comment startled Ed. He dismissed his reaction as foolish, as reading too much into nothing, and he let the ponderosa pine and saltgrass speeding by on the shoulder of the refurbished interstate lull his mind. A jet took off from the military air base on the outskirts of the city, trailing exhaust. The air force and some fast-attack elements of the navy were legally allowed to use carbon fuels.

Sy followed the climbing jet. "It's hard to imagine that every car on this road, on every road, everywhere, and every plane in the sky, and every boat, burned carbon fuel for more than a century. Thank the Mother we've come to our senses."

Ed closed his eyes and rested his head against the door post.

For an instant, he detected muskiness. Sy was close to Natalie's age, maybe three or four years older, with a face a perfect balance of wisdom and innocence.

"We still have work to do, that jet for one." Sy crunched a celery stick delicately. "It's ironic that half of the Bureau of Environmental Security's own vehicle fleet still burns gasoline. Did you know that?"

"No, I didn't." A part of Ed thought Sy's voice ought to annoy him, but it didn't. It was restful.

Sy paused, as if hesitating. Ed opened his eyes in anticipation. "You were going to say something?"

"Thank you, Ed," Sy said.

"For what?"

"For working on the dam removal. It's important work, and it's important to me."

"With any luck, we'll be done with most of it in a year or so." *And I will be ZephyrCom's rising star of a CEO. Maybe.*

"I don't mean to pry, but you look troubled, Ed. Can I help?"

Sy twisted her body toward him, encouraging him to speak. Ed folded his hands in his lap. "I'm fine. It's been a busy couple of days, and I'm still sorting it out."

Sy reached into her bag and pulled out a packaged juice. "I've never had a chance to tell you about our plans after the dam is gone. Are you interested?"

"Of course." Ed said the words to be polite. He didn't care that much about life after the dam. He doubted he would stick around. He liked Sy, but she was after something.

"We've been dependent on the impounded water for so long that there's nothing to replace agriculture without some help, and the recreation economy is based on a lake, not a flowing river. The local economy is going to hurt."

"I thought all River Defenders cared about was restoring the river to its natural flow."

"Humans have distorted nature here, but that doesn't mean we want Utility to die. Many of the people I work with have lived in Utility all their lives. They just want the town to think ahead."

Even a conservative town such as Utility has its progressives.

Sy sipped her drink. "We talk to the BES and the government regularly, and we're confident that they're going to provide grants and loans to transition the community to an economy compatible with the local ecology."

"And that means?"

"Tourism, small-scale agriculture not dependent on irrigation, and riparian restoration. It's been done at the other dam removal projects. You'd think they've all failed, if you listened to the resisters in Utility." The last phrase was said with a heavy dose of cynicism. It sounded out of character coming from Sy.

"Changes like those are going to displace a lot of people. No wonder they're upset."

"I'm not proud of that," Sy said. She lifted her chin, as if working up courage. "The river was never meant to support a town of 40,000. Utility needs to be smaller to find a true balance with its surroundings."

"People like Covington Rast will fight you to the bitter end."

Sy shot him a look of anger. "People like Cov Rast will have to adjust." Her face softened. "The climate is different now, literally and politically. He is on the wrong side of history."

"It seems change is inevitable, as far as Utility is concerned."

"The plan is missing one thing, Ed. It needs someone people trust to lead it."

Oh, hell. "If you're looking for a recommendation, Grace Cromer would be my choice. She's mayor, after all."

"People don't believe she's interested in Utility's welfare, at bottom. They're suspicious of her because she made lots of money while she was away and came back to become mayor. They think she's lording her success over them."

"Connie Gasca is a good administrator. I'm dependent on her."

Sy's skepticism was evident. "She has... baggage with many people. Not with me, but..."

"What kind of baggage?" Ed couldn't imagine why people might object to Connie.

Sy ignored the question. "I had someone else in mind."

"I think I know who you mean," Ed said.

"Oh?"

"Come on, Sy. You've been working up to it for the last 15 minutes. You want me to stick around after the dam is gone."

"Why not you?"

"I might have other plans."

"Like what?"

This is what Sy really wants to know: How committed am I to the deconstruction? "I haven't made any decisions yet. Right now, I'm focused on Arroyo Grande Dam."

"And Junie."

"Of course. Junie is at the center of my life." Ed shifted in his seat. He might not have said the same thing before Marcy's death. "Besides, why should people in Utility trust me? I'm an outsider. Parochial people don't welcome strangers."

"You grew up here, Ed."

"And left. And came back, like Grace, after making a fortune." *Though I lost mine, unlike Grace.* "I've felt the eyes on my back. Half the town wonders why you left in the first place, and the other half wonders why you'd want to come back. At the end of the day, everyone looks at you sideways. No, I don't have the necessary credibility to be a leader here."

"Believe or not, Ed, many people in Utility respect you. You're already a leader, despite what you think. Most local people are practical, even if they don't like the removal. You took a project in complete disarray and put it on track. Everyone sees that. The fact that you saved downtown from a raging monster helped."

"That's an exaggeration. All I did was bash an AI's brains out."

"The point is, of all people in Utility, you could lead the town into a positive future compatible with the environment."

"Why don't *you* lead the post-dam restoration?"

"Me?" Sy's shock was genuine.

"You mean you've never considered it?"

The public car crawled past an AI-managed truck convoy going a few kilometers per hour slower in the right lane. Sy watched the train go by. "I have my own baggage."

"You mean the environmental group?"

Sy tapped the door handle, as if debating how much to reveal. "I'm an outsider, too. I'm not... I don't have the respect that you do."

Ed had no idea what she was talking about, but he recognized that her statement was meant as a way to keep her distance. A silence formed between Ed and Sy, as if both waited for the next move. Ed considered how things had changed in just a few months. He came to Utility bankrupt, *persona non grata* in the energy world, with a new job on a project bound for disaster. Today, he had a job offer from a friend and sometime lover that gave him a chance to return to a world where people made the future. And now, a woman who sent shivers up his spine held out the opportunity to take a town on a new path, to make a smaller-scale difference, but still change the lives of many for the better. *What do I care about most? Saving the planet, or saving a town with a woman as beautiful as Sy Ioannu?*

"You should ask what Junie thinks."

"Thanks, I will." *She may be the one who decides for all of us.*

As the public car sped west from Spokane, the lowering clouds let go of the load of the moisture they carried from the Pacific Ocean. Rain dappled the car's windows. The Cascade Range acted like a filter as the winter cold fronts moved east, and most of the rain fell on the west side. The mountains allowed some of the precious water to slip onto the Columbia Plateau. In years past, farmers and foresters could count on snow to store water and let it trickle out of the hills over months, but the Warming eliminated the snow pack, except on the highest peaks. Now the water sloughed off the hills and desert like dead skin, and even a light rain could wash out low-lying areas.

Ed puzzled at the lack of network traffic, until he realized that he had left his powerful AI filters on. He called up the menu in his minds-eye, and switched to a default filter. A series of pings flashed by as the network caught up. The bulk were from Connie Gasca.

Ed texted: `Connie, I'm about an hour from town. I just got your messages. Can you send me images of what you found?`

Ed texted back and forth with his operations manager. Sy watched, knowing that Ed was catching up with business, but she noticed the concern on Ed's face. "Trouble?"

"Sy, do you mind if I'm dropped off at the site?"

"Of course not. Is there anything I can help with?"

Ed didn't answer as he exchanged more information with Connie and the Grant County Sheriff's Department. Sy instructed the car's AI to drive for the dam site, and when they arrived, the rain was steady. Ed jumped out of the car.

"Sy, I've got a favor to ask. Can you take my luggage to my apartment? Junie's there. She can let you in."

"What's wrong?"

"I'll tell you later."

The hood on Ed's light jacket was not meant to keep out a good rain as he bypassed the office and a pair of sheriff's department cruisers. The air temperature was cold enough to add a few slushy snowflakes to the rain. The equipment yard was an unholy mess of mud. Rivulets of chocolate-brown water crisscrossed the yard. Ed's shoes were ruined by the time he reached an open shed where some of the most valuable equipment was stored. Connie was in the building with a uniformed sheriff's deputy.

"Let's see what we've got, Connie," Ed said.

Connie led him back outside to an immense crane, one of the two diesel-fueled pieces of equipment operated under a BES special license. Electric motor and battery technology still couldn't match the power diesel engines could generate to lift loads of 200 metric tons or more. Connie stopped at the fuel tank and took off the cap. "Someone poured sugar or salt into the fuel tank." A crystalline substance clung to the lip of the filler hose.

"Shit."

"It's worse. Whoever did this managed to override the engine security codes and start up the motor."

"Just like the bulldozer in town."

"Some of the fuel got into the fuel lines and into the engine," Connie continued. "There's also crystals in the crankcase."

Ed added it up. "The engine's destroyed."

"It'll have to be torn down and rebuilt."

"Christ."

"There's more. Someone hacked into the local network and erased all the on-board storage for the entire robot inventory."

"We can restore from backup, right?"

"Yes, but each bot will have to be reconfigured and tested. That's the safety protocol. The government is pretty strict about it."

"How long will that take?"

"A few days."

"Not so bad."

"I'm sorry, I meant a few days for each bot."

"There's hundreds of them!" Ed cursed again.

The sheriff's deputy stepped into the conversation. His cap was covered with plastic to keep off the rain. His avatar said "Cavil, 344." The number matched the number on his badge. "Do you know anyone who might have done this, sir?"

"Only half the town." Ed shivered, exhaustion catching up to him. "No, I don't mean that, but there's lot of people who won't be sorry this happened. How did they get onto the site?"

"They cut through the fence," Cavil said. "Whoever it was disabled the security system, too."

"We managed to get that back online pretty quickly," Connie said. "And nothing's missing, as far as we can tell."

The three walked back to the open shed. The outside temperature warmed a degree or two. The accumulation of wet snow was melting quickly.

"It's a classic monkey-wrenching, I'd say." The deputy wiped droplets off the screen of his hand-sized tab. "Somebody is angry with the company, or the project. Have you fired anyone recently from this job?"

Ed looked at Connie.

"No one in the last few weeks. The workforce has been pretty steady."

"Any threats, verbally, email, otherwise?"

Ed thought of the threats against him and the dam. *I should've checked on Junie.* "We get a fair amount of hate email and hacking attempts."

The deputy cleared his throat. "I'll have to inform the BES investigators. Some of this looks like an environmental crime, and that's their jurisdiction."

"They probably already know about it." Ed addressed the deputy, who looked young, but world weary. "You called it a monkey-wrenching. I thought that was done by environmental activists against logging companies or oil companies."

"That was back in the mid-20th century," the deputy said. "These days, it's often people who have a beef with the BES or green companies." The deputy excused himself and promised to contact Connie and Ed for formal statements.

196

"At least no one was hurt," Ed said.

"We're lucky. The bots aren't safe, but no one would've known until they were booted up. The saboteur left a message that alerted the guys who showed up for the early shift."

"What kind of message?"

Connie led him outside to the side of the big shed. Drops of cold rain trickled down Ed's collar. The saboteur had scrawled in large, uneven letters on the side of the shed: STOP KILLING UTILITY, OR WE'LL KILL YOU.

CHAPTER 16

♦ ♦ ♦

RAIN PELTED THE TRIPLE-PANED WINDOW of Don Rast's kitchen, distracting Junie from her tablet. Don asked for more homework help, and they practiced differential equations. His grandfather snored on the couch in the living room. Don straightened as if jolted by an electric shock. "Christ, no."

Don's sleeves were rolled up and the hair was coarse when Junie touched his arm by instinct. "What is it?"

"A text from the colony. Come on, I need your help."

The forwarded text and image appeared in Junie's minds-eye. "Oh, god." *I hope the little girl and her mom are alright.*

Don threw on a rain slicker and gave a spare to Junie two sizes too large. They raced to the barn and booted up the equines. The flesh-and-blood horses were too valuable to risk in a rainstorm. Don slaved Daisy to Silver and Junie felt as if she were back at Girl Scout camp towed on an inner tube behind a fast boat on the lake. The robots didn't trot or gallop, but the trail was difficult to see in the pouring rain and Junie held on to Daisy's neck as they traveled at a fast walk that sometimes became a trot. Daisy's metal skin was wet and slick. Junie couldn't anticipate her moves and she was afraid of falling off at every sharp turn.

"Don, slow down!"

They arrived at the lip of the wash and the pace eased as the robots picked their way down the embankment to the stream bed. The devastation shocked Junie. Splintered planks and sheet metal bent like aluminum foil spread across the floor of the wash. Naked dolls, torn shirts, half a couch, dismembered robot pets, nothing was whole in the ruins. It was if the Year of Storms had returned to destroy one last community, finishing the work that had obliterated the East Coast from Newark to New Haven. The revolting smell forced a cough, and when she realized the stench's meaning, she tumbled off Daisy and vomited into the root ball of an upended cottonwood. Junie recognized the mangled face of the elder woman she had met with the man named Peter on her first visit to the village of the disidentified. The woman's skin was gray against the caramel of the smooth stones of the wash. Junie had never seen death before, not even small animals or pets. The trade in caged animals had ended a decade before she was born.

Don fared better, but his face blanched and he tied a dust mask over his mouth as he approached Peter.

"I found her body under a fallen log," Peter said, as if reporting last year's weather.

"I've brought some food and the emergency supplies." Don pointed at the packs on Silver and Daisy. "Is anyone else missing?"

"We haven't found any of our animals."

Don's voice broke. "Animals are smarter than people. Maybe they escaped into the hills."

"No. No, there's no reason to hope." Peter blinked as he shrugged in his mud-caked coat. "I'm not sure. A few people worried about a flash flood when the rain started coming down hard. They went up into higher ground."

The rain became a fine mist, retarding time.

"Should we call the police?" Junie wiped her mouth on the wet sleeve of her slicker.

"No!" Peter's stunned apathy disappeared. "The sheriff tolerates us, as long as we keep quiet. The bessies probably know we're here, but I'd rather not stir the hornet's nest."

Peter's plea was the same as the mother's back at the highway, rank with the fear of separation.

Don tugged at Silver's reins. "Let's go see if anyone else needs help."

"I can't leave her, Don." Peter glanced at the body of his companion.

"We'll come back for her." Don rummaged in the pack and found a tarp, which he draped over the body. Junie helped him anchor the tarp with stones.

The three picked their way around the torn branches, plastic chairs, and tangled electrical cable. They came to an open area, which Junie remembered from her first visit. It passed as a kind of square to the unnamed village. A half-dozen adults and children bent over the debris like stoop laborers in old photos. Junie searched their faces for the mother and child, as well as the dissed man below the horse sculptures, and she was disappointed. A dog chewed and swallowed. Don gathered loose lumber and made an ankle-high pile.

"What are you doing?" Peter sounded a mild panic.

"You've got to build a fire. It'll be freezing tonight."

"No, the Carbon Laws..."

Don pointed at a tangle of aluminum. "Your solar bank is scrap, Peter. The batteries are dead. There's no power for the heaters. You have to take the chance."

Even in the twilight, Peter's eyes glistened as Don fed the fire. Feeling useless, Junie gathered a few sticks and laid them on the tiny blaze. Abruptly, Peter dropped onto a smooth boulder and cried. Junie struggled against her own tears.

Not including herself and Don, Junie counted ten people at the fire: eight adults and two children, aged about five and ten. One of the adults' arms was in a splint. Another had a bandaged laceration. One found a grate from a grill, put it over the fire, and set a dented pot of water on it to boil. Don's emergency supplies included tea bags and cups, and within a half-hour, tea was warming bellies. Darkness cloaked the destruction from view, and Junie imagined the settlement as she had first seen it, poor but orderly.

Two adults and their 13-year-old boy were missing. One of the missing adults was a relative of Don's. One person, Peter's mother, was dead. Hers was the body under the tarp a dozen meters away. He talked about how she defied all the rules and regulations and followed her son to the camp. "She never complained and always helped anyone who asked, dissed or not, if she could."

People said different things about my mother. She recalled her confusion and pain at her mother's funeral, as well as her annoyance at the cloying affection of people she had never met before, at least since she was a baby. "Your mother loved to climb solo," her father explained. "She knew everything there was to know about that climb, but no one saw her fall. She probably just slipped." The casket was closed. *Were they hiding something horrible from a ten-year-old child?*

"Juniper," her father said the next day, after all the relatives and friends disappeared, "your mother loved you more than anything. So do I."

A week later, he was off on a business trip, and Junie was staying at a friend's house. She missed her mother, but she missed her father more.

How was it that these people were sentenced to social death? What did they do to deserve it? The other dissed men and women in the camp talked openly about their misdeeds. One had used the wrong mixture of fertilizer on his fields. A once-in-a-decade rainstorm came and washed the fertilizer into a stream, causing an algae bloom and killing a thousand spawning salmon. He was convicted of "species decimation" and disidentified. The Bureau of Environmental Security carried out the sentences for violations of the Carbon Laws and other crimes against the natural world. Junie heard rumors about the bessies' harshness, but after the Warming gripped the earth like a vise, everyone agreed that protection of the remaining biosphere was more important than ever.

The flash flood was unfair to these people, Junie thought, because they had nothing to begin with. Junie's self-assurance was farcical in the face of an unprovoked attack by nature. *Would I be so useless if another big earthquake hit San Francisco?* Junie huddled with the cup of tea in both hands, nudged against Don in part to ward off the cold and to keep him close.

She let herself believe she wanted to be near him. In the public car on the way to his house that evening, she composed a brief email to Alex. Breaking off the relationship was easier than she expected. She agreed with him, she wrote, that maybe it was better to move on. She'd once helped a girlfriend compose a break-up email full of spite and drama. Junie didn't want that, and though pushing the "send" was hard, it also offered relief. Don's presence was soothing balm on her wounds.

The night deepened, and the dissed drifted off one by one to makeshift shelters. Junie yawned and called for the clock in her minds-eye, forgetting that the network was far away. Don said his goodnights and headed for Silver. Junie followed him.

"Are we going back?"

"We're staying the night. There's no reason to take chances in the dark." He opened one of the saddlebags on Silver's flank. "Help me with this tent and sleeping bag."

Bag? Singular?

Unwelcome thoughts of Alex welled up, but Junie set aside her anxiety and laid out the fabric. It self-assembled into a two-person domed shelter. Don unrolled the bag and arranged it inside. He removed a flat, square, packaged item from Silver's saddlebag and unfolded a wool blanket. "Natural wool still makes the best kind of blankets." He folded the blanket in half lengthwise. "You take the bag. I'll have the blanket." Don opened the tent's flap. "After you."

"Um, I need a minute or two."

"Oh, okay. I'll wait for you." Don ducked into the tent. "Take this flashlight."

A flicker inside the tent outlined Don against the fabric as he moved around. Junie stepped away, her flash boring a tunnel in the dark. The latrine was fresh and half-civilized with sanitizer. Junie pushed away the horror of the flash flood and imagined herself at Girl Scout camp finding her way to a biffy in the small hours.

Faint coyote yelps punctuated the dark. Junie flicked off the light, and her eyes drifted upward. The ribbon of the Milky Way stretched across the sky. The river of stars bridged the black walls of the wash. Her summer camping trips were in hills near the cities, and city lights obscured the stars, despite campaigns against light pollution. Here, in the desert of the Columbia Plateau, few artificial lights competed with the stars, and they seemed near enough to pluck like grapes from a vine. She'd been fascinated by the stars ever since a trip with her parents to the desert at age eight or nine. She read about them in books her father bought her, and she put "planetary astronomy" on her college applications. On this night, however, the cold fires in the sky reminded her of the reflections of the campfire in the eyes of the dissed, like florets in a field of desolation. *I hope that mom and her little girl are safe.*

"Junie? Are you okay?" Don's voice came out of the darkness tinged with worry.

"I'm fine." Weak light from the open flap of the tent guided her inside. "I'm tired." The bag lay on one side, unzipped and ready for her. Don lay inside the blanket, his head on a rolled-up sweater. He smiled, as if seeing Junie after a long absence. She sat on the sleeping bag and waited.

"Oh, sorry," Don said. He turned his back to give Junie privacy.

Junie removed her muddy boots and her rain slicker. "Don?"

"Yeah?"

"I may be leaving."

Don turned over. "Leaving?" Surprise edged the word.

"You can't tell anybody."

"Okay."

"There's this project, and Dad's really interested. I can tell."
Junie told Don about the trip to the ZephyrCom facility. "I don't
know for sure, if I'm going back home... I mean, Sierra Vista."

"But..." Don sat up and crossed his legs.

"He went down there to talk to some people about it."

"Um, who?"

"The woman's name is Natalie Wong. She's as rich as they
come. She and Dad have gone out a few times."

"So he wants to be with her?"

"I don't think that's it. He's just excited about a new business.
He misses all that stuff."

"I guess he doesn't like it here." Junie imagined Don was sorry
that they might be apart. *Maybe he would miss me?*

"He's here, we're here, because he needed a job. We were out
of money. You can't tell anyone about this." Junie's last words were
hasty.

"I promise I won't repeat it." Don hid his hands under a fold of
the blanket. "Do you want to leave?"

Junie brought her knees to her chest, wrapping her arms
around them to make a ball, like a hedgehog defending itself
against a threat. She chewed her lower lip. "I don't know." *You are
the only reason I would stay.* She was not ready to reveal this to the
young man who looked at her as if she was the only girl in
existence.

After a long silence, Don said, "It would be great if you
stayed, but I get it if you have to go."

The tiny lamp in the tent filled Don's face with a reddish
warmth. He had wanted her with him to help with what he found at
the wash. Junie felt as if she had nothing to offer, but Don didn't
seem to care. She reached out to him and brushed his cheek with
the the back of her fingers. He closed his eyes, and the kiss was

instinctive, as if preordained. It lasted a brief moment before another thought of Alex intruded. *No. Alex and I are done.* The echo of this desire was hollow as the sound of it mixed with Tiffany's long-ago warning at the football game about rebound love.

They said goodnight to each other again, and Don rolled over, his back to Junie. The tent defined a world within a world, two young people and a camp light between them, helping people for whom help was forbidden. *Am I safe here?* She thought of the stars above her, unchanging and steady on the human scale, and Junie never felt safer, except as a five-year-old snuggled under the arm of her father when he read her stories before bed. Don was different, a rougher, quieter boy—*No, a man*—but his kindness was endearing. The dark green blanket draped over his broad shoulders and back was far more inviting than the empty sleeping bag. She crawled in beside him and fell asleep.

◆ ◆ ◆

The next day dawned chilly and clear, with hints of frost on the bare branches of the overturned cottonwoods. The trickle of water in the creek hinted nothing of the deadly torrent 36 hours before. Don said the creek would dry up within a few days as he found some self-heating, freeze-dried food bars. After adding a few milliliters of bottled water, the chocolate and banana bar was hot enough to burn Junie's tongue. It warmed her better than the packaged coffee.

After breakfast, the pair helped Peter and the others organize more of the village, and in the morning light with a full belly, the world was less chaotic. For one thing, the mother and child Junie had worried over appeared at the fire. They were bedraggled and exhausted, but otherwise fine. Junie and the woman didn't speak, the mother respecting the regulations, but Junie offered a broad smile to the baby. *The Mother bless them both.*

For his part, Peter's eyes were hollow and red. The community collected his mother's body and buried it on a cobble and sand shelf above the highest level of the flood. Junie heard the helicopter first and a few minutes later a military vehicle drove over a sand bar into the square. "Military" wasn't quite the right word, because it was forest green and a dull gold tulip was painted on the side.

"BES." Peter swallowed.

The back of the vehicle opened and three men in uniforms of forest green, two of them with stasers, emerged. The men with stasers were helmeted. The third wore a peaked cap. A security robot, shaped like a headless ostrich, stepped out of its cubby in the vehicle's flank and took a position on a small rise.

The officer addressed Don and Junie. "Please lower your privacy filters for identification."

Unlike last night, Junie's minds-eye showed an active, strong network signal with a government tag. She saw the avatars of Don, the equines, the officer, and the helmeted BES police, but none over Peter and the other dissed. Junie complied with the order. Her minds-eye indicated a scan in progress.

"Why are you here?" The officer's manner was polite, but insistent. The name over his avatar was "Bridgestone."

"We're on a camping trip," Don said.

"Your documents file does not show a permit."

Junie opened a private minds-eye channel between herself and Don. We don't have...

"Maintain open communications during our discussion or you will be arrested and interrogated."

Junie's heart jumped. *The BES never failed to intimidate ordinary people.*

"We forgot to get a permit," Don said. "It was only one night. It's my fault."

The officer's eyes narrowed, as if weighing the truth of Don's explanation. Bridgestone glanced over the scene, letting his eyes fall on each of the dissed, still as statues. "Three bodies were found five kilometers downriver from the creek's outlet. One was a juvenile male."

A dissed woman covered her mouth with her hand, holding back emotion.

Bridgestone returned his attention to Junie and Don. The forest green of his uniform matched the old leaves on the sagebrush. "You two are the only individuals in the area. Did you see anything?"

"No, sir." Don said.

"The boy's ID chip was damaged. The two adults were dissed." Absently, the officer touched his forehead. "Records on them do not exist."

Bridgestone stepped around piles of debris, alternately glancing at and avoiding eye contact with Peter and the others. "The bodies are considered a hazardous waste spill, and we were called to investigate whether there might be other bodies." The tulip and pips on his collar glinted in the sunlight. The pistol on his hip was tight in its holster. "It seems possible that the boy could've have been camping out as well, and the site was hit by a flash flood. However, I don't see any permits for the area." He shrugged. "The others are—unimportant—apart from disposing of the corpses."

The officer clasped his hands behind his back. "Mr Rast, I urge you to return home with your equines immediately. I'll remind you that the law mandates a one-year jail sentence for aiding a disidentified. If the accused is a disidentified juvenile, he is treated as an adult. Do I make myself clear?"

Sweat glistened on Don's temple. He glanced at Junie. "Yes, sir. I'll remember."

"You, Miss Wye, have been reported missing."

"What?"

"The report was filed early this morning by your father. Mr Wye is the project manager at the dam removal, correct?"

"Project superintendent." *Get your facts straight, Officer Friendly.*

"Because you're a juvenile, I'm directed to bring you to the local sheriff's office."

"Wait! Don?" Junie was near panic. "Am I being arrested?"

"No, Miss Wye," the officer said calmly.

Unnoticed, the security robot moved behind Junie and Don.

"Mr Rast," Bridgestone said, "I suggest you organize an outing of clean-up volunteers for this area. I wouldn't want to write any citations for neighbors or make arrests related to all this garbage." His face came up to Peter's. "Or hazardous waste." The officer turned on his heel. "Miss Wye, come with me, please."

The robot's presence nudged Junie forward. She wanted to send a text to Don, but she held back because of Bridgestone's warning. Despite the absence of network contact, she felt Don's eyes on her.

"Don't worry about me, Junie. I'll catch up to you."

Junie felt at once reassured and frightened as she climbed into the back of the armored vehicle. The doors closed behind her, leaving her in a tangy, metallic darkness.

CHAPTER 17

◆ ◆ ◆

"WHERE THE HELL HAVE YOU BEEN?" Ed Wye restrained a yell when the doors of the public car closed on him and Junie. The shout might've released the hours of tension and anxiety, but it would've drawn stares in his visitor's spot outside the Grant County Sheriff's Department headquarters. He raced to the courthouse after getting a text at work saying she was waiting for him. "I was worried sick about you."

"Why? I've been out all night before." Junie's hair was wild and her clothes were spattered with mud.

Not while saboteurs and terrorists are making threats against us. "You were off the grid all night. You've never been off the grid that long."

He'd resisted telling her details about the threats, thinking that she was stressed enough with the move, school, and Alex. Now he second-guessed himself, wondering if telling her more might've made her more cautious and communicative. He didn't want to constantly look over his shoulder, thought Rossmann believed the resisters would get more desperate as the project progressed. "I have no idea where you are when you're not on the network."

Sy reported to Ed that she had arrived at his apartment to deliver his luggage, pinged the security AI with no answer, and knocked with no answer. Distracted by the monkey-wrenching, Ed didn't think much of it. He went straight to bed when he got home, but sleep was fitful, and when he got up at 06:00 and checked her room, her always-unmade bed was cold and calls to her went unanswered. She hadn't checked in at school, and Tiffany and Trudy had no idea where she was. Fantasies about finding her body in a ditch after a flash flood plagued him. He punched "911" to report her missing. Ninety minutes later, a call came in from the sheriff's office.

"I was with Don Rast." Junie was defensive, but not defiant. She let out a noise of disgust as she looked in the vanity mirror.

Cov Rast's craggy face invaded Ed's imagination, and the father was prepared to rage, convinced the old man had put the grandson up to something with his daughter. Nothing linked the Rasts to the threats or the sabotage, beyond the elder's irrational opposition, but Ed wouldn't wait for facts if he saw the slightest hint that the boy touched Junie. "Juniper, did he hurt you?"

"No," she snapped. "He's the nicest guy I've ever met. He wouldn't hurt a fly." She insisted he was a perfect gentleman.

How can she be so naive?

His thoughts turned to how she had shown up at the sheriff's department. The deputy who released Junie to Ed said almost nothing about the circumstances. He offered only that a female BES officer had brought Junie in. "You owe me an explanation, little girl."

Junie kept her gaze on the hills surrounding Utility, as if trying to see beyond them.

"At least give me an outline of what happened. Some of the roads were washed out. Was that it?"

The girl shook her head No.

"All I want to know is that you were safe."

"I was perfectly safe."

No, you're not. Ed sighed. "How were the bessies mixed up in this?"

Now came the defiance, expressed as a cynical wave over her face. "They're cold and cruel. That's all I want to say."

That's the Junie Wye I know. "I'm still not hearing an

explanation."

"Fine. I was with Don helping him with homework. We started talking about camping and we both like going outdoors. So we went camping."

That doesn't ring true. "What? In the rain?"

"He had all the stuff. We took the equines. It was just an overnight."

"But the bessies..."

"They happened to show up. Some kind of investigation. They insisted I come back with them. What was I supposed to do?"

"Jesus Christ, Junie. It's the BES. You don't screw around with them. Are you in trouble? What did you do?"

"Nothing! Why are you accusing me? The bessies are nothing but bullies who get off on scaring people."

It was hard to disagree with Junie, but if the sheriff or BES suspected her of some crime, he would've heard something by now. That was assuming they wanted to pursue a case. The news chans were full of stories about the trouble caused by the rainstorm. One person was dead. The authorities' hands were full, but something was wrong. *She's not telling me everything. Should I expect her to?*

The car rolled into one of the reserved spaces at Ed and Junie's apartment building. Seconds after opening the front door, Junie was in the shower and Ed was texting the office with the news that Junie was safe and home. Ramesh, Grace, and others pinged back emo-sigs of relief and joy. Connie was out on her own family emergency. Ed heard a knock on the front door. The avatar was Sy's.

"I'm sorry, Ed." Sy's face was drawn and her eyes bloodshot when Ed opened the door. "I was so worried that I hardly slept last night. Texting and calls weren't..."

"It's okay, Sy." Ed stepped aside and let her in.

"If it were Mason, I'd be frantic. I had to come over."

Ed was happy to see Sy. He needed another adult, another

parent, to hear his story. *Natalie wouldn't know what I was talking about.* They went to the kitchen and Ed ordered tea from the kettle AI. After he detailed everything that happened, he realized he had unloaded his emotions on Sy as well: frustration, anger, fear, worry. *I'm failing again, this time with Junie.* Offloading his fears was something he hadn't done with anyone, not even Marcy, at least since the early years of their marriage.

Sy listened without saying a word. *It's not just that I needed to unload. It's as if she drew it out of me, and I feel better.*

Junie walked into the kitchen in a robe and slippers. "Oh, sorry." Her eyes flicked from Ed to Sy and back. "I should've checked the network before walking in."

"No, Junie." Sy gathered her purse and coat. "It's alright. I'm the one intruding. You and your father have had a tough night. I should leave..."

"I was going to make coffee," Junie said.

The offer had an extra note of affection, Ed noticed, making it more than a polite invitation. Sy's face softened, in silent gratitude. Ed was glad that Junie was earning a few euros a week watching Mason for Sy, and he sensed a budding friendship. "Wait, Sy." The words came out of Ed's mouth reflexively. "I mean, you're not intruding."

Sy regarded her lithe hands. "Listen, let me take you both out to breakfast."

"You're kind to offer." Ed had not eaten anything since a snack when he got home from work in the wee hours, but anything sounded better than a bot-made breakfast after the all-night worry.

"I should be getting to school," Junie said.

"The day is half over, Junie," Sy said. "You need a good meal. There's a new place downtown opened up by a chef who worked in Palo Alto." Sy turned to Ed. "It'll remind you of home. You know, comfort food."

Junie perked up. "Dad, I'm starving."

Ed and Sy finished their tea while Junie dressed, and when they arrived at Café Izakaya, located in an ancient brick building a block from the courthouse. Junie was overjoyed at finding a New Popular Japanese eatery with traditional steamed rice and miso soup. The *wakame* reminded her of the ocean. By the end of the meal, Junie's laughter and Sy's smiles had pushed the strain of the past 24 hours out of Ed's mind. A routine ping from the office reminded him that activities at the job site were at a standstill. "I need to get to work, Sy. Thanks so much for the meal."

"Yes, thank you," Junie added.

"My pleasure. But..." The bracelet on Sy's wrist clinked on the glass of the table. "I have a small favor to ask, Ed. I know you need to get to the office, but there's something I've been wanting to show you for months. The weather's perfect and I was hoping..."

"Can it wait for a few days until things settle down?"

"It could, but the rainstorm makes it an amazing sight. I don't want to say anything more, or it'll ruin the effect."

"Dad, let's go. Sy's been nice to us."

Ramesh sent a message saying BES investigators looking into the sabotage were crawling over the site like roaches. He was handing over reams of technical information about the robots and the entire operation. *Let Ramesh deal with the bessies.* "I'm up for it."

♦ ♦ ♦

Sy ordered a four-person public car and Junie dozed as the vehicle headed into the hills above Utility, roughly following the Columbia River upstream. The road dipped close to the river bed exposed by the drawdown, and rivulets of water—dregs from the rainstorm—drained across the mudflat to the main channel. When the road climbed back into the hills, it passed farmstead after abandoned farmstead, some with "For sale" signs flapping in the breeze. Rows of overgrown fruit trees filled the spaces between the empty houses and barns.

"Cov Rast owns some of these orchards," Sy said, "but the government has been cutting back on his water allocations."

Junie opened her eyes and listened.

"He may own most of the orchard land in Grant and Douglas counties, but the amount that can produce enough fruit to make a profit to keep going is shrinking."

Ed imagined the old man feeling squeezed as if he were a cider apple.

The car climbed high into the bluffs on the west side of the river. The macadam road leveled out on a plain that stretched for kilometers in every direction. A haze obscured the foothills and peaks of the Cascade Range further west, and nothing except clumps of sagebrush, greasewood, and tufts of brown grass stretched east as far as the eye could see. The car slowed and turned onto a gravel road with a hump in the middle.

"This track isn't on the local maps, Sy,"

"Don't worry, Ed. I was here a few days ago. It's good."

Junie watched the track ahead of the car.

After a few hundred meters, the track dipped into a depression that turned into an arroyo. Ed remembered the maps of the upper reaches of the Arroyo Grande impoundment. He called up one stored in his minds-eye. It showed Utility in two places: the current town site and the old town's submerged location a kilometer upstream on the ancient river's original course. Ed zoomed in on several side canyons filled with water. A few were fed with streams originating in the mountains. Some of the canyons were likely exposed. The AI picked through a few narrow spaces and stopped, complaining about the road conditions.

"We'll walk the rest of the way," Sy said. "It's an easy hike."

The trio donned coats with hoods, but the sun warmed them. Ed pocketed a bottle of water from the car's emergency kit and followed Sy down a thin trail in the dirt. Wind lowed through the rocks.

"This is a little tricky." Sy held out her hands to balance herself. She reached out, first for Junie, then for Ed. Her skin was smooth and her touch electric. The sound spiked into a roar, and a fine mist floated in waves across the trail. "Be careful. The water can make the rocks slippery. See that outcropping? Stand there, and you'll see it."

Ed edged toward the outcrop of rock. It was only a few meters away, but as he approached, he saw the drop-off, and the roar was deafening. The viewpoint stood above a torrent that boiled and raged toward the river. The muddy water flowed down in stages, alternating powerful whitewater with pools that effervesced as if carbonated.

Sy touched his arm, pointed above their heads, and shouted in his ear. "Look at the walls. See the boundary between the light and dark? That's the old level of the impoundment."

Before the drawdown, the falls were submerged.

"The rain brought it back to life. Before the dam, there was a stream here, even during the dry months."

Ed could hardly believe his eyes. Junie was transfixed on the scene. She edged closer to the drop-off.

"No, Junie," Ed said.

"We can get a little closer." Sy drew them off to the trail. "This way."

The roar subsided, and Ed was drawn toward the river, almost as if carried by the water of the convulsing creek. The trail curved around a head-high, water-carved stone, and the roar blasted Ed. Droplets of water struck him as if blown by a hurricane. He pulled up the hood of his coat, and he heard another sound: laughter. Junie let the splashing water from the creek soak her hair and she shook it like a horse shaking its mane. Sy watched both of them, a smile creasing her face, as if she had reached a long-sought goal.

A chill settled on Ed, and he motioned to Sy. Junie shivered as well, but she was as happy as the day Ed and Marcy had let her splash naked in the Pacific Ocean on a family trip when she was four. Sy produced a towel and gave it to Junie. Ed took the towel from his daughter after she wiped her face and neck. "You planned this, didn't you?"

"I looked for an opportunity," Sy said. "I didn't think it would come so soon."

Ed thought a moment. "It's amazing."

The shadows lengthened, and the three hikers moved up the trail toward the car. Ed brought up the rear of the small train, with Sy leading. Though he didn't know her exact age, he realized she couldn't be more than a year or two older than Marcy, had she lived. It was too easy to make a simple substitution of Sy for Marcy, but he had never done it before with any woman whom he'd dated after Marcy's death. *Certainly not Natalie.* He discarded the silly notion of an unconscious search for a new mother for Junie. The child was beyond such need, but the sense of respect he saw between the young woman and maturer woman was gratifying in the way a father notices a child mastering knowledge beyond the expected. It helped Ed rationalize a desire for Sy that agitated his body and mind.

"Look over there." Junie pointed at two figures in an open area below a basalt column. "Are they in trouble?" One of the figures appeared bent over the other.

"We should check," Sy said.

The network signal was weak, but the avatar over the standing figure popped in. "Connie?" Ed said in surprise.

A moment later, he came up to his operations manager, who knelt next to her grandfather, Bob Gasca, whom he had last seen at the high school. The elder stared down the arroyo toward the river. His seat offered a view of the entire falls.

"Connie!" Ed repeated.

"I'm sorry, Ed. I know I'm supposed to be at work, but Grandfather got someone to drop him at the cutoff, and I found him here."

"Is he alright? Do you want us to call 9-1-1?"

The old man croaked, "I'm fine, Concepción. I just want to sit a minute."

Tears fell down Bob's cheeks.

"Connie, is he okay? He's crying."

She nestled closer to her grandfather. "None of us ever thought we'd see this again. We thought it was lost forever."

Sy stood back, as if she knew exactly what Connie meant. Junie watched, water dripping from her hair like a sea nymph's.

"I don't understand," Ed said.

Connie turned to Ed. Tears welled up in her eyes. She wiped them away, but she smiled. "Before the dam came, my people came here every spring to fish for salmon with nets. The falls gave us everything we needed to survive."

The old man moved his hands, as if dipping into a bucket of water. "The dam took it away, but we never forgot."

"Now it's back," Connie said. "It's alive again. We're alive again. This place, our home, it's alive again."

"But the fish are gone, Connie. They've been gone for a century."

"They'll come back," Bob said. "We survived. They did too. I know it."

All of life boils down to survival: Yourself, your family, your people, your way of life. The indigenous people of the Columbia River saw their ways nearly wiped out when the dam was built. In addition, the dam builders sacrificed the salmon, which eventually went extinct. Time passed, and the powerful decided to mend the rift with Mother Nature, and take down the dams. The way of life built by those who benefited from the dam was now threatened. Reconciling these conflicts and contradictions was enough to drive a man mad, but Ed's eyes were focused on one thing, the wonderment on Junie's face.

CHAPTER 18

♦ ♦ ♦

"I APOLOGIZE FOR THE SURPRISE, Mr Wye, but I wanted to attend to the problem personally."

Problem? Ed shifted his feet to regain his balance.

The deputy inspector general extended his hand. Gerard Rossmann had summoned Ed to his Bureau of Environmental Security office to discuss a vague "concern about operations." Rossmann's grip was strong, with an added squeeze that reminded the recipient of his status, beyond the green uniform and the golden BES tulip. "Please, won't you join me in the conference room?"

Ed felt as if he were being led to into surgery for disidentification.

Grace Cromer was already in the meeting room. Her eyes softened when they met Ed's, but they were harder when they regarded Rossmann. "With respect, Gerard, I don't have time for pleasantries. You wanted to see Ed and myself?"

Ed admired Grace for her courage. Ordinary people, Ed among them, called the enforcers of environmental law "bessies" when frustrated or annoyed by their antics. Extremists called them "green shirts," and cartoons showed men and women like Rossmann in uniforms with the death's head of the Schutzstaffel and Gestapo of Nazi Germany. Ed thought the image obscene, but a memory popped into his mind of a meeting years previous with an angry investor from a major New York West bank. The banker was footing the bill for one of Ed's failures; BES was bankrolling the dam removal. Rossmann's face had the same set as the investor.

Ed's mouth was dry, but Grace was unperturbed, at least on the outside.

"I'll come to the point, Mr Wye. I wanted to hear first-hand what's being done to speed up the restart of the dam removal."

How many disidentification orders has he signed with those hands? Ed cleared his throat. "We've reprogrammed about a third of the AI modules in the construction equipment. It's taking longer than expected."

"Why is that?" The question demanded as much as it requested information.

"The protocols are pretty strict, General. We don't want the state inspectors pulling our license or the union making trouble about rushed work and the affects on safety. We have a timeline..."

"...that is wholly inadequate. You are months behind schedule."

Blood rose into Ed's face. Rossmann was trying to intimidate him, and Ed fought the butterflies churning in his stomach. "We could use more engineering support."

"From whom?"

"What about you?" Ed borrowed some courage from Grace.

"You are a brave man." The grin on Rossmann's face transformed into a sneer. "You are in no position to make demands."

"It's only a request."

"Or make requests."

Grace intervened in the building tension. "I believe Ed and his people are doing the best they can. The damage by the saboteur was far worse than originally thought. Have you found the culprit, Gerard? I'm told that your people have combed through the systems like swine looking for truffles."

By his look of disgust, Rossmann didn't like the metaphor, but Ed liked how Grace turned the general's aggression back on him. Grace did not take kindly to bullying. When they were at Riverside

Elementary School, she knocked a boy's tooth out after he attempted to extort candy from a kindergartner. "What about this Slane fellow?"

"He's been eliminated as a suspect in the bot vandalism. The mods to the AI have a different fingerprint."

"Is he still in jail?"

"He was released weeks ago. Of course, he's skipped town, though we can find him easily enough, if necessary."

Ed's chest tightened. That meant that the person or persons making threats against him and Junie were still out there and as dangerous as ever.

Rossmann betrayed embarrassment. "Admittedly, our investigation has been as slow and fruitless as your progress toward finishing this project." Rossmann's affect changed to pride over his counterpunch to Grace's jab. "But we have time, while you do not."

Ed cocked his head. "I don't understand."

"This project is very high on the agenda of the Interior Ministry."

"You said as much a few months ago," Grace said.

"I would even say it's the ministry's top priority. Restoring the Columbia River to its wild state, or close to it, would be remembered for generations." Rossmann leaned over the table, placing his folded hands in front of him, as if in fervent prayer. "You have three months from today's date to breach the dam so that the river runs unimpeded."

"Three months!" Ed was dumbfounded. "You can't be serious. I was given two years."

Rossmann gritted his teeth. "The project has been under way for more than a year. Our deadline is more than generous."

"You're..." Ed almost said "insane." "...being unreasonable. I've brought the project back to its original schedule before the sabotage, but you're telling me to speed up."

"You'll have to bring your decisive instincts to bear, won't you, Mr Wye?"

"Do you know how many thousands of cubic meters of concrete we have to get through?"

"How do you expect us to do this?" Grace kept calm, but there was angst in her speech.

"Can't you just blow it up?" Rossmann waved his hands as if demonstrating flying debris.

The suggestion slammed into Ed like a bullet. "You're serious." The inspector general's impatience was palpable, as well as his ignorance.

Rossmann read Ed's expression. "Your methodology doesn't concern me. I want a free-running river."

"What you're asking is..." Ed wasn't sure how to finish the sentence.

"Tough, but not impossible, Mr Wye." Rossmann rose from his chair. "You've a reputation as a brilliant engineer, if a failed businessman." He pointed a thick finger at Ed. "Don't fail *me*."

Ed was glad he had disabled the emo-sig plug-in for his network avatar. If he did, Rossmann would have seen the attribute for contempt.

The conference room door clicked shut behind Rossmann before Ed spoke to Grace. "What the hell was that?"

"He's been on every elected and appointed official's back around here for years. He seems to think we live in a backwater full of backsliders. You'd think we were 19th century oil barons."

"There isn't an oil deposit or coal deposit within 300 kilometers." Ed was annoyed.

"The point is, he's ambitious, and the dam removal is his entree into an appointment at the Capital. That's what he really cares about. We're getting in his way."

"Maybe he's worried that the saboteurs will stop him somehow. Maybe he thinks they're about to do something stupid, and he's trying to beat them to the punch." Ed fingered an empty water glass from the set on the table. "I have no idea how I'm going to take down that dam in three months. I'd almost have to 'blow it up.'" Ed mocked Rossmann's explosive gesture.

A silence fell between the two friends, but it was laced with tension. Ed hadn't spoken to Grace since he'd returned from San Francisco. Natalie pinged him once or twice, but their conversations were strained. *I don't know what I want now. Ever since Sy showed me the falls... Junie is more distant, and it's more than growing up.*

"Have you thought any more about ZephyrCom?" Grace was tentative.

"Day and night, Grace. Day and night." Ed wiped his face with his hands. "Rossmann says I'm decisive. He doesn't know me very well."

"Natalie is losing her patience, Ed."

Ed rose from his chair and opened the conference door. He found a bit of his own courage, despite his nagging uncertainty. "She has a right to withdraw her offer, if she wants to. I'm not..." He glanced around the room and the hallway. *The walls have eyes and ears.* "We should talk about this somewhere else."

"Coffee then?"

Ed nodded, and they headed for the building lobby and an adjacent strip mall. The elevator door opened and Cov Rast was yelling something at the receptionist. Rast spotted Ed and Grace and lost interest in the receptionist.

"You bastard!" Cov ambled stiffly over to Ed, rage distorting his face. "Motherfucking bastard!"

Ed froze while Cov erupted. "You're taking away my water." Spittle landed on Ed's shirt.

Grace placed a hand on Cov's chest, as if protecting Ed. "Back off, Cov."

"Look at this!" Waving a mangled piece of paper in fury, Cov managed to share a file over the public network with Ed and Grace. It was an order from the BES water managers.

The green-uniformed receptionist came up. "Is there a problem?" A BES security bot loped toward the group.

"These water thieves..." Still addressing Ed, Cov glanced at the receptionist, who was as guiltless as a sparrow. "...have cut off my water from the river. I need that water. My fruit trees will die without that water." The receptionist shrank under Cov's screams into a frightened boy and offered to take Cov's name and network ID. "To hell with you," Cov retorted.

Cov about-faced and again approached Ed. "You're the worst of them, but I've got you by the balls. I'll send *you* to a hell you can't even imagine."

Ed shook his head in puzzlement. He hadn't stolen any water from anybody. There was the draw down of the impoundment, but that was necessary for the deconstruction.

"Wye, I know about you." Cov's growl was wolf-like. "I know everything about you. Everything. I'm going to tell everyone. You don't care about this town, about anything or anyone within a hundred miles. All you care about is repairing your precious reputation. You're washed up, a complete failure. Everyone knows it. Take down the dam and the ZephyrCom job is yours. You'll be back on top of the world, living off the work of other people." Cov roared in anger. "You're destroying me, and I'm going to return the favor!"

Grace's face pinched. "That's crazy, Cov."

"You're even worse." Cov pointed at Grace as if accusing her of murder. "Backroom deals. Putting your dirty money in this wind power scheme. Pushing Wye here to take down the dam even faster so you can double what you already have too much of. Meanwhile, my family gets nothing, my farm shrivels into nothing." Cov's voice choked. "You and the green shirts have wanted all along to wreck people like me and towns like this. You're killers!"

At that moment, a Utility PD cruiser disgorged two officers at the building's entrance.

Watching them out of the corner of his eye, the engineer tried to sort out Cov's words. They were a tangle of truths, falsehoods, and misinterpretations, like a game of telephone played with family secrets no one wanted to acknowledge.

"What's the trouble here?" The taller of the two officers said. They touched their caps at the sight of the mayor.

"Just a small disagreement," Grace said.

"I'm sorry to interrupt, but we need to tell you that a body's been found at the dam."

The officer approached Cov. "There's a name on its clothing, sir." The officer offered the name, and Cov's face drained of color.

Cov rode in the cruiser to the dam site. Ed and Grace followed in her private car. Ed and Grace heard the name, but they were unsure what it meant, other than upsetting Cov further. Ed told his company car AI to return to the site on its own. *A body? If it were a construction accident, I'd know about it already.* An ambulance parked inside the gate, but the attendant sat in the shade chewing a mist stick. The EMT-bot was deployed but inactive. Next to the ambulance was a black panel van with Grant County government license plates. The group walked into the main building and Ed found Ramesh. A reprogrammed bot had discovered the body and sent an automated kill command to the other bots. The operators confirmed the presence of human remains.

Rossmann's deadline and the altercation at the BES office was forgotten as a winter sun beat down on the group, which wore blaze orange vests and hard hats. The quickest way to the scene was via an access cage lifted and then lowered by a crane, a hair-raising trip in the breeze that blew chilly off the impoundment's remnant behind the coffer. Ed unclipped his safety harness and the trio—Grace and Cov included—stepped gingerly on the rough surface of the blasted and jack-hammered concrete. A phalanx of

demolition bots was lined up on the other side of a crime scene
barrier. Workers in hard-hats looked on as a sour-faced man
wearing a sheriff's department jacket made notes on a tablet. He
bent down to the concrete and brushed away debris from polished
metal that reflected the sunlight.

Sour-face came over to Ed and Grace. The words "Grant
County Coroner" were printed on his left breast. "Madame
Mayor." He nodded at Ed. "You're Wye, the superintendent."

"Yes. This is Covington Rast."

The coroner extended his hand. "I'm sorry, Mr Rast."

"Let me see."

The coroner guided them to a smoothed out space on the
concrete covered with a foam pad. Cov, with Ed supporting him,
knelt on the pad. Ed peered over the old man's shoulder. The
coroner pointed out features of the skeleton with a stylus. "The
skull and mandible are pretty obvious. This is the clavicle and
scapula, and there's a neck bone here. These voids were left over
after the concrete set and the soft tissue decayed. I found fragments
of fabric. Over here," the coroner pointed to a brownish spot, "is a
piece of wood, possibly from a tool."

"I don't see..."

"We called you after we found this on his—we're presuming
it's a male skeleton—on his safety helmet. The helmet is
aluminum, which is the right for the time period." The coroner
brushed dust off the hardhat above a narrow brim.

Ed bent lower, and in the bright sunlight, he made out four
faded, hand-painted letters in red: RAST.

The coroner brushed concrete dust off his sleeve. "We've
always heard stories about workers who fell into the concrete and
drowned. We thought of them as urban legends. We know that 77
men were killed while the dam was under construction, but all the
bodies were accounted for. I guess they missed this one."

Ed breathed out.

"I've thought of the stories as a metaphor for the dangerous work," The coroner continued. "Exaggerations told in a bar after a shift. Horrible injuries were common in those days. There probably is real blood mixed in with the concrete."

Cov Rast rested on his haunches, staring over the edge of the dam downstream. Light glittered off the water. His eyes were unfocused. "It's Julian."

"Who?" Grace said.

"You mean you can identify him?" the coroner said.

"It's Julian Rast, Julius Rast's younger brother. There were family stories..."

Cov Rast reached out his hand for help, and he grabbed Ed's arm to get to his feet. "Julian came out to work on the farm, then took a job building the dam. He disappeared one day. He was kind of the black sheep of the family at the time, and everyone thought he had drifted off somewhere. But he's here." Cov stared down at the silent bones and the hard-hat, half-sunk into the concrete. "He stayed."

Ed wasn't sure what to say. "We'll take care of it, Mr Rast. We'll stop work until we can recover your relative and we can give him a proper burial."

Cov turned to Ed. Unlike his rage in the BES office, his eyes blazed the coldness of hatred. "Don't you go anywhere near Julian. Not within ten feet." He hissed through is teeth. "First you destroy me, and now you desecrate a grave. My blood is in this land, and his blood is in this dam. You're a monster. Every last one of you!" Cov swept a hand across the assemblage, like a revival preacher. "I'll stop this crime against me and my family, if it's the last thing I do."

The intensity in Cov Rast's eyes almost turned Ed into a believer.

CHAPTER 19

♦ ♦ ♦

JUNIE STIRRED HER MISO SOUP with a spoon while Tiffany and Trudy shared a plate of *korokke* at Café Izakaya. With chopsticks, Junie's friends touched each of the fish balls to a dipping bowl of soy sauce. A notification in her minds-eye made her smile: `Physics tutoring, Don's house, 11:00 Saturday.`

"What are you grinning about?" Tiffany said.

I'll be alone with him tomorrow. "None of your business."

"You're thinking about Don Rast again."

"So you can read minds now?"

"I know you too well."

"You're nothing but a gossip."

"I'll admit it," Tiffany said. "I'm a gossip. I happen to enjoy it."

"I suppose you won't restrain yourself about me and Don."

"I don't spread gossip about my friends."

"Just about innocent strangers and your enemies."

Tiffany shrugged. "Everyone knows that gossip serves a social purpose. It's been shown by sociologists to reinforce social ties and enforce the rules."

"Wow." Junie's eyes widened. "What brand of mist have you been swallowing?"

"Can I help it if I like to read?"

"So gossip is a good thing?" Trudy said.

"Putting people down is not a good thing, necessarily, but

gossip helps people feel like they're a member of the group. It helps define who's breaking the rules, like who's too big for their britches."

"Like who?" Junie slurped her soup.

Tiffany lowered her voice and her head, as if ducking flying debris. "Syren Ioannu."

Junie tensed at the name. Even after their conversation and her caring manner after the fight with Alex, Junie was unsure how to think about Sy, or any middle-aged woman, for that matter. Sy was beautiful—*too beautiful*—and Junie respected her subtle grace and intelligence. She was also an affectionate mother to Mason, and Junie had seen parents neglect children even as they kept them fed, clothed, and sheltered in the privileged neighborhoods of Silicon Valley. On the other hand, Junie suspected that her father's attraction to Sy was a path to disaster, though she couldn't put her finger on the reason.

Junie also respected Sy's role as a leader in River Defenders. The parents of Tiffany and Trudy and eighty or ninety percent of the adults disliked her or ignored the environmental group, though Junie detected a grudging acceptance as time passed. Kids uncertain about their own feelings reflected their parents' feelings, and there were fewer cutting remarks about Sy and RD in the c-tribes these days. The dam was coming down, whether Utility liked it or not, and at least the Defenders were talking about what life could be like afterward. *Dad is helping Sy, indirectly.* The deniers and opponents just kept denying and opposing, mostly by habit.

"I'm not sure I want to hear any gossip about Sy Ioannu."

"Don't be so self-righteous, Juniper Wye." Tiffany sucked the last drop of soda. "It's science."

Why don't I want to hear the gossip? On the way back from the visit to the falls out in the desert, as Junie shared images of the falls with her c-tribes, she noticed how Sy and her father talked. He seemed attracted and distracted at the same time, as if trying to solve two problems at once in his head. She guessed it had to do with the trip to San Francisco and Natalie Wong. *She's a control freak, but Dad likes her.* Sy, on the other hand, had a polite manner with her father, but she was waiting for something. She had an agenda. It was old-fashioned, and manipulative. She was pushing him to finish the dam removal, and she was lonely. *Yes, he's the smartest unattached man in this benighted hamlet.*

"Fine, Tiffany. What sort of lies have you heard about a middle-aged woman with a four-year-old?"

Trudy leaned in, mimicking Tiffany. "They're not lies. They're true."

Tiffany folded her arms in a huff. "My sources are extremely reliable."

"Sorry! Tell me, for chrissakes."

Tiffany relaxed. "Well, you know that she's a cyprian."

Junie wanted to blurt out that she knew Sy's history, at least the important parts. On the other hand, her conversation in the solarium felt private, and Junie didn't want to break confidences. "Is that your gossip? There's cyprians in every town. The Cyprian Association started in San Francisco, you know. I've been to their headquarters."

"No kidding?" Trudy was wide-eyed.

"I haven't actually been inside their headquarters—no one under 18 allowed—but I've been by it a hundred times." Junie remembered the modern building that only hinted at the legitimatized sex trade the members represented.

"Cyprians aren't a dime a dozen here like they are in Bay Area," Tiffany said. "My mom says that since California breakup, San Francisco has descended into a Sodom and Gomorrah."

"Has your mom ever been there?"

"No, I don't think so."

Junie made a skeptical sound. "Take it from someone who grew up there. No one is walking the streets soliciting sex. The CA got rid of all that."

"No one is walking the streets here either," Tiffany said.

"How do you know?"

"Well, I don't see..."

"Don't be so sure of yourself." The truth was, Junie hadn't seen any sex trade in Utility, legitimate or illegitimate. Junie knew what to look for. CA social workers visited every high school junior class in the Bay Area and explained how to stay out of the illegitimate sex trade and report pimps and child trafficking. Sy didn't say anything about whether she was a practicing cyprian, only that her grandmother and mother built the CA and that Sy had done something terrible to get her kicked out of the family. *The details are none of my business.* Junie did a quick network search of the local region for a CA office or registered cyprians, but none turned up. That wasn't unusual. Most practicing cyprians outside the big cities preferred referrals to advertising, even if it was just a listing in a directory. It was a way of accommodating local values. "It wouldn't surprise me if Sy Ioannu preferred to keep her practice quiet."

"Actually, she's retired."

"Retired?"

"It was a forced retirement."

Even if this was gossip, Junie thought, the possibility that Sy had been forced out of the CA was something new. "I don't believe it. She doesn't seem the type."

"Believe it. You'll never guess why."

"Shock me."

"An illegal DNA tattoo."

"That's bullshit." Junie cracked up. "Only the super-rich can afford adding animal genes to their DNA, and Sy Ioannu is not rich. Have you seen her house?"

"No."

"It's nice, but it's not the house of someone who has that kind

231

of money."

"How do you know this?" Tiffany was suspicious.

"I've been watching her kid sometimes while she goes out."

Trudy's eyes grew wider. "You don't suppose she, uh, does her cyprian thing while you're babysitting, do you?"

Junie considered the idea, then shook her head. "She's got a kid. Parents don't take those kinds of risks."

"How do you know she wasn't super-rich years ago," Tiffany said. "but lost everything after getting kicked of the whores union?"

"I don't like that word."

"Whatever, the point is that she was kicked out."

Junie shrugged. "So what if she was? What did she actually do to her DNA?"

Tiffany twisted her face in uncertainty. "I don't know. Mom just said..."

Trudy shushed her friend. "You're not supposed to..."

Tiffany backtracked. "I mean, I heard that the tattoo wasn't visible and apparent. That's what the law says it has to be, so that people know."

"I've seen pictures of people who look like birds, with actual feathers." Junie remembered some of the news chan stories. "There's rumors of a Russian criminal with huge canine teeth who eats raw meat and has striped skin."

"But after that serial killer who had modified his saliva into something like snake venom," Tiffany said, "the government made a law that DNA tattoos could only change appearance, not function."

"So it was secret? What Ioannu did?" Trudy went wide-eyed again.

"Duh! The rumor is that it was her body chemistry."

Junie dismissed Tiffany's assertion. "People drink alcohol and sniff mist. That changes your body chemistry."

"Not permanently," Trudy said.

"Maybe she did something like the Abkhazians did with their Olympic athletes," Tiffany said.

"That would be truly stupid. Altering the basketball team's DNA to boost their eye-hand coordination shortened their lives by years," Junie said. "Sy Ioannu is smarter than that." *I think she is.*

"It's cheating," Trudy added. "That's why that Ioannu woman was kicked out of the CA. She's a shape shifter, pure and simple. Whatever she did, it gave her an unfair advantage over the other whores in the union. She could earn more money than whores with no modifications."

"Stop using that word." Junie snatched the last fish ball from Tiffany's plate. "You and your lunatic mom are confusing DNA tattoos with genetic therapies. Those fix genetic diseases. Those aren't always visible."

Tiffany seemed doubtful. "I hadn't thought of that. What kind of diseases?"

Trudy spoke up as if afraid she wouldn't be heard. "Inherited diseases, cancer, anything that involves mutations."

"That's chemistry, right?" Tiffany said.

"Everything that happens in a living thing is basically chemistry." As she took a picture of herself biting a rice ball with her com ring, Trudy stated the fact with more confidence that Junie had seen before. The quieter half of T 'n T wanted to be a biologist.

"So, Tif, maybe your so-called gossip is just about someone who was sick and got it fixed." *Is Sy sick? Is Mason sick?*

"Ok, but why would she be kicked out of the, um, CA for getting fancy medicine?"

Junie didn't know the answer. *What is Sy Ioannu doing to my dad?*

A serve-bot trundled by, its wheels clacking over the uneven floor of the old building. The evening crowd was showing up, and the Izzy's owner sometimes gave customers a dirty look if they occupied a table too long.

"Time for me to go, ladies," Junie declared.

The girls exchanged goodbyes and Junie waited a few minutes for the bus. The day was relatively cool and the heater lulled Junie into that state between dozing and full sleep, when dreams and desire mix. She and Don sat on a blanket set for a picnic at a beach near Half Moon Bay. An orange sun promised to meld with the horizon. A breeze hissed through the pampas grass. Each of the lovers drank one of the new Malay beverages, and their faces nearly touched. Junie bit into a strawberry Don offered, and the sweet red juice dribbled down his finger. She sucked on his finger and he licked her chin. Another, deeper hunger overtook them. *This is what the poets say love is.* Her sense of joy and freedom with Don, magnified by the sun and the breeze, wrecked her respect for the rules and regs of anything. In a flash, she dropped all her clothes, giggling like a maniac, and she ran for the surf, in the same way she did ages ago with her mother and father watching. Don ran after her, naked as anything, and he caught up with her. As the warm soothing water buoyed them, he kissed her as if she was the only woman on the planet. The surf splashed, and she churned her way out of the waves onto the beach.

Junie's minds-eye lit up with the warning about her stop. Her heart pounded from the vivid fantasy and she breathed deep. Junie gripped the handholds as if the bus bucked like a horse, though it was steady as a rock. She stepped off in front of her apartment complex. She blinked under the relentless sun. In the parking lot, she spotted the private car, and she gulped.

I am a complete and utter idiot.

The two-seater was an older model, white, and well-cared for. He'd spent months restoring the old car, even finding a copy of the original AI and installing it.

Alex. My god! Alex!

The months apart vanished as if they had never existed. The

distance, the fight, the anxiety, were like leaves blown away in a storm. *Breakup? What breakup?* All of Junie's worry disappeared. She raced up a path into the complex, uncaring whether she ran into a random old lady or a landscape bot. She'd push anyone and everything aside to see Alex.

She turned a corner and he was sitting at the bottom of the stairs leading to her front door. She yelped in delight, and he jumped up in half-surprise. She dropped her purse and her bag with tablets and half a to-go bento box from the Izzy and leaped at Alex. They wrapped their arms around one another like embracing octopuses. *He smells like home, like ocean air mixed with wool, warm and spicy.* He wore the same half-centimeter beard that was in fashion when she left San Francisco. "Alex, you're here."

"I couldn't wait to see you any longer. I skipped school and just drove."

"You should've told me..."

"I thought I'd surprise you. I even blocked off my net connection so you wouldn't see me."

"I'm so happy." *That's what I'm supposed to say.* A pinprick of doubt, irritating and insistent, begged for Junie's attention. "I've missed you so much. Were you waiting long?"

"No. I just got here. Maybe ten minutes. I was going to ping you and then you showed up."

"Alex." Their kiss was long and deep, and her body felt as if parts would shake loose. Calls, texts, vids, pings, even sig-ups were nothing compared to his touch and scent and tongue and blue-gray eyes. She wanted to melt into his body. Junie let go, but only to breathe.

Alex breathed as well. "I've waited for months to kiss you. I laid awake at night for hours just thinking about you. I thought I'd forgotten what touching you was like."

The memory of the photo with Alex—*and the slut*—wormed its way into Junie's awareness, but she let it pass like the ant that raced across the sidewalk in front of her into a clump of grass.

"You look a little different." Alex scrunched his face. "You're not wearing the same clothes when you left."

"Well, I've had to adapt."

"You look, um, great, but I think I like the old look better."

Junie let the comment hang in the air, then dismissed it with a metaphorical wave. *Alex and I are together now. Everything is perfect.* The teenagers sat on the concrete stairs, bent into each other like two willows, arms and legs entangled.

A cough.

"Dad!"

"Hi, Junie."

The couple unraveled themselves. "Dad, you remember Alex?"

"I do." The middle-aged manager and the almost-graduated high school senior shook hands.

"He wanted to surprise me."

"I hope it was a pleasant surprise."

The comment puzzled Junie. "Of course it was."

"Sure. Of course. Are you guys up for pizza?"

The delivery bot arrived twenty minutes later, giving Junie, Alex, and Ed a chance to catch up. Alex was accepted into Cal-Berkeley, and he planned to study biomechanics and cyberbotics. Junie hadn't heard from any of the schools she had applied to, but no one was worried about whether she might make it into one or more of them. She settled on an interest in the heavens, and she'd spent a lot of time lately watching videos and documentaries about dark matter planets and anti-stars. Junie and Alex did most of the talking, mostly to each other. Ed said little, preferring to listen, and worry crossed his face. *Work is so hard on him. He'll be happier once the dam project is done.* Her father sighed.

Junie had the presence of mind to switch her net privacy controls to absolute solitude, save for Alex. Ed went back to his office to catch up, and as the light outside faded, Junie and Alex decided to watch a holo-movie. Junie didn't care what he picked, but Alex was nice enough to avoid stories about enviro-cops chasing down oil smugglers, or some other action thing. They watched an ancient 2-D movie about L.A. back in the twenty-teens, but she was soon dozing in Alex's arms. He stirred and she woke and they necked, ignoring the old-timey music and scenes of crazy people swimming in pools wasting zillions of gallons of water and maniacally driving cars without AI programming. If it had been possible to drink Alex, to consume him, to take him into her soul like some kind of spirit vampire, she would have.

She wanted Alex in her bed. Alex wanted it too. It would not be the first time for her and Alex, but she could not do it. An unwelcome thought of Don invaded her mind, and she wanted to swat it away like a pesky mosquito. *Don is only a dear, special friend.* A corner of her heart accused her of lying to herself about the young farmer who was handsome, strong, and as kind as as spring sunrise, but Junie was not ready to admit her guilt.

Perhaps she needed to get to know Alex again before lovemaking. After all, seven or eight months had passed since they had last seen each other. *Alex is holding back, too, because...* She couldn't finish the thought, but she and Alex satisfied themselves with touches in each other's secret places. Alex didn't say how long he was staying, but Junie decided to be patient. *Not my strength, but...* Again, she couldn't finish the thought. It was like leaving a high-value test question unanswered, and she didn't like it. Her life, perfect only an hour ago, devolved into a jumble.

"Everything's okay now, right?" Alex said.

They spent the night on the couch in the living room. Rattling dishes woke Junie. They were covered with a blanket, but Junie didn't remember getting one.

"Pancakes, anyone?"

He hasn't made pancakes since we moved here. "Sure, Dad."

Saturday promised to be hot, and she kissed Alex on the curve of his jaw. They padded into the kitchen, and Junie waited while the squeezer bot finished filling a glass with orange juice. Alex laid into a stack of four pancakes.

Ed set a similar stack in front of Junie. "I have to go into work, as usual, Junie-girl. What sort of plans do you have today?"

The couple glanced at each other. Alex shrugged. "I dunno. Maybe a tour of the town, the mall, Café Izzy." Junie shrugged.

"Sounds like fun." Ed set the dirty dishes in the washer and dried his hands on a towel. His face had a question on it. "Junie, did you..."

"What, Dad?"

Ed flicked his gaze away from Alex and shook his head. "Nothing, sweetheart. Time for me to go. Have a good day." The shadow of concern lingered. Junie couldn't fathom it.

In Alex's car, Junie spoke instructions to the rescued AI, which needed repeats in two places. The old AIs were buggy as hell, and Alex was proud that he was able to get it to work at all. The car sped on its programmed route, starting with the locked-up high school. Junie surprised herself on how much she knew about Utility's streets, parks, monuments, and its people after only a few months in the area.

"It's an okay town, but you sound like you love it," Alex said.

"Don't think it for a second. I'm just happy you're here." Doubt again nagged Junie, not about her happiness at seeing Alex, but the denial of her feelings about Utility. Conflicting emotions about Don stalked her like a predator, and she struggled to keep them at arm's length.

The sun cast harsh shadows, and rays caromed off the red basalt bluffs. They drove through downtown and Junie pointed out where Ed had killed the bulldozer. At a public overlook at the dam project, Alex was enthralled with a descriptive net vid in his minds-eye, while Junie paced, bored. She heard about the project all the time from Ed and the local news chans. The vid was BES propaganda, as far as Junie was concerned.

"Very cool, about the river finally running free," Alex said. "Your dad's cool, too."

Junie smiled. "There's an old waterfall that's reappeared a few kilometers up the road that follows the reservoir. The local Indians used to fish there."

"Yeah, the vid had pictures."

Junie didn't remember that detail from the vid. *Maybe Dad had it added.*

"I'm getting hungry."

"There's Café Izzy, but the mall's food court is closer."

"Let's try the mall. I've never been big on the new style Japanese food."

Junie didn't remember that detail, either.

Alex's car was parked in the lot, which was separated from the overlook by a short, but winding trail. Junie led the way, and as she came around a curve, she saw a ragged figure digging in the trash can. She ignored him at first, but when he lifted his head, she recognized him. He had a tulip welt on his forehead, raised so that it lightened the tone of his weathered and tanned skin. *God, it's Peter from the village.* Junie stopped in her tracks, and Alex bumped into her.

"What's wrong?" Alex said.

Junie and Peter's eyes met, but he shuffled off after gathering up a torn canvas bag with scraps of food and recyclables. *It was Peter I saw at the horse sculpture, forever ago.* Don had taken her to the village twice more, and the second time, Junie brought a portable telescope borrowed from school. She showed the children a partial solar eclipse on a piece of scrap cotton sheet. The whole community marveled at the semicircular bite the invisible moon took out of the sun's disk. The awe of the moment broke down the barriers of distrust and disdain her old world had trained her to feel toward the dissed. She learned the name of the little girl she snatched away from the highway traffic: Corinne.

Alex raised his voice. "Junie! What's the matter? Do you hear a rattlesnake or something?"

The question snapped her out of a trance. "Don't you see..."

"See what?"

His back to Junie, Peter slung the bag over his shoulder. A tin can dropped out and clattered on the gravel.

"I don't see anything, Junie. I don't hear anything, either. Are you alright?"

"What do you mean?" *Why doesn't he see Peter?* "Oh." *Because Peter is disidentified, a non-person, invisible to human society.* "Sorry, Alex. Maybe it's the heat. I'm thirsty." *I'm sorry, Peter, my friend.*

"There's water in the car."

They met up with Tiffany at the mall food court shortly after Tif's shift ended. She worked in one of the big stores as a merchandizing intern to meet a college entrance requirement. Tiffany watched Alex eat a tofu salad, admiring and skeptical at the same time.

"So, you're going to Cal-Berkeley," she said. "Congrats."

Alex shrugged. "I've been working for it since sixth grade. My mom knows the assistant provost." He took another mouthful. "Where are you going to college?"

Tiffany named a regional school.

"Hmm."

Junie detected an eye roll. "Tiffany is the best mathematician in the senior class."

"Cool." Alex was not impressed. Sierra Vista turned out math geniuses by the truckload.

Tiffany offered a "What?" shrug and look, as if to say Alex was on the bad side of stuck-up. Junie wasn't about to argue with her. Alex had a streak of arrogance, which Junie accepted as part of the package. He hadn't said all that much during the day, and his reaction to Peter bugged her. While not unfriendly to Tiffany, he wasn't interested in learning anything more about her, Junie's best friend in Utility. *Maybe he's just tired from the long drive and busy night.* "Let's look around."

"Yeah, the view here is uninspiring," Tiffany sniffed. "See you later, Junie."

Junie and Alex strolled through the mall, eventually finding the specialty store where Tiffany and Trudy found conservative clothes for Junie after her first day at school. "What do you think?" Junie laid a blouse across her front.

Alex shrugged.

"What's wrong with you?" The question came out too quickly. "I mean, are you okay?"

"I'm fine." He fingered a t-shirt.

"No, you're not."

Alex brushed past a sale rack and exited the store.

"Wait!" Junie chased after Alex. She feared he was upset. *Maybe I should've slept with him last night.* "Are you mad at me? Did I say something?"

"No." He stopped under a potted tree.

"Dammit, Alex. What's wrong? Talk to me." Back home, Alex was voluble, but not chatty. They hadn't really talked since he arrived in Utility.

"You're different."

"Different?"

"This store. It's weird. I used to love the way you dressed. It was sexy. Now..." He swept his hand, gesturing to her outfit. "...it's, I don't know, dull."

"Dull?" Of course she'd changed the way she dressed. "Ok, so I dress different. People here were helping me fit in." She brightened. "Look, when we get back to the apartment, I'll change into something from home. I've kept all my old clothes." *I know just what skirt and top he'd like.*

"Are we going to hang out with your friends?"

"I don't know. Maybe."

"I don't get your goat-roper friends."

"What the fuck?" Junie's hands went to her hips. Tiffany and Trudy weren't as urbane as her friends in Sierra Vista, but they hung out nearly every day. Junie loved them like sisters.

Alex's face drooped. "I mean, they're okay, but they aren't very ambitious." With a sneer, he repeated the name of Tiffany's preferred college.

His attitude shocked Junie. "Maybe her parents don't have the connections you do, mister 'Mom knows the provost.'" Junie turned on her heel and headed for the food court.

"Wait, Junie!"

"You're an asshole." Junie yelled the insult over her shoulder and marched down the walkway, her stomach churning with hurt and anger. *He never said things like that back home. We hung out with each others' friends all the time.* She remembered thinking of Utility as a MON and the people as culchies as she drove the highway into town on the day she arrived. Guilt washed over her when she saw Tiffany chatting with Trudy and someone else at a table. The third person was hidden by a hot dog cart.

"Junie, I'm sorry." Alex picked up his pace to catch up. "I shouldn't have said that."

I have changed. She let Alex take her in his arms. They embraced in forgiveness. "I'm sorry I called you an asshole."

"That's okay."

"My friends are nice. You'll see."

Junie took Alex's hand. After two steps, Junie saw the third person at the table: Don Rast.

He stood the required distance from T 'n T. He was hunched slightly, as if he were embarrassed or begging. Trudy looked uncomfortable, but Tiffany was speaking to him. Don spotted Junie and Alex. "Hey!"

The clock in Junie's minds-eye barked at her: 14:04. Junie's broken promise to help Don with his homework confronted her like an accusing vice principal.

"Did you forget?" Don said.

"No, I..."

Tiffany glared at Junie.

"Yes, I guess so. I'm sorry."

"I came looking for you because..." Don stopped himself. "I didn't see you on the net, and I..."

"I maxed the privacy... Wait. Were you worried?"

Don blinked, unable to admit his fear openly.

"You were. You're so sweet." *Would Alex have felt the same way and come looking for me?*

"You've always shown up before. I thought you might be with Tiffany or Trudy." Don's eyes noticed Junie's fingers as they separated from Alex's. "Who's he?"

Don's dissed status loomed as a warning. Alex had ignored Peter, like the rules said. Junie was supposed to ignore Don, too, but he was as close a friend as Tiffany and Trudy. *Closer. Much closer.* She glanced at Alex. This time, he was staring at Don, less inclined to ignore a peer who wasn't as ragged as the usual dissed man or woman.

"Juniper, Don asked you a question."

In an instant, Junie hated Tiffany for her cruelty. Tiffany nailed the dilemma: Answer Don and break the rules that Alex and everyone followed, or tell Don that Alex was her boyfriend. *That would hurt him, I know it, and I'd rather cut my wrists than hurt him.*

Junie ran. As fast as her feet could carry her. She dodged moms with strollers, other kids she recognized from school, and cleaning bots. She ignored flashing red warnings in her minds-eye about mall rules against running and horseplay. She ignored the pings from Alex and his yells for her to stop. She couldn't run and reset the privacy controls at the same time so she could say she was sorry to Don. Everything in the world had gone wrong, and there was nothing she could do. Her tears flowed as fast as her feet carried her into the hot sun. A weather alert told her of heat danger, the first such alert of the year. A flash caught her eye, and a bus rolled toward her, the tires drumming on the heat-caused ridges of the pavement. Without a thought, Junie halted, and the buses' AI recognized her request to board.

The coach followed its familiar route. Junie was alone, and no one approached her, but the landmarks were familiar and the route updates in her minds-eye comforting. She left her privacy controls at maximum, adding Alex to her list of blocked contacts. She wanted nothing to do with anyone, at least until she could sort things out. Tiffany was a cruel bitch. Trudy was emotionally dense. Thinking of Don or Alex only hurt. *Dad tried to warn me.* A mental image of her mother came to Junie, but it was as fuzzy as an out-of-focus vid. *I have no one to talk to about anything.* Her anger and frustration rose as the day replayed in her mind. She grew antsy, leaning forward in her seat as if ready to take off in a race to forget all her troubles. The bus stopped to let off a passenger. Junie jumped out of her seat, ready to run, and she found herself, completely by accident, at the iron gate to Sy Ioannu's garden.

CHAPTER 20

♦ ♦ ♦

THE TASTE OF MARGINAL PANCAKES lingered in Ed's mouth, metallic and unpleasant, as he took in the view from his office at the dam. *Do I protect my daughter from the inevitable?* He liked Alex well enough, but it occurred to him that the emotional danger posed by Alex to his daughter felt more concrete than a vague threat by a wannabe terrorist.

"Connie and Ramesh, come in to my office, please." Ed focused on work. He couldn't save Junie from herself.

Ed's operations and engineering leads took chairs at the office table with their boss. Ed tapped a pencil on the table top to distract himself from a daydream about another fight between Junie and Alex. "I know I ask you this every day, but where are we on the job plan?"

The strain had aged Connie during the nine months since Ed's arrival. The death of her grandfather was the hardest blow. Ed attended the funeral, and Bob Gasca was buried on the reservation the day the tribes sued the government to regain control over Wanapum Falls as a "sacred cultural site." Most people thought the tribe would win in a few years. A visitors center was already in the concept stages. Ed attended the initial public meeting. *Sy was there, but Cov Rast was not.* Connie sighed. "We've removed 31 percent of the concrete in the wedge."

"What's the rate?"

"As fast as we can go. We've got so many operators and bots that they're bumping into each other to get broken concrete hauled out. The shop stewards are threatening to file grievances over safety margins. One of the bots got pushed though a safety barrier today and fell fifty meters. It'll have to be scrapped."

"You've taken the crews off the powerhouse demolitions, right?"

"Every man, woman, and bot."

"How's the coffer holding up?" Ed said.

Ramesh leaned forward. "The spring runoff is lower than expected so far. The coffer's in good shape."

Thank God for small favors. Ed took a while to warm up to Ram. He was an affable perfectionist, though Ed sensed a chip on his shoulder in the set of his eyes. He had a well of duty that never ran dry, but the water, as it were, was chilly. Ed had yet to meet his wife and child. He was also a creative man. He figured out a way to lift out the section of concrete containing Julian Rast's bones so an archaeologist could remove them without damaging them.

"How's that study I asked for coming?"

Ramesh shifted in his seat. "Ed, it's a terrible idea."

Ed lifted his hand to slap the table, but he calmed himself, instead laying the palm down flat without a sound. "You've told me a million times, Ram, but I want to see numbers on boosting the explosives and setting them in deeper holes."

"Fine," Ramesh said with less frustration that you might expect. "The study's done."

"Done?" Ed was taken aback. "Why didn't you tell me?"

"Because it's a shit idea and it could get people killed."

Ed rose from his chair and watched the activity on the dam site. A permanent haze of dust floated above the roughly V-shaped wedge that demo robots were digging out of the center of the dam. *I need this to work. I have to get this done, or I'm nothing.* "I may not have a choice, Ram. Not if Rossmann demands it."

"The risks of structural failure triple if we follow that scenario. Is Rossmann willing to chance it?"

"I don't think he cares. He just wants the dam down."

"We should go above his head, complain to the Interior Ministry."

"No. It would piss him off. They all back him, anyway."

"Ed..."

"No! Just give me the damned numbers, or I'll find someone who will."

"Ok."

Ed regretted what he said to Ramesh. The man was one of the most talented engineers he had ever known. He might recommend him to Natalie if he decided not to... "I'm sorry. I shouldn't have said that." Ed sat back in his chair. "Please tell me what you found."

Ramesh breathed out and touched keys on the holo-emitter. They displayed the equations and a pair of charts.

"Fucking Christ," Ed said. He had been here before. It was the point where he had to commit or back away. If he hadn't committed in his last venture, he might not have gone bankrupt and wound up in this job and torn Junie away from all she knew. *Or met Sy Ioannu.* In his entrepreneurial past, the choice was usually in the context of a meeting with investors, or owners of an obscure but promising technology he championed. Natalie Wong was pushing him toward one of those points, and he didn't like it. *Taking those risks haven't amounted to anything for so long, I've forgotten what success feels like.* "If we started today, how long would it take to set up?"

"You're not seriously thinking of doing this?" Ramesh has the same look on his face as someone surprised by the stench of food left too long in the break room refrigerator.

Ed rationalized his decision. "If we don't do this, Rossmann will find people willing to do it. We'll all be out of a job, and Rossmann will make sure that we never work on a government project again." *Natalie might change her mind about me.*

Connie kept her gaze down during the argument, but Ed noticed her eyes flicking upward as a point was made. She was quiet, competent, and heard every word said.

"What do you think, Connie?" Ed's question meant she had the last word.

"I keep thinking about my grandfather and the falls. The dam's time is over, whether we take it down with one shot or piece by piece." Connie put her interlaced fingers on the table's edge. "If we put the field engineers on triple shifts, we can get everything ready by..." She gave a timeline that was tight, but reasonable, to Ed's ears.

"I can't be a part of this." Ramesh pushed himself away from the table. "I don't want it on my conscience if something goes wrong."

"Ram, don't." The thought of losing his best engineer hurt Ed. "I need you here. Help us make this work."

"I don't know. I'll have to think about it." The young man departed.

Silence and the decision to move ahead with a dangerous plan hung over the table like a fiend.

Connie said, "Have you heard about Ram?"

Ed blinked. "No. What about him?"

"He sent his family away. His little boy was threatened at kindergarten. His wife got a string of disgusting com messages. He's pretty upset."

"Why didn't he say anything?"

"He's always been private about his home life."

"Do you think he's going to quit?"

Connie shrugged.

"You're staying, aren't you?" Connie, like Ram, was irreplaceable. Losing her would set the project back a year or more. *Same with Ram.*

"I don't have any place else to go. This is my home."

As Connie closed the door behind her, a sense of isolation descended on Ed. He knew he could finish this job, but he couldn't do it without Connie and Ramesh's help. He never invested impulsively, and he had worked hard in his last company to anticipate and mitigate every important risk, but all his thought and caution had bankrupted him anyway. Now he was faced with another long shot. The stakes weren't money this time. It was property, maybe lives, certainly his career and reputation. *If this goes south, how will it affect Junie?* Everything was on the table, again, and all the signs said failure was a better-than-even possibility.

The email appeared simultaneously with a message on the public network addressed to him. The email address was anonymized and the sending avatar on the message was masked, probably three or four times over. The thread of Ed's anxiety tightened when the voice call came in a few seconds later. "You're running out of time. Stop the work on the dam now. Get out of Utility." The voice was human, but no one Ed recognized.

The voice was different every time. Same with the sending email address, and the masked avatar. The threat's content, though, was always on point. *It's too consistent to be different people.* More complicated than simple fear, the effect was disorientation, like feeling lost in your own neighborhood. He never acclimated to it, despite its persistence. One time, he thought a car had followed him home. DMV tracking showed an occupied public car had taken a route identical to his at about the same time, except for the first few blocks, and its destination, but the cops could find no connection to criminal activity. In recent weeks, the threats grew more frequent. Now they came daily. Junie said nothing, and Ed assumed she would complain if someone threatened her.

If someone did threaten Junie, I might have to quit, or send her back to San Francisco.

Ed spent the rest of the afternoon working with Ram's

calculations and simulations. He found ways to improve the results from the shaped charges that boosted the safety margin by two percentage points. As he tapped the tab, the latest threat drifted back into his awareness as if pulled in by a magnet inside his mind, no matter how hard he tried to dismiss it. Instead, he tried to solve the riddle. Cov Rast was too smart for thuggish behavior. Maybe someone working for Rast? Don Rast liked Junie too much to threaten Ed in that way. Was Slane back in the area?

By the time he surfaced from his concentration on Ramesh's report, night had fallen. The office was dark, except for the glow of sleeping holo-emitters. The demolition bots, the operators, and the supervisors continued to pound away at Arroyo Grande Dam. Hunger tickled him, and he yawned. Despite the security lights in the parking lot, the clear night seemed darker than normal. A chill penetrated his coat. Winter was holding on. He scanned the lot and adjacent equipment yard, and he saw a patrolling security bot, its green ready light dim but sharp. A shed cast a half-shadow on his vehicle as he sent the unlock command over the network.

"When are you going to listen to me?"

The voice startled Ed and he twisted toward it.

"Don't move any closer." The voice was distorted. Same with the figure's face, as if it was covered with thousands of tiny mirrors. Light from a security lamp glinted off the slide of the figure's automatic pistol. "Raise your hands so I can see them."

Ed complied. His heart pounded, but the man's attitude—the person seemed to be male, by his shoulders and carriage—lacked resolution, as if he didn't believe in what he was doing. The gun, however, had the fanatic's certainty. Ed's eyes fixed on the end of the barrel. He had the terrifying feeling that the gun was pointed at more than him. It was pointed at Junie, Sy, Ramesh, Connie, Grace, Natalie, Rossmann, even Cov Rast. "Christ, don't shoot. Please."

Gloved fingers opened and closed on the gun, and the man

adjusted his stance, as if preparing to run. "I don't want to shoot you."

The reassurance wasn't convincing. "My wallet is in my coat..."

"I don't want your money or codes."

"My apartment network password..." *I hope Junie's out.*

"Not that either."

"What..." *Try to scare him?* "There's a security bot near. It's armed with a staser." Ed glanced at the gate, open to let him leave.

"The bot can't see me. I've made sure of that. It'll walk right past, as if I were you."

"How..."

"None of your business."

Ed relaxed, but his heart still pounded. *Maybe the gun is just to scare me.* "I don't know what you want, friend, but you can leave now, and no one will know you were here."

"You will."

"I'll never tell."

"Maybe. Maybe not."

"What would I say? A man with a gun, in the shadows, a mask on his face, running away in the dark."

The man hesitated, as if debating a decision. "I have nothing against you, Mr Wye. But I want you to quit. Go back to California. You don't belong here. Take the job with ZephyrCom and leave."

"How do you know about that?"

The man chuckled. "It's a small town, Ed. Haven't you figured that out? Word gets around."

For two seconds, a car's headlights drove away the shadows, and Ed made out a figure of average height dressed in black, his head covered in a navy or black balaclava. Even his eyes were covered. The word "ninja" came to mind, and Ed almost laughed at the absurdity of it, if it weren't for the gun.

"I was hired to finish a job, friend. I can't just quit," Ed said. *Not and have a hope in hell of working again.*

"You can and you will." The man's statement, muffled by the headgear, smelled of desperation.

"Take it easy."

"Listen, I'm not your enemy. I don't want you to be blamed."

Ed cocked his head, hesitating to speak. "Blamed? I don't understand. What did I do?"

"Nothing. But you'll be blamed for what's going to happen."

Ed's palms sweat at this new danger. His mind raced. "What's wrong? What have I done to you?"

"Nothing, I'm telling you. But I don't want other people to be hurt by what I'm doing. That's why you have to leave. That's why I want this project shut down. If it keeps going, I'll have to take my revenge. I won't have a choice. If you quit, the bessies will think twice about what they're doing."

"You're sure about that? The BES isn't known for backing down."

"They need you."

Ed tried to process what the man meant by "revenge." Was he after BES for taking down the dam? Did he have something against Connie, or Grace, or Ramesh, or even Sy? Did Rossmann do something to him?

A flash of recognition broke into Ed's mind. "Are you..? Did you..?" He was about to say "sabotage," but thought better of it. "Did you modify the AI programming on the construction bots?"

Silence.

"And what about the bulldozer downtown, and the welding protocols on the coffer?"

The saboteur drew a breath, as if readying himself to speak, then exhaled without a word.

"It didn't work. You probably know that. It slowed us down a bit, but we're back at full capacity. We might even get the job done faster."

Ed regretted his boast, afraid it might give the shooter an excuse to pull the trigger. "I mean that we're back on schedule." *Not a lie. I haven't actually decided on the one-shot option.* "The project's at full capacity again."

The man glanced away, as if uncertain what to do next. The gun barrel lowered a millimeter. *Don't do anything stupid, Ed Wye.* "Look, I don't think you really want to hurt anybody. I only want to go home and eat dinner with my daughter and—"

"Shut up." The man regained his composure. "Listen to me." He cocked the pistol, and Ed swallowed. "This is my last warning. Leave Utility. Leave Grant County. Don't ever come back." He waved the pistol toward the car. "Get in."

"Wait!" *Where is he going to kill me?*

"Don't argue."

Ed pulled the door open.

"Slowly. Keep your hands visible."

The project superintendent sat in the left front passenger seat. "Close the door and turn your face to the back. Stay still."

Ed followed the man's direction. The saboteur would shoot him in the back of the head, and he took a short breath, making a tiny whimper, as he realized his last moments had come. *Junie!*

Seconds passed. A reflection in a building window caught his eye. A pair of headlights on and off, left then right, independently, as if something had passed in front of them. A car parked about a hundred meters south of the gate flicked its lights to bright and drove off.

Ed breathed out, and terror flooded into him like a tsunami. He cried out to release the tension and covered his face with his hands, tears flowing freely. "Oh, god. He could've killed me. I could've died." He wanted to embrace Junie as if it was the last time he would ever see her. The wave passed, and he shuddered as the adrenaline wore off.

Ed remained in the car for ten minutes, not moving, fearful the man might return. Nothing happened, and the engineer risked opening the car door. A few insects and a distant *crack-crack-crack* from the demolition disturbed the quiet. He shone a flashlight from the glove compartment toward the place where the saboteur had stood. As Ed studied the cut fabric of the cyclone fence, the security bot ambled past, as if nothing was wrong.

Ed leaned against the fence pole. "That guy could completely wreck us if he wanted to." He found a bottle of water in the trunk of the car. He shivered, drenched in sweat. Thirst overcame him, and he drank half the bottle in one gulp. He wiped his forehead, and perspiration glistened on his palm.

The night insects, the steady, but distant beat of the demo bots, and the cold beauty of the sky above dampened Ed's anxiety. He sent a note to Connie about the fence, and a note to himself to contact the Utility police in the morning.

He climbed back into the car, and a text arrived. I know it's late, but dinner tonight? Mason is with a friend.

Ed jumped on the invitation. He needed to escape.

◆ ◆ ◆

"You look like hell," Sy said, letting Ed by. "Are you sick?"

Ed didn't think to clean himself up after his encounter in the parking lot. He didn't even look in the car's mirrors. Driving straight to Sy's house was like running home to his parents' house after a dog frightened him, but he couldn't help himself. "I'm fine."

"No, you're not. You're pale." Sy touched his forehead. "No fever, but you're dehydrated."

Ed smelled cooking tomatoes. "I haven't eaten dinner. And I need a drink."

"Some ice water first. Then a glass of wine."

In the kitchen, the thick smell of pasta sauce almost made Ed faint with pleasure. Pasta boiled on the stove and the fragrance of fresh bread permeated the symphony of scents. A candle stuck in an old bottle decorated the table.

He told her the story of the assault. It took half a bottle of Chianti. Sy said little, except to encourage him to continue. Ed felt the residue of fear dissipate. The incident receded, as if it happened years previous, instead of an hour. *I've never talked to a woman like this, not even Marcy. It's magic.*

Spaghetti and meatballs. Sy could not have picked a better meal to comfort Ed. The meatballs were small, in the Swedish style, and they weren't meat, which Ed preferred. In spite of this, he wolfed it down. He leaned back in his chair, sated. His host was calm, but attentive. Ed grinned. "And how was your day?"

They laughed together.

"Let's move to the living room." Sy brought the bottle and the glasses, and she wove her way through the compact house, dance-like and effortless. They relaxed on the sofa, drinks in hand. She reclined on the opposite end from Ed, resting her head on her palm, one foot tucked under her seat. *She's enchanting.* Ed coughed, unwilling to give away his feelings.

"Something wrong?"

Ed shook his head. "No, not at all. A long, difficult day."

"You're tired. Should I call up your car?"

"No! I mean, I'd rather be here than home."

Sy grinned and lowered her eyes. "How's Junie? Doing well in school?"

"Mmm." Ed nodded. "She could do better, but..." He shrugged.

"She's a smart girl."

"That's what everybody says."

"As smart as her dad."

"Well..." Ed sipped the wine. His mouth was dry.

"She's going a great job with Mason. He looks forward to seeing her."

"She loves Mason."

"I remember when I was that young. I was a little boy crazy. My mother texted me every night at 20-hundred, if I wasn't home, checking on me, begging me to come home. I had three or four boyfriends in the space of about six months, sometimes two at once."

"What did your father think?"

"He was too busy managing the family business to notice."

"I'm sorry."

"I'm over it, just like I got over the breakups and the drama when I was seventeen."

"You should talk to Junie about her love life."

Sy grinned. "Actually, I have, a couple of times. This afternoon, too. She somehow wound up here. She was pretty upset about Alex and Don. She has a strong moral sense. She felt guilty."

Ed startled as if a secret had come out. He checked the time in his minds-eye and wondered if he should follow the lead of Sy's mother and check on Junie. He didn't. "I'm sorry you had to hear all that."

"Nonsense. I hope Mason grows up to be half the person Junie is."

Ed finished the wine in his glass.

Sy poured more. She sipped from her glass. Her lips were lush and full. "Listen, Ed, I know you'd probably rather not talk about work, after what happened tonight."

Ed sighed.

"I can tell there's so much on your mind. Junie. Rossmann. Other things."

Does everyone know about Natalie Wong and ZephyrCom? "I admit that I wish I had an adult to talk to other than people who work for me or people whom I report to." *I'm sweating again.*

256

"It's difficult when you don't have someone to share your troubles with, someone who wants to know about them for no other reason than she cares about you."

"She?"

"Or he." She shrugged.

Why not share? "The thing is, I have an important decision to make." *Two important decisions.*

"About work?"

"Yes."

"Tell me. Maybe I can help."

Ed related the rising pressure on him to finish the dam removal—leaving out the role Sy and River Defenders played—and the sabotage of the bots that set the project back by six weeks. He added his hypothesis about his assailant as the saboteur and his strange remark about revenge. He worried he could not complete the job without taking a huge risk with the safety of people and property downstream. For the moment, Ed kept the open secret of ZephyrCom to himself.

Sy edged closer to him, as if to hear better and read his body language with more precision. She set her glass of wine on the coffee table, as if she needed both hands for what she prepared to do next. Her posture was open; she set her hands on her lap in a yogi-like pose. She appeared genuinely interested in his story, looking him in the eyes and cocking her head to pick up the timbre of his voice.

"I'm sorry there's so much pressure on you right now," Sy said after Ed had finished his story. "I come from a world where pressure is anathema. Sometimes you have to work hard, maintain a fast pace, and show results, but after all is said and done, you need to relax and let life—by that I mean breathing, seeing, hearing, touching—happen without demands."

"Sounds utopian."

"Utopias are an ideal, but ideals are unobtainable in their

purest form. It's like trying to reach for infinity. We do what we can."

"What do you think I should do?" *About both things? The dam and ZephyrCom.* The words in his mind wanted to jump from his tongue. Saying things out loud made them more urgent and concrete, and speaking might force him into the wrong choice. He wasn't ready.

"I can't tell you what to do, Ed. I will say that you are doing important work in Utility, despite what your enemies say. Restoring the earth is a noble, heroic task. Heroes take calculated risks to reach their goals."

"Lately, all of my risks have ended in failure." Ed lifted his eyes to Sy and something had changed about her. He saw every jet-colored hair on her scalp, every shade in her blue-violet irises, each skin cell on her face, as if his vision was magnified, like an old comic book superhero. His skin danced with sensations, as if a someone, perhaps Sy, drew a soft brush across the back of each hand. It wasn't the alcohol, he decided, and neither of them had chewed a mist stick.

"Ed, I'm glad you're in Utility, doing this job. I hope you'll see it through."

The engineer's hand lay flat on the sofa cushion between him and Sy. It was an unintended invitation, but Sy responded, placing her hand over his. A current, mild but powerful, permeated every cell of his body. His heart pounded again, but not in fear. It was anticipation as delicious as the first sight of the spaghetti and meatballs. The thought made him chuckle, and the sound encouraged Sy to edge closer. She leaned in to him, opened her mouth slightly, but stopped a finger's width from his mouth. *She's a sadist. She's torturing me with every breath.* The thoughts lay on the edge of his consciousness. They were the thoughts of an observer, not a guardian. Whatever part of his personality protected him from excess fled.

The next hour was a blur. Time was stretched and compressed in the same 60 minutes, an impossibility for the rational mind, but the sub-networks governing the rational part of his mind shut themselves off, allowing him to surrender every synapse to Sy Ioannu and accept time as an illusion. A part of him noticed that she did not surrender to him, though she did nothing to control his action and reaction. It was a dance, sensual and sexual, which she practiced and understood like an artist, better yet, a connoisseur, and she gladly shared her passion.

A handful of his rational cells rebelled, like hecklers, and they shouted their skeptical opinions into his consciousness. Something was not exactly right, like a sensor off by a thousandth of a degree. Ed had made love with his share of women, but the experience with Sy was so far above the range of his adult life that he couldn't classify it. You can't shut off a man's engineer-ness with a touch. The evening was immeasurable, an impossibility, like the absence of time.

The worry was tiny, like a mite on an elephant. Sy breathed softly beside him, though Ed suspected she dozed rather than slept. Disturbing her was unthinkable. He found his coat and called his car to take him home. Closing Sy's front door behind him, he waited in the dark on her porch for its headlights.

One thing I know for sure, I'm going to finish taking down that dam.

CHAPTER 21

♦ ♦ ♦

"WHERE WERE YOU LAST NIGHT?"

Ed rolled over on his bed. Junie stood in the doorway of his room in jeans and a t-shirt. A towel was wrapped around her head. Sunbeams streamed on Ed's fully-clothed body, and he squinted. "I was out."

"You were offline. You left work late and drove into town. Then you disappeared."

The backtrace features of the com system were a blessing and a curse. *I suppose I deserve the scrutiny.* "I was at Sy's house." He didn't feel like discussing the encounter in the parking lot.

"She's got a network signal blocker not even the BES spooks can penetrate."

"You're exaggerating." Ed rolled off the bed into a sitting position. He felt tired, but fresh, and inexplicably defensive. "And I don't see that it's your business, little girl."

Junie's eyes narrowed. "Wait. Did you fuck her?"

Ed tended to ignore profanity, but whenever it came out of his daughter's mouth, he winced. "I don't think it's necessary to say it like that."

"So you did fuck her. Jesus."

Ed searched his memory over the past 12 hours. The assault came back, but it was fuzzy. He remembered dinner. *Did I pass out? I don't feel like I have a hangover.* "I had a few drinks."

"She blew your mind, didn't she?"

Ed ran his fingers through his hair and the memory flooded

back. He froze as the sensations returned, only a little less intense than the moment they happened. He closed his mouth after he realized he was gaping.

"Big mistake, daddy-o. She's got you by the balls."

"Junie, language, for chrissakes. Yeah, okay, we slept together, but we're two adults."

"You'd better hear this." Junie explained what T 'n T had told her about Syren Ioannu, about her DNA tattoos and her shape shifting.

"You're letting your imaginations run away with you." Ed stood up, expecting wooziness from a hangover, but instead, certain muscles ached, as if they hadn't been worked in years. "Oh, man."

"You know she's a fallen cyprian."

"So?" Junie's father stepped past his daughter into the bathroom. "I thought you young people were past all prejudice."

"I don't mean that. She was kicked out of the CA."

Ed shut the door to the bathroom and stripped. He set the shower timer to five minutes, despite the cost of the extra water.. *I feel like indulging myself.* "How do you know she didn't resign voluntarily?"

"Dad, Tiffany's mom works for the police department. Dad!"

Arguing over the noise of the shower didn't appeal to Ed. He couldn't take the gossip of a few teenage girls seriously, even if one of them was his only child. Junie was not one to spread rumors, however, which meant she believed what Tiffany had told her.

After shaving, brushing his teeth, and running a systems check of his com implants, Ed refilled the coffee maker with Arabica beans. Junie sat at the table with a tab. "There you are. I thought you were never coming out."

"I felt like slowing down a bit today."

"She's done something to you."

"You could say that. I like her." *She's more than a friend to me, though.*

"She's hiding something from you, and she's a sneak."

"Juniper, I'd be careful who you call a 'sneak.' She's been good to you."

"Listen, Dad, if she's modified her DNA to make her sex pheromones more powerful, you can't be certain that she's not manipulating you in some way."

"And this is new in human history?"

"The DNA tattoo is. Yeah, women have used sex to get their way since forever, but at least the playing field was level."

"You're sure about that." Junie was a smart girl, but her lack of experience showed. "There's natural variations in a person's abilities. I suppose that could be true of sexual and empathetic powers as well."

Doubts crossed Junie's face. He set down a cup of coffee for himself and her. "I appreciate you looking out for me."

"Have you told her about the job offer from Natalie?"

"Of course not. That's no one's business but mine."*She knows about it, though. Of that, I'm certain.* "You haven't talked about it with your friends, have you?"

"I didn't need to. Tiffany told me."

The saboteur knew about it, too. "Christ."

"Sy runs the local chapter of River Defenders, right? She wants that dam down as badly as the bessies. She'd want you to stick around to finish the project. They lost two superintendents before you came along. So, she has an interest in making you feel good about staying."

This girl is scary. "Sy and I both have an interest in seeing the dam down. It's my job and the project is something she believes in. She doesn't have to manipulate me to get that done."

"Ugh! You don't get it. She's doing everything she can to get you to turn down the job at... Whatever the place is called."

"ZephyrCom." Ed sighed. "Let's say you're right, that she's

manipulating me. Getting me to stick around seems a pretty weak reason. I want to finish the job anyway, and I don't want to disrupt your life again."

"Haven't you figured out yet that I don't want to be here? That I want to go home to my friends?" Junie folded her arms, as if she didn't believe her own argument.

"There. You see? You're letting your imagination run wild."

Junie pushed around the half-empty mug. "I don't trust her, Dad. She's nice enough, but she wants something."

"Everybody wants something." *I wanted to be respected again.* A flicker of bright green from the kitchen window caught his attention. The oak tree on the common lawn showed its first young leaves of the spring. The shoots were the opposite of the dark green of the old leaves before they turned brown with the onset of winter. The memory of the old leaves triggered thoughts of the BES uniform, and an image of Gerard Rossmann came to mind. Ed shuddered, remembering his last encounter with the deputy inspector general. Rossmann and Sy knew each other a long time ago. *Does he want something from her? Does she want something from him? Am I part of the transaction?* Ed shook his head, sweeping away cobwebs from the night before.

Ed felt something was missing. He turned his attention back to Junie. "Why are you so angry, sweetheart? This isn't about Sy Ioannu, or my private life, is it?" He refreshed his coffee, and noticed the empty chair next to his daughter. "Say, where's Alex?"

Junie's face fell. "He's gone home. We're done."

"Oh, shit." Ed glanced out the window. Alex's car was not in its parking spot. He set down his coffee mug and took the chair next to Junie at the table. *This is why she's so angry. The break is final.*

Junie struggled to control her emotions. "I feel like everything is falling apart. I loved my life back home, but Utility isn't so bad, once you get to know people. I hate Alex now. He betrayed me, and I'm afraid that Sy is playing games with you. She might betray you too. I don't want to hate her. She's an amazing woman."

Ed agreed with Junie about Sy. Keeping her at arm's length suited him, but she was more and more in his thoughts. After so many years watching people in the business world manipulate and scheme and occasionally stab partners in the back, Ed believed he could spy dissembling, whatever its form. Yes, it was possible Sy Ioannu was faking an interest in him—cyprians were trained illusionists—but Ed didn't see any warning signs of deception. He did, however, believe she was holding back on the whole story.

"Junie-girl, you'll have to trust that I can handle Sy. Besides, I'm not so sure it matters whether she's a shape shifter or not. She was wrong to hide her DNA modifications, but she can't reverse them without risking cancer or something worse. She's paid for her mistake, in a sense, if her cyprian license and membership in the CA was revoked. She's also lost her family, and now she has a child to care for. That's a powerful incentive to do the right thing."

Junie kept her eyes on the mashed, tear-soaked paper tissue in her hands.

"I'm sorry about Alex. Maybe it was never meant to work, even if we had stayed in Sierra Vista."

Junie's eyes shifted, considering the possibility.

"And what about Don Rast?"

"I don't want to think about him. He might betray me—us—too. His grandfather hates you."

"I don't know Don very well, but if he's anything like his grandfather, he's his own man. He'll be a good friend."

♦ ♦ ♦

The traditional day of rest didn't apply to the Arroyo Grande Dam removal project. The entire crew, office staff included, was told to spend at least part of Saturdays and Sundays in the office until further notice. The deconstruction crew was on three shifts, 24 hours a day, seven days a week, and now that the reprogramming issues were resolved, they were happy—the operators, the mechanics, the supervisors, the safety crew, the lower level officer workers—double overtime on Sunday was the icing on the cake. The salaried people—the engineers, the IT professionals, the managers, including Ed—suffered. The original BES contract had incentive bonuses, but the new deadline made the bonuses moot. Their pay and benefits didn't change. Nonetheless, costs skyrocketed as the teams pulled out the stops to find spare cranes, bots, dozers, and people. Red ink spread over the budget like blood from an open wound. Ed feared a BES auditor would shut down the project, but all the bills were paid on time and in full. Rossmann was finding a way to keep the bureaucracy happy, which was yet another sign he intended to get his way.

Still, it was Sunday, and the mellowing effects of the previous night convinced Ed to go into the office a couple of hours later than he might have otherwise. The decibel level in the open area of the office was subdued, compared to a normal workday. Connie approached him, and worry creased her brow. The circles under her eyes were hellish. *She'll probably hate me when this is all over.* "What is it, Connie?"

The operations manager whispered the news, and Ed glanced at his office. The door was closed. He sighed. "Thanks. Come and get me if I don't come out in an hour or so."

Connie lifted a corner of her mouth. She knew he was being facetious. *Maybe I'm not.*

Ed stood at his office door, collected himself, and opened it.

"It's about time, Edward Wye." Natalie Wong said. She stood by the window that looked out over the buzz of activity on the dam. "Punctuality and predictability were always two of your virtues. What happened?"

"Natalie!" Ed embraced the investor, his possible new boss,

and unrequited lover. "If you told me you were coming, I would've been here at my usual time."

"So why were you late?"

"Natalie, that's not your business." Ed hung his jacket on the coat hook next to Natalie's light wrap. "It's Sunday, for one thing."

"Don't tell me you've started going to church."

"Lots of opportunities here. A church on every corner, practically. There's talk that the musalla downtown is in line for mosque status." Natalie's business jacket over a blouse and fitted jeans was her way of acknowledging the titular day of rest.

"You're not serious..."

Ed had no religious impulses. He was gently mocking Natalie. "Had you there, didn't I?"

Natalie huffed and sat on the narrow sofa against a wall. "Score one for you. For a second, I thought this town had got its hooks into you."

Highlights of the morning discussion with Junie replayed in Ed's mind. Natalie's assertion had a ring of truth to it. "I'm just here doing a job. I've made a few friends, and I like the people I work with."

Natalie frowned, unhappy with Ed's reply. "May I have a cup of coffee, Eddie?"

"Sure." Ed fussed with his office pot. "Why are you here, Natalie? I don't think you'd fly all the way here for a social call."

"Why not? We're friends, right? Don't you like visits from your friends?"

"Natalie, we've known each other for a couple of decades. You've never done this before, at least with me."

She pulled a powdered mist packet from her jacket pocket and added it to her coffee. "You don't belong here, Eddie. I'm here to remind you of that."

She's nervous, maybe even scared. "What's wrong?"

"Nothing's wrong, but it's been months since we talked about

266

ZephyrCom and I got tired of texts and emails and video chats. Visiting people in person is a lost art. I decided to revive it by coming to see you."

"It is nice to see you. I mean that."

Natalie flashed a smile. "You're a gentleman, Eddie, but we need to talk business."

Ed took the empty spot next to Natalie on the sofa. She put her hand on Ed's. Compared to Sy's, Natalie's touch was like a centipede's. "Eddie, a lot has happened behind the scenes since you were in San Francisco."

"Oh-oh. You mean ZephyrCom is on hold?" *Deals die all the time. This might be a blessing in disguise.*

"Just the opposite. The New York West guys you met were impressed with you, and with the project. They're recruited more investors, including the Bengaluru Group."

The news stunned Ed. "Holy Jesus." The engineer's excitement rose. "It's the biggest investment bank in South Asia, by orders of magnitude."

"It's the biggest deal I've ever made, Eddie, by orders of magnitude." Natalie sipped the coffee and scrunched her face. "That's awful." She fumbled in a pocket, unwrapped a mist stick, and sucked on it. "There's more. I'd like to show you something. I need your holo-emitter."

Ed saw the request in his minds-eye, and he signed off on the security personally. A file transferred to his account.

"Play the file, will you?"

The emitter glowed with cool light and the 3-D image of a Chinese woman in her late 40s. Her face was serene and confident, like that of a powerful wife of a nobleman in some prior dynasty. "She looks familiar, Natalie."

"She should. You met her in Beijing almost 20 years ago."

Ed flashed on a long weekend in the Chinese capitol full of handshakes and toasts. One member of the Guangzhou delegation was a pretty, if formal, mechanical engineer, a rarity in China even after 200 years of communism. During a reception, Ed and her chatted in a corner about generator efficiency. In the image on Ed's emitter, she was flanked by two younger men in early middle age. "She's done well, looks like."

"She's the PRC's Deputy Minister for Environmental Protection. China-watchers say she could be President someday." Natalie nodded at the image. "Listen."

The woman spoke in calm, thoughtful tones. Natalie's voice was respectful, even deferential. The timestamp on the recording was three days ago.

"My Mandarin's pretty rusty, Natalie. I heard 'contract,' and not much more."

"That's the key word. I met her last month in Beijing." Natalie swallowed. "You know me, Eddie. I'm not intimidated by anything or anybody, but I was terrified."

Ed put his free hand over hers. *She came to me for support.*

"Terrified in a good way, if that's possible. She gave me 15 minutes. She remembered you." She turned back to the emitter.

The conversation continued for a few minutes, and one of the functionaries laid a tab in front of the minister, who asked a question. Ed heard her say "Mister Wye."

"Christ."

"People like your worker bees think high finance and innovation are all about money and who's got it. You and I know that's only part of it, and not the biggest part. What matters most is who's your friend, who believes in you, and who you know. It's never been more true than now. Financiers like the Chinese care first about who's running the show. I told you that your reputation was still strong outside North America. They believe in you, and in me."

Ed swallowed.

"You've got to quit this hellhole and come to San Francisco. I need you, Eddie. It's a new start for you, and it's my dream." She squeezed Ed's hand. "I don't have much time."

"The Chinese set a deadline."

"I only have a few days. I need you, Eddie. I need you on the team. And I'm prepared to pay for it."

"What do you mean?"

"Check your personal com account."

The com's message loader showed one labeled "Deposit." The encrypted message made Ed gulp. "Jesus, Natalie. I don't know what to say."

"'Thank you' is good enough, but I'm curious. How will you spend your ¥50 million consulting fee?"

If Ed were the impulsive sort, he would've handed in his resignation there and then. He didn't however, because his beloved Junie was falling in love with Don Rast. *And I might be falling in love with Sy Ioannu.* "I'm… This is..."

Natalie tapped the table with a long fingernail. She clenched her jaw, as if bottling up an unspeakable emotion. Ed's breathing grew short.

"You don't understand, Eddie," Natalie snapped. "I'm not going to take 'No' for an answer. I've staked my whole reputation on ZephyrCom. I'm going to do whatever it takes to get you."

Ed gathered his courage. "I appreciate your position, Natalie, but I've also got investments to manage: Junie, and now this project. I can't abandon either."

"I'm not making myself clear, am I?" Natalie's eyes blazed. "ZephyrCom is far more important to me and to the planet than the deconstruction of a useless dam in a backwater town. You're wasting your time and talent here. I'll find a way to poach you from Rossman if it's the last thing I do."

"Is that a threat?"

"Take it however you want. You know me. I get what I want, by any means necessary."

That's what always scared Ed about Natalie. When things went her way, she was warm, friendly, and generous. When things stood in her way, she called on a cold malevolence in her heart that rivaled the blackest pit. Ed didn't know where it came from. Perhaps it had grown as she grew more powerful. Failure to her was a painful insult to her self-worth. It reminded her of her isolation.

Ed knew he could not fill that hole, but his opinion might not matter to Natalie Wong.

CHAPTER 22

♦ ♦ ♦

COV RAST DIDN'T RELISH MEETING with Slane, and he was exhausted by the ten-hour drive into the wilds of western Alberta, despite a two-hour siesta. Frustrated by the steady progress of his enemies at the dam, the elder sensed he was nearing his last options. His natural pessimism receded when Slane texted him, but the revengeful towboat captain insisted he held something that couldn't and shouldn't be shared over the com net.

In the cheapest room at a rundown motel, Slane reached into the pocket of his jacket, removed a frayed, coffee-stained envelope, and handed it to Cov.

"What the fuck is this?"

"Research on Wye."

The envelope contained electronic documents. Cov swiped idly through them. "Looks like patent filings and legal stuff." A sheaf of pages clipped together. "What's with the paper? Not even governments use paper anymore."

"Remember that contact I told you about? The one in the engineering firm? He wouldn't give me the electronic versions. I promised him I'd destroy those once you saw them." Slane pointed to the sheaf of papers.

Rast credited Slane for his amateur sleuthing, though he supposed he had little else to do while keeping his distance from the bessies. "Where'd he get them?"

"He didn't say and I didn't ask."

Cov didn't care how Slane got them, only that they were

authentic. "They're the real thing. You're sure of it."

"As much as I can be."

"And that's supposed to help me believe whatever's in here?" Cov blew out a breath and shuffled through the papers. The legalese reminded him of the report he got from the coroner confirming the bones encased in the dam belonged to his cousin Julian. The DNA analysis was conclusive. *What else will surprise me?* Whispers reached him that the BES had narrowed down a list of suspects in the sabotage, but no one had come calling to his door. Though he would never condone the kind of violence and property destruction practiced by the saboteurs, a part of him was grateful. Who was his secret ally?

Slane brushed off Cov's doubts about the document's legitimacy. "The best stuff is on the last page. It's a supplemental report by the patent office, but it was never filed with the court. It's not part of the official record."

Cov scanned the final page. The text was fuzzy, as if someone had taken an out-of-focus picture of it and transferred it to paper. As he read it, his jaw dropped. "Jesus fucking Christ. If this is true..."

Cov's pessimism receded further, like a tide ebbing.

Slane fingered a mist stick. "The patent office investigator says so."

"Why was it left out of the record?"

"That's the biggest mystery. Did he forget? Was the report lost somehow?" Slane's voice dropped in volume. "Or maybe the cop was forced to hide it. Or lose it. Or he was bribed."

"Bribed?"

"Just a guess."

Cov reread the phrasing. It was in lawyer-speak, but the meaning wasn't lost on Cov. The patent office was questioning how Wye acquired the patents he claimed to own. "It doesn't matter. It might be enough."

"Enough for what?"

"To raise doubts, to get people asking questions, to get rid of Wye and stop the project." Cov was excited. *There's hope yet.*

"Maybe, but you should look at the other docs too."

Cov paged through them, laying them on the bed one after the other. His eyes started to hurt. *Damn surgeons and their transplants are worthless.* "Give me the gist, Slane."

"They have to do with Sy Ioannu."

Cov's heart nearly stopped. He thought of Mason.

"She was stripped of her cyprian license eight years ago after she was accused of enhancing her DNA to gain an illegal competitive advantage over other cyprians."

I already know all this, but Slane doesn't know that. "Her bad luck she was found out."

"I was in Spokane a couple of months ago and saw her."

"Is she practicing? You sly dog." A mental image of Slane screwing his grandson's mother disgusted him.

"You're an ass, Rast. She was with Gerard Rossmann."

"So what? Rossmann's probably screwed a hundred cyprians."

Slane grew impatient. "Listen to me, Rast. Look at the top page of the DOL doc."

Cov sighed and opened the Department of Licensing e-document. "It's an application for renewal of a cyprian license."

"Ioannu filed that a year ago. Did you know the bessies have to sign off on it?"

Cov was nonplussed. "What the hell for? BES is all about enforcing the Carbon Laws and the environmental regulations."

"It's very hard to get a cyprian license. You have to get a dozen signatures from dog catcher on up to the governor-general. It was part of the deal for getting prostitution legalized in Pacific West."

Cov remembered the debate. It went on for a decade. "Forget the history lesson. I don't see the connection."

"Ioannu needs Rossmann's signature."

"You're not making any sense, Slane. Life in the boonies has addled you."

"What if Ioannu is trading, um, services, for Rossmann's signature? Or maybe he's getting her to do something for him?"

"Christ on a stick, Slane. Get to the point."

"You've heard the rumors going around about Ioannu and Wye. They're more than just friends. A little tête-à-tête between a genetically altered whore and a lonely newcomer might be enough to keep him around."

Cov thought for a moment. "That's awful thin reasoning, Slane. Awful thin. Maybe they just like each other." Don and Junie came to mind. The boy was with her more often than with his grandfather these days. He didn't like it, but he doubted Don would listen to a grandfatherly warning and stop seeing her.

"Maybe you're right, Rast, but I can't imagine a judge would look kindly on a deputy inspector general of the BES pushing hard to take down a dam who's hanging around with a cyprian whose license was stripped and whose application for reinstatement is sitting on his desk." Slane caught his breath. "It stinks to high heaven."

The image of Rossmann and Ioannu mooning at each other made Cov smile. "You might have something there, Slane."

The towboat captain nodded.

Cov was having none of it. "Let me get this straight. First, you accuse Wye of patent fraud." He stole a glance at the papers. "Then you tell me a cock and bull story about the whore seducing Wye to keep him interested in the dam deconstruction in hopes of getting her cyprian license back." Cov sniggered. "Sound likes a crock of shit to me." *Some of it, anyway.* "What is it you really want, Slane?"

"I've told you, Rast. We both want Wye gone and the dam saved. I've just given you evidence that will send Wye packing and get Rossmann fired. What else do you want, a picture of Wye and

274

Ioannu fucking?"

Slane made Cov retch, but the elder was not about to reject out of hand the possibility that Slane might have found something that could end his misery. He needed an expert opinion. Without telling Slane, Cov pinged his attorney. *It's time I did some real damage.*

CHAPTER 23

♦ ♦ ♦

ED WYE AWOKE WITH A START. The wall of water in his dream crashed on him and soaked him in cold sweat. He lay on the couch in his office, licking his dry lips, the image of four-year-old Junie rolling like a log in the surging water dissolving as his mind cleared. *I'm not ready for this.* Dawn streamed through his office window as the spring sun rose over Arroyo Grande, predicting another hot day and highlighting its importance. A wag in the office dubbed it D-Day, for demolition day, the day the Arroyo Grande Dam came down.

I've missed something. I know it.

Ed wished he were a thousand kilometers away. The day he'd worked for had come, and he was afraid of it. Tempted on the one hand to call Natalie and accept the ZephyrCom offer, and on the other hand to tell Junie to grab her go bag and run off with him to Nunavut or some other godforsaken New Arctic Settlement, he rose from the couch, feeling as if he'd aged five years in the last five weeks. The staff and crew had pulled 16-hour days and a half-dozen all-nighters, including last night. Ed fell asleep at his desk around 03:00; he didn't remember moving to the couch. He shuffled into the office bathroom, noticing Connie prone on the break room sofa, her face in the crook where the sofa arm met the sofa back, as if hiding from the future.

A shower, shave, fresh clothes dropped off by Junie the day before, and a mist stick rejuvenated him. What felt like a disaster in the making had a certainty of success in the space of twenty minutes. Connie had started a pot of coffee, and after apologizing for disturbing her, he walked out to the observation point and marveled at the clarity of the sky, the way the undulating top of the basalt cliffs met the blue of the sky, and the hundred shades of yellow, red, and orange on the cliffs' vertical striations. Ed perceived the rush of the impoundment water through the diversion channel as breathy tranquility. A songbird flitted by, found his perch, and called, as if taking credit for the quiet left behind by the silent demolition bots while laying claim to a patch of scrub in anticipation of the day's result. *Sy would love this moment.*

Is Ramesh with you?

Connie's text prompted Ed to look about. He's not out here.

He's not in the office and not on the network.

Maybe he went home.

He's not answering my pings.

Ed sent his own message to his head engineer, but the response came back *Unavailable.* Problems with the com net in rural areas were unusual, if not uncommon. Maybe he went offline for some rest.

It's not like him.

No one had been themselves for the past week, but Ed had noticed a particular snappishness in Ram. Ed chalked it up to the strain of the project and missing his family, which had flown to India to stay with distant relatives. Ed picked up strained conversations in Hindi, and though he didn't understand a word, he imagined the female voice on the other end of the call to be Ram's wife or possibly his mother. Ed did not pry into Ram's affairs, though he wondered why Ram didn't use his minds-eye implants to keep the squabbles private.

We've got a couple of hours before we run the final checks. He'll turn up. Connie, however, was right, Ed reflected. Ramesh wasn't someone to unplug, even for a short time. The engineer was one of the most dedicated workers Ed had ever met, to a fault. Engineers were an obsessive clan, by nature and by training, and Ed had to order him home once or twice when exhaustion cut into Ram's performance. It was as if Ram had more at stake than simply completing a major project under an impossible deadline. His attitude reminded Ed of his own desire to reach his goal and use his achievement as a springboard back into Silicon Valley. Perhaps Ram was trying to prove to the deniers and obstructionists that he couldn't be intimidated into giving up. Ed shrugged. The two had never discussed politics, though the fire in Ram's belly burned a shade too brightly, in Ed's opinion.

Ed's lack of concern changed into a fidgety impatience when Ram failed to respond to pings after an hour of trying. He didn't show even after most of the engineering and staff had taken their places for the final checks and countdowns. Connie's growing alarm spread among the office staff and the foremen and women. No one could find Ramesh. Ed toyed with the idea of reporting him missing, but he couldn't believe that it wasn't just some weird glitch with the com net or a public car that had blown a tire with Ram as the unlucky passenger. He would've called in, though.

Ed's anxiety spiked when Gerard Rossmann's forest-green, tulip-logoed sedan pulled into the space reserved for VIPs. Though Ed did not plan to make D-Day a media event, as he had with the first blast in the winter, he invited Rossmann to witness the project's climax. With Ramesh absent, the big day might have to be postponed. Ed put on his best nonchalant face. "Good morning, General."

"Superintendent." The BES officer and his project manager shook hands, as much to show conviviality to the staff as a standard greeting. The general was in a good mood. "I'm excited to see the fruit of your work."

Ed cleared his throat. "General, we may have to delay today's blasting."

The general's face fell. The disappearance of his smile gave his face a skeletal cast. "Why is that?"

"Our chief engineer seems to have taken the day off." Ed regretted his bad joke.

"You allowed this?"

"I meant that he hasn't shown up for work."

Instead of growing cross, Rossmann looked inwardly, as if weighing a new piece of information about a problem.

"We've tried to reach him," Ed added, "but he hasn't responded."

"Is he important to the blasting?"

"He practically designed the entire thing. He knows it better than anyone, myself included."

"No one else knows how it works?" Rossmann scolded.

"All the engineering staff—" Ed swept his hand across the room of desks, holo-emitters glowing. "—know the systems backwards and forwards."

Rossmann scanned the room, moving his eyes back and forth. "Then let's proceed."

"Sir, Ramesh Chandra's work is critical to the project's success. If something should go wrong—"

"Let's hope it doesn't. I want you to proceed, Wye."

Every eye in the room was on Ed. Would he let a BES bully humiliate the project superintendent in front of everyone? "General, a word in my office, if you don't mind."

Ed opened the door in an invitation. Rossmann huffed, but didn't protest. Ed's office smelled of dirty socks and pencil erasers.

"General, our plan is good, but it's high risk. I need every person at their place. Ramesh needs to be here."

"I doubt he's coming to work today."

Ed gaped, disbelieving. "Say that again."

"He's absconded to avoid arrest."

Ed closed the blinds to his inside window. *I'm living in a nightmare.* "Have you lost your mind?"

"Careful, Mr Wye. While you were pounding away at the dam's concrete, we were drilling deeper into Mr Chandra's activities." Rossmann lowered himself onto Ed's couch with a restrained grunt. Ed wondered if the piece of furniture was still damp from his bad dream the night before. Rossmann didn't hint either way.

"Are you sure it wasn't Slane?"

"Quite certain. He's a saboteur, too, but his style was like a chainsaw sculptor compared to a Michelangelo." Rossmann picked at a loose green thread on the couch. "Besides, we've been blocking his access to any of the dam's networking systems, and he's been busy with... other things."

"You let Slane go free hoping he'd lead you to other conspirators." Recollections of the threats and the intruder churned Ed's stomach.

"Indeed. It turns out Utility has more secret conspiracies than a dog has fleas." Rossmann pulled on the loose thread, and a hole appeared in the upholstery. Ed thought his behavior juvenile. "Chandra's sabotage to the coffer dam and the demolition bots was extremely sophisticated. Layers of dead ends, trap doors, and other programming gymnastics, too arcane for me to fully understand. But my BES engineers managed to unravel the Gordian knot, and Chandra held the bitter end. The sad thing is, he apparently saw that we were on his trail. He's lit out, as the saying goes."

Ed steadied himself against the wall. Rossmann's accusation was impossible for him to accept. How could his best colleague, equaled only by Connie, have betrayed him so deeply? Ed couldn't believe a man as intelligent and hard-working as Ramesh Chandra wished harm to the project. Sure, he could see how some of Ram's behavior might be seen as disloyal or perhaps careless. From

Rossmann's perspective, sending his family to India, as far away from Utility as possible, might pave the way for an escape if he were discovered. Maybe the furtive arguments in Hindi were really discussions for a conspiracy about to bear fruit. Perhaps Ram's churlish attitude revealed his true feelings about the project, and Ed didn't see what was happening. He remembered that Ramesh was at the hearing before the dozer went loco. *Rossmann's not going mad. I am.*

"If what you're saying is true, General Rossmann, everything we've planned for today is compromised."

"Not to worry, Wye."

"I have to worry, Rossmann. It's my neck on the block. We can't go through with it. We'll have to tear it all down and start over."

"You're over-reacting, Wye. My engineers have been watching every move by your team, not just Chandra's. Everyone's quite impressed with your ideas. Brilliant, I'd say."

I should've guessed Rossmann would keep an eye on us. "I'm not as smart as you think I am."

"Don't underestimate yourself. Proceed, and everything will be fine."

"How can I proceed after everything you've said?"

"Once we were certain that Chandra was hiding something, our engineers set up a software decoy to keep him thinking that no one knew what he was doing. In reality, we were cleaning things up and even added an improvement or two."

The officer's arrogance enraged Ed. Rossmann and the Bureau of Environmental Security had breathed down his neck for most of a year, and now they were interfering under his nose. He couldn't accept that Ramesh would stab him in the back, but Rossmann's confidence chipped away at his resistance. Ed kept his bile down. "Why haven't you arrested Ram, if you knew what he was doing?"

"Chandra is a brilliant civil engineer, but his AI skills are that of a journeyman." Rossmann turned thoughtful. "We're certain he's had help, but we haven't been able to trace it to its source. We were hoping he'd give it away somehow, but he's been extraordinarily careful. I wish he were on our side. He'd make an excellent confidential informer."

Ed glanced through the crack between the closed blinds and the window frame. The staff had gathered in clumps, probably speculating on what Ed and Rossmann were debating. *Which one of them is betraying me now?* He caught himself, disgusted with his own selfishness. "I can't go through with the demolition, Rossmann."

"You can and you will."

"Not until I'm satisfied that the systems aren't compromised."

Rossmann stood and faced his superintendent. "I give you my word that all is well. Proceed."

"I can't. I don't trust you."

"Trust is irrelevant. I want that dam down. Proceed or I will see that you never work again. You'll live like a disidentified, even if you aren't formally dissed."

Rossmann's intensity convinced Ed of his earnestness. *What would happen to Junie if he made good on his threat?* "If it goes wrong, it's on your head."

"Those in power never place blame where it belongs, but I accept your condition."

Ed hesitated when put his hand on the door, as if fearing to open a portal to some hell. With Rossmann standing behind him like a demon, he felt he had no choice but to obey.

As he stood in the open door, Connie and the staff—minus Ramesh Chandra—regarded Ed as if he were a condemned man. "Start the final checks," Ed said. "The countdown starts in ten minutes."

"What about Ram?" Connie said.

"Ram is… away and won't be coming back."

"What are you saying? What's happened?"

Aware of a looming Rossmann behind him, Ed snapped, "Don't argue with me. Get to work, all of you. You have nine minutes."

The demo techs ran through their checklists, and Ed was ready to order a 60-second countdown. As he composed the message, a text came through the network.

BY ORDER OF THE EASTERN DISTRICT COURT OF THE PACIFIC WEST DIVISION, A TEMPORARY INJUNCTION IS GRANTED TO RAST, ET AL...

The universe is determined to fuck me over. Ed spied a sheriff's deputy striding through the open office. He locked eyes with the superintendent.

"Mr Wye, you've been served." The deputy ignored Rossmann and handed Ed a manila envelope. Rossmann kept still.

Ed removed a document, studied the heading, and swiped through to the signature. He set himself on the edge of a desk. The language was vague, something about ensuring public confidence in transparent and scientific decision-making. "General, I've been ordered to stop all demolition activities on Arroyo Grande Dam. I'm to appear in court next week. You too."

"I'm aware of the proceedings."

"You knew this was coming?" Ed was confused.

"He most certainly did." Covington Rast took over where the deputy left off. Rast's presence wound up the tension. "I told you, Wye, that I would do everything I could to stop this project, and now I have the law behind me." One thing Ed liked about Cov Rast: He didn't give a shit who you were or what office you held. Ed bet the old man fought until he had nothing left.

"Your legal standing in this issue is highly questionable, Mr Rast," Rossmann said. "The fact that you have a sympathetic backwoods judge issuing orders means nothing." The officer folded his hands behind his back. "BES attorneys have already taken the order to the Court of Appeals in San Francisco. These tactics never work, Mr Rast. The courts have ruled a dozen times that the government and the Bureau have the authority to carry out policy with respect to dam removals and any other actions it deems protects or enhances the environment in response to climate change."

"Not when there's evidence of incompetence or corruption."

Ed wheeled on Cov. "What the hell are you talking about?"

"You are unqualified for this job, Wye. You're a patent thief."

Oh God, not that again.

"Grace Cromer is a past investor in your failed business ventures. That suggests a conflict of interest. She hired you. You owe her something. And Rossmann here"—Cov waved at the inspector general as if he were an insect—"has hired a delicensed cyprian to persuade you to ignore a fat job offer in order to finish a project you'd abandon if you could."

"You're crazy, Rast!" Ed's reputation was under attack again. "So what if I'd rather be doing something else? I'm here doing my job, aren't I? Wait a minute..." Ed's jaw dropped. "Are you talking about Sy Ioannu? She wants the dam down, too. Why would Rossmann hire a cyprian to keep me here?"

"Insurance, Wye. The dam comes down by Rossmann's deadline, he uses his connections in the Cyprian Association to get her license reinstated. *Quid pro quo.*"

"You've gone senile." Despite the crazy story, Ed winced. *Was Sy just doing Rossmann's bidding?*

"For an experienced businessman, Mr Rast, your ignorance surprises me." Rossmann stepped forward. "You, of all people, ought to understand that doing business often means promises made off the books, handshakes between people with favors to trade, a wink and a nod on occasion to move things forward."

"Tell it to the judge, General. He'll decide whether your backroom dealings are just 'doing business' or something worse."

"I don't think your complaint will get that far."

Ed retreated to a corner of the conference room while Cov and the general fenced. The reflections on the eastern wall of the canyon above the impoundment rendered an image worthy of the 19th century impressionists. Cov wasn't prone to fantasies. He accused Ed of falling into the age-old trap of emotional attachment to a professional whose business was sexual gratification. It embarrassed Ed. Sy was a cyprian, perhaps retired or on some kind of sabbatical, particularly with a child to care for, but Ed thought they were friends, and the night with her was simply two lonely adults sharing a fleeting moment of intimacy. The DNA tattoo charge was a rumor, nothing more. His anger rose, but he was angry at himself more than Sy. He felt the world was pressing down on him.

A text arrived in Ed's minds-eye: IN THE MATTER OF RAST VS BUREAU OF ENVIRONMENTAL SECURITY, THE INJUNCTIVE ORDER IS VACATED, BY ORDER OF THE NINTH CIRCUIT...

Ed switched off his texting app, exhausted with the machinations of lawyers, bureaucrats, and complainers, such as Covington Rast, who started to rave. Ed was sick of it all. He wanted to leave the building and take a stroll next to the peaceful surface of the reservoir. His upbeat mood of the morning had vanished into a black hole. He hadn't felt this tired since the final judgment came down awarding him the patent rights Roger Saar stole from him. It had taken all his might and most of his fortune to prove his innocence and get that supplemental report quashed. Its lies and half-truths would have shamed P.T. Barnum, but it was a Pyrrhic victory, and it had come back to haunt him. Few things in his career had gone right since then. On his worst days, he was ready to jump off a bridge. First Marcy, then Junie, kept him going, encouraging him to find ways of climbing out of his hole. He wasn't quite ready to fold in this game. *Today is my last chance.*

"Ed?" Connie tugged at his sleeve. "Are you okay?"

"I'm fine, Connie."

"General Rossmann's been trying to get your attention."

"What?" Ed blinked.

"Mr Wye, we need to proceed with the demolition. The court..."

Ed's fears reformed like a returning cancer, but his brain clicked. *Maybe I can take advantage of this and postpone the blast.* "With respect, General, I'm wondering if we should wait until I consult with all the parties. I'm not sure I understand all the issues." It was a cover-your-ass statement, but with so many people weighing in, and the inherent risks in their plan, a time-out was a logical choice.

Rossmann pulled Ed aside and whispered in his ear. The general's eyes glistened with intimidation. "Pull the trigger, or I will make sure that we share a cell in whatever hellish prison we're sent to."

The thought frightened Ed more than disidentification. *He's afraid, too, but of what? Failure?*

Rossmann lifted his voice so all could hear. "I'd like to assure everyone that I have absolute legal authority in this matter. Let me be very clear. The Columbia River will run free. That is what the world wants. That is what everyone wants. Please proceed, Mr Wye."

Ed gripped the edge of a chair behind one of the technicians. The 3-D displays floated above the holo-emitters. *I'm just a cog in a big machine, but I will spin, and maybe good will come of it.* "Let's do a 60-second countdown." Ed pressed on.

"You're going to regret this, Wye." Rast's growl underlined the warning, but it had a lassitude that sounded like air hissing from a tire.

One of the techs called out the time remaining at 10-second intervals. For the last 10 seconds, he counted down to zero.

Nothing happened. The room was silent as the grave.

Ed ran over to the terminal and reached over the technician's shoulder. "The dashboard says everything went off without a hitch. There's even nominal feedback from the sensing stations." He touched a key on another terminal, which switched the displays to camera views all over the site. Nothing stirred, not even dust from the light breeze.

"What kind of stunt are you pulling, Wye?"

"Nothing, I—"

"Try again. Restart the countdown..." Rossmann paused with the glassy-eyed effect from a distraction in his minds-eye. "Wait a moment..."

The old dam visitors center shuddered and a hurricane of dust and pebbles enveloped the vehicles in the construction yard. A helo set down in their midst and disgorged BES officers in SWAT gear and a squad of security bots.

"Our AI spotted a fault and stopped the firing signal." Rossmann said. He blinked. "Chandra's here." With that, Rossmann bolted for the main door. His personal sec-bot followed him. Ed followed as well, finding Rossmann conferring with an officer in lieutenant's insignia. Rossmann barked an order as another helo roared overhead. He turned to Ed. "Get back inside, Wye. Chandra might be armed."

"Not a chance. I know him."

"Then stay out of the way."

The scene calmed as the sec-bots and the armed bessies spread out to search for Ramesh. Ram, are you on the site? Ed couldn't resist reaching out to his friend, or the person whom he once thought of as a friend. *No, he's still my friend, my colleague.* He knew the BES was listening, and Ed received no response to his ping, but he was compelled to search for Ram himself. He knew the site better than Rossmann and his goons, but he saw no sign of the engineer in every place he checked. A thought occurred to him. He walked back to the old visitors center, hoping to give the impression of obeying Rossmann's command to return to the office.

Inside, he motioned Connie over. "Keep everyone at their desks. Don't let anyone move." Connie nodded, he face twisted with concern. "Everything will be alright," Ed assured.

The superintendent stepped purposefully to the network closet, once an old telephone switch room, where the project kept its bio-logic networking devices and servers. After the construction bots were attacked, the room's shielding against cyber-attacks was strengthened. It could also serve as a refuge. The room was in a corner, the door camouflaged by discarded office furniture. He laid his thumb on the DNA reader, and the door opened with a click. He closed the door behind him. He flicked on the light, but it illuminated only part of the room. The servers hummed, but Ed smelled sweat. "Ram, I think you're in here."

Three seconds passed, and the engineer emerged from a deep shadow. His face was a mask of terror overlain by a fanatic determination. "You weren't supposed to find me. The shielding..."

"I guessed where you might be. This is the best place to hide. It also gives you access to the network and the project's AIs."

Ramesh Chandra swallowed hard.

"Ram, what are you doing? I don't understand."

"It has nothing to do with you."

"The whole fucking BES is after you. There's an army out there that wants to kill you."

"It's Rossmann I want. I tried to warn you."

"If you want Rossmann dead, why are you sabotaging the project?"

"I don't want to kill him. I want to destroy him."

"How is sabotaging the project going to do that? He'll just have someone else take down the dam."

"No, you don't understand, Ed." Ram seemed to waver, as if drunk or high on mist. "Rossmann is a murderer. He killed thousands of my people."

Ed noticed the tablet in Ram's hand, but said nothing.

"Have you ever wondered about him? He's only been in Utility for a few years. Despite his grand title, this is practically Siberia to a man like him. He was sent here to keep him out of sight, did you know that?"

Ed shook his head.

"He took down a dam in India ten years ago. Not many people know about it on this side of the world, especially the fact that he killed thousands, maybe tens of thousands when the flood swept away whole towns and whole families." Ram's eyes filled with tears. "He killed my family, destroyed my ancestral village. I've lived in Pacific West all my life, my parents too, but that was our home, that tiny dusty village below a dam that had made them prosperous and independent. I'll destroy him for what he did to us."

The tablet in Ram's hand beeped. He grimaced, a smile with no joy. "Ah, we're ready. Shall we take down the Arroyo Grande Dam, Ed?"

"That was the whole idea."

"True, but I won't take it down like you planned. I'll take it down my way."

Ed grasped what he meant and blanched. "Ram, please don't."

"I'm sorry, Ed. It has to be this way."

"The BES knows what you've been doing. They've set out some kind of decoy."

"Natalie was right. You do have a streak of naivete."

"Natalie? Natalie Wong? What's she got to do with this?"

Ram ignored the question. "I've been watching the watchers, Ed. I've stepped around them, like a soccer player dribbling a ball past a blind defender."

A distant thud broke the silence of the utility closet. Muffled voices came through the door.

"Rossman's coming, Ram." Ed figured out the significance of

the tablet and held out his hand. "Give me the tab, Ram. It's over."

Ram edged toward the door. Tempted to call out to Rossmann, Ed rejected the idea because it might provoke Ram. He blanked on what else to do, though memories from the last few months fell in a pattern. Ramesh's presence at the hearing in the courthouse, his decision to send his family away to protect them not from threats, but from the BES; his "failure" to show up for work; Rossmann's elimination of suspects until only Ramesh remained. Ram's story filled in the blanks, though Ed couldn't grasp the engineer's need for revenge for a crime that seemed as far removed from Ed as the depredations of English invaders against his Irish ancestors. It didn't matter. Ram was ready to finish what he'd started. "Ram, the tab."

Ed had no weapon, no training for self-defense, and when Ram rushed him, he ducked. Ram didn't need the extra push to get Ed out of the way as he caromed to the door. Ed gathered himself and ran after the engineer, who collided with the old furniture, scattering boxes and sending screeches from chair legs bouncing into the high-ceiling room. Ed called to him to stop, warning him of danger, but Ram made straight for the main door.

As he drew even with a metal cabinet, the object exploded, sending shrapnel in all directions. The sec-bot's staser blast had missed the man, but it didn't matter. Ram sprawled on the concrete floor. Shouts and screams replaced the booming echoes. Ed crawled toward Ram, half-afraid of another staser shot, but unwilling to ignore Ramesh's moans. A finger-length shard of metal stuck out from his neck, throbbing with his heartbeat, blood leaking around its jagged edge. Ed bent over the dying man. "Ram, we'll get help. You'll make it."

Ram's hand clenched and relaxed. Ed glanced toward it. A few centimeters beyond was the tab. Ed reached for it. *Can I disarm it?*

"No!" Ram's voice was cut short, as if the pain of his injuries prevented him giving full throat. "Don't touch it."

"Ram, I have to stop you. Don't make the same mistake Rossmann made." Ed reached for the tab again.

"Ed, no. Stop, please."

Ed halted.

"I don't want you to be blamed." Ram winced with pain.

Ed wondered where Rossmann and the bessies were. Wouldn't they take Ram into custody right now? Would Rossmann find a way to solve his problem without the inconvenience of an arrest and trial? He reached for the tab.

"You'll set off the explosives, if you touch it. It's sensitive to my DNA print. Only I can put my hand on it."

Ed gulped. He'd almost caused a disaster. "Ram, you have to stop your program. You can't hurt innocent people. I know you. You're a good man. If I helped you get the tablet, will you stop the blast?"

Ram studied his boss for a moment, eyes glistening with tears. Blood pooled under his neck. He nodded.

Ed breathed out and guided Ram's hand to the tablet. Ram adjusted his head, despite the injury, and he gathered the tablet with his fingers. He lifted his other hand and swiped and touched. Ed watched, but he could not follow what Ram was doing.

A second later, which Ed remembered as the world turning inside out, the floor of the visitors center shifted, and the air trembled. Horrified, Ed regarded Ram. "Why?"

Ram's breathing was fast and shallow. The tablet clattered as it hit the floor. "Obligations, Ed. Obligations." Ram's breathing stopped and his eyes rolled back.

A kiloton of energy shook the Arroyo Grande Dam, shattering the concrete like porcelain, shaking the ground so hard that Ed lost his balance, even as he knelt over Ram's body. Ed's plan was a series of blasts over 10 seconds or so, minimizing excess vibrations, while grinding the dam into interlocking chunks of concrete that could be broken and hauled away by the demolition crew. It was basically a highly controlled one-time application of his earlier step-by-step approach. Ram had set off the charges within milliseconds of each other, as if a Titan from Greek mythology had swung a massive hammer to the top of the dam, destroying it in one blow.

In a flash of recognition, Ed grasped Ram's core idea. It had nothing to do with the dam itself, which was enveloped in a shroud of white dust. The sound of metal tearing, like the screams of children, drifted up from the construction pit on the upstream side of the dam. He glanced at a camera monitor nearby, but he had already predicted what happened next. Within a few beats of the intense vibrations, the welds and bracing of the interlocking metal sheets of the coffer dam failed, and they bent aside like riot-control bots giving way to a pressing crowd, allowing a wall of water to slide into the pit. The invasion appeared to happen slowly, like a dancer taking a turn on a stage, but the horde was soon at the ramparts. Millions of tons of water headed straight for the pulverized dam, now a barrier in name only.

CHAPTER 24

POETS ARE FULL OF SHIT. Junie's conclusion came to her while viewing the river from a jumble of flat rocks arranged as if a non-human creature had designed a set of outdoor furniture 100,000 years ago. She lounged on the boulders, head tilted back to catch the sun with her face. *Poets are liars.* Back in San Francisco, a few days after Junie and Alex spent their first day together without the distractions or camouflage of mutual friends, he sent her a poem. It talked about first meetings, curiosity, and the difficulty of thinking about anything else but her. It was a great sales job, and Junie was hooked. Alex was the typical analytical man. He relied on the words of ne'er-do-well scribblers who articulated what he could not. For a couple of months or so, he sent her poems or books of poems as if on a schedule. It was an advertising campaign, a drumbeat of pretty packaging meant to dress up ordinary things, or to mask flaws and dangers. Then he stopped, as if the deal were closed.

If the world ever brings back hangings, let the poets be first on the gallows.

Don was next to her at the rocky outcrop locals called "the sofa and chairs." He peered through binoculars at the dam site. Overhead, security drones buzzed them every few minutes. So did buzzards.

"What are they waiting for?" Don scratched the back of his head.

"It's a complicated business, blowing up a dam," Junie said.

Don wiped the lens on the binoculars with a micro-fiber cloth. He and Alex were alike in many ways. Both suited Junie's tastes: curly-haired, tall, broad-shouldered, quiet. Unlike Alex, Don did not rely on dead strangers to say what he felt. That's not to say choosing words was his strength. Junie knew Don for what he did, not what he said. He worked hard, and with her help, he'd raised his grades in his math-centered courses. With graduation around the corner, Don wanted to do well as he waited for responses to his letters of application to college. Don was as smart as Alex, but in an earthier, rougher manner that was authentic for its lack of gleam. Gifts and poems made love prettier, but did they add to its shine? Junie slapped herself in the arm. *I'm such an idiot.* She was on the edge of love again, but unlike the frantic, grasping love with Alex, the emotion with Don was soft, reticent, hushed, and far more powerful.

"Why did you hit yourself?" Don saw the movement of her fist.

"Nothing. Bugs."

Junie shaded her eyes from the sun under her broad hat. Despite Don's insistent curiosity, she couldn't focus on the dam. As the morning wore on, the hardness of the sun and the rocks interrupted with a hard truth: she had changed. *I've changed for the better.* Junie rested her chin in her hand as light played on the impoundment behind the dam. Not long after the breakup, Don had pinged her, and she told him about the planned Big Bang. They skipped school to watch the blast from the viewpoint.

She still pined for the Bay Area—Utility's choice in restaurants hadn't improved since the Izzy opened, though she'd developed a taste for the vanilla soy milk shakes at the Dew Drop Inn—and her old friends rarely contacted her. Less than a year had passed since her arrival, but Tiffany had become a best friend, with Trudy a close second. Sy Ioannu was a friend too, but Junie was still skeptical of the cyprian's motives.

Daisy and Silver, the equine robots, stood a few paces away from the sofa and chairs. If they had been flesh and blood, they might have chewed on the short clumps of new grass around the rocks. As robots, they stood almost still, apart from swishing tails that signaled their stand-by status. Below, the partially demolished Arroyo Grande Dam was silent. Junie and Don were too far away to hear the river rushing through the diversion channel, but the snow-white streams of water from the pump outlets were visible along the length of the coffer.

Don lowered the glasses, excited. "Look there." He pointed over the impoundment. "A helicopter. No, two." He put the glasses back up to his eyes like a twelve-year-old. "They've got the BES seals on them."

Junie had not invited Don to her bed, but it was only a matter of time. The fire for Alex had burned hot for months, and embers take time to cool. She wanted to care for this new flame, like an ancient priestess. *I couldn't leave Utility now.*

"The helos are headed for the dam." Don sighed. "Maybe they canceled the blast."

The woman brushed the point on the man's face where his neck met his jaw. "A while longer, okay? This is so important to my dad. I want to tell him I saw it." *It's important that you're sharing this moment with me.*

"Hang on." Don handed the binoculars to Junie. "Take a look."

In less than a minute, the site was swarming with bessies and bots. Junie texted her father. What's happening? The app returned an "unreachable" error. *Security block.* "It's like they're searching for somebody."

"Why would they have guns?"

A rumble shook the basalt stone that served as her chair. The vibrations felt as if they came from miles below. The dam disappeared in a wispy cloud that resembled chalk dust rising from a child's clapping hands.

"Christ on a stick." Junie handed the binoculars to Don and pointed. "That can't be right."

Don peered through the optics. He lowered them, as if not trusting his eyes. "The coffer dam. It's failing."

The coffer collapsed across its length, and water smashed into the dam. The flood hesitated for three seconds before the broken concrete gave way, and a 10,000-ton slurry of water, concrete, and dust flowed through a gap like crepe batter. The transformation shocked Junie. Everything had gone terribly wrong. "My god, Don, should we tell somebody?"

"There's people downstream. Parts of the town." His face was pale, even in the blazing sun. "I'll call 9-1-1. I'll post messages on my c-tribes."

Junie stood and stepped forward, as if to get a better look. Her sensations alternated between helplessness and a desire to act, though not necessarily run. As she posted messages on all her tribes, even the Bay Area groups, water poured through the gap in the dam as if it came out of the mouth of a monstrous pitcher. Sweat trickled down her belly.

Don was stricken. His voice shook. "All that water. It'll back up into the side canyons."

The emergency pushed out all thoughts of Don, Alex, and love. "Fuck. The colony. The com signals don't reach there. They have no idea what's coming."

"How do we warn Peter and the others?"

An image of little Corinne, the girl she'd rescued on the busy road, came to Junie, and she bolted from her stance and mounted Daisy. "Come on! We have to tell them." She set off at a full gallop, uncaring that she had never ridden the equine at a gallop. Sunlight glinted off its copper-gold skin, despite the fine coating of trail dust. Her minds-eye showed Don behind her, and she wished he'd set the robot at a higher skill level. Daisy could run like a racehorse for hours. Junie barely held on, and she bounced in the saddle like a rag doll, stabs of pain shivering up her back. She told the equine its destination. *Come on!*

The trail hugged the edge of the canyon, and Junie caught glimpses of the forward edge of the wave as it rolled down the river bed. Girl and robot raced the deadly torrent. The river's course was relatively flat, which slowed the leading chaos of trees, stones, and chunks of concrete. The water spread out over the narrow flood plain, but it was pulling away from Junie and Daisy. The river made a wide turn, which meant the colony was closer as the crow files. Junie ordered the bot to take the most direct route, but the machine was hard-coded to take the trails it knew.

The twists and turns slowed Junie and Daisy down, and the girl noticed the drones, whirring about like the horse flies in Don's barn. They broadcast messages, but Junie tuned them out. She dipped into a shallow wash and rose up to its crest on the other side. A moment later, a government helicopter buzzed her before returning to the river's course. Distracted, she stopped for a moment to gaze up at it. The flood's jagged edge churned forward.

The equine turned away from the river, and Junie recognized the landscape. With Don and Silver ten meters behind her, Daisy slowed, picking her way around loose rubble and broken stones. Junie urged the robot with commands: haptic with her legs, aural with her voice, and digital with her minds-eye. The robot's responses led Junie to imagine it wanted to reach Corinne and the colonists as bad as she did.

Junie found the illegal hamlet's hidden canyon, and a few meters below its lip, the public com signals faded. She heard the beginnings of an emergency evacuation message, and her last received text read: THIS IS NOT A TEST. THE GOVERNMENT HAS ISSUED A WARNING... Maybe Don's call had saved some people. A few paces away, Silver and Don tramped through the sand and sage.

Surefooted and confident, Daisy reached the bottom of the arroyo, and at Junie's urging, it trotted through the short trees and brush. Junie sent text messages to Peter and the dissed colonists, but the messages stayed put when her implants failed to find the com signal carriers. She wanted to call out, but she was out of breath. Adrenalin made her shaky, and her hands were sore from gripping the pommel and reins. Junie spotted a hut of discarded lumber on a bank, higher up that the old shelters swept away in the flash flood months before. Corinne ran out with a huge smile, hair bouncing, happy to see her friend again.

"Corinne! Where's your mom?" The woman emerged from the hut. "Get to higher ground. There's another flood coming."

Peter emerged from the hut holding a plate. Daisy halted in a crackle of stones. Junie's breathing was thin from the ride. "You've got to move up the bank."

"Why? What's happening?"

"Please!" She gulped, frustrated that Peter didn't understand the danger.

Silver pulled up next to Daisy.

Peter grabbed Silver's halter. "Don...?"

"The dam. It's gone. The coffer too."

Junie's breath came easier. "The water is coming here."

Peter straightened, in charge. "Both of you. Go to the other huts downstream. I'll go upstream and get people moving as fast as I can." He ushered Corinne and her mother back into the hut, instructing them to grab whatever they could. Sensing the emergency, Corinne was crying.

Junie and Don split up and stopped at all the huts they could find. Some had smokeless cooking fires. A few huts were empty. People greeted Junie with a wave. *These people are important to me.* Junie announced Peter's evacuation order. "Another flood!" No one hesitated or argued, as if threats of disaster were as normal as dawn and dusk.

Down the wash toward the river's main course, Junie stopped to see if she missed any huts. Sweat dripped down her face, converting the dirt clinging to her skin to streaks of mud. She swallowed a last swig of water from a canteen. Daisy's constantly adjusting actuators hissed as her hooves adjusted to the uneven ground. Junie heard another sound, a steady gurgle, growing louder. She was near the dry streambed of the unnamed creek. A reflection caught her eye. A trickle of water flowed *uphill*. Equally repulsed and curious, Junie dismounted to get a closer look. Bits of leaves, motes of soil, and a flailing insect floated on the water's surface as it snaked around the rounded stones.

The helicopter flew over her again.

Junie saw the charcoal-gray wall a second before it hit her. The meter-high wave scuttled among the bigger stones, pushing over trees and tearing out the sage. It knocked her flat on her backside. *I'm going to have butt bruises for a month.* The slosh of muck tasted dirty as it soaked her, and its cold sucked at her body like a vampire. Junie witnessed a tsunami once at Big Sur. An earthquake across the Pacific Ocean launched it, a small one, a meter in height, and Junie watched the marching waves, caused when the floor of the sea lifted. The wave that carried her in the anonymous arroyo was nothing like the short wave-length, regular, wind-driven ocean waves that kissed the beach day and night. Thousands of people watched the tsunami hit the cliffs along the spectacular California coast. This was a mini-tsunami, a micro-tsunami. A tsunami in the desert. The water lifted her over the larger rocks, knocking her against downed trees and boulders. A sharp pain struck her lower back. Her head surfaced, and she gasped. Daisy tumbled end over end, the equine's legs flailing, but Junie heard no screams. The bot's avatar had an alarm signal over it. Junie's legs were numb.

For a moment, the stream carried Junie on its surface like pallbearers. She bobbed. The sky stopped moving. Muffled voices, shouts, called her name, and Don and Peter reached out to her. She floated, like she did in Rast High's swimming pool. The world felt distant, as if she were in orbit above it, floating. Her minds-eye complained of errors. Don held a long pole or the branch of a tree stripped of leaves. Junie gathered he wanted her to grab it, but she was too cold, and her arms wouldn't obey. The sky moved again, spinning, as did the trees that stuck out of the water in odd ways, and the water carried her away from Don. *I'm going backwards, and downhill.* Her back hurt and her head rang and her hair was tangled around her face. Don followed her along the bank, howling, but he was receding, growing smaller, blending into the cottonwoods and red basalt and lichen, and he disappeared behind a clump of rocks. She furrowed her brow, and a choked chuckle emerged from her blue lips. *Two men out of my life.* The gritty water plugged her ears and filled her mouth and nose and she had an impulse to sneeze, but her lungs did nothing. *Life sucks and then you die. Goodbye, Don Rast. I love you.*

CHAPTER 25

"DID WE EVER CONDUCT THAT EVACUATION DRILL?" Ed's words bounced out of his mouth as he ran towards the site office, Connie close behind. Broken concrete cackled as pieces fell into the raging cataract that was once a dam. "Well? Did we?"

"No, we didn't," Connie said. "The push to finish the job..."

"It wasn't a priority," Ed said. "Of course not." He blamed no one but himself. It never occurred to him that someone might want to take the dam down in the way Ramesh did. Most people wanted to keep the dam intact, not destroy it, and those who wanted the dam down weren't the type to risk lives and property downstream. *Or so I thought.*

He had no time for reflection. The site office was a version of Bedlam. Engineers and office workers rushed from desk to desk. Holo-emitters displayed maps and documents. People spoke into their coms, desperate to convince listeners that the worst had happened. Ed remembered that Junie was going to watch the demolition, but he told her the best view was on a bluff overlooking the site. *She might be afraid, but she's safe.*

The bessies had already removed Ram's body.

Cov Rast was not in sight, either.

Ed said, "The first thing we need to do is notify every law enforcement agency..."

Connie interrupted. Her exhaustion had vanished, as if adrenalin had refueled her. "No. We need to contact the state emergency management office. I met with their rep several months ago to talk about contingencies."

"Great. Do it, Connie, but I'm not taking any chances. Another thing. Ping and message and call every local media outlet you can think of. I'm not waiting for the emergency managers to act."

"Yes, sir."

In his minds-eye, Ed rolled through an array of live video feeds from the site's security and monitoring systems. Some of the images were dark, the cameras destroyed in the collapse and the flood. "Where's Rossmann?"

"Right here, Mr Wye."

Ed wheeled on the inspector general, who appeared at death's door. "What's wrong with you?"

"There'll be an investigation. I was in charge of the project."

"This wasn't your doing. You saw what happened."

Rossmann's smile hinted at terrifying knowledge. "You don't know the Bureau, do you, Wye?"

"Look, if you help me, maybe we can salvage your job." Ed pointed at the helo in the equipment yard. "I need to get a view of what's left of the dam and track the wavefront. I need the helicopter."

Rossmann shook his head. "I'll be blamed. Understand?"

"General, you can save some lives. Give me the helo."

The impoundment drained through the V-shaped gap, but the remnants of the dam constricted the flow to a steady rate, rather than letting all the water out at once. *Maybe we can do some predictions.* "Ram!" Ed stopped himself. Ram was dead. "Connie! I need you." A monitor in the conference room showed a news chans' drone over the river. It flew over a group of inundated houses. One of them collapsed. A crawl warned everyone within a kilometer of the river to head to higher ground. *Connie got through.* She appeared from a group of cubicles. "Connie, get one of the engineers to calculate a flow rate through the gap. Maybe we can warn the towns further downstream, give them a timeline."

I need better visibility into the situation. "Rossmann!"

"The helicopter's yours, Wye." The blades on the helo wound up.

Ed patted Rossmann's arm. "Thanks."

"This isn't what I wanted, Wye."

"Focus on the problem at hand, General."

Outside, Rossmann yelled over the noise of the turbine. He had collected himself. "The enforcement teams are trained in search and rescue."

Ed wondered if Rossmann had an ulterior motive for helping. *No better motive than survival.* "We need to warn people on the river."

"We'll repeat the com-based warning messages from drones."

"Anyplace where the coverage is weak."

Both climbed into the helo. Rossmann ordered it downriver. Ed could do nothing at the wrecked dam site. Connie sent him some estimates of the wavefront's arrival at major settlements on the river, though it had already passed the neighborhoods of Utility closest to the river, leaving destruction behind. The pilot flew the copter with her hands on the controls, something Ed had never seen before. AIs usually did all the work. There was no time to program the AI. Rossmann caught Ed's concern. "Don't worry, Wye. We've worked on several, er, special projects. She's the best."

Ed checked the news chans to see if warnings were getting through. One chan rotated among images of people scrambling to get away from the water, houses floating downstream like leaves in forest stream, and a body floating face down. The mayor of a downriver hamlet threw a punch at a reporter. One of the drones circled a rescue scene.

"Sir, something interesting." The pilot addressed Rossmann, but Ed could hear. "Check your three o'clock."

Ed and Rossmann gazed out of the right side of the copter. Two beige clouds followed each other on a trail that hugged the edge of the bluffs. "Horses and riders." A flash glinted off the lead animal. Ed put his hand on the window, as if trying to touch something he recognized. "Christ! That's my daughter." He tried pinging her. Nothing came back. "Pilot, can you get closer?"

The copter banked and swooped over the riders. Ed could not get a response from the com, but he was certain. "That's her alright. Don Rast is following her. Where are they going?"

"Wye, we're not here for sightseeing. We've got to watch the river." Rossmann ordered the pilot back to the wavefront.

The aircraft flew downriver at about 300 meters, giving Ed a view of the flooding. As he guessed, the constriction of the gap in the dam steadied the flow, though the initial front of water and debris had swept everything before it. Emergency vehicles raced on the roads. A building was on fire. Some of the flow backed into coulees and washes as the river's level rose.

"Sir, a word?"

Rossmann listened a moment and glanced at Ed. "I'll have to keep you out of this conversation, Wye."

Ed nodded, imagining a dressing-down from a higher-up that had to be kept private. Rossmann came back on. "We're turning back."

"Trouble with the helo?"

"No. A group of... people. They probably haven't got the warnings."

"I don't understand."

"Your daughter and the Rast boy might be there."

The helicopter gained altitude, cleared the walls of the canyon, and came around almost 180 degrees. The pilot guided the aircraft across the desert, making straight for one of the deeper gashes in the desert floor. She dipped down close to the edges of the wash and slowed to a hover.

Ed pointed. "There, I see them." Figures scrambled up the banks. "There's Don with his horse."

"It's a bot."

Ed couldn't tell the difference at this height. "I don't see Junie."

Rossmann gave an order, and the pilot drifted downstream. "What's that?" He pointed.

Both men spotted another wavefront, smaller than the main one of the river. The new front crept inexorably up the wash, making for a sharp bend in the otherwise dry stream bed.

"There she is!" Ed's daughter had dismounted, unaware of the wavefront a few dozen meters away. He pinged Junie again. He'd get a hint of a carrier wave, and her avatar would light up for a second before going offline again. "Junie!"

The wavefront came around the corner and swept Junie off her feet. Ed watched horrified as the debris-choked mess tossed her and the equine like dolls. Ed screamed at the window while Rossmann barked orders at the pilot. The copter hovered over the scene, but the coulee was too narrow for the pilot to get any lower.

"Look there," Rossmann called, "by those trees."

Don Rast and another man in ancient clothes were holding a pole or a tree branch out to Junie, but she didn't reach for it. "Junie-girl, take the branch!" Ed shouted at his daughter, uncaring that she could never hear him from inside the helicopter. One moment, he was in charge of managing a disaster, the next moment, he was helpless as a puppy. He grabbed the door handle, desperate to get to his daughter. Rossmann pulled him away. "Ed, we're at 50 meters. You'll be killed if you fall." Ed pounded at the door when he saw the water begin to recede, as if in a draining bathtub, pulling everything with it, including his daughter's body.

"Sir, I've got to move away or I might hit something." A rising column of rock loomed ahead of the helo.

"Do it," Rossmann said.

"No! No!" Ed screamed. "I have to get down there and help her." Don chased after her down the stream bed, but stopped. Ed could see him calling out. Junie had disappeared.

"Ed, we'll head back to the river and watch for Junie."

Ed wiped his face. Tears of frustration and terror stained it.

"We'll find her, Ed."

The BES helicopter hovered over the confluence of the normally dry stream and the river for a quarter hour. They searched slowly along the banks of the stream and the river, but saw nothing. Ed's panic waned to numbness, and he ignored every attempt to get him to focus on the unfolding man-made disaster. Finding and rescuing Junie was all that mattered to him. He flashed to memories of Marcy's death, how she'd died instantly on the rocks at Yosemite. It had taken Ed, her friends and rescuers two days to reach her body. Perhaps it was the distance in time, or the difference in kind, but the potential of losing Junie was far worse for Ed than the actual loss of Marcy. *I cherished Marcy, but I adore my daughter.*

Ed, we've found Junie. The text was from Cov Rast. Can you come? The text included xGPS coordinates.

"Got it," the pilot said. "But we can't stay long. Fuel's getting low." The copter moved downriver, and within thirty seconds, Ed saw the figures on the riverbank: two BES paramilitary officers and Cov Rast. His grandson was still up the canyon. At Cov's feet was a figure covered with a thermal blanket.

The copter settled on an old paved road a dozen meters above the river bank. Dust and bits of sagebrush flew in an artificial storm. Ed lost sight of the group, reviving his panic, but they reappeared with a stretcher next to the door. The paramilitaries loaded the prone figure into the cabin. Cov climbed into the copter with arthritic stiffness. The old man asked to go to the community hospital. The pilot acknowledged, and the helo left the paras behind. Cov ignored Rossmann.

"Junie, my girl. Junie!" Ed touched her hair, the only part of her not bruised or matted with blood. Part of him wouldn't accept

306

that the mangled form was Juniper Wye, his lovely, intelligent, stubborn daughter, 18 going on 25, senior at Julius Rast High School, a preschooler just yesterday. He half-expected her to open her eyes and spit out a sarcastic joke. Instead, she was motionless, held in place by straps on the rescue stretcher. Her avatar, finally available on the com network, shrieked a medical emergency.

Cov yelled into his headset microphone to be heard over the helo noise. "I saw her auto emergency beacon when I crossed the bridge. There's an access road to the river bank. That's where I found her."

Ed kept his eyes on his daughter, but he sensed Cov's worry and sympathy. "How did she get there?"

"I don't know. She was with Don this morning."

A flash of anger rose in Ed as he remembered the galloping horse-bots and riders, but he dismissed the feeling. *He tried to help her back in the wash.* "What was she doing with him? Who were those people?"

Rossmann glanced at Rast, then looked away.

"There's a colony of dissed people there," Rast said. "Some of them are friends and relatives of mine. The bessies sent..." Rast raised his voice, then held back, recognizing the greater importance of the emergency over his private resistance to the BES. "Don visited them and brought them supplies. Junie was helping."

Nothing Cov said made sense to Ed. He knew she was spending time with Don, but she never mentioned Cov's "colony." In any case, he didn't care. Ed kept his focus on Junie. Her eyes were closed, as if asleep. His hand did not stir from her hair for the entire flight, even though he felt the dampness of blood. Touching her reassured him she was still alive, that he could protect her from the angel of death. The hospital's helipad came into view and he told the pilot to be careful. The pilot nodded, though Ed reflected on a trifle of shame that he would tell a professional how to do her

307

job. *She's ferrying my daughter, and her survival is all that matters to me.*

Orderlies and nurses rushed to the copter door and placed Junie on a rolling stretcher. Ed followed them, only noticing Cov again when they reached the emergency room. As the only hospital within 300 kilometers, Utility Medical Center was equipped to handle all but the worst trauma victims, and it was bursting at the seams. The orderlies ignored everything around them as they rushed Junie down the hall and into a room marked "Surgery 2." A nurse put her hand on Ed's chest. "I'm sorry, sir. That's as far as you can go."

"That's my daughter."

"The doctor will be out as soon as she can."

Ed's anger rose again. "That's my daughter. I want to know what's going on now."

"Ed." Cov touched his arm. "Let's go. We'll just have to wait."

Ed let Cov guide him to the waiting area. He remembered it from the dozer incident. *People said I saved the town.* Nurses tended to minor wounds or covered victims with thermal blankets. Cov took one of two empty chairs. "You might as well sit, Ed. It's going to be a while."

Rossmann had disappeared. The helo was gone.

Ed stared down the hall toward the operating room, unable to take his gaze off the last place he had seen his daughter alive. All the while, his minds-eye queue warnings blinked, insisting on answers to hundreds of pings and messages backed up in his com. He could've shut the warnings off, or blocked them by modifying one of the filters he used in San Jose, but he had learned to ignore them as if they were an itchy mosquito bite. *Connie can handle things if I have to say goodbye to Junie.* He covered his face and sniffed.

"It's alright, Ed." Cov laid a reassuring hand on Ed's shoulder. "I'd do the same if it were my grandson." The elder folded his hands between his knees. "I had no idea this could happen. Never in a million years."

Cov's gravelly voice irritated Ed as the quiet in the waiting room urged him to calm. Cov's use of Ed's first name—never done before—struck him as insincere, even insulting. Fear over Junie's injury chipped at Ed's professional mien around the powerful man, but the elder spoke as if chastened by what had happened.

"I wanted the dam to stay, but I never wanted violence. I hate the bessies, but causing the deaths of innocent people..."

Ed winced at the last few words.

"...that's just evil, not worth it..."

Ed half-listened to Rast, an enemy trying to be a friend, if only because they both had children about the same age who were friends, perhaps more. "It wasn't Rossmann's fault. He pushed me to take down the dam, but he didn't want this either. Somebody else wanted justice, but his own kind." He told Cov a truncated version of Ram's story.

Guilt pricked at Ed's soul. He hadn't cared much about the politics or the consequences of taking down the dam. *Maybe I should have.* He came to Utility to do a job, repair his reputation, and move on, maybe to a new life at ZephyrCom, back in the world where he belonged. *I wanted a fresh start. I took another big risk. I bet everything. Now I might lose everything.*

"I'll be truly sorry, Ed, if Junie..." Rast couldn't finish the sentence.

Time dragged, day turned into night, and Cov fell asleep on the waiting room couch. Ed's resentment faded. The old man didn't need to stay, but he'd taken an emotional hit as well, and Ed believed the elder's sympathy to be sincere. The project superintendent wondered if he should pull himself together and help Connie and the others back at the office, but every time he opened a message or composed an email, a mental image of Junie's broken body overwhelmed him.

He left messages from Sy Ioannu unopened.

"I heard about Junie." Grace Cromer stood before Ed, her face pale as the moon, echoing the dried concrete slurry on her clothes. "I should've come earlier."

"You have other things on your mind." Ed's exhaustion, emotional and physical, stretching back to the day he'd taken the job nearly a year before, knocked down a barrier he hadn't perceived. *Why was Grace the only one of my business contacts who ever stuck with me?* He thought it was an old, enduring friendship, pure and simple, but it was more. Memories of Roger Saar offered the insight: Grace was in love with his old professor. "Are you here because of Junie, or are you keeping your enemies closer?"

Grace lowered herself into a chair and sighed with sorrow and guilt. "Yesterday, I might have said the latter, but when I heard about Junie, all I could think of is that she might have been my daughter." Grace laughed at herself. "It's a stupid, juvenile thing to think, 30 years after breaking up with you." She shrugged. "I really did believe in those patents you held, even if they didn't belong to you. They were the work of genius."

"Grace, those patents..."

"No, Ed, let's not fight now." Grace brushed away loose hairs. "Yes, I invested in your ventures mostly to keep you close, to keep you from drifting away, as people tend to do. I was in love with Roger. We were going to get married. Then he killed himself. I blamed you. I hoped that you'd do something or say something that would give me a chance to prove your theft, if not murder, but after today, I'm starting to think I've wasted a lot of energy."

In the same way as Grace, Ed didn't want to get into an argument over pieces of paper that meant nothing in the face of all that happened, especially to Junie. Ed reached out to Grace, but she flinched, got up, and walked away. It was too soon for a reconciliation.

Working up his courage, Ed scrolled through the last dozen messages from Connie, more from boredom than interest. The wavefront from the collapse traveled 50 kilometers downstream, killing livestock, taking down bridges, carrying away cars whose AI systems had no idea how to interpret the flood, washing away dam-independent hydropower facilities. But the warnings got through. People further downriver moved to higher ground, and responders reported fewer and fewer rescue calls. The impoundment was 90 percent drained, and the office reported a decreasing flow rate. As long as people gave it a wide berth, the river destroyed things, not human beings, though many people lost all they owned. Dozens did not hear the warnings, or the warnings did not come in time. Their bodies piled along the river's shore like driftwood.

A woman in a white smock slow marched toward Ed from deep down the hall that led to the operating rooms. Ed imagined the woman was a messenger from outside reality. Her face was relaxed, if tired, and she kept her gaze on Ed, as if she knew his thoughts. He had never seen her before. The woman stopped at the entrance to the waiting room. "Mr Wye?" Ed realized she had identified him by his avatar. Her avatar showed her name as "Dr Selig." Ed stood.

"Will you walk with me, please?"

Ed halted. "I want to know now what's happened to Junie. She's alive?"

"Mr Wye, is there someone you can speak with, a minister, or a close friend?"

"Why would you ask that?" His throat closed. *I don't know who to talk to. Sy?*

Selig touched his arm. "Mr Wye, your daughter will be fine."

All of Ed's defenses crumbled. He collapsed against a cabinet, barely keeping himself from falling to the polished floor. In an instant, the imaginary scenarios of accompanying his daughter's

311

body to the undertaker, seeing her lying in a coffin, setting her remains next to her grandparents and Marcy, evaporated. He cried as if his own private dam had burst, but the flood washed away his worst fears. "I'm sorry, doctor."

"Not to worry, Mr Wye." Selig handed him a clean cloth to wipe his tears. "There is more, though. She is badly hurt. She has a serious skull fracture, and her lower spine was crushed. She is paralyzed from about here down." The doctor put her hand on her back near her kidneys.

Fresh fears filled Ed's imagination. "Is it permanent?"

"She's stabilized, and we've contacted the best surgeon in Seattle. We've already started treatment. Time is of the essence."

"I want to see her."

"Of course. This way."

Selig led him into the ICU, and he saw Junie encased in a full body trauma auto-doc. She floated in a milky liquid that mimicked amniotic fluid, as warm and comforting as her mother's before she was born. Only her face, tinged with gray, was exposed to air. Ed wanted more than anything to take her hand and stroke her hair, but her hand was submerged in stem cell solution and her hair shorn and head bandaged. He sat on a chair next to the bed. He covered his eyes, but the tears flowed freely. He blamed himself for everything, for taking a job in desperation, for failing to do the job without hurting people, for taking Junie away from her friends and school, for almost killing her, the person he loved above all others. *I'm a fuck-up. That's all I am. A fuck-up.*

Selig stood by, leaving him alone without leaving his side. A heart monitor marked time, as did the *whoosh* of her respirator. His daughter was still as a carving, though he thought he saw her eyes move under her lids. *Is she dreaming? Of what? Of whom?* When she was a baby, she had the usual nightmares of small children, and more than once crawled into bed with him and Marcy when she was in kindergarten. Ed chuckled under his breath when he thought of her sleeping these days. It was impossible to get her up before 07:00. She was having less trouble getting up these days. More motivated. Something to do. Someone to see.

The brush of a foot on the polished floor caught his attention. Don Rast stood at the door. His clothes were dusty, but his face and hands were clean. Behind him was his grandfather. The younger man was close enough for Ed to touch. Don worked his mouth as if to say something, but no words emerged. He tried again. "She saved those people, Mr Wye."

"Saved them?"

"The colony was flooded, but everyone got to high ground." Don told Ed about seeing the dam collapse, and the run to the colony. Ed didn't understand the details, but Junie had done something extraordinary.

Don crushed his ball cap in his anxiety. "I tried to save her, Mr Wye. I reached out to her—" Don's hands opened and closed as if he was reliving that moment. "—but she was too far away. I'm sorry." He wiped his eyes with the back of his hand.

Cov Rast hung back in the shadows.

Ed acknowledged Don. "You did your best."

"Sir, may I stay a while?"

Junie's father measured the man before him. He was tall, strong, good looking, and smart. Junie had picked well. Ed wished he'd spoken to Don more before now, even as a part of Ed wanted to tell Don to leave. Ed would watch over his daughter and keep the darkness away. Another part of Ed knew that Junie loved both her father and this young man, and that Don was not replacing him, so much as letting the father rest while he watched against the terrors around them. *If I am a failure, it's not with Junie.* Ed got to his feet and stood aside, letting Don keep his own watch.

CHAPTER 26

♦ ♦ ♦

THE SUBORBITER CONCOURSE at Hong Kong International
Airport welcomed Ed as a minor principality might welcome a
deputy prime minister of a foreign government. The restrained,
deferential smiles of the white-gloved ushers intended to impress
presidents, monarchs, and the most powerful CEOs, however,
failed to ease the tension in Ed's gut. Natalie Wong responded with
the enthusiasm emo-sig when he invited her to meet, though she
wanted to see him in China, not California. He did not know what
to expect, now that he understood what she was capable of. Natalie
might not let him go home alive.

It was Rossmann's idea. An air ambulance had taken Junie
and Ed to the university medical center in Seattle, where surgeons
worked fifteen hours to repair her spinal cord. They directed the
nanobots to weave together each thread of nerve like old women
with knitting needles. In the recovery room, Junie's cheeks had the
pale yellow cast of post-surgery intensive care. It was the color of
her father's dread. Her lips were slack and her head was wrapped in
gauze, turban-like, but covering her eyes. Unlike the moment in
the emergency room, Ed had no idea if she dreamed or lived in a
state as close to death as a human being could, despite the warmth
of her fingers.

"You're going to pay a price for this," Junie had said on the
day she arrived in Utility, angry and resentful at a change she didn't
want. *If only I hadn't taken her out of her world.*

When he left her side three days after her body was crushed by the river, she was still in a coma. Rossmann was insistent when he showed up at the hospital.

"We've examined Chandra's tablet and minds-eye implants and we believe we've identified his main contact." They spoke in the cafeteria.

Ed gave himself a moment to process the information. "It's hard for me to believe, General. I've known Natalie Wong for 20 years. She's hard-nosed, but not a terrorist."

"Do you know why she took up with Chandra?" Doctors, nurses, patients, and visitors gave the general sidelong glances. A BES officer always meant trouble, but Rossmann ignored their nervousness.

Ed said, "I can't imagine why, except that Ram was a brilliant engineer. She liked having smart people around her."

"She wanted *you* with her, correct?" Rossmann detailed all he knew about ZephyrCom and her pursuit of Ed Wye, because of his experience as a CEO and his stature as an important patent holder.

"Yes, that's true, but I never gave her an answer either way."

"It's time you did."

A suborbiter ticket appeared in Ed's minds-eye. The destination was open. Rossmann wanted to work fast, and he didn't care about the expense, similar to his attitude about the cost of the dam deconstruction. "Ironic, isn't it, General? You hired Syren Ioannu to seduce me as a way to keep me on the project until it was done, and now you're sending me to take the job you hoped I'd reject." Ed challenged Rossmann to put all his cards on the table.

"My relationship with Ms Ioannu is more nuanced that you suspect, Wye, but I didn't discourage her from approaching you. It served my purpose, and hers."

"Hers?"

"Believe it or not, Wye, she likes you."

Though Ed hid his feelings, the statement thrilled him. Ramesh's betrayal, as well as the losses caused by the disaster, infuriated and depressed him, but he knew in his heart that he was not responsible. He'd done the job he was hired to do, at least until Ramesh's sabotage. The facts supported his case, should he ever be charged with a crime or otherwise taken to court. It was a small thing at this point. Junie was all that mattered to him now. "I don't know what you want from me, Rossmann. I can't leave Junie. She's stable, but the doctors won't know the results of the surgery for days. She might be paralyzed for life. She needs me."

"I respect your priorities, Wye, but there are far larger issues at stake. Apart from destroying government property, the uncontrolled demolition of the dam wrecked dozens of kilometers of restored riparian habitat along the river. That's a crime the Bureau can't ignore."

"I suppose it's pointless for me to refuse to help you."

"If you do, you'll be charged with negligence. Your career will be over."

"What might *you* be charged with?"

The question took Rossmann aback. "I don't know what you mean."

"For one thing, you worried out loud that you might be blamed for the dam's destruction and aftermath. I take it that my help might cover your ass. Then there's Ramesh's accusations. He told me just before he died that you had destroyed his ancestral village in India and many more. He accused you of mass murder. He wanted revenge."

A shadow crossed Rossmann's face. "I regret what happened in India, Wye. Chandra probably didn't tell you that the Indian authorities declined to prosecute anyone. People were warned for years to leave. The Indian government understood what was most important: saving the planet."

Are these the sacrifices we have to make to care for the earth? Ed kept his doubts about the answer to his question to himself.

"At least let me talk to my lawyer before I buy into your

game."

"You can do it on the suborbiter."

After Sy and Don agreed to substitute for him at Junie's side, Ed emailed Natalie, who invited him to Hong Kong. Ed's attorney, an old friend in the firm that had shepherded Ed's bankruptcies, called him during the brief period of weightlessness as the suborbiter traced the top of its parabola over the Pacific Ocean from San Francisco to Hong Kong. The lawyer advised him to do whatever Rossmann wanted.

Ed's virtual passport was stamped automatically when the suborbiter landed. One of the ushers was a serious but relaxed young woman. As she escorted him, he guessed she was a BES agent, but they spoke no more than pleasantries. The concourse was quiet, lined with elegant art, and peppered with subdued advertising. One poster, designed in another nostalgic revival of 20th century socialist realism, touted the PRC's glorious achievements in the genetic engineering of climate-change-tolerant apples. *I wonder what Cov Rast would think of that.*

As she did for his visit to her months prior, Natalie sent her private car to pick him up. As he climbed in, Ed caught the stern look from his escort, and he read Rossmann's double message: "Don't leave before getting what I want," and "Be careful." The car let him off at the lobby of a luxury high-rise in Kowloon. The heat and humidity of late spring descended on the city, and it combined with the knot in Ed's stomach to squeeze sweat from every sweat gland. Natalie's valet met him at the glass doors.

"Good to see you again, Merson."

"Madame is expecting you." The tiny smile on the tall man's gaunt face was no comfort.

Natalie found him in the lobby. "Eddie!" Beaming, she lifted her arms in greeting.

They touched cheeks. Ed hoped his skin wasn't a sticky as he imagined. "I'm sorry for the short notice."

"No worries, my dearest Eddie. I'm so glad you've come. How is Junie? She must be doing better already, or you would've stayed home."

Sy had texted him that Junie was still in a coma, but the doctors felt more optimistic as the hours progressed.

"She's as well as you can expect, but I didn't want to wait to talk to you about ZephyrCom."

"That's my Eddie. Always business, business, business."

Am I still that man? On the planes to Spokane to gather belongings and San Francisco to the suborbiter launch facility, and aboard the suborbiter to Hong Kong, Ed conducted an autopsy of his time in Utility. Junie's injury and surgery brought everything he'd done into sharper focus. He questioned every decision he made through the dam's collapse. Unsatisfied with the answers, he challenged every decision he'd made since Junie's birth, his marriage to Marcy, even his graduate research and dispute with Roger Saar. *Was I wrong to fight him? Is that how I started down this path to this place?* All of his work over 20 years and more had amounted to nothing, less than nothing, if Junie didn't survive. The possibility brought a lump to his throat he feared would give away his true motivations to Natalie.

"Is everything all right, Eddie?" Natalie's concern was genuine.

"Yes. I'm tired, is all."

"And you're worried about Junie."

"Yes, I am."

"She's strong. She'll pull through. Listen, you must be hungry, but we won't tire you out further. There's a neighborhood farmer's market a block away. Let's get some noodles and talk. Then I'll put you to bed."

A slight breeze from Victoria Harbor cooled down the neighborhood a degree. The neon and LED lights from the shops and restaurants cast harsh evening shadows. Ed was glad for his short-sleeved shirt and khaki pants, despite the trickle of sweat on his spine. Natalie was dressed in a silk blouse and light slacks.

"You seem at home here," Ed observed.

"My ancestors came from the Pearl River, remember?"

Ed recalled the photo in Natalie's San Francisco apartment. The word "ancestors" brought back Ramesh's accusation. "Part of us always seems tied to where we're from."

"You've grown used to Utility," Natalie said.

"Acclimated, yes."

"You don't belong there, Eddie. Your talents are wasted on the dam project. You're destined to work with me on ZephyrCom."

Ed wanted to dispute Natalie's claim on his life, but that went against his plan. Instead, he said, "I see that you were right all along. I'm sorry."

"No need to apologize. We need friends to give us perspective. That's all I did."

Strolling at a measured pace, the pair passed a fruit vendor, and one of the apple boxes caught Ed's eye. They were the golden apples with the red streaks touted by the poster in the concourse. The teenaged vendor bowed slightly and offered a thin slice to Natalie and Ed. The fruit was sweet, tart, and exquisite. "Pricey," he said.

"It's the 'human-handled' certification. Very trendy, but expensive."

Happy for the momentary distraction, a flurry of ideas came to Ed. He ordered a box shipped to Utility. "For Junie," he said to Natalie, partly as misdirection.

"A nice gift. Apple a day and all that."

Another ten paces brought them to an open-air eatery. Ed ordered noodles. Natalie chose *dim sum*.

"Now, to business, my dear Eddie."

Rossmann's instructions echoed in Ed's imagination. His appetite waned, but he kept eating.

"Let me be direct. I propose you become CEO of ZephyrCom immediately. You'll be the face the company needs. You'll move here to Hong Kong and we'll work with the authorities in Beijing on permits and, uh, incentives for building the wind farms with our technology."

"Incentives?"

Natalie grinned. "One must take care of one's friends."

She wants me to hand out bribes. "Go on."

"That's really all there is. I need your stature and reputation."

"What about running the show? Am I just a figurehead?"

"You'll have operational responsibilities, but you know me, Eddie. I'll be the power behind the throne." She bit off a morsel of steamed bun.

"Hmm."

"Don't worry, Eddie. You'll be very well compensated. I've also inquired about Junie's admittance to China's best universities. She's a shoe-in."

Could I tear Junie away from her friends again? What if she said No? "I see. You're very persuasive, Natalie."

"I see us as partners, Eddie."

"With you as senior partner."

Natalie giggled with the anticipation of a bettor winning a race.

Casting back to their talk in San Francisco in her apartment after dinner, Ed wondered if she still wanted a personal partnership. He waited for her to broach the subject, but she never did.

"What if we meet resistance?

"From whom?"

"The authorities. Local townspeople. Someone is always upset or feels ignored."

"I always get what I want. You know that."

"Or else?" An ember of anger heated in Ed's chest. Here was

Natalie at her core. Ruthless, cruel, and ambitious to the point of homicide.

"Or else what?"

"One of my engineers, Ramesh Chandra, said something to me before he died."

Natalie was perplexed, but the facts came to her. "You mean the man who caused the Arroyo Grande Dam to collapse? An awful accident. I was sorry to hear about it."

No, you were overjoyed. "He mentioned your name."

That brought Natalie up short, if only for a half-second. "Are you sure?"

"He said you thought I was naive."

Natalie's chewing slowed. She took a sip of water. The glass left a ring of condensation on the table. "That's ridiculous."

"It's something you'd say."

"Eddie, you have to admit that sometimes you act more like a child than an adult. You can be quite selfish."

The words sliced at his heart like a knife. After all that had happened, especially Junie's injury, he'd posed the question to himself. Did his ambitions and decisions hurt Junie? Was he so keen on getting back to the world of Silicon Valley that he failed to see how she might be endangered? "I suppose we all have our weaknesses."

"That's why we need strong friends, to balance our weaknesses."

I know your weakness, the thing that blinds you. "You like to win, whatever it takes, don't you?"

"Don't scold me, Eddie. You wouldn't be here if it weren't for me."

"I wasn't scolding you."

"Sure sounds like it."

"Did you know Ramesh Chandra?"

"I know thousands of people."

"Did you help Ramesh take down the dam?"

Natalie regarded Ed as if re-evaluating a critical decision. "Even if I did, what would I gain by angering the BES?"

"Me. Or rather my reputation to people important to you."

"True, it's a non-fungible asset I need to close the deal with the Chinese government. I've only got a few days left to make this happen." Natalie shifted in her seat. A pained look came over her face. "Eddie, you're upsetting me."

Ed hoped Rossmann had made contact with the Environmental Protection Ministry. The deputy minister needed to know why Ed was in Hong Kong. "Admit it. You helped Ramesh Chandra."

"I need you. Here. Now."

"How did you help him?"

"I didn't help him."

"Then one of your companies or employees helped him. Was it Merson?"

Natalie laughed. "Merson is my valet, not my operative."

Ed's frustration grew. He wasn't getting what he needed. "I can't work for you if you aren't honest with me."

"Don't threaten me, Eddie."

"I want to know what I'm getting into. Did you help Ramesh Chandra?"

Natalie sighed. "Oh, very well, Eddie. I have a distant cousin who is a former cryptographer with the People's Liberation Army. He does contract work for me. He was contacted by Chandra via the dark com. My cousin told me what Chandra wanted, something about communications security, but the man didn't say anything about blowing up a dam. I thought it was harmless."

"But you knew he was on the dam project. And you knew that he was out for revenge against Rossmann, didn't you?"

"I did my due diligence."

"You thought whatever Chandra was doing might help you get your hooks into me."

"You make it sound corrupt." Natalie's face reflected distaste. "I hedged my bets."

"Your bet nearly killed my daughter."

"I truly regret that, Eddie. You must believe me, but there were larger issues at stake than an obsolete dam in a backwater county."

This cut to the chase for Ed. Natalie had no interest in anything but herself. She was a monster. "What could be more important than the life of my child?" Faces passing to and fro in front of the restaurant turned his way.

Natalie looked around her. "Eddie, there's no need to raise your voice. What I did was intended to help you and Junie, to get you out of a wilderness."

Ed forced himself to calm down. "And make you even richer and more powerful."

"I like to run up the score."

A commotion interrupted the conversation. A uniformed officer appeared in the back of the restaurant. Flashing blue lights reflected off the buildings across the street. Out of nowhere, Merson was at Natalie's side. "Madame! We need to leave." He pointed a pistol at Ed's chest.

"Eddie, what have you done?"

A black security bot loped toward the restaurant, its oval form distorted by the neon. Passers-by screamed and ran. Distracted, Merson glanced away, and Ed bolted. Merson followed his target, but the machine fired first. The staser blast vaporized the valet's forearm. The gun clattered to the floor, his hand still gripping it. Natalie screamed as blood from Merson's arm sprayed her pale blouse. Trying to run, Ed slipped in the spattered blood and fell to the floor. In an instant, a half-dozen human officers in BES uniforms stood over Ed, Natalie, and Merson's writhing body. Natalie's screams drowned out every other noise in the restaurant. Ed pushed himself away from her, as if she were possessed by a demon.

Rossmann loomed over the trio, outfitted in helmet and flak jacket. His eyes lighted on each of his targets. Ed thought he should feel comforted and safe. Instead, it was terror at what the general might do next. Merson had passed out, blood leaking from the stump of his arm. Natalie covered her face with hands soaked in her valet's blood.

"Natalie Wong," Rossmann declared, "you are under arrest for crimes against the ecosystem of the Columbia River." He let a victorious smirk crawl across his face.

CHAPTER 27

◆ ◆ ◆

JUNIE CALLED UP THE LATEST OBSERVATIONS from the JOVE deep space telescope array to update the data in her final paper of the semester. She shooed away the night insects attracted to her glowing screen as she kept her eye out for Don. He was late from the picking, and she hated it when he was gone past twilight. The BES's dark sky requirements, while good for astronomers and nocturnal creatures, made night travel riskier. She shook off her anxiety and focused on her chemistry results. She loved her toughest class, because her professor at Stanford knew all there was to know about teasing out the chemical signatures of life on other worlds. The stem cells rebuilding her spinal cord for the past two years sparked her interest in exo-chemistry and the question of how life had arisen on the exo-planets.

Even as she healed, her father passed through a period of personal trial and grief. For a year, he was under administrative arrest, ordered by a judge to install an app in his com implants that pinged his whereabouts night and day to the court as the investigation into the dam collapse proceeded. It was a virtual shackle. An additional gag order from the judge bottled up his sorrow and guilt. He couldn't talk to anyone about the case, even his daughter. And his anger at Ramesh's betrayal ate at him.

At a hearing in the Grant County Courthouse, he told the story of the sting against Natalie Wong, and how the BES had tapped into a live stream of data from his minds-eye. It recorded enough damning evidence from her father's conversation with Natalie in

325

Hong Kong for an arrest. His leg quivered with nervousness as he spoke.

In the end, Ramesh Chandra was labeled a terrorist by the BES. Ed shouldered part of the blame for not seeing the signs of Ramesh's perfidy. Gerard Rossmann was relieved of any responsibility; He was merely implementing government policy.

Rodrigo Slane was never heard from again.

Merson—that's how he wanted his name recorded—turned state's evidence in return for an artificial arm and hand.

Natalie Wong was disidentified. The law prohibited anyone from speaking her name in public or private again.

Junie searched the darkness again for Don. `Where are you, culchie?` The text carried Junie's private term of endearment for her lover. She no longer used the word in public to avoid hurting the locals' sensibilities.

Don didn't respond to Junie's ping.

Covington Rast died a few weeks after the verdict. The doctors blamed a massive stroke, but Junie wondered if the old man's life drained away with the water behind the Arroyo Grande Dam. Cov wanted only close family and friends to say goodbye to him. Don asked Junie, Ed, Sy and Mason to come to the service. The local farmers co-op organized the affair.

"He was wrong about the dam, but you have to respect him," Ed said to Sy in the Rast family home.

"Covington loved Utility," Sy said. "Its people were his people. Its history was his history. His family was the most important thing in his life. That's why he wanted to be buried here. He was a good man, deep in his heart."

"He hated you."

"I thought so, too, but now I'm not sure. He never said so, but I think he secretly loved Mason. A man who loves a place like his own flesh and blood couldn't deny his own flesh and blood. That's why he left Mason land and money. A part of me believes he had good feelings for me, in spite of his distrust."

Don laid his grandfather to rest next to his grandmother Arlene. They reposed in the family plot on a hillside that overlooked his great-great-grandfather's original purchase of land. Near Cov were the bones of Julian Rast, the distant relative found entombed in the dam. The river was a silvery ribbon below.

Though the old man was gone, Junie felt his presence, as well as the presence of all the Rasts over the last two centuries. It was hard not to think he was nearby, offering advice, carping on problems, enjoying his legacy. With him passed an era.

As the new head of the Rast family said his thanks and goodbyes to people paying their respects, Junie joined the conversation under an gnarled apple tree, said to be the oldest on the property.

"You two ought to admit the obvious and be a couple." Junie's bald statement startled her father.

"Your painkillers are speaking for you," Ed said, embarrassed.

"A mist-truth," Sy added.

Junie persisted. "It's not only true, it ought to be true. You belong together." She set aside her misgivings about Sy as the elder woman proved as strong a pillar of support for her father as the daughter. Rossmann, before he was promoted out of the BES' Pacific West district, fulfilled his promise to reinstate Sy's cyprian license, and she had moved ahead—discreetly—with her plans for a ganeum. The collapse had muted the voices resisting change, but she understood that the entertainment services she proposed would only be accepted if they came slowly, quietly, as part of a overall revival of Utility on a different economic base. As head of the local River Defenders, she was also on an advisory committee helping with the river's final stages of restoration.

"Don needs your help, both of you. Me, too," Junie said. "The business is now his. The land, the orchards, everything. He's alone."

"He's not alone, Junie," Sy said. "Mason is his brother. We're his family now."

"Don wants to keep the business going," Junie added. "He's making plans to visit Shaanxi. He's looking for new tree fruit hybrids."

"The Chinese have done some amazing things with genetics," Sy said. "Adaptations to higher summer temps, less water usage, higher yields with fewer resources and tougher growing conditions. Don't you agree, Ed?"

Ed folded his arms and stayed quiet. Sy's comment was a reference to the box of fruit he'd sent back from Hong Kong. He'd told Junie the real reason he'd shipped the box, but the investigation, the gag order, and the electronic shackles sapped his energy, and he never followed up on his ideas.

"Thing is, Don's a grower, not a businessman, if you get my meaning," Junie said.

The seed was planted. By the time Don had settled the last of his grandfather's affairs, Ed had written a new business plan, which Don accepted. Junie's father flew down to the Bay Area and looked up his old contacts. Few of them knew anything about the ag business, and many were perplexed by his interest in such an un-sexy industry. Nonetheless, he convinced a small group of angels to invest, among them Grace Cromer.

"Junie-girl," he said when he returned, "we can make this work."

Starlight penetrated the spaces between the branches of pear, peach, and apple trees. The actuators of Junie's exo-skeleton hissed in mild complaint as she eased herself off her chair at the outdoor table. The AI interpreted the impulses from the sciatic and other nerves in her lower back, as well as her motor cortex, to assist her legs and hips. The computer stressed her back, hips, and legs enough to strengthen her muscles and promote healing without causing pain, though Junie noted soreness in her reporting logs.

The design had much in common with the exo that Connie Gasca's father used, though his was intended as a substitute for withered legs and dead areas of the brain, not to heal them.

Stepping inside the warehouse, Junie donned a coat hanging on a hook. The temperature was two degrees Celsius and the relative humidity 90 percent, optimal for keeping apples fresh up to four months. Her father was on a forklift moving empty fruit boxes off shelves. His face was determined as he concentrated on the work. He could've programmed the AI for the tasks, but he enjoyed working with heavy equipment. He said it gave him a sense of accomplishment.

"Don's been out there a long time, Dad." Junie said. "How long does it take to pick apples?"

Ed set the forklift's brake and stepped off. "Enough time to convince well-off people in Seattle, Portland, Anchorage, and everywhere else to pay premium prices in specialty stores for fruits picked by hand. Tiffany says so after every meeting with retailers. I've seen this myself in the markets and online. The 'human-handled' movement is gaining steam."

"I see." Junie played ignorant to get him to talk. She understood perfectly what he and Tiffany had worked out.

"Cov was a good businessman, but Rast Orchards was failing, and not because the BES was taking his water. He wasn't adapting fast enough to the new environment. We can prevent a failure by taking advantage of new cultivars to expand the business and jump on the newest trends. The numbers add up. I've seen human-handled fruit and vegetables selling by the truckload in San Francisco. We've already got orders."

"But the workers we use, Dad. Isn't that a problem?"

Ed removed his gloves and shoved them in a pocket of his overalls. "We think we have a... well, an understanding with the authorities. If we're discreet, they won't bother us. And we can still get the 'human-handled' certification."

"Seems very risky."

"Yes, there's risk. Don wants to try anyway. You know him. Once he wants to do something, it's hard to stop him. Just like his granddad." Ed shared an email with his daughter via the com network. "We got this today. Trudy sent photos and a quality analysis of the first apples we sent to a Seattle wholesaler Cov worked with for decades. The wholesaler ordered ten boxes for immediate shipment."

Trudy couldn't resist throwing in a selfie with her taking a huge bite from one of the apples.

Junie kept up with her best friends on various c-tribes. She also heard occasionally from her father's old colleagues on the deconstruction project, though she rarely relayed news. It brought back bad memories for him, but she decided one bit of news was too important to keep to herself. "Dad, did you see the post Connie shared?"

For a half-second, Ed stopped swiping through a document, and Junie feared she had crossed a line. The shadow on his face was brief, but telling. He respected the deconstruction operations supervisor. He never blamed her or any of the other engineers and staff, apart from Ramesh, for the sabotage that destroyed the Arroyo Grande Dam. The shadow was grief, or a memory of what might have been. "I don't keep up as much on things as I should."

Junie bit her lip. "The first ZephyrCom generator installations went online today. There's photos. She was interviewed in the Chinese media."

Her father stayed on task, then sighed, without taking his eyes off the document. "I'm glad for her. She deserves it."

"She sent me a private ping." Junie paused.

"Well?"

"She just said 'Say thanks for me to Ed. He made the project happen as much as anyone.'"

"Well, then." Ed's tone was soft, if noncommittal. "Her

grandfather would've been proud of her." Bob Gasca had died a week after the tribal government won control of the re-emerged falls they regarded as sacred. Though she had powerful ties to Utility and the tribes, Connie decided she needed to see something of the world, though she promised to come back if she felt lonely or isolated.

"Dad, how are you doing?"

"What do you mean?"

"Ever since Hong Kong, you've never talked about going back to Silicon Valley. I thought that's what you wanted."

"I thought so, too, for a long time. But after Natalie, and Ramesh, and your injury..." He shrugged and rested his stubbled chin in his palm. "I guess it wasn't meant to be."

"But are you happy?"

Ed was thoughtful. "My definition of happiness is changing, but I know this much." He brightened. "You and Don are my future, now."

"And Sy?"

"Yes, she's part of my future, too. And Mason."

Junie fought back tears. "Thanks, Dad."

Father and daughter heard the crunch of gravel outside the warehouse. The main door rolled up, though the strip curtain kept the cold inside.

"Don?" Junie said.

"No, it's Peter."

Frustrated, Junie saw two or three moving shadows, which resolved into Peter and a half-dozen other men and women. "Where's Don?"

"He's with another group behind us."

Next to Peter was a robot cart with five large boxes of fruit. "Take a look."

The light was good enough to see the red streaks on a yellow bed. Junie selected and bit an apple. "A little tart, but that'll go away by the time we deliver." She took another bite. "Softish?"

Ed sampled his own apple. "The next saplings we get have new genes to firm up the flesh, but Tiffany says consumers are okay with slightly soft, just not too soft."

"We'll see," Junie said. "Let's get these boxes inside."

Peter slipped his hands into his pockets while Ed ordered the cart to a shelf and started the forklift. The dissed man stared at his dusty boots for a moment, then lifted his gaze. His welt cast a shadow on his forehead. "Junie, you've saved us twice now."

"I don't understand."

"Right before you got hurt, and when you gave us these jobs."

"I didn't—"

"I don't mean to embarrass you, but Don told us that you had the idea for giving us the work once your dad thought of the 'human-handled' angle. It actually makes *us* feel human again. I just wanted to say thank-you, that's all."

"You're sweet, but it seemed obvious to me."

"One more thing, Junie. I never told anyone this, but I knew Cov Rast for almost half a century before he died. I'm sorry Cov didn't get to know you better. He'd have loved you like a daughter."

Junie smiled in acknowledgment, but what Peter didn't know was that Cov had tried. Once he saw how Don felt about her, he seemed to melt a bit, like ice cream left out of a freezer for a few minutes. Cov texted her, sent her flowers on her birthday, and gave her local history ebooks for passing the time during physical therapy. He could not bring himself to visit her in person while she was in recovery. His reluctance puzzled her, until she realized that it might be too painful. *Perhaps Don and I reminded him too much of him and his wife when they were young.* After a time, she observed a sentimental streak in his personality as wide at the Columbia River itself. *Not unlike the love the people of Utility have for the river. God bless them and their restoration work.*

Voices caught her attention again, and a group of dissed

walked through the curtain with two more carts. Don wasn't with them. "Where is he?"

The workers directed Junie outside, and she pushed through the hanging strips of plastic. Don was under a security lamp, studying a pad, making notes. He looked ghost-like, as if his grandfather were inhabiting his body for a moment. In a strange way, all his ancestors inhabited his body, if you thought of it at a chemical level, or a genetic level. A hundred years, or a thousand years, or the whole history of life on earth lived in this man, the same as it lived in her own history, though on a slightly different path. If her studies of exo-planets were right, creatures ten-thousand light years away had their own ways of coding history in living things, and passing that history by encouraging disparate paths to merge, become one, and create another.

"Why didn't you respond to my text?"

"Sorry. Distracted by work. Forgive me?"

Junie forgave Don without thinking about it. She stood on her toes and reached to his forehead. She didn't really need the exo any more, but the doctors insisted on a few more weeks. Her headaches had gone months ago. With practiced fingers, she brushed away a dark lock of his curly hair. The welt had disappeared, leaving a perfect man even more perfect, if such a thing were possible. She kissed him, believing in perfection with all her heart.

EPILOGUE

◆ ◆ ◆

VICE INSPECTOR GENERAL GERARD ROSSMANN of the Bureau of Environmental Security permitted himself a feeling of pride as he sipped champagne on the balcony of a conference center 100 kilometers from the Yangtze River. Ordinarily, he kept emotions such as pride in check. Everything he did and felt was in service to the earth, not himself. Today, however, was special. Around him, dignitaries from across China raised their glasses in a toast to the project he oversaw. Among the VIPs was the Chinese Deputy Minister for Environmental Protection, a woman of 40 or so who carried herself like one of the princesses of the Forbidden City.

"A glorious day, wouldn't you agree, General?"

"Indeed, Minister. I'm honored to be a part of it."

"You made it happen."

"I had nothing to do with it, Minister." Rossmann's modesty was a step in a diplomatic dance. In fact, if he hadn't taken over from the previous occupant of his post, the Yangtze River would still be a prisoner after today. "You made the final decision. I'd say you were the heroine."

"Nonsense."

In the distance, the blades of wind generators sliced through the hazy sky. "As the champion of the new technology brought to your country by ZephyrCom and other energy companies, Minister, China would still be dependent on outdated, environmentally destructive energy strategies, such as hydroelectric dams."

"Your flattery is well-practiced, General, but my motivations are purely patriotic."

"Of course, Minister."

"I do have regrets, though. I so wanted Mr Wye on the project."

The mild rebuke was familiar to Rossmann. "Yes, it was regrettable that he turned down all your entreaties. I never understood why."

"You don't have children, do you?"

"No, ma'am."

"I have a little boy and a little girl. I think I would go mad if something happened to them. I sympathize with his decision to stay home."

"Still, the opportunity for Mr Wye..."

"His recommendation of Ms Gasca as the project superintendent under you was excellent, though it took some time for my colleagues to warm up to her. Indigenous people make some Chinese nervous. We're culturally distrustful of outsiders with no history."

"She's done a brilliant job, you must admit."

"I was disappointed when I was told she plans to return to Pacific West and her home town after the final phase of restoration work is under way."

"Some people have a powerful attraction to their place of origin." Rossmann had no such feelings. He considered himself a citizen of his planet.

"I envy her. One day I shall retire to my ancestral village in Guangdong province."

"Not for many years, I hope."

A chime sounded.

"Should we move to the dais, Minister?"

The two officials climbed the short flight of stairs to a platform with a lectern and a small side table. On the table was a tab in a crimson sleeve. Above them and over the hundred or so VIPs were screens showing the wide expanse of the yellowish Yangtze River, cut in half by a concrete wall. In the early 21st century, misguided leaders of China spanned the river with a hydroelectric and flood-control dam that turned out to be the largest ever constructed as measured by electricity output. No one had ever dared to build a dam as big again. Rossmann reflected on the terrible price paid by the river and land for human arrogance and greed, not only here, but across the planet on ten thousand rivers and streams. Today, however, the obscene wound of the Three Gorges Dam would start to heal.

Via the screen, Rossmann watched the lazy river, drawn down to its pre-dam level by a diversion channel. His heart picked up its pace as the minister spoke briefly and touched the tab. He'd worked his whole life for such moments. The dam in India, the Arroyo Grande Dam, and now this monster. A few seconds later, without a sound because of the distance, the dam vanished in a dirty cloud of concrete dust.

AUTHOR'S NOTE

Thank you so much for reading *Restoration*. I sincerely hope you enjoyed it. Writing is a challenging and rewarding experience, and I'd like to hear your feedback. Please take a moment to review my book on Amazon, Goodreads, or your favorite book review site. You can follow me on Facebook (@AuthorJGFollansbee), Twitter (@Joe_Follansbee), and Instagram (@jgfollansbee). You can also follow me on my personal blog. Tell your friends!

Restoration is the third full-length novel in my dystopian thriller series, *Tales From A Warming Planet*. The first and second novels, *Carbon Run* and *City of Ice and Dreams*, are available now on Amazon. You'll also enjoy the novelette *The Mother Earth Insurgency*, published in 2017.

Thank you!

– Joe Follansbee, Spring 2018

Carbon Run
"A very exciting read" (4.5 stars) — *A Page to Turn*
Buy now on Amazon!

City of Ice and Dreams
"Can't wait to see what comes next from this author." (5 stars) —
Goodreads review
Buy now on <u>Amazon</u>.

COMING IN 2018

♦ ♦ ♦

The Mother Earth Insurgency: A Collection of Tales from a Warming Planet

To get early information about release dates, visit my personal blog, http://joefollansbee.com, and sign up for my reader newsletter.

ABOUT THE AUTHOR

◆ ◆ ◆

J.G. FOLLANSBEE IS THE AUTHOR of science fiction and speculative fiction novels set on an Earth and in a society transformed by climate change. A writer who publishes independently, Follansbee explores themes of survival, justice, and tolerance with strong female protagonists and antagonists. Mr. Follansbee supports meaningful clean energy and transportation policies that combat the damaging effects of climate change. He lives in Seattle.

www.ingramcontent.com/pod-product-compliance
Lightning Source LLC
Chambersburg PA
CBHW021444240626
47153CB00001B/280